O. Henry

The Gift of the Magi and Other New York Stories

e-artnow 2018

Reading suggestions (available from e-artnow as Print & eBook)

James Knowles
The Legends of King Arthur and His Knights

Mark Twain
A Connecticut Yankee in King Arthur's Court

Charles Dickens
Barnaby Rudge

Rudyard Kipling
Plain Tales from the Hills: Rudyard Kipling Collection - 40+ Short Stories (The Tales of Life in British India)

O. Henry
The Gift of the Magi and Other New York City Stories

Rudyard Kipling
Plain Tales from the Hills: 40+ Short Stories Collection (The Tales of Life in British India)

Washington Irving
The Complete Short Stories of Washington Irving: The Sketch Book of Geoffrey Crayon, Bracebridge Hall, Tales of a Traveler, The Alhambra, Woolfert's Roost & The Crayon Papers Collections (Illustrated)

Nathaniel Hawthorne, O. Henry
Of Love, Life & Happiness: A Thanksgiving Collection

Robert Louis Stevenson
The Complete Short Stories of Robert Louis Stevenson

O. Henry
The Complete O. Henry Short Stories (Rolling Stones + Cabbages and Kings + Options + Roads of Destiny + The Four Million + The Trimmed Lamp + The Voice of the City + Whirligigs and more)

O. Henry

The Gift of the Magi and Other New York Stories

The Skylight Room, The Voice of The City, The Cop and the Anthem, A Retrieved Information, The Last Leaf, The Ransom of Red Chief, The Trimmed Lamp and more

e-artnow, 2018
Contact: info@e-artnow.org
ISBN 978-80-268-9048-5

Contents

A Retrieved Reformation	11
The Cop And The Anthem	15
The Duplicity Of Hargraves	19
The Gift Of The Magi	27
The Last Leaf	31
The Ransom Of Red Chief	35
The Skylight Room	41
The Trimmed Lamp	45
The Whirligig Of Life	51
A Harlem Tragedy	55
The Making Of A New Yorker	59
The Voice Of The City	63
Biography of O. Henry	67
Chapter One: The Life And The Story	68
Chapter Two: Vogue	70
Chapter Three: Ancestry	73
Chapter Four: Birthplace And Early Years	84
Chapter Five: Ranch And City Life In Texas	101
Chapter Six: The Shadowed Years	119
Chapter Seven: Finding Himself In New York	134
Chapter Eight: Favourite Themes	144
Chapter Nine: Last Days	160

A Retrieved Reformation

A guard came to the prison shoe-shop, where Jimmy Valentine was assiduously stitching uppers, and escorted him to the front office. There the warden handed Jimmy his pardon, which had been signed that morning by the governor. Jimmy took it in a tired kind of way. He had served nearly ten months of a four year sentence. He had expected to stay only about three months, at the longest. When a man with as many friends on the outside as Jimmy Valentine had is received in the "stir" it is hardly worth while to cut his hair.

"Now, Valentine," said the warden, "you'll go out in the morning. Brace up, and make a man of yourself. You're not a bad fellow at heart. Stop cracking safes, and live straight."

"Me?" said Jimmy, in surprise. "Why, I never cracked a safe in my life."

"Oh, no," laughed the warden. "Of course not. Let's see, now. How was it you happened to get sent up on that Springfield job? Was it because you wouldn't prove an alibi for fear of compromising somebody in extremely high-toned society? Or was it simply a case of a mean old jury that had it in for you? It's always one or the other with you innocent victims."

"Me?" said Jimmy, still blankly virtuous. "Why, warden, I never was in Springfield in my life!"

"Take him back, Cronin!" said the warden, "and fix him up with outgoing clothes. Unlock him at seven in the morning, and let him come to the bull-pen. Better think over my advice, Valentine."

At a quarter past seven on the next morning Jimmy stood in the warden's outer office. He had on a suit of the villainously fitting, ready-made clothes and a pair of the stiff, squeaky shoes that the state furnishes to its discharged compulsory guests.

The clerk handed him a railroad ticket and the five-dollar bill with which the law expected him to rehabilitate himself into good citizenship and prosperity. The warden gave him a cigar, and shook hands. Valentine, 9762, was chronicled on the books, "Pardoned by Governor," and Mr. James Valentine walked out into the sunshine.

Disregarding the song of the birds, the waving green trees, and the smell of the flowers, Jimmy headed straight for a restaurant. There he tasted the first sweet joys of liberty in the shape of a broiled chicken and a bottle of white wine — followed by a cigar a grade better than the one the warden had given him. From there he proceeded leisurely to the depot. He tossed a quarter into the hat of a blind man sitting by the door, and boarded his train. Three hours set him down in a little town near the state line. He went to the café of one Mike Dolan and shook hands with Mike, who was alone behind the bar.

"Sorry we couldn't make it sooner, Jimmy, me boy," said Mike. "But we had that protest from Springfield to buck against, and the governor nearly balked. Feeling all right?"

"Fine," said Jimmy. "Got my key?"

He got his key and went upstairs, unlocking the door of a room at the rear. Everything was just as he had left it. There on the floor was still Ben Price's collar-button that had been torn from that eminent detective's shirt-band when they had overpowered Jimmy to arrest him.

Pulling out from the wall a folding-bed, Jimmy slid back a panel in the wall and dragged out a dust-covered suit-case. He opened this and gazed fondly at the finest set of burglar's tools in the East. It was a complete set, made of specially tempered steel, the latest designs in drills, punches, braces and bits, jimmies, clamps, and augers, with two or three novelties, invented by Jimmy himself, in which he took pride. Over nine hundred dollars they had cost him to have made at ——, a place where they make such things for the profession.

In half an hour Jimmy went down stairs and through the café. He was now dressed in tasteful and well-fitting clothes, and carried his dusted and cleaned suit-case in his hand.

"Got anything on?" asked Mike Dolan, genially.

"Me?" said Jimmy, in a puzzled tone. "I don't understand. I'm representing the New York Amalgamated Short Snap Biscuit Cracker and Frazzled Wheat Company."

This statement delighted Mike to such an extent that Jimmy had to take a seltzer-and-milk on the spot. He never touched "hard" drinks.

A week after the release of Valentine, 9762, there was a neat job of safe-burglary done in Richmond, Indiana, with no clue to the author. A scant eight hundred dollars was all that was secured. Two weeks after that a patented, improved, burglar-proof safe in Logansport was opened like a cheese to the tune of fifteen hundred dollars, currency; securities and silver untouched. That began to interest the rogue-catchers. Then an old-fashioned bank-safe in Jefferson City became active and threw out of its crater an eruption of banknotes amounting to five thousand dollars. The losses were now high enough to bring the matter up into Ben Price's class of work. By comparing notes, a remarkable similarity in the methods of the burglaries was noticed. Ben Price investigated the scenes of the robberies, and was heard to remark:

"That's Dandy Jim Valentine's autograph. He's resumed business. Look at that combination knob — jerked out as easy as pulling up a radish in wet weather. He's got the only clamps that can do it. And look how clean those tumblers were punched out! Jimmy never has to drill but one hole. Yes, I guess I want Mr. Valentine. He'll do his bit next time without any short-time or clemency foolishness."

Ben Price knew Jimmy's habits. He had learned them while working up the Springfield case. Long jumps, quick getaways, no confederates, and a taste for good society — these ways had helped Mr. Valentine to become noted as a successful dodger of retribution. It was given out that Ben Price had taken up the trail of the elusive cracksman, and other people with burglar-proof safes felt more at ease.

One afternoon Jimmy Valentine and his suit-case climbed out of the mail-hack in Elmore, a little town five miles off the railroad down in the blackjack country of Arkansas. Jimmy, looking like an athletic young senior just home from college, went down the board sidewalk toward the hotel.

A young lady crossed the street, passed him at the corner and entered a door over which was the sign, "The Elmore Bank." Jimmy Valentine looked into her eyes, forgot what he was, and became another man. She lowered her eyes and coloured slightly. Young men of Jimmy's style and looks were scarce in Elmore.

Jimmy collared a boy that was loafing on the steps of the bank as if he were one of the stockholders, and began to ask him questions about the town, feeding him dimes at intervals. By and by the young lady came out, looking royally unconscious of the young man with the suit-case, and went her way.

"Isn't that young lady Polly Simpson?" asked Jimmy, with specious guile.

"Naw," said the boy. "She's Annabel Adams. Her pa owns this bank. What'd you come to Elmore for? Is that a gold watch-chain? I'm going to get a bulldog. Got any more dimes?"

Jimmy went to the Planters' Hotel, registered as Ralph D. Spencer, and engaged a room. He leaned on the desk and declared his platform to the clerk. He said he had come to Elmore to look for a location to go into business. How was the shoe business, now, in the town? He had thought of the shoe business. Was there an opening?

The clerk was impressed by the clothes and manner of Jimmy. He, himself, was something of a pattern of fashion to the thinly gilded youth of Elmore, but he now perceived his shortcomings. While trying to figure out Jimmy's manner of tying his four-in-hand he cordially gave information.

Yes, there ought to be a good opening in the shoe line. There wasn't an exclusive shoe-store in the place. The drygoods and general stores handled them. Business in all lines was fairly good. Hoped Mr. Spencer would decide to locate in Elmore. He would find it a pleasant town to live in, and the people very sociable.

Mr. Spencer thought he would stop over in the town a few days and look over the situation. No, the clerk needn't call the boy. He would carry up his suit-case, himself; it was rather heavy.

Mr. Ralph Spencer, the phœnix that arose from Jimmy Valentine's ashes — ashes left by the flame of a sudden and alterative attack of love — remained in Elmore, and prospered. He opened a shoe-store and secured a good run of trade.

Socially he was also a success, and made many friends. And he accomplished the wish of his heart. He met Miss Annabel Adams, and became more and more captivated by her charms.

At the end of a year the situation of Mr. Ralph Spencer was this: he had won the respect of the community, his shoe-store was flourishing, and he and Annabel were engaged to be married in two weeks. Mr. Adams, the typical, plodding, country banker, approved of Spencer. Annabel's pride in him almost equalled her affection. He was as much at home in the family of Mr. Adams and that of Annabel's married sister as if he were already a member.

One day Jimmy sat down in his room and wrote this letter, which he mailed to the safe address of one of his old friends in St. Louis:

Dear Old Pal:

I want you to be at Sullivan's place, in Little Rock, next Wednesday night, at nine o'clock. I want you to wind up some little matters for me. And, also, I want to make you a present of my kit of tools. I know you'll be glad to get them — you couldn't duplicate the lot for a thousand dollars. Say, Billy, I've quit the old business — a year ago. I've got a nice store. I'm making an honest living, and I'm going to marry the finest girl on earth two weeks from now. It's the only life, Billy — the straight one. I wouldn't touch a dollar of another man's money now for a million. After I get married I'm going to sell out and go West, where there won't be so much danger of having old scores brought up against me. I tell you, Billy, she's an angel. She believes in me; and I wouldn't do another crooked thing for the whole world. Be sure to be at Sully's, for I must see you. I'll bring along the tools with me.

Your old friend,

Jimmy.

On the Monday night after Jimmy wrote this letter, Ben Price jogged unobtrusively into Elmore in a livery buggy. He lounged about town in his quiet way until he found out what he wanted to know. From the drugstore across the street from Spencer's shoe-store he got a good look at Ralph D. Spencer.

"Going to marry the banker's daughter are you, Jimmy?" said Ben to himself, softly. "Well, I don't know!"

The next morning Jimmy took breakfast at the Adamses. He was going to Little Rock that day to order his wedding-suit and buy something nice for Annabel. That would be the first time he had left town since he came to Elmore. It had been more than a year now since those last professional "jobs," and he thought he could safely venture out.

After breakfast quite a family party went downtown together — Mr. Adams, Annabel, Jimmy, and Annabel's married sister with her two little girls, aged five and nine. They came by the hotel where Jimmy still boarded, and he ran up to his room and brought along his suit-case. Then they went on to the bank. There stood Jimmy's horse and buggy and Dolph Gibson, who was going to drive him over to the railroad station.

All went inside the high, carved oak railings into the banking-room — Jimmy included, for Mr. Adams's future son-in-law was welcome anywhere. The clerks were pleased to be greeted by the good-looking, agreeable young man who was going to marry Miss Annabel. Jimmy set his suit-case down. Annabel, whose heart was bubbling with happiness and lively youth, put on Jimmy's hat, and picked up the suit-case. "Wouldn't I make a nice drummer?" said Annabel. "My! Ralph, how heavy it is? Feels like it was full of gold bricks."

"Lot of nickel-plated shoe-horns in there," said Jimmy, coolly, "that I'm going to return. Thought I'd save express charges by taking them up. I'm getting awfully economical."

The Elmore Bank had just put in a new safe and vault. Mr. Adams was very proud of it, and insisted on an inspection by every one. The vault was a small one, but it had a new, patented door. It fastened with three solid steel bolts thrown simultaneously with a single handle, and had a time-lock. Mr. Adams beamingly explained its workings to Mr. Spencer, who showed a courteous but not too intelligent interest. The two children, May and Agatha, were delighted by the shining metal and funny clock and knobs.

While they were thus engaged Ben Price sauntered in and leaned on his elbow, looking casually inside between the railings. He told the teller that he didn't want anything; he was just waiting for a man he knew.

Suddenly there was a scream or two from the women, and a commotion. Unperceived by the elders, May, the nine-year-old girl, in a spirit of play, had shut Agatha in the vault. She had then shot the bolts and turned the knob of the combination as she had seen Mr. Adams do.

The old banker sprang to the handle and tugged at it for a moment. "The door can't be opened," he groaned. "The clock hasn't been wound nor the combination set."

Agatha's mother screamed again, hysterically.

"Hush!" said Mr. Adams, raising his trembling hand. "All be quite for a moment. Agatha!" he called as loudly as he could. "Listen to me." During the following silence they could just hear the faint sound of the child wildly shrieking in the dark vault in a panic of terror.

"My precious darling!" wailed the mother. "She will die of fright! Open the door! Oh, break it open! Can't you men do something?"

"There isn't a man nearer than Little Rock who can open that door," said Mr. Adams, in a shaky voice. "My God! Spencer, what shall we do? That child — she can't stand it long in there. There isn't enough air, and, besides, she'll go into convulsions from fright."

Agatha's mother, frantic now, beat the door of the vault with her hands. Somebody wildly suggested dynamite. Annabel turned to Jimmy, her large eyes full of anguish, but not yet despairing. To a woman nothing seems quite impossible to the powers of the man she worships.

"Can't you do something, Ralph — *try*, won't you?"

He looked at her with a queer, soft smile on his lips and in his keen eyes.

"Annabel," he said, "give me that rose you are wearing, will you?"

Hardly believing that she heard him aright, she unpinned the bud from the bosom of her dress, and placed it in his hand. Jimmy stuffed it into his vest-pocket, threw off his coat and pulled up his shirtsleeves. With that act Ralph D. Spencer passed away and Jimmy Valentine took his place.

"Get away from the door, all of you," he commanded, shortly.

He set his suit-case on the table, and opened it out flat. From that time on he seemed to be unconscious of the presence of any one else. He laid out the shining, queer implements swiftly and orderly, whistling softly to himself as he always did when at work. In a deep silence and immovable, the others watched him as if under a spell.

In a minute Jimmy's pet drill was biting smoothly into the steel door. In ten minutes — breaking his own burglarious record — he threw back the bolts and opened the door.

Agatha, almost collapsed, but safe, was gathered into her mother's arms.

Jimmy Valentine put on his coat, and walked outside the railings towards the front door. As he went he thought he heard a faraway voice that he once knew call "Ralph!" But he never hesitated.

At the door a big man stood somewhat in his way.

"Hello, Ben!" said Jimmy, still with his strange smile. "Got around at last, have you? Well, let's go. I don't know that it makes much difference, now."

And then Ben Price acted rather strangely.

"Guess you're mistaken, Mr. Spencer," he said. "Don't believe I recognize you. Your buggy's waiting for you, ain't it?"

And Ben Price turned and strolled down the street.

The Cop And The Anthem

On his bench in Madison Square Soapy moved uneasily. When wild geese honk high of nights, and when women without sealskin coats grow kind to their husbands, and when Soapy moves uneasily on his bench in the park, you may know that winter is near at hand.

A dead leaf fell in Soapy's lap. That was Jack Frost's card. Jack is kind to the regular denizens of Madison Square, and gives fair warning of his annual call. At the corners of four streets he hands his pasteboard to the North Wind, footman of the mansion of All Outdoors, so that the inhabitants thereof may make ready.

Soapy's mind became cognisant of the fact that the time had come for him to resolve himself into a singular Committee of Ways and Means to provide against the coming rigour. And therefore he moved uneasily on his bench.

The hibernatorial ambitions of Soapy were not of the highest. In them there were no considerations of Mediterranean cruises, of soporific Southern skies drifting in the Vesuvian Bay. Three months on the Island was what his soul craved. Three months of assured board and bed and congenial company, safe from Boreas and bluecoats, seemed to Soapy the essence of things desirable.

For years the hospitable Blackwell's had been his winter quarters. Just as his more fortunate fellow New Yorkers had bought their tickets to Palm Beach and the Riviera each winter, so Soapy had made his humble arrangements for his annual hegira to the Island. And now the time was come. On the previous night three Sabbath newspapers, distributed beneath his coat, about his ankles and over his lap, had failed to repulse the cold as he slept on his bench near the spurting fountain in the ancient square. So the Island loomed big and timely in Soapy's mind. He scorned the provisions made in the name of charity for the city's dependents. In Soapy's opinion the Law was more benign than Philanthropy. There was an endless round of institutions, municipal and eleemosynary, on which he might set out and receive lodging and food accordant with the simple life. But to one of Soapy's proud spirit the gifts of charity are encumbered. If not in coin you must pay in humiliation of spirit for every benefit received at the hands of philanthropy. As Caesar had his Brutus, every bed of charity must have its toll of a bath, every loaf of bread its compensation of a private and personal inquisition. Wherefore it is better to be a guest of the law, which though conducted by rules, does not meddle unduly with a gentleman's private affairs.

Soapy, having decided to go to the Island, at once set about accomplishing his desire. There were many easy ways of doing this. The pleasantest was to dine luxuriously at some expensive restaurant; and then, after declaring insolvency, be handed over quietly and without uproar to a policeman. An accommodating magistrate would do the rest.

Soapy left his bench and strolled out of the square and across the level sea of asphalt, where Broadway and Fifth Avenue flow together. Up Broadway he turned, and halted at a glittering café, where are gathered together nightly the choicest products of the grape, the silkworm and the protoplasm.

Soapy had confidence in himself from the lowest button of his vest upward. He was shaven, and his coat was decent and his neat black, ready-tied four-in-hand had been presented to him by a lady missionary on Thanksgiving Day. If he could reach a table in the restaurant unsuspected success would be his. The portion of him that would show above the table would raise no doubt in the waiter's mind. A roasted mallard duck, thought Soapy, would be about the thing — with a bottle of Chablis, and then Camembert, a demi-tasse and a cigar. One dollar for the cigar would be enough. The total would not be so high as to call forth any supreme manifestation of revenge from the café management; and yet the meat would leave him filled and happy for the journey to his winter refuge.

But as Soapy set foot inside the restaurant door the head waiter's eye fell upon his frayed trousers and decadent shoes. Strong and ready hands turned him about and conveyed him in silence and haste to the sidewalk and averted the ignoble fate of the menaced mallard.

Soapy turned off Broadway. It seemed that his route to the coveted island was not to be an epicurean one. Some other way of entering limbo must be thought of.

At a corner of Sixth Avenue electric lights and cunningly displayed wares behind plate-glass made a shop window conspicuous. Soapy took a cobblestone and dashed it through the glass. People came running around the corner, a policeman in the lead. Soapy stood still, with his hands in his pockets, and smiled at the sight of brass buttons.

"Where's the man that done that?" inquired the officer excitedly.

"Don't you figure out that I might have had something to do with it?" said Soapy, not without sarcasm, but friendly, as one greets good fortune.

The policeman's mind refused to accept Soapy even as a clue. Men who smash windows do not remain to parley with the law's minions. They take to their heels. The policeman saw a man half way down the block running to catch a car. With drawn club he joined in the pursuit. Soapy, with disgust in his heart, loafed along, twice unsuccessful.

On the opposite side of the street was a restaurant of no great pretensions. It catered to large appetites and modest purses. Its crockery and atmosphere were thick; its soup and napery thin. Into this place Soapy took his accusive shoes and telltale trousers without challenge. At a table he sat and consumed beefsteak, flapjacks, doughnuts and pie. And then to the waiter be betrayed the fact that the minutest coin and himself were strangers.

"Now, get busy and call a cop," said Soapy. "And don't keep a gentleman waiting."

"No cop for youse," said the waiter, with a voice like butter cakes and an eye like the cherry in a Manhattan cocktail. "Hey, Con!"

Neatly upon his left ear on the callous pavement two waiters pitched Soapy. He arose, joint by joint, as a carpenter's rule opens, and beat the dust from his clothes. Arrest seemed but a rosy dream. The Island seemed very far away. A policeman who stood before a drug store two doors away laughed and walked down the street.

Five blocks Soapy travelled before his courage permitted him to woo capture again. This time the opportunity presented what he fatuously termed to himself a "cinch." A young woman of a modest and pleasing guise was standing before a show window gazing with sprightly interest at its display of shaving mugs and inkstands, and two yards from the window a large policeman of severe demeanour leaned against a water plug.

It was Soapy's design to assume the role of the despicable and execrated "masher." The refined and elegant appearance of his victim and the contiguity of the conscientious cop encouraged him to believe that he would soon feel the pleasant official clutch upon his arm that would insure his winter quarters on the right little, tight little isle.

Soapy straightened the lady missionary's ready-made tie, dragged his shrinking cuffs into the open, set his hat at a killing cant and sidled toward the young woman. He made eyes at her, was taken with sudden coughs and "hems," smiled, smirked and went brazenly through the impudent and contemptible litany of the "masher." With half an eye Soapy saw that the policeman was watching him fixedly. The young woman moved away a few steps, and again bestowed her absorbed attention upon the shaving mugs. Soapy followed, boldly stepping to her side, raised his hat and said:

"Ah there, Bedelia! Don't you want to come and play in my yard?"

The policeman was still looking. The persecuted young woman had but to beckon a finger and Soapy would be practically en route for his insular haven. Already he imagined he could feel the cozy warmth of the station-house. The young woman faced him and, stretching out a hand, caught Soapy's coat sleeve.

"Sure, Mike," she said joyfully, "if you'll blow me to a pail of suds. I'd have spoke to you sooner, but the cop was watching."

With the young woman playing the clinging ivy to his oak Soapy walked past the policeman overcome with gloom. He seemed doomed to liberty.

At the next corner he shook off his companion and ran. He halted in the district where by night are found the lightest streets, hearts, vows and librettos. Women in furs and men in greatcoats moved gaily in the wintry air. A sudden fear seized Soapy that some dreadful enchantment had rendered him immune to arrest. The thought brought a little of panic upon it, and when he came upon another policeman lounging grandly in front of a transplendent theatre he caught at the immediate straw of "disorderly conduct."

On the sidewalk Soapy began to yell drunken gibberish at the top of his harsh voice. He danced, howled, raved and otherwise disturbed the welkin.

The policeman twirled his club, turned his back to Soapy and remarked to a citizen.

"'Tis one of them Yale lads celebratin' the goose egg they give to the Hartford College. Noisy; but no harm. We've instructions to lave them be."

Disconsolate, Soapy ceased his unavailing racket. Would never a policeman lay hands on him? In his fancy the Island seemed an unattainable Arcadia. He buttoned his thin coat against the chilling wind.

In a cigar store he saw a well-dressed man lighting a cigar at a swinging light. His silk umbrella he had set by the door on entering. Soapy stepped inside, secured the umbrella and sauntered off with it slowly. The man at the cigar light followed hastily.

"My umbrella," he said, sternly.

"Oh, is it?" sneered Soapy, adding insult to petit larceny. "Well, why don't you call a policeman? I took it. Your umbrella! Why don't you call a cop? There stands one on the corner."

The umbrella owner slowed his steps. Soapy did likewise, with a presentiment that luck would again run against him. The policeman looked at the two curiously.

"Of course," said the umbrella man — "that is — well, you know how these mistakes occur — I — if it's your umbrella I hope you'll excuse me — I picked it up this morning in a restaurant — If you recognise it as yours, why — I hope you'll —"

"Of course it's mine," said Soapy, viciously.

The ex-umbrella man retreated. The policeman hurried to assist a tall blonde in an opera cloak across the street in front of a street car that was approaching two blocks away.

Soapy walked eastward through a street damaged by improvements. He hurled the umbrella wrathfully into an excavation. He muttered against the men who wear helmets and carry clubs. Because he wanted to fall into their clutches, they seemed to regard him as a king who could do no wrong.

At length Soapy reached one of the avenues to the east where the glitter and turmoil was but faint. He set his face down this toward Madison Square, for the homing instinct survives even when the home is a park bench.

But on an unusually quiet corner Soapy came to a standstill. Here was an old church, quaint and rambling and gabled. Through one violet-stained window a soft light glowed, where, no doubt, the organist loitered over the keys, making sure of his mastery of the coming Sabbath anthem. For there drifted out to Soapy's ears sweet music that caught and held him transfixed against the convolutions of the iron fence.

The moon was above, lustrous and serene; vehicles and pedestrians were few; sparrows twittered sleepily in the eaves — for a little while the scene might have been a country churchyard. And the anthem that the organist played cemented Soapy to the iron fence, for he had known it well in the days when his life contained such things as mothers and roses and ambitions and friends and immaculate thoughts and collars.

The conjunction of Soapy's receptive state of mind and the influences about the old church wrought a sudden and wonderful change in his soul. He viewed with swift horror the pit into which he had tumbled, the degraded days, unworthy desires, dead hopes, wrecked faculties and base motives that made up his existence.

And also in a moment his heart responded thrillingly to this novel mood. An instantaneous and strong impulse moved him to battle with his desperate fate. He would pull himself out of the mire; he would make a man of himself again; he would conquer the evil that had taken possession of him. There was time; he was comparatively young yet; he would resurrect his old eager ambitions and pursue them without faltering. Those solemn but sweet organ notes had set up a revolution in him. Tomorrow he would go into the roaring downtown district and find work. A fur importer had once offered him a place as driver. He would find him tomorrow and ask for the position. He would be somebody in the world. He would —

Soapy felt a hand laid on his arm. He looked quickly around into the broad face of a policeman.

"What are you doin' here?" asked the officer.

"Nothin'," said Soapy.

"Then come along," said the policeman.

"Three months on the Island," said the Magistrate in the Police Court the next morning.

The Duplicity Of Hargraves

When Major Pendleton Talbot, of Mobile, sir, and his daughter, Miss Lydia Talbot, came to Washington to reside, they selected for a boarding place a house that stood fifty yards back from one of the quietest avenues. It was an old-fashioned brick building, with a portico upheld by tall white pillars. The yard was shaded by stately locusts and elms, and a catalpa tree in season rained its pink and white blossoms upon the grass. Rows of high box bushes lined the fence and walks. It was the Southern style and aspect of the place that pleased the eyes of the Talbots.

In this pleasant, private boarding house they engaged rooms, including a study for Major Talbot, who was adding the finishing chapters to his book, "Anecdotes and Reminiscences of the Alabama Army, Bench, and Bar."

Major Talbot was of the old, old South. The present day had little interest or excellence in his eyes. His mind lived in that period before the Civil War, when the Talbots owned thousands of acres of fine cotton land and the slaves to till them; when the family mansion was the scene of princely hospitality, and drew its guests from the aristocracy of the South. Out of that period he had brought all its old pride and scruples of honour, an antiquated and punctilious politeness, and (you would think) its wardrobe.

Such clothes were surely never made within fifty years. The major was tall, but whenever he made that wonderful, archaic genuflexion he called a bow, the corners of his frock coat swept the floor. That garment was a surprise even to Washington, which has long ago ceased to shy at the frocks and broadbrimmed hats of Southern congressmen. One of the boarders christened it a "Father Hubbard," and it certainly was high in the waist and full in the skirt.

But the major, with all his queer clothes, his immense area of plaited, ravelling shirt bosom, and the little black string tie with the bow always slipping on one side, both was smiled at and liked in Mrs. Vardeman's select boarding house. Some of the young department clerks would often "string him," as they called it, getting him started upon the subject dearest to him — the traditions and history of his beloved Southland. During his talks he would quote freely from the "Anecdotes and Reminiscences." But they were very careful not to let him see their designs, for in spite of his sixty-eight years, he could make the boldest of them uncomfortable under the steady regard of his piercing gray eyes.

Miss Lydia was a plump, little old maid of thirty-five, with smoothly drawn, tightly twisted hair that made her look still older. Old fashioned, too, she was; but ante-bellum glory did not radiate from her as it did from the major. She possessed a thrifty common sense; and it was she who handled the finances of the family, and met all comers when there were bills to pay. The major regarded board bills and wash bills as contemptible nuisances. They kept coming in so persistently and so often. Why, the major wanted to know, could they not be filed and paid in a lump sum at some convenient period — say when the "Anecdotes and Reminiscences" had been published and paid for? Miss Lydia would calmly go on with her sewing and say, "We'll pay as we go as long as the money lasts, and then perhaps they'll have to lump it."

Most of Mrs. Vardeman's boarders were away during the day, being nearly all department clerks and business men; but there was one of them who was about the house a great deal from morning to night. This was a young man named Henry Hopkins Hargraves — every one in the house addressed him by his full name — who was engaged at one of the popular vaudeville theatres. Vaudeville has risen to such a respectable plane in the last few years, and Mr. Hargraves was such a modest and well-mannered person, that Mrs. Vardeman could find no objection to enrolling him upon her list of boarders.

At the theatre Hargraves was known as an all-round dialect comedian, having a large repertoire of German, Irish, Swede, and black-face specialties. But Mr. Hargraves was ambitious, and often spoke of his great desire to succeed in legitimate comedy.

This young man appeared to conceive a strong fancy for Major Talbot. Whenever that gentleman would begin his Southern reminiscences, or repeat some of the liveliest of the anecdotes, Hargraves could always be found, the most attentive among his listeners.

For a time the major showed an inclination to discourage the advances of the "play actor," as he privately termed him; but soon the young man's agreeable manner and indubitable appreciation of the old gentleman's stories completely won him over.

It was not long before the two were like old chums. The major set apart each afternoon to read to him the manuscript of his book. During the anecdotes Hargraves never failed to laugh at exactly the right point. The major was moved to declare to Miss Lydia one day that young Hargraves possessed remarkable perception and a gratifying respect for the old regime. And when it came to talking of those old days — if Major Talbot liked to talk, Mr. Hargraves was entranced to listen.

Like almost all old people who talk of the past, the major loved to linger over details. In describing the splendid, almost royal, days of the old planters, he would hesitate until he had recalled the name of the Negro who held his horse, or the exact date of certain minor happenings, or the number of bales of cotton raised in such a year; but Hargraves never grew impatient or lost interest. On the contrary, he would advance questions on a variety of subjects connected with the life of that time, and he never failed to extract ready replies.

The fox hunts, the 'possum suppers, the hoe downs and jubilees in the Negro quarters, the banquets in the plantation-house hall, when invitations went for fifty miles around; the occasional feuds with the neighbouring gentry; the major's duel with Rathbone Culbertson about Kitty Chalmers, who afterward married a Thwaite of South Carolina; and private yacht races for fabulous sums on Mobile Bay; the quaint beliefs, improvident habits, and loyal virtues of the old slaves — all these were subjects that held both the major and Hargraves absorbed for hours at a time.

Sometimes, at night, when the young man would be coming upstairs to his room after his turn at the theatre was over, the major would appear at the door of his study and beckon archly to him. Going in, Hargraves would find a little table set with a decanter, sugar bowl, fruit, and a big bunch of fresh green mint.

"It occurred to me," the major would begin — he was always ceremonious — "that perhaps you might have found your duties at the — at your place of occupation — sufficiently arduous to enable you, Mr. Hargraves, to appreciate what the poet might well have had in his mind when he wrote, 'tired Nature's sweet restorer,' — one of our Southern juleps."

It was a fascination to Hargraves to watch him make it. He took rank among artists when he began, and he never varied the process. With what delicacy he bruised the mint; with what exquisite nicety he estimated the ingredients; with what solicitous care he capped the compound with the scarlet fruit glowing against the dark green fringe! And then the hospitality and grace with which he offered it, after the selected oat straws had been plunged into its tinkling depths!

After about four months in Washington, Miss Lydia discovered one morning that they were almost without money. The "Anecdotes and Reminiscences" was completed, but publishers had not jumped at the collected gems of Alabama sense and wit. The rental of a small house which they still owned in Mobile was two months in arrears. Their board money for the month would be due in three days. Miss Lydia called her father to a consultation.

"No money?" said he with a surprised look. "It is quite annoying to be called on so frequently for these petty sums. Really, I —"

The major searched his pockets. He found only a two-dollar bill, which he returned to his vest pocket.

"I must attend to this at once, Lydia," he said. "Kindly get me my umbrella and I will go down town immediately. The congressman from our district, General Fulghum, assured me some days ago that he would use his influence to get my book published at an early date. I will go to his hotel at once and see what arrangement has been made."

With a sad little smile Miss Lydia watched him button his "Father Hubbard" and depart, pausing at the door, as he always did, to bow profoundly.

That evening, at dark, he returned. It seemed that Congressman Fulghum had seen the publisher who had the major's manuscript for reading. That person had said that if the anecdotes, etc., were carefully pruned down about one half, in order to eliminate the sectional and class prejudice with which the book was dyed from end to end, he might consider its publication.

The major was in a white heat of anger, but regained his equanimity, according to his code of manners, as soon as he was in Miss Lydia's presence.

"We must have money," said Miss Lydia, with a little wrinkle above her nose. "Give me the two dollars, and I will telegraph to Uncle Ralph for some tonight."

The major drew a small envelope from his upper vest pocket and tossed it on the table.

"Perhaps it was injudicious," he said mildly, "but the sum was so merely nominal that I bought tickets to the theatre tonight. It's a new war drama, Lydia. I thought you would be pleased to witness its first production in Washington. I am told that the South has very fair treatment in the play. I confess I should like to see the performance myself."

Miss Lydia threw up her hands in silent despair.

Still, as the tickets were bought, they might as well be used. So that evening, as they sat in the theatre listening to the lively overture, even Miss Lydia was minded to relegate their troubles, for the hour, to second place. The major, in spotless linen, with his extraordinary coat showing only where it was closely buttoned, and his white hair smoothly roached, looked really fine and distinguished. The curtain went up on the first act of "A Magnolia Flower," revealing a typical Southern plantation scene. Major Talbot betrayed some interest.

"Oh, see!" exclaimed Miss Lydia, nudging his arm, and pointing to her programme.

The major put on his glasses and read the line in the cast of characters that her finger indicated.

Col. Webster Calhoun.... H. Hopkins Hargraves.

"It's our Mr. Hargraves," said Miss Lydia. "It must be his first appearance in what he calls 'the legitimate.' I'm so glad for him."

Not until the second act did Col. Webster Calhoun appear upon the stage. When he made his entry Major Talbot gave an audible sniff, glared at him, and seemed to freeze solid. Miss Lydia uttered a little, ambiguous squeak and crumpled her programme in her hand. For Colonel Calhoun was made up as nearly resembling Major Talbot as one pea does another. The long, thin white hair, curly at the ends, the aristocratic beak of a nose, the crumpled, wide, ravelling shirt front, the string tie, with the bow nearly under one ear, were almost exactly duplicated. And then, to clinch the imitation, he wore the twin to the major's supposed to be unparalleled coat. High-collared, baggy, empire-waisted, ample-skirted, hanging a foot lower in front than behind, the garment could have been designed from no other pattern. From then on, the major and Miss Lydia sat bewitched, and saw the counterfeit presentment of a haughty Talbot "dragged," as the major afterward expressed it, "through the slanderous mire of a corrupt stage."

Mr. Hargraves had used his opportunities well. He had caught the major's little idiosyncrasies of speech, accent, and intonation and his pompous courtliness to perfection — exaggerating all to the purposes of the stage. When he performed that marvellous bow that the major fondly imagined to be the pink of all salutations, the audience sent forth a sudden round of hearty applause.

Miss Lydia sat immovable, not daring to glance toward her father. Sometimes her hand next to him would be laid against her cheek, as if to conceal the smile which, in spite of her disapproval, she could not entirely suppress.

The culmination of Hargraves's audacious imitation took place in the third act. The scene is where Colonel Calhoun entertains a few of the neighbouring planters in his "den."

Standing at a table in the centre of the stage, with his friends grouped about him, he delivers that inimitable, rambling, character monologue so famous in "A Magnolia Flower," at the same time that he deftly makes juleps for the party.

Major Talbot, sitting quietly, but white with indignation, heard his best stories retold, his pet theories and hobbies advanced and expanded, and the dream of the "Anecdotes and Reminiscences" served, exaggerated and garbled. His favourite narrative — that of his duel with Rathbone Culbertson — was not omitted, and it was delivered with more fire, egotism, and gusto than the major himself put into it.

The monologue concluded with a quaint, delicious, witty little lecture on the art of concocting a julep, illustrated by the act. Here Major Talbot's delicate but showy science was reproduced to a hair's breadth — from his dainty handling of the fragrant weed — "the one-thousandth part of a grain too much pressure, gentlemen, and you extract the bitterness, instead of the aroma, of this heaven-bestowed plant" — to his solicitous selection of the oaten straws.

At the close of the scene the audience raised a tumultuous roar of appreciation. The portrayal of the type was so exact, so sure and thorough, that the leading characters in the play were forgotten. After repeated calls, Hargraves came before the curtain and bowed, his rather boyish face bright and flushed with the knowledge of success.

At last Miss Lydia turned and looked at the major. His thin nostrils were working like the gills of a fish. He laid both shaking hands upon the arms of his chair to rise.

"We will go, Lydia," he said chokingly. "This is an abominable — desecration."

Before he could rise, she pulled him back into his seat. "We will stay it out," she declared. "Do you want to advertise the copy by exhibiting the original coat?" So they remained to the end.

Hargraves's success must have kept him up late that night, for neither at the breakfast nor at the dinner table did he appear.

About three in the afternoon he tapped at the door of Major Talbot's study. The major opened it, and Hargraves walked in with his hands full of the morning papers — too full of his triumph to notice anything unusual in the major's demeanour.

"I put it all over 'em last night, major," he began exultantly. "I had my inning, and, I think, scored. Here's what the *Post* says:

His conception and portrayal of the old-time Southern colonel, with his absurd grandiloquence, his eccentric garb, his quaint idioms and phrases, his moth-eaten pride of family, and his really kind heart, fastidious sense of honour, and lovable simplicity, is the best delineation of a character role on the boards to-day. The coat worn by Colonel Calhoun is itself nothing less than an evolution of genius. Mr. Hargraves has captured his public.

"How does that sound, major, for a first nighter?"

"I had the honour" — the major's voice sounded ominously frigid — "of witnessing your very remarkable performance, sir, last night."

Hargraves looked disconcerted.

"You were there? I didn't know you ever — I didn't know you cared for the theatre. Oh, I say, Major Talbot," he exclaimed frankly, "don't you be offended. I admit I did get a lot of pointers from you that helped me out wonderfully in the part. But it's a type, you know — not individual. The way the audience caught on shows that. Half the patrons of that theatre are Southerners. They recognized it."

"Mr. Hargraves," said the major, who had remained standing, "you have put upon me an unpardonable insult. You have burlesqued my person, grossly betrayed my confidence, and misused my hospitality. If I thought you possessed the faintest conception of what is the sign manual of a gentleman, or what is due one, I would call you out, sir, old as I am. I will ask you to leave the room, sir."

The actor appeared to be slightly bewildered, and seemed hardly to take in the full meaning of the old gentleman's words.

"I am truly sorry you took offence," he said regretfully. "Up here we don't look at things just as you people do. I know men who would buy out half the house to have their personality put on the stage so the public would recognize it."

"They are not from Alabama, sir," said the major haughtily.

"Perhaps not. I have a pretty good memory, major; let me quote a few lines from your book. In response to a toast at a banquet given in — Milledgeville, I believe — you uttered, and intend to have printed, these words:

The Northern man is utterly without sentiment or warmth except in so far as the feelings may be turned to his own commercial profit. He will suffer without resentment any imputation cast upon the honour of himself or his loved ones that does not bear with it the consequence of pecuniary loss. In his charity, he gives with a liberal hand; but it must be heralded with the trumpet and chronicled in brass.

"Do you think that picture is fairer than the one you saw of Colonel Calhoun last night?"

"The description," said the major frowning, "is — not without grounds. Some exag — latitude must be allowed in public speaking."

"And in public acting," replied Hargraves.

"That is not the point," persisted the major, unrelenting. "It was a personal caricature. I positively decline to overlook it, sir."

"Major Talbot," said Hargraves, with a winning smile, "I wish you would understand me. I want you to know that I never dreamed of insulting you. In my profession, all life belongs to me. I take what I want, and what I can, and return it over the footlights. Now, if you will, let's let it go at that. I came in to see you about something else. We've been pretty good friends for some months, and I'm going to take the risk of offending you again. I know you are hard up for money — never mind how I found out; a boarding house is no place to keep such matters secret — and I want you to let me help you out of the pinch. I've been there often enough myself. I've been getting a fair salary all the season, and I've saved some money. You're welcome to a couple hundred — or even more — until you get —"

"Stop!" commanded the major, with his arm outstretched. "It seems that my book didn't lie, after all. You think your money salve will heal all the hurts of honour. Under no circumstances would I accept a loan from a casual acquaintance; and as to you, sir, I would starve before I would consider your insulting offer of a financial adjustment of the circumstances we have discussed. I beg to repeat my request relative to your quitting the apartment."

Hargraves took his departure without another word. He also left the house the same day, moving, as Mrs. Vardeman explained at the supper table, nearer the vicinity of the downtown theatre, where "A Magnolia Flower" was booked for a week's run.

Critical was the situation with Major Talbot and Miss Lydia. There was no one in Washington to whom the major's scruples allowed him to apply for a loan. Miss Lydia wrote a letter to Uncle Ralph, but it was doubtful whether that relative's constricted affairs would permit him to furnish help. The major was forced to make an apologetic address to Mrs. Vardeman regarding the delayed payment for board, referring to "delinquent rentals" and "delayed remittances" in a rather confused strain.

Deliverance came from an entirely unexpected source.

Late one afternoon the door maid came up and announced an old coloured man who wanted to see Major Talbot. The major asked that he be sent up to his study. Soon an old darkey appeared in the doorway, with his hat in hand, bowing, and scraping with one clumsy foot. He was quite decently dressed in a baggy suit of black. His big, coarse shoes shone with a metallic lustre suggestive of stove polish. His bushy wool was gray — almost white. After middle life, it is difficult to estimate the age of a Negro. This one might have seen as many years as had Major Talbot.

"I be bound you don't know me, Mars' Pendleton," were his first words.

The major rose and came forward at the old, familiar style of address. It was one of the old plantation darkeys without a doubt; but they had been widely scattered, and he could not recall the voice or face.

"I don't believe I do," he said kindly — "unless you will assist my memory."

"Don't you 'member Cindy's Mose, Mars' Pendleton, what 'migrated 'mediately after de war?"

"Wait a moment," said the major, rubbing his forehead with the tips of his fingers. He loved to recall everything connected with those beloved days. "Cindy's Mose," he reflected. "You worked among the horses — breaking the colts. Yes, I remember now. After the surrender, you took the name of — don't prompt me — Mitchell, and went to the West — to Nebraska."

"Yassir, yassir," — the old man's face stretched with a delighted grin — "dat's him, dat's it. Newbraska. Dat's me — Mose Mitchell. Old Uncle Mose Mitchell, dey calls me now. Old mars', your pa, gimme a pah of dem mule colts when I lef' fur to staht me goin' with. You 'member dem colts, Mars' Pendleton?"

"I don't seem to recall the colts," said the major. "You know I was married the first year of the war and living at the old Follinsbee place. But sit down, sit down, Uncle Mose. I'm glad to see you. I hope you have prospered."

Uncle Mose took a chair and laid his hat carefully on the floor beside it.

"Yassir; of late I done mouty famous. When I first got to Newbraska, dey folks come all roun' me to see dem mule colts. Dey ain't see no mules like dem in Newbraska. I sold dem mules for three hundred dollars. Yassir — three hundred.

"Den I open a blacksmith shop, suh, and made some money and bought some lan'. Me and my old 'oman done raised up seb'm chillun, and all doin' well 'cept two of 'em what died. Fo' year ago a railroad come along and staht a town slam ag'inst my lan', and, suh, Mars' Pendleton, Uncle Mose am worth leb'm thousand dollars in money, property, and lan'."

"I'm glad to hear it," said the major heartily. "Glad to hear it."

"And dat little baby of yo'n, Mars' Pendleton — one what you name Miss Lyddy — I be bound dat little tad done growed up tell nobody wouldn't know her."

The major stepped to the door and called: "Lydia, dear, will you come?"

Miss Lydia, looking quite grown up and a little worried, came in from her room.

"Dar, now! What'd I tell you? I knowed dat baby done be plum growed up. You don't 'member Uncle Mose, child?"

"This is Aunt Cindy's Mose, Lydia," explained the major. "He left Sunnymead for the West when you were two years old."

"Well," said Miss Lydia, "I can hardly be expected to remember you, Uncle Mose, at that age. And, as you say, I'm 'plum growed up,' and was a blessed long time ago. But I'm glad to see you, even if I can't remember you."

And she was. And so was the major. Something alive and tangible had come to link them with the happy past. The three sat and talked over the olden times, the major and Uncle Mose correcting or prompting each other as they reviewed the plantation scenes and days.

The major inquired what the old man was doing so far from his home.

"Uncle Mose am a delicate," he explained, "to de grand Baptis' convention in dis city. I never preached none, but bein' a residin' elder in de church, and able fur to pay my own expenses, dey sent me along."

"And how did you know we were in Washington?" inquired Miss Lydia.

"Dey's a cullud man works in de hotel whar I stops, what comes from Mobile. He told me he seen Mars' Pendleton comin' outen dish here house one mawnin'."

"What I come fur," continued Uncle Mose, reaching into his pocket — "besides de sight of home folks — was to pay Mars' Pendleton what I owes him."

"Owe me?" said the major, in surprise.

"Yassir — three hundred dollars." He handed the major a roll of bills. "When I lef' old mars' says: 'Take dem mule colts, Mose, and, if it be so you gits able, pay fur 'em'. Yassir — dem was his words. De war had done lef' old mars' po' hisself. Old mars' bein' 'long ago dead, de debt descends to Mars' Pendleton. Three hundred dollars. Uncle Mose is plenty able to pay now. When dat railroad buy my lan' I laid off to pay fur dem mules. Count de money, Mars' Pendleton. Dat's what I sold dem mules fur. Yassir."

Tears were in Major Talbot's eyes. He took Uncle Mose's hand and laid his other upon his shoulder.

"Dear, faithful, old servitor," he said in an unsteady voice, "I don't mind saying to you that 'Mars' Pendleton' spent his last dollar in the world a week ago. We will accept this money, Uncle Mose, since, in a way, it is a sort of payment, as well as a token of the loyalty and devotion of the old regime. Lydia, my dear, take the money. You are better fitted than I to manage its expenditure."

"Take it, honey," said Uncle Mose. "Hit belongs to you. Hit's Talbot money."

After Uncle Mose had gone, Miss Lydia had a good cry — for joy; and the major turned his face to a corner, and smoked his clay pipe volcanically.

The succeeding days saw the Talbots restored to peace and ease. Miss Lydia's face lost its worried look. The major appeared in a new frock coat, in which he looked like a wax figure personifying the memory of his golden age. Another publisher who read the manuscript of the "Anecdotes and Reminiscences" thought that, with a little retouching and toning down of the high lights, he could make a really bright and salable volume of it. Altogether, the situation was comfortable, and not without the touch of hope that is often sweeter than arrived blessings.

One day, about a week after their piece of good luck, a maid brought a letter for Miss Lydia to her room. The postmark showed that it was from New York. Not knowing any one there, Miss Lydia, in a mild flutter of wonder, sat down by her table and opened the letter with her scissors. This was what she read:

Dear Miss Talbot:

I thought you might be glad to learn of my good fortune. I have received and accepted an offer of two hundred dollars per week by a New York stock company to play Colonel Calhoun in "A Magnolia Flower."

There is something else I wanted you to know. I guess you'd better not tell Major Talbot. I was anxious to make him some amends for the great help he was to me in studying the part, and for the bad humour he was in about it. He refused to let me, so I did it anyhow. I could easily spare the three hundred.

Sincerely yours,

H. Hopkins Hargraves,

P.S. How did I play Uncle Mose?

Major Talbot, passing through the hall, saw Miss Lydia's door open and stopped.

"Any mail for us this morning, Lydia, dear?" he asked.

Miss Lydia slid the letter beneath a fold of her dress.

"The *Mobile Chronicle* came," she said promptly. "It's on the table in your study."

The Gift Of The Magi

One dollar and eighty-seven cents. That was all. And sixty cents of it was in pennies. Pennies saved one and two at a time by bulldozing the grocer and the vegetable man and the butcher until one's cheeks burned with the silent imputation of parsimony that such close dealing implied. Three times Della counted it. One dollar and eighty-seven cents. And the next day would be Christmas.

There was clearly nothing to do but flop down on the shabby little couch and howl. So Della did it. Which instigates the moral reflection that life is made up of sobs, sniffles, and smiles, with sniffles predominating.

While the mistress of the home is gradually subsiding from the first stage to the second, take a look at the home. A furnished flat at $8 per week. It did not exactly beggar description, but it certainly had that word on the lookout for the mendicancy squad.

In the vestibule below was a letter-box into which no letter would go, and an electric button from which no mortal finger could coax a ring. Also appertaining thereunto was a card bearing the name "Mr. James Dillingham Young." The "Dillingham" had been flung to the breeze during a former period of prosperity when its possessor was being paid $30 per week. Now, when the income was shrunk to $20, the letters of "Dillingham" looked blurred, as though they were thinking seriously of contracting to a modest and unassuming D. But whenever Mr. James Dillingham Young came home and reached his flat above he was called "Jim" and greatly hugged by Mrs. James Dillingham Young, already

introduced to you as Della. Which is all very good.

Della finished her cry and attended to her cheeks with the powder rag. She stood by the window and looked out dully at a grey cat walking a grey fence in a grey backyard. Tomorrow would be Christmas Day, and she had only $1.87 with which to buy Jim a present. She had been saving every penny she could for months, with this result. Twenty dollars a week doesn't go far. Expenses had been greater than she had calculated. They always are. Only $1.87 to buy a present for Jim. Her Jim. Many a happy hour she had spent planning for something nice for him. Something fine and rare and sterling — something just a little bit near to being worthy of the honour of being owned by Jim.

There was a pier-glass between the windows of the room. Perhaps you have seen a pier-glass in an $8 flat. A very thin and very agile person may, by observing his reflection in a rapid sequence of longitudinal strips, obtain a fairly accurate conception of his looks. Della, being slender, had mastered the art.

Suddenly she whirled from the window and stood before the glass. Her eyes were shining brilliantly, but her face had lost its colour within twenty seconds. Rapidly she pulled down her hair and let it fall to its full length.

Now, there were two possessions of the James Dillingham Youngs in which they both took a mighty pride. One was Jim's gold watch that had been his father's and his grandfather's. The other was Della's hair. Had the Queen of Sheba lived in the flat across the airshaft, Della would have let her hair hang out the window some day to dry just to depreciate Her Majesty's jewels and gifts. Had King Solomon been the janitor, with all his treasures piled up in the basement, Jim would have pulled out his watch every time he passed, just to see him pluck at his beard from envy.

So now Della's beautiful hair fell about her, rippling and shining like a cascade of brown waters. It reached below her knee and made itself almost a garment for her. And then she did it up again nervously and quickly. Once she faltered for a minute and stood still while a tear or two splashed on the worn red carpet.

On went her old brown jacket; on went her old brown hat. With a whirl of skirts and with the brilliant sparkle still in her eyes, she fluttered out the door and down the stairs to the street.

Where she stopped the sign read: "Mme. Sofronie. Hair Goods of All Kinds." One flight up Della ran, and collected herself, panting. Madame, large, too white, chilly, hardly looked the "Sofronie."

"Will you buy my hair?" asked Della.

"I buy hair," said Madame. "Take yer hat off and let's have a sight at the looks of it."

Down rippled the brown cascade. "Twenty dollars," said Madame, lifting the mass with a practised hand.

"Give it to me quick," said Della.

Oh, and the next two hours tripped by on rosy wings. Forget the hashed metaphor. She was ransacking the stores for Jim's present.

She found it at last. It surely had been made for Jim and no one else. There was no other like it in any of the stores, and she had turned all of them inside out. It was a platinum fob chain simple and chaste in design, properly proclaiming its value by substance alone and not by meretricious ornamentation — as all good things should do. It was even worthy of The Watch. As soon as she saw it she that it must be Jim's. It was like him. Quietness and value — the description applied to both. Twenty-one dollars they took from her for it, and she hurried home with the 87 cents. With that chain on his watch Jim might be properly anxious about the time in any company. Grand as the watch was, he sometimes looked at it on the sly on account of the old leather strap that he used in place of a chain.

When Della reached home her intoxication gave way a little to prudence and reason. She got out her curling irons and lighted the gas and went to work repairing the ravages made by generosity added to love. Which is always a tremendous task, dear friends — a mammoth task.

Within forty minutes her head was covered with tiny, closelying curls that made her look wonderfully like a truant schoolboy. She looked at her reflection in the mirror long, carefully, and critically.

"If Jim doesn't kill me," she said to herself, "before he takes a second look at me, he'll say I look like a Coney Island chorus girl. But what could I do — oh! what could I do with a dollar and eighty-seven cents?"

At 7 o'clock the coffee was made and the frying-pan was on the back of the stove hot and ready to cook the chops.

Jim was never late. Della doubled the fob chain in her hand and sat on the corner of the table near the door that he always entered. Then she heard his step on the stair away down on the first flight, and she turned white for just a moment. She had a habit for saying little silent prayers about the simplest everyday things, and now she whispered: "Please God, make him think I am still pretty."

The door opened and Jim stepped in and closed it. He looked thin and very serious. Poor fellow, he was only twenty-two — and to be burdened with a family! He needed a new overcoat and he was without gloves.

Jim stopped inside the door, as immovable as a setter at the scent of quail. His eyes were fixed upon Della, and there was an expression in them that she could not read, and it terrified her. It was not anger, nor surprise, nor disapproval, nor horror, nor any of the sentiments that she had been prepared for. He simply stared at her fixedly with that peculiar expression on his face.

Della wriggled off the table and went for him.

"Jim, darling," she cried, "don't look at me that way. I had my hair cut off and sold because I couldn't have lived through Christmas without giving you a present. It'll grow out again — you won't mind, will you? I just had to do it. My hair grows awfully fast. Say 'Merry Christmas!' Jim, and let's be happy. You don't know what a nice — what a beautiful, nice gift I've got for you."

"You've cut off your hair?" asked Jim, laboriously, as if he had not arrived at that patent fact yet even after the hardest mental labor.

"Cut it off and sold it," said Della. "Don't you like me just as well, anyhow? I'm me without my hair, ain't I?"

Jim looked about the room curiously.

"You say your hair is gone?" he said, with an air almost of idiocy.

"You needn't look for it," said Della. "It's sold, I tell you — sold and gone, too. It's Christmas Eve, boy. Be good to me, for it went for you. Maybe the hairs of my head were numbered," she went on with sudden serious sweetness, "but nobody could ever count my love for you. Shall I put the chops on, Jim?"

Out of his trance Jim seemed quickly to wake. He enfolded his Della. For ten seconds let us regard with discreet scrutiny some inconsequential object in the other direction. Eight dollars a week or a million a year — what is the difference? A mathematician or a wit would give you the wrong answer. The magi brought valuable gifts, but that was not among them. This dark assertion will be illuminated later on.

Jim drew a package from his overcoat pocket and threw it upon the table.

"Don't make any mistake, Dell," he said, "about me. I don't think there's anything in the way of a haircut or a shave or a shampoo that could make me like my girl any less. But if you'll unwrap that package you may see why you had me going a while at first."

White fingers and nimble tore at the string and paper. And then an ecstatic scream of joy; and then, alas! a quick feminine change to hysterical tears and wails, necessitating the immediate employment of all the comforting powers of the lord of the flat.

For there lay The Combs — the set of combs, side and back, that Della had worshipped long in a Broadway window. Beautiful combs, pure tortoise shell, with jewelled rims — just the shade to wear in the beautiful vanished hair. They were expensive combs, she knew, and her heart had simply craved and yearned over them without the least hope of possession. And now, they were hers, but the tresses that should have adorned the coveted adornments were gone.

But she hugged them to her bosom, and at length she was able to look up with dim eyes and a smile and say: "My hair grows so fast, Jim!"

And them Della leaped up like a little singed cat and cried, "Oh, oh!"

Jim had not yet seen his beautiful present. She held it out to him eagerly upon her open palm. The dull precious metal seemed to flash with a reflection of her bright and ardent spirit.

"Isn't it a dandy, Jim? I hunted all over town to find it. You'll have to look at the time a hundred times a day now. Give me your watch. I want to see how it looks on it."

Instead of obeying, Jim tumbled down on the couch and put his hands under the back of his head and smiled.

"Dell," said he, "let's put our Christmas presents away and keep 'em a while. They're too nice to use just at present. I sold the watch to get the money to buy your combs. And now suppose you put the chops on."

The magi, as you know, were wise men — wonderfully wise men — who brought gifts to the Babe in the manger. They invented the art of giving Christmas presents. Being wise, their gifts were no doubt wise ones, possibly bearing the privilege of exchange in case of duplication. And here I have lamely related to you the uneventful chronicle of two foolish children in a flat who most unwisely sacrificed for each other the greatest treasures of their house. But in a last word to the wise of these days let it be said that of all who give gifts these two were the wisest. Of all who give and receive gifts, such as they are wisest. Everywhere they are wisest. They are the magi.

The Last Leaf

In a little district west of Washington Square the streets have run crazy and broken themselves into small strips called "places." These "places" make strange angles and curves. One street crosses itself a time or two. An artist once discovered a valuable possibility in this street. Suppose a collector with a bill for paints, paper and canvas should, in traversing this route, suddenly meet himself coming back, without a cent having been paid on account!

So, to quaint old Greenwich Village the art people soon came prowling, hunting for north windows and eighteenth-century gables and Dutch attics and low rents. Then they imported some pewter mugs and a chafing dish or two from Sixth avenue, and became a "colony."

At the top of a squatty, three-story brick Sue and Johnsy had their studio. "Johnsy" was familiar for Joanna. One was from Maine; the other from California. They had met at the *table d'hôte* of an Eighth street "Delmonico's," and found their tastes in art, chicory salad and bishop sleeves so congenial that the joint studio resulted.

That was in May. In November a cold, unseen stranger, whom the doctors called Pneumonia, stalked about the colony, touching one here and there with his icy fingers. Over on the east side this ravager strode boldly, smiting his victims by scores, but his feet trod slowly through the maze of the narrow and moss-grown "places."

Mr. Pneumonia was not what you would call a chivalric old gentleman. A mite of a little woman with blood thinned by California zephyrs was hardly fair game for the red-fisted, short-breathed old duffer. But Johnsy he smote; and she lay, scarcely moving, on her painted iron bedstead, looking through the small Dutch windowpanes at the blank side of the next brick house.

One morning the busy doctor invited Sue into the hallway with a shaggy, gray eyebrow.

"She has one chance in — let us say, ten," he said, as he shook down the mercury in his clinical thermometer. "And that chance is for her to want to live. This way people have of lining-up on the side of the undertaker makes the entire pharmacopeia look silly. Your little lady has made up her mind that she's not going to get well. Has she anything on her mind?"

"She — she wanted to paint the Bay of Naples some day," said Sue.

"Paint? — bosh! Has she anything on her mind worth thinking about twice — a man, for instance?"

"A man?" said Sue, with a jew's-harp twang in her voice. "Is a man worth — but, no, doctor; there is nothing of the kind."

"Well, it is the weakness, then," said the doctor. "I will do all that science, so far as it may filter through my efforts, can accomplish. But whenever my patient begins to count the carriages in her funeral procession I subtract 50 per cent. from the curative power of medicines. If you will get her to ask one question about the new winter styles in cloak sleeves I will promise you a one-in-five chance for her, instead of one in ten."

After the doctor had gone Sue went into the workroom and cried a Japanese napkin to a pulp. Then she swaggered into Johnsy's room with her drawing board, whistling ragtime.

Johnsy lay, scarcely making a ripple under the bedclothes, with her face toward the window. Sue stopped whistling, thinking she was asleep.

She arranged her board and began a pen-and-ink drawing to illustrate a magazine story. Young artists must pave their way to Art by drawing pictures for magazine stories that young authors write to pave their way to Literature.

As Sue was sketching a pair of elegant horseshow riding trousers and a monocle on the figure of the hero, an Idaho cowboy, she heard a low sound, several times repeated. She went quickly to the bedside.

Johnsy's eyes were open wide. She was looking out the window and counting — counting backward.

"Twelve," she said, and a little later "eleven;" and then "ten," and "nine;" and then "eight" and "seven," almost together.

Sue looked solicitously out the window. What was there to count? There was only a bare, dreary yard to be seen, and the blank side of the brick house twenty feet away. An old, old ivy vine, gnarled and decayed at the roots, climbed half way up the brick wall. The cold breath of autumn had stricken its leaves from the vine until its skeleton branches clung, almost bare, to the crumbling bricks.

"What is it, dear?" asked Sue.

"Six," said Johnsy, in almost a whisper. "They're falling faster now. Three days ago there were almost a hundred. It made my head ache to count them. But now it's easy. There goes another one. There are only five left now."

"Five what, dear. Tell your Sudie."

"Leaves. On the ivy vine. When the last one falls I must go, too. I've known that for three days. Didn't the doctor tell you?"

"Oh, I never heard of such nonsense," complained Sue, with magnificent scorn. "What have old ivy leaves to do with your getting well? And you used to love that vine so, you naughty girl. Don't be a goosey. Why, the doctor told me this morning that your chances for getting well real soon were — let's see exactly what he said — he said the chances were ten to one! Why, that's almost as good a chance as we have in New York when we ride on the street cars or walk past a new building. Try to take some broth now, and let Sudie go back to her drawing, so she can sell the editor man with it, and buy port wine for her sick child, and pork chops for her greedy self."

"You needn't get any more wine," said Johnsy, keeping her eyes fixed out the window. "There goes another. No, I don't want any broth. That leaves just four. I want to see the last one fall before it gets dark. Then I'll go, too."

"Johnsy, dear," said Sue, bending over her, "will you promise me to keep your eyes closed, and not look out the window until I am done working? I must hand those drawings in by tomorrow. I need the light, or I would draw the shade down."

"Couldn't you draw in the other room?" asked Johnsy, coldly.

"I'd rather be here by you," said Sue. "Besides I don't want you to keep looking at those silly ivy leaves."

"Tell me as soon as you have finished," said Johnsy, closing her eyes, and lying white and still as a fallen statue, "because I want to see the last one fall. I'm tired of waiting. I'm tired of thinking. I want to turn loose my hold on everything, and go sailing down, down, just like one of those poor, tired leaves."

"Try to sleep," said Sue. "I must call Behrman up to be my model for the old hermit miner. I'll not be gone a minute. Don't try to move 'till I come back."

Old Behrman was a painter who lived on the ground floor beneath them. He was past sixty and had a Michael Angelo's Moses beard curling down from the head of a satyr along the body of an imp. Behrman was a failure in art. Forty years he had wielded the brush without getting near enough to touch the hem of his Mistress's robe. He had been always about to paint a masterpiece, but had never yet begun it. For several years he had painted nothing except now and then a daub in the line of commerce or advertising. He earned a little by serving as a model to those young artists in the colony who could not pay the price of a professional. He drank gin to excess, and still talked of his coming masterpiece. For the rest he was a fierce little old man, who scoffed terribly at softness in any one, and who regarded himself as especial mastiff-in-waiting to protect the two young artists in the studio above.

Sue found Behrman smelling strongly of juniper berries in his dimly lighted den below. In one corner was a blank canvas on an easel that had been waiting there for twenty-five years to receive the first line of the masterpiece. She told him of Johnsy's fancy, and how she feared she would, indeed, light and fragile as a leaf herself, float away when her slight hold upon the world grew weaker.

Old Behrman, with his red eyes, plainly streaming, shouted his contempt and derision for such idiotic imaginings.

"Vass!" he cried. "Is dere people in de world mit der foolishness to die because leafs dey drop off from a confounded vine? I haf not heard of such a thing. No, I will not bose as a model for your fool hermit-dunderhead. Vy do you allow dot silly pusiness to come in der prain of her? Ach, dot poor lettle Miss Johnsy."

"She is very ill and weak," said Sue, "and the fever has left her mind morbid and full of strange fancies. Very well, Mr. Behrman, if you do not care to pose for me, you needn't. But I think you are a horrid old — old flibbertigibbet."

"You are just like a woman!" yelled Behrman. "Who said I will not bose? Go on. I come mit you. For half an hour I haf peen trying to say dot I am ready to bose. Gott! dis is not any blace in which one so goot as Miss Yohnsy shall lie sick. Some day I vill baint a masterpiece, and ve shall all go away. Gott! yes."

Johnsy was sleeping when they went upstairs. Sue pulled the shade down to the window-sill, and motioned Behrman into the other room. In there they peered out the window fearfully at the ivy vine. Then they looked at each other for a moment without speaking. A persistent, cold rain was falling, mingled with snow. Behrman, in his old blue shirt, took his seat as the hermit-miner on an upturned kettle for a rock.

When Sue awoke from an hour's sleep the next morning she found Johnsy with dull, wide-open eyes staring at the drawn green shade.

"Pull it up; I want to see," she ordered, in a whisper.

Wearily Sue obeyed.

But, lo! after the beating rain and fierce gusts of wind that had endured through the livelong night, there yet stood out against the brick wall one ivy leaf. It was the last on the vine. Still dark green near its stem, but with its serrated edges tinted with the yellow of dissolution and decay, it hung bravely from a branch some twenty feet above the ground.

"It is the last one," said Johnsy. "I thought it would surely fall during the night. I heard the wind. It will fall to-day, and I shall die at the same time."

"Dear, dear!" said Sue, leaning her worn face down to the pillow, "think of me, if you won't think of yourself. What would I do?"

But Johnsy did not answer. The lonesomest thing in all the world is a soul when it is making ready to go on its mysterious, far journey. The fancy seemed to possess her more strongly as one by one the ties that bound her to friendship and to earth were loosed.

The day wore away, and even through the twilight they could see the lone ivy leaf clinging to its stem against the wall. And then, with the coming of the night the north wind was again loosed, while the rain still beat against the windows and pattered down from the low Dutch eaves.

When it was light enough Johnsy, the merciless, commanded that the shade be raised.

The ivy leaf was still there.

Johnsy lay for a long time looking at it. And then she called to Sue, who was stirring her chicken broth over the gas stove.

"I've been a bad girl, Sudie," said Johnsy. "Something has made that last leaf stay there to show me how wicked I was. It is a sin to want to die. You may bring me a little broth now, and some milk with a little port in it, and — no; bring me a hand-mirror first, and then pack some pillows about me, and I will sit up and watch you cook."

An hour later she said.

"Sudie, some day I hope to paint the Bay of Naples."

The doctor came in the afternoon, and Sue had an excuse to go into the hallway as he left.

"Even chances," said the doctor, taking Sue's thin, shaking hand in his. "With good nursing you'll win. And now I must see another case I have downstairs. Behrman, his name is — some kind of an artist, I believe. Pneumonia, too. He is an old, weak man, and the attack is acute. There is no hope for him; but he goes to the hospital to-day to be made more comfortable."

The next day the doctor said to Sue: "She's out of danger. You've won. Nutrition and care now — that's all."

And that afternoon Sue came to the bed where Johnsy lay, contentedly knitting a very blue and very useless woolen shoulder scarf, and put one arm around her, pillows and all.

"I have something to tell you, white mouse," she said. "Mr. Behrman died of pneumonia to-day in the hospital. He was ill only two days. The janitor found him on the morning of the first day in his room downstairs helpless with pain. His shoes and clothing were wet through and icy cold. They couldn't imagine where he had been on such a dreadful night. And then they found a lantern, still lighted, and a ladder that had been dragged from its place, and some scattered brushes, and a palette with green and yellow colors mixed on it, and — look out the window, dear, at the last ivy leaf on the wall. Didn't you wonder why it never fluttered or moved when the wind blew? Ah, darling, it's Behrman's masterpiece — he painted it there the night that the last leaf fell."

The Ransom Of Red Chief

It looked like a good thing: but wait till I tell you. We were down South, in Alabama — Bill Driscoll and myself — when this kidnapping idea struck us. It was, as Bill afterward expressed it, "during a moment of temporary mental apparition"; but we didn't find that out till later.

There was a town down there, as flat as a flannel-cake, and called Summit, of course. It contained inhabitants of as undeleterious and self-satisfied a class of peasantry as ever clustered around a Maypole.

Bill and me had a joint capital of about six hundred dollars, and we needed just two thousand dollars more to pull off a fraudulent town-lot scheme in Western Illinois with. We talked it over on the front steps of the hotel. Philoprogenitiveness, says we, is strong in semi-rural communities; therefore and for other reasons, a kidnapping project ought to do better there than in the radius of newspapers that send reporters out in plain clothes to stir up talk about such things. We knew that Summit couldn't get after us with anything stronger than constables and maybe some lackadaisical bloodhounds and a diatribe or two in the *Weekly Farmers' Budget* . So, it looked good.

We selected for our victim the only child of a prominent citizen named Ebenezer Dorset. The father was respectable and tight, a mortgage fancier and a stern, upright collection-plate passer and forecloser. The kid was a boy of ten, with bas-relief freckles, and hair the colour of the cover of the magazine you buy at the news-stand when you want to catch a train. Bill and me figured that Ebenezer would melt down for a ransom of two thousand dollars to a cent. But wait till I tell you.

About two miles from Summit was a little mountain, covered with a dense cedar brake. On the rear elevation of this mountain was a cave. There we stored provisions. One evening after sundown, we drove in a buggy past old Dorset's house. The kid was in the street, throwing rocks at a kitten on the opposite fence.

"Hey, little boy!" says Bill, "would you like to have a bag of candy and a nice ride?"

The boy catches Bill neatly in the eye with a piece of brick.

"That will cost the old man an extra five hundred dollars," says Bill, climbing over the wheel.

That boy put up a fight like a welter-weight cinnamon bear; but, at last, we got him down in the bottom of the buggy and drove away. We took him up to the cave and I hitched the horse in the cedar brake. After dark I drove the buggy to the little village, three miles away, where we had hired it, and walked back to the mountain.

Bill was pasting court-plaster over the scratches and bruises on his features. There was a fire burning behind the big rock at the entrance of the cave, and the boy was watching a pot of boiling coffee, with two buzzard tail-feathers stuck in his red hair. He points a stick at me when I come up, and says:

"Ha! cursed paleface, do you dare to enter the camp of Red Chief, the terror of the plains?"

"He's all right now," says Bill, rolling up his trousers and examining some bruises on his shins. "We're playing Indian. We're making Buffalo Bill's show look like magic-lantern views of Palestine in the town hall. I'm Old Hank, the Trapper, Red Chief's captive, and I'm to be scalped at daybreak. By Geronimo! that kid can kick hard."

Yes, sir, that boy seemed to be having the time of his life. The fun of camping out in a cave had made him forget that he was a captive himself. He immediately christened me Snake-eye, the Spy, and announced that, when his braves returned from the warpath, I was to be broiled at the stake at the rising of the sun.

Then we had supper; and he filled his mouth full of bacon and bread and gravy, and began to talk. He made a during-dinner speech something like this:

"I like this fine. I never camped out before; but I had a pet 'possum once, and I was nine last birthday. I hate to go to school. Rats ate up sixteen of Jimmy Talbot's aunt's speckled hen's eggs. Are there any real Indians in these woods? I want some more gravy. Does the trees moving make the wind blow? We had five puppies. What makes your nose so red, Hank? My father has lots of money. Are the stars hot? I whipped Ed Walker twice, Saturday. I don't like girls. You dassent catch toads unless with a string. Do oxen make any noise? Why are oranges round? Have you got beds to sleep on in this cave? Amos Murray has got six toes. A parrot can talk, but a monkey or a fish can't. How many does it take to make twelve?"

Every few minutes he would remember that he was a pesky redskin, and pick up his stick rifle and tiptoe to the mouth of the cave to rubber for the scouts of the hated paleface. Now and then he would let out a war-whoop that made Old Hank the Trapper shiver. That boy had Bill terrorized from the start.

"Red Chief," says I to the kid, "would you like to go home?"

"Aw, what for?" says he. "I don't have any fun at home. I hate to go to school. I like to camp out. You won't take me back home again, Snake-eye, will you?"

"Not right away," says I. "We'll stay here in the cave a while."

"All right!" says he. "That'll be fine. I never had such fun in all my life."

We went to bed about eleven o'clock. We spread down some wide blankets and quilts and put Red Chief between us. We weren't afraid he'd run away. He kept us awake for three hours, jumping up and reaching for his rifle and screeching: "Hist! pard," in mine and Bill's ears, as the fancied crackle of a twig or the rustle of a leaf revealed to his young imagination the stealthy approach of the outlaw band. At last, I fell into a troubled sleep, and dreamed that I had been kidnapped and chained to a tree by a ferocious pirate with red hair.

Just at daybreak, I was awakened by a series of awful screams from Bill. They weren't yells, or howls, or shouts, or whoops, or yawps, such as you'd expect from a manly set of vocal organs — they were simply indecent, terrifying, humiliating screams, such as women emit when they see ghosts or caterpillars. It's an awful thing to hear a strong, desperate, fat man scream incontinently in a cave at daybreak.

I jumped up to see what the matter was. Red Chief was sitting on Bill's chest, with one hand twined in Bill's hair. In the other he had the sharp case-knife we used for slicing bacon; and he was industriously and realistically trying to take Bill's scalp, according to the sentence that had been pronounced upon him the evening before.

I got the knife away from the kid and made him lie down again. But, from that moment, Bill's spirit was broken. He laid down on his side of the bed, but he never closed an eye again in sleep as long as that boy was with us. I dozed off for a while, but along toward sun-up I remembered that Red Chief had said I was to be burned at the stake at the rising of the sun. I wasn't nervous or afraid; but I sat up and lit my pipe and leaned against a rock.

"What you getting up so soon for, Sam?" asked Bill.

"Me?" says I. "Oh, I got a kind of a pain in my shoulder. I thought sitting up would rest it."

"You're a liar!" says Bill. "You're afraid. You was to be burned at sunrise, and you was afraid he'd do it. And he would, too, if he could find a match. Ain't it awful, Sam? Do you think anybody will pay out money to get a little imp like that back home?"

"Sure," said I. "A rowdy kid like that is just the kind that parents dote on. Now, you and the Chief get up and cook breakfast, while I go up on the top of this mountain and reconnoitre."

I went up on the peak of the little mountain and ran my eye over the contiguous vicinity. Over toward Summit I expected to see the sturdy yeomanry of the village armed with scythes and pitchforks beating the countryside for the dastardly kidnappers. But what I saw was a peaceful landscape dotted with one man ploughing with a dun mule. Nobody was dragging the creek; no couriers dashed hither and yon, bringing tidings of no news to the distracted parents. There was a sylvan attitude of somnolent sleepiness pervading that section of the external outward surface of Alabama that lay exposed to my view. "Perhaps," says I to myself, "it has not yet been discovered that the wolves have borne away the tender lambkin from the fold. Heaven help the wolves!" says I, and I went down the mountain to breakfast.

When I got to the cave I found Bill backed up against the side of it, breathing hard, and the boy threatening to smash him with a rock half as big as a cocoanut.

"He put a red-hot boiled potato down my back," explained Bill, "and then mashed it with his foot; and I boxed his ears. Have you got a gun about you, Sam?"

I took the rock away from the boy and kind of patched up the argument. "I'll fix you," says the kid to Bill. "No man ever yet struck the Red Chief but what he got paid for it. You better beware!"

After breakfast the kid takes a piece of leather with strings wrapped around it out of his pocket and goes outside the cave unwinding it.

"What's he up to now?" says Bill, anxiously. "You don't think he'll run away, do you, Sam?"

"No fear of it," says I. "He don't seem to be much of a home body. But we've got to fix up some plan about the ransom. There don't seem to be much excitement around Summit on account of his disappearance; but maybe they haven't realized yet that he's gone. His folks may think he's spending the night with Aunt Jane or one of the neighbours. Anyhow, he'll be missed to-day. Tonight we must get a message to his father demanding the two thousand dollars for his return."

Just then we heard a kind Of war-whoop, such as David might have emitted when he knocked out the champion Goliath. It was a sling that Red Chief had pulled out of his pocket, and he was whirling it around his head.

I dodged, and heard a heavy thud and a kind of a sigh from Bill, like a horse gives out when you take his saddle off. A niggerhead rock the size of an egg had caught Bill just behind his left ear. He loosened himself all over and fell in the fire across the frying pan of hot water for washing the dishes. I dragged him out and poured cold water on his head for half an hour.

By and by, Bill sits up and feels behind his ear and says: "Sam, do you know who my favourite Biblical character is?"

"Take it easy," says I. "You'll come to your senses presently."

"King Herod," says he. "You won't go away and leave me here alone, will you, Sam?"

I went out and caught that boy and shook him until his freckles rattled.

"If you don't behave," says I, "I'll take you straight home. Now, are you going to be good, or not?"

"I was only funning," says he sullenly. "I didn't mean to hurt Old Hank. But what did he hit me for? I'll behave, Snake-eye, if you won't send me home, and if you'll let me play the Black Scout to-day."

"I don't know the game," says I. "That's for you and Mr. Bill to decide. He's your playmate for the day. I'm going away for a while, on business. Now, you come in and make friends with him and say you are sorry for hurting him, or home you go, at once."

I made him and Bill shake hands, and then I took Bill aside and told him I was going to Poplar Cove, a little village three miles from the cave, and find out what I could about how the kidnapping had been regarded in Summit. Also, I thought it best to send a peremptory letter to old man Dorset that day, demanding the ransom and dictating how it should be paid.

"You know, Sam," says Bill, "I've stood by you without batting an eye in earthquakes, fire and flood — in poker games, dynamite outrages, police raids, train robberies and cyclones. I never lost my nerve yet till we kidnapped that two-legged skyrocket of a kid. He's got me going. You won't leave me long with him, will you, Sam?"

"I'll be back some time this afternoon," says I. "You must keep the boy amused and quiet till I return. And now we'll write the letter to old Dorset."

Bill and I got paper and pencil and worked on the letter while Red Chief, with a blanket wrapped around him, strutted up and down, guarding the mouth of the cave. Bill begged me tearfully to make the ransom fifteen hundred dollars instead of two thousand. "I ain't attempting," says he, "to decry the celebrated moral aspect of parental affection, but we're dealing with humans, and it ain't human for anybody to give up two thousand dollars for that forty-pound chunk of freckled wildcat. I'm willing to take a chance at fifteen hundred dollars. You can charge the difference up to me."

So, to relieve Bill, I acceded, and we collaborated a letter that ran this way:

Ebenezer Dorset, Esq.:

We have your boy concealed in a place far from Summit. It is useless for you or the most skilful detectives to attempt to find him. Absolutely, the only terms on which you can have him restored to you are these: We demand fifteen hundred dollars in large bills for his return; the money to be left at midnight tonight at the same spot and in the same box as your reply — as hereinafter described. If you agree to these terms, send your answer in writing by a solitary messenger tonight at half-past eight o'clock. After crossing Owl Creek, on the road to Poplar Cove, there are three large trees about a hundred yards apart, close to the fence of the wheat field on the right-hand side. At the bottom of the fence-post, opposite the third tree, will be found a small pasteboard box.

The messenger will place the answer in this box and return immediately to Summit.

If you attempt any treachery or fail to comply with our demand as stated, you will never see your boy again.

If you pay the money as demanded, he will be returned to you safe and well within three hours. These terms are final, and if you do not accede to them no further communication will be attempted.

TWO DESPERATE MEN.

I addressed this letter to Dorset, and put it in my pocket. As I was about to start, the kid comes up to me and says:

"Aw, Snake-eye, you said I could play the Black Scout while you was gone."

"Play it, of course," says I. "Mr. Bill will play with you. What kind of a game is it?"

"I'm the Black Scout," says Red Chief, "and I have to ride to the stockade to warn the settlers that the Indians are coming. I'm tired of playing Indian myself. I want to be the Black Scout."

"All right," says I. "It sounds harmless to me. I guess Mr. Bill will help you foil the pesky savages."

"What am I to do?" asks Bill, looking at the kid suspiciously.

"You are the hoss," says Black Scout. "Get down on your hands and knees. How can I ride to the stockade without a hoss?"

"You'd better keep him interested," said I, "till we get the scheme going. Loosen up."

Bill gets down on his all fours, and a look comes in his eye like a rabbit's when you catch it in a trap.

"How far is it to the stockade, kid?" he asks, in a husky manner of voice.

"Ninety miles," says the Black Scout. "And you have to hump yourself to get there on time. Whoa, now!"

The Black Scout jumps on Bill's back and digs his heels in his side.

"For Heaven's sake," says Bill, "hurry back, Sam, as soon as you can. I wish we hadn't made the ransom more than a thousand. Say, you quit kicking me or I'll get up and warm you good."

I walked over to Poplar Cove and sat around the postoffice and store, talking with the chawbacons that came in to trade. One whiskerando says that he hears Summit is all upset on account of Elder Ebenezer Dorset's boy having been lost or stolen. That was all I wanted to know. I bought some smoking tobacco, referred casually to the price of black-eyed peas, posted my letter surreptitiously and came away. The postmaster said the mail-carrier would come by in an hour to take the mail on to Summit.

When I got back to the cave Bill and the boy were not to be found. I explored the vicinity of the cave, and risked a yodel or two, but there was no response.

So I lighted my pipe and sat down on a mossy bank to await developments.

In about half an hour I heard the bushes rustle, and Bill wabbled out into the little glade in front of the cave. Behind him was the kid, stepping softly like a scout, with a broad grin on his face. Bill stopped, took off his hat and wiped his face with a red handkerchief. The kid stopped about eight feet behind him.

"Sam," says Bill, "I suppose you'll think I'm a renegade, but I couldn't help it. I'm a grown person with masculine proclivities and habits of self-defense, but there is a time when all systems of egotism and predominance fail. The boy is gone. I have sent him home. All is off. There was martyrs in old times," goes on Bill, "that suffered death rather than give up the particular graft they enjoyed. None of 'em ever was subjugated to such supernatural tortures as I have been. I tried to be faithful to our articles of depredation; but there came a limit."

"What's the trouble, Bill?" I asks him.

"I was rode," says Bill, "the ninety miles to the stockade, not barring an inch. Then, when the settlers was rescued, I was given oats. Sand ain't a palatable substitute. And then, for an hour I had to try to explain to him why there was nothin' in holes, how a road can run both ways and what makes the grass green. I tell you, Sam, a human can only stand so much. I takes him by the neck of his clothes and drags him down the mountain. On the way he kicks my legs black-and-blue from the knees down; and I've got to have two or three bites on my thumb and hand cauterized.

"But he's gone" — continues Bill — "gone home. I showed him the road to Summit and kicked him about eight feet nearer there at one kick. I'm sorry we lose the ransom; but it was either that or Bill Driscoll to the madhouse."

Bill is puffing and blowing, but there is a look of ineffable peace and growing content on his rose-pink features.

"Bill," says I, "there isn't any heart disease in your family, is there?"

"No," says Bill, "nothing chronic except malaria and accidents. Why?"

"Then you might turn around," says I, "and have a took behind you."

Bill turns and sees the boy, and loses his complexion and sits down plump on the round and begins to pluck aimlessly at grass and little sticks. For an hour I was afraid for his mind. And then I told him that my scheme was to put the whole job through immediately and that we would get the ransom and be off with it by midnight if old Dorset fell in with our proposition. So Bill braced up enough to give the kid a weak sort of a smile and a promise to play the Russian in a Japanese war with him is soon as he felt a little better.

I had a scheme for collecting that ransom without danger of being caught by counterplots that ought to commend itself to professional kidnappers. The tree under which the answer was to be left — and the money later on — was close to the road fence with big, bare fields on all sides. If a gang of constables should be watching for any one to come for the note they could see him a long way off crossing the fields or in the road. But no, sirree! At half-past eight I was up in that tree as well hidden as a tree toad, waiting for the messenger to arrive.

Exactly on time, a half-grown boy rides up the road on a bicycle, locates the pasteboard box at the foot of the fence-post, slips a folded piece of paper into it and pedals away again back toward Summit.

I waited an hour and then concluded the thing was square. I slid down the tree, got the note, slipped along the fence till I struck the woods, and was back at the cave in another half an hour. I opened the note, got near the lantern and read it to Bill. It was written with a pen in a crabbed hand, and the sum and substance of it was this:

Two Desperate Men.

Gentlemen: I received your letter to-day by post, in regard to the ransom you ask for the return of my son. I think you are a little high in your demands, and I hereby make you a counter-proposition, which I am inclined to believe you will accept. You bring Johnny home and pay me two hundred and fifty dollars in cash, and I agree to take him off your hands. You had better come at night, for the neighbours believe he is lost, and I couldn't be responsible for what they would do to anybody they saw bringing him back. Very respectfully,

EBENEZER DORSET.

"Great pirates of Penzance!" says I; "of all the impudent —"

But I glanced at Bill, and hesitated. He had the most appealing look in his eyes I ever saw on the face of a dumb or a talking brute.

"Sam," says he, "what's two hundred and fifty dollars, after all? We've got the money. One more night of this kid will send me to a bed in Bedlam. Besides being a thorough gentleman,

I think Mr. Dorset is a spendthrift for making us such a liberal offer. You ain't going to let the chance go, are you?"

"Tell you the truth, Bill," says I, "this little he ewe lamb has somewhat got on my nerves too. We'll take him home, pay the ransom and make our getaway."

We took him home that night. We got him to go by telling him that his father had bought a silver-mounted rifle and a pair of moccasins for him, and we were going to hunt bears the next day.

It was just twelve o'clock when we knocked at Ebenezer's front door. Just at the moment when I should have been abstracting the fifteen hundred dollars from the box under the tree, according to the original proposition, Bill was counting out two hundred and fifty dollars into Dorset's hand.

When the kid found out we were going to leave him at home he started up a howl like a calliope and fastened himself as tight as a leech to Bill's leg. His father peeled him away gradually, like a porous plaster.

"How long can you hold him?" asks Bill.

"I'm not as strong as I used to be," says old Dorset, "but I think I can promise you ten minutes."

"Enough," says Bill. "In ten minutes I shall cross the Central, Southern and Middle Western States, and be legging it trippingly for the Canadian border."

And, as dark as it was, and as fat as Bill was, and as good a runner as I am, he was a good mile and a half out of Summit before I could catch up with him.

The Skylight Room

First Mrs. Parker would show you the double parlours. You would not dare to interrupt her description of their advantages and of the merits of the gentleman who had occupied them for eight years. Then you would manage to stammer forth the confession that you were neither a doctor nor a dentist. Mrs. Parker's manner of receiving the admission was such that you could never afterward entertain the same feeling toward your parents, who had neglected to train you up in one of the professions that fitted Mrs. Parker's parlours.

Next you ascended one flight of stairs and looked at the second-floor-back at $8. Convinced by her second-floor manner that it was worth the $12 that Mr. Toosenberry always paid for it until he left to take charge of his brother's orange plantation in Florida near Palm Beach, where Mrs. McIntyre always spent the winters that had the double front room with private bath, you managed to babble that you wanted something still cheaper.

If you survived Mrs. Parker's scorn, you were taken to look at Mr. Skidder's large hall room on the third floor. Mr. Skidder's room was not vacant. He wrote plays and smoked cigarettes in it all day long. But every room-hunter was made to visit his room to admire the lambrequins. After each visit, Mr. Skidder, from the fright caused by possible eviction, would pay something on his rent.

Then — oh, then — if you still stood on one foot, with your hot hand clutching the three moist dollars in your pocket, and hoarsely proclaimed your hideous and culpable poverty, nevermore would Mrs. Parker be cicerone of yours. She would honk loudly the word "Clara," she would show you her back, and march downstairs. Then Clara, the coloured maid, would escort you up the carpeted ladder that served for the fourth flight, and show you the Skylight Room. It occupied 7×8 feet of floor space at the middle of the hall. On each side of it was a dark lumber closet or storeroom.

In it was an iron cot, a washstand and a chair. A shelf was the dresser. Its four bare walls seemed to close in upon you like the sides of a coffin. Your hand crept to your throat, you gasped, you looked up as from a well — and breathed once more. Through the glass of the little skylight you saw a square of blue infinity.

"Two dollars, suh," Clara would say in her half-contemptuous, half-Tuskeenial tones.

One day Miss Leeson came hunting for a room. She carried a typewriter made to be lugged around by a much larger lady. She was a very little girl, with eyes and hair that had kept on growing after she had stopped and that always looked as if they were saying: "Goodness me! Why didn't you keep up with us?"

Mrs. Parker showed her the double parlours. "In this closet," she said, "one could keep a skeleton or anaesthetic or coal—"

"But I am neither a doctor nor a dentist," said Miss Leeson, with a shiver.

Mrs. Parker gave her the incredulous, pitying, sneering, icy stare that she kept for those who failed to qualify as doctors or dentists, and led the way to the second floor back.

"Eight dollars?" said Miss Leeson. "Dear me! I'm not Hetty if I do look green. I'm just a poor little working girl. Show me something higher and lower."

Mr. Skidder jumped and strewed the floor with cigarette stubs at the rap on his door.

"Excuse me, Mr. Skidder," said Mrs. Parker, with her demon's smile at his pale looks. "I didn't know you were in. I asked the lady to have a look at your lambrequins."

"They're too lovely for anything," said Miss Leeson, smiling in exactly the way the angels do.

After they had gone Mr. Skidder got very busy erasing the tall, black-haired heroine from his latest (unproduced) play and inserting a small, roguish one with heavy, bright hair and vivacious features.

"Anna Held'll jump at it," said Mr. Skidder to himself, putting his feet up against the lambrequins and disappearing in a cloud of smoke like an aerial cuttlefish.

Presently the tocsin call of "Clara!" sounded to the world the state of Miss Leeson's purse. A dark goblin seized her, mounted a Stygian stairway, thrust her into a vault with a glimmer of light in its top and muttered the menacing and cabalistic words "Two dollars!"

"I'll take it!" sighed Miss Leeson, sinking down upon the squeaky iron bed.

Every day Miss Leeson went out to work. At night she brought home papers with handwriting on them and made copies with her typewriter. Sometimes she had no work at night, and then she would sit on the steps of the high stoop with the other roomers. Miss Leeson was not intended for a skylight room when the plans were drawn for her creation. She was gay-hearted and full of tender, whimsical fancies. Once she let Mr. Skidder read to her three acts of his great (unpublished) comedy, "It's No Kid; or, The Heir of the Subway."

There was rejoicing among the gentlemen roomers whenever Miss Leeson had time to sit on the steps for an hour or two. But Miss Longnecker, the tall blonde who taught in a public school and said, "Well, really!" to everything you said, sat on the top step and sniffed. And Miss Dorn, who shot at the moving ducks at Coney every Sunday and worked in a department store, sat on the bottom step and sniffed. Miss Leeson sat on the middle step and the men would quickly group around her.

Especially Mr. Skidder, who had cast her in his mind for the star part in a private, romantic (unspoken) drama in real life. And especially Mr. Hoover, who was forty-five, fat, flush and foolish. And especially very young Mr. Evans, who set up a hollow cough to induce her to ask him to leave off cigarettes. The men voted her "the funniest and jolliest ever," but the sniffs on the top step and the lower step were implacable.

*

I pray you let the drama halt while Chorus stalks to the footlights and drops an epicedian tear upon the fatness of Mr. Hoover. Tune the pipes to the tragedy of tallow, the bane of bulk, the calamity of corpulence. Tried out, Falstaff might have rendered more romance to the ton than would have Romeo's rickety ribs to the ounce. A lover may sigh, but he must not puff. To the train of Momus are the fat men remanded. In vain beats the faithfullest heart above a 52-inch belt. Avaunt, Hoover! Hoover, forty-five, flush and foolish, might carry off Helen herself; Hoover, forty-five, flush, foolish and fat is meat for perdition. There was never a chance for you, Hoover.

As Mrs. Parker's roomers sat thus one summer's evening, Miss Leeson looked up into the firmament and cried with her little gay laugh:

"Why, there's Billy Jackson! I can see him from down here, too."

All looked up — some at the windows of skyscrapers, some casting about for an airship, Jackson-guided.

"It's that star," explained Miss Leeson, pointing with a tiny finger. "Not the big one that twinkles — the steady blue one near it. I can see it every night through my skylight. I named it Billy Jackson."

"Well, really!" said Miss Longnecker. "I didn't know you were an astronomer, Miss Leeson."

"Oh, yes," said the small star gazer, "I know as much as any of them about the style of sleeves they're going to wear next fall in Mars."

"Well, really!" said Miss Longnecker. "The star you refer to is Gamma, of the constellation Cassiopeia. It is nearly of the second magnitude, and its meridian passage is —"

"Oh," said the very young Mr. Evans, "I think Billy Jackson is a much better name for it."

"Same here," said Mr. Hoover, loudly breathing defiance to Miss Longnecker. "I think Miss Leeson has just as much right to name stars as any of those old astrologers had."

"Well, really!" said Miss Longnecker.

"I wonder whether it's a shooting star," remarked Miss Dorn. "I hit nine ducks and a rabbit out of ten in the gallery at Coney Sunday."

"He doesn't show up very well from down here," said Miss Leeson. "You ought to see him from my room. You know you can see stars even in the daytime from the bottom of a well.

At night my room is like the shaft of a coal mine, and it makes Billy Jackson look like the big diamond pin that Night fastens her kimono with."

There came a time after that when Miss Leeson brought no formidable papers home to copy. And when she went out in the morning, instead of working, she went from office to office and let her heart melt away in the drip of cold refusals transmitted through insolent office boys. This went on.

There came an evening when she wearily climbed Mrs. Parker's stoop at the hour when she always returned from her dinner at the restaurant. But she had had no dinner.

As she stepped into the hall Mr. Hoover met her and seized his chance. He asked her to marry him, and his fatness hovered above her like an avalanche. She dodged, and caught the balustrade. He tried for her hand, and she raised it and smote him weakly in the face. Step by step she went up, dragging herself by the railing. She passed Mr. Skidder's door as he was red-inking a stage direction for Myrtle Delorme (Miss Leeson) in his (unaccepted) comedy, to "pirouette across stage from L to the side of the Count." Up the carpeted ladder she crawled at last and opened the door of the skylight room.

She was too weak to light the lamp or to undress. She fell upon the iron cot, her fragile body scarcely hollowing the worn springs. And in that Erebus of the skylight room, she slowly raised her heavy eyelids, and smiled.

For Billy Jackson was shining down on her, calm and bright and constant through the skylight. There was no world about her. She was sunk in a pit of blackness, with but that small square of pallid light framing the star that she had so whimsically and oh, so ineffectually named. Miss Longnecker must be right; it was Gamma, of the constellation Cassiopeia, and not Billy Jackson. And yet she could not let it be Gamma.

As she lay on her back she tried twice to raise her arm. The third time she got two thin fingers to her lips and blew a kiss out of the black pit to Billy Jackson. Her arm fell back limply.

"Goodbye, Billy," she murmured faintly. "You're millions of miles away and you won't even twinkle once. But you kept where I could see you most of the time up there when there wasn't anything else but darkness to look at, didn't you?...Millions of miles...Goodbye, Billy Jackson."

Clara, the coloured maid, found the door locked at 10 the next day, and they forced it open. Vinegar, and the slapping of wrists and burnt feathers proving of no avail, some one ran to 'phone for an ambulance.

In due time it backed up to the door with much gong-clanging, and the capable young medico, in his white linen coat, ready, active, confident, with his smooth face half debonair, half grim, danced up the steps.

"Ambulance call to 49," he said briefly. "What's the trouble?"

"Oh, yes, doctor," sniffed Mrs. Parker, as though her trouble that there should be trouble in the house was the greater. "I can't think what can be the matter with her. Nothing we could do would bring her to. It's a young woman, a Miss Elsie — yes, a Miss Elsie Leeson. Never before in my house —"

"What room?" cried the doctor in a terrible voice, to which Mrs. Parker was a stranger.

"The skylight room. It —"

Evidently the ambulance doctor was familiar with the location of skylight rooms. He was gone up the stairs, four at a time. Mrs. Parker followed slowly, as her dignity demanded.

On the first landing she met him coming back bearing the astronomer in his arms. He stopped and let loose the practised scalpel of his tongue, not loudly. Gradually Mrs. Parker crumpled as a stiff garment that slips down from a nail. Ever afterward there remained crumples in her mind and body. Sometimes her curious roomers would ask her what the doctor said to her.

"Let that be," she would answer. "If I can get forgiveness for having heard it I will be satisfied."

The ambulance physician strode with his burden through the pack of hounds that follow the curiosity chase, and even they fell back along the sidewalk abashed, for his face was that of one who bears his own dead.

They noticed that he did not lay down upon the bed prepared for it in the ambulance the form that he carried, and all that he said was: "Drive like h———l, Wilson," to the driver.

That is all. Is it a story? In the next morning's paper I saw a little news item, and the last sentence of it may help you (as it helped me) to weld the incidents together.

It recounted the reception into Bellevue Hospital of a young woman who had been removed from No. 49 East——— street, suffering from debility induced by starvation. It concluded with these words:

"Dr. William Jackson, the ambulance physician who attended the case, says the patient will recover."

The Trimmed Lamp

Of course there are two sides to the question. Let us look at the other. We often hear "shopgirls" spoken of. No such persons exist. There are girls who work in shops. They make their living that way. But why turn their occupation into an adjective? Let us be fair. We do not refer to the girls who live on Fifth Avenue as "marriage-girls."

Lou and Nancy were chums. They came to the big city to find work because there was not enough to eat at their homes to go around. Nancy was nineteen; Lou was twenty. Both were pretty, active, country girls who had no ambition to go on the stage.

The little cherub that sits up aloft guided them to a cheap and respectable boardinghouse. Both found positions and became wage-earners. They remained chums. It is at the end of six months that I would beg you to step forward and be introduced to them. Meddlesome Reader: My Lady friends, Miss Nancy and Miss Lou. While you are shaking hands please take notice — cautiously — of their attire. Yes, cautiously; for they are as quick to resent a stare as a lady in a box at the horse show is.

Lou is a piecework ironer in a hand laundry. She is clothed in a badly-fitting purple dress, and her hat plume is four inches too long; but her ermine muff and scarf cost $25, and its fellow beasts will be ticketed in the windows at $7.98 before the season is over. Her cheeks are pink, and her light blue eyes bright. Contentment radiates from her.

Nancy you would call a shopgirl — because you have the habit. There is no type; but a perverse generation is always seeking a type; so this is what the type should be. She has the high-ratted pompadour, and the exaggerated straight-front. Her skirt is shoddy, but has the correct flare. No furs protect her against the bitter spring air, but she wears her short broadcloth jacket as jauntily as though it were Persian lamb! On her face and in her eyes, remorseless type-seeker, is the typical shopgirl expression. It is a look of silent but contemptuous revolt against cheated womanhood; of sad prophecy of the vengeance to come. When she laughs her loudest the look is still there. The same look can be seen in the eyes of Russian peasants; and those of us left will see it some day on Gabriel's face when he comes to blow us up. It is a look that should wither and abash man; but he has been known to smirk at it and offer flowers — with a string tied to them.

Now lift your hat and come away, while you receive Lou's cheery "See you again," and the sardonic, sweet smile of Nancy that seems, somehow, to miss you and go fluttering like a white moth up over the housetops to the stars.

The two waited on the corner for Dan. Dan was Lou's steady company. Faithful? Well, he was on hand when Mary would have had to hire a dozen subpoena servers to find her lamb.

"Ain't you cold, Nance?" said Lou. "Say, what a chump you are for working in that old store for $8. a week! I made $18.50 last week. Of course ironing ain't as swell work as selling lace behind a counter, but it pays. None of us ironers make less than $10. And I don't know that it's any less respectful work, either."

"You can have it," said Nancy, with uplifted nose. "I'll take my eight a week and hall bedroom. I like to be among nice things and swell people. And look what a chance I've got! Why, one of our glove girls married a Pittsburg — steel maker, or blacksmith or something — the other day worth a million dollars. I'll catch a swell myself some time. I ain't bragging on my looks or anything; but I'll take my chances where there's big prizes offered. What show would a girl have in a laundry?"

"Why, that's where I met Dan," said Lou, triumphantly. "He came in for his Sunday shirt and collars and saw me at the first board, ironing. We all try to get to work at the first board. Ella Maginnis was sick that day, and I had her place. He said he noticed my arms first, how round and white they was. I had my sleeves rolled up. Some nice fellows come into laundries. You can tell 'em by their bringing their clothes in suit cases; and turning in the door sharp and sudden."

"How can you wear a waist like that, Lou?" said Nancy, gazing down at the offending article with sweet scorn in her heavy-lidded eyes. "It shows fierce taste."

"This waist?" cried Lou, with wide-eyed indignation. "Why, I paid $16. for this waist. It's worth twenty-five. A woman left it to be laundered, and never called for it. The boss sold it to me. It's got yards and yards of hand embroidery on it. Better talk about that ugly, plain thing you've got on."

"This ugly, plain thing," said Nancy, calmly, "was copied from one that Mrs. Van Alstyne Fisher was wearing. The girls say her bill in the store last year was $12,000. I made mine, myself. It cost me $1.50. Ten feet away you couldn't tell it from hers."

"Oh, well," said Lou, good-naturedly, "if you want to starve and put on airs, go ahead. But I'll take my job and good wages; and after hours give me something as fancy and attractive to wear as I am able to buy."

But just then Dan came — a serious young man with a ready-made necktie, who had escaped the city's brand of frivolity — an electrician earning 30 dollars per week who looked upon Lou with the sad eyes of Romeo, and thought her embroidered waist a web in which any fly should delight to be caught.

"My friend, Mr. Owens — shake hands with Miss Danforth," said Lou.

"I'm mighty glad to know you, Miss Danforth," said Dan, with outstretched hand. "I've heard Lou speak of you so often."

"Thanks," said Nancy, touching his fingers with the tips of her cool ones, "I've heard her mention you — a few times."

Lou giggled.

"Did you get that handshake from Mrs. Van Alstyne Fisher, Nance?" she asked.

"If I did, you can feel safe in copying it," said Nancy.

"Oh, I couldn't use it, at all. It's too stylish for me. It's intended to set off diamond rings, that high shake is. Wait till I get a few and then I'll try it."

"Learn it first," said Nancy wisely, "and you'll be more likely to get the rings."

"Now, to settle this argument," said Dan, with his ready, cheerful smile, "let me make a proposition. As I can't take both of you up to Tiffany's and do the right thing, what do you say to a little vaudeville? I've got the rickets. How about looking at stage diamonds since we can't shake hands with the real sparklers?"

The faithful squire took his place close to the curb; Lou next, a little peacocky in her bright and pretty clothes; Nancy on the inside, slender, and soberly clothed as the sparrow, but with the true Van Alstyne Fisher walk — thus they set out for their evening's moderate diversion.

I do not suppose that many look upon a great department store as an educational institution. But the one in which Nancy worked was something like that to her. She was surrounded by beautiful things that breathed of taste and refinement. If you live in an atmosphere of luxury, luxury is yours whether your money pays for it, or another's.

The people she served were mostly women whose dress, manners, and position in the social world were quoted as criterions. From them Nancy began to take toll — the best from each according to her view.

From one she would copy and practice a gesture, from another an eloquent lifting of an eyebrow, from others, a manner of walking, of carrying a purse, of smiling, of greeting a friend, of addressing "inferiors in station." From her best beloved model, Mrs. Van Alstyne Fisher, she made requisition for that excellent thing, a soft, low voice as clear as silver and as perfect in articulation as the notes of a thrush. Suffused in the aura of this high social refinement and good breeding, it was impossible for her to escape a deeper effect of it. As good habits are said to be better than good principles, so, perhaps, good manners are better than good habits. The teachings of your parents may not keep alive your New England conscience; but if you sit on a straight-back chair and repeat the words "prisms and pilgrims" forty times the devil will flee from you. And when Nancy spoke in the Van Alstyne Fisher tones she felt the thrill of *noblesse oblige* to her very bones.

There was another source of learning in the great departmental school. Whenever you see three or four shopgirls gather in a bunch and jingle their wire bracelets as an accompaniment to apparently frivolous conversation, do not think that they are there for the purpose of criticizing the way Ethel does her back hair. The meeting may lack the dignity of the deliberative bodies of man; but it has all the importance of the occasion on which Eve and her first daughter first put their heads together to make Adam understand his proper place in the household. It is Woman's Conference for Common Defense and Exchange of Strategical Theories of Attack and Repulse upon and against the World, which is a Stage, and Man, its Audience who Persists in Throwing Bouquets Thereupon. Woman, the most helpless of the young of any animal — with the fawn's grace but without its fleetness; with the bird's beauty but without its power of flight; with the honey-bee's burden of sweetness but without its — Oh, let's drop that simile — some of us may have been stung.

During this council of war they pass weapons one to another, and exchange stratagems that each has devised and formulated out of the tactics of life.

"I says to 'im," says Sadie, "ain't you the fresh thing! Who do you suppose I am, to be addressing such a remark to me? And what do you think he says back to me?"

The heads, brown, black, flaxen, red, and yellow bob together; the answer is given; and the parry to the thrust is decided upon, to be used by each thereafter in passages-at-arms with the common enemy, man.

Thus Nancy learned the art of defense; and to women successful defense means victory.

The curriculum of a department store is a wide one. Perhaps no other college could have fitted her as well for her life's ambition — the drawing of a matrimonial prize.

Her station in the store was a favored one. The music room was near enough for her to hear and become familiar with the works of the best composers — at least to acquire the familiarity that passed for appreciation in the social world in which she was vaguely trying to set a tentative and aspiring foot. She absorbed the educating influence of art wares, of costly and dainty fabrics, of adornments that are almost culture to women.

The other girls soon became aware of Nancy's ambition. "Here comes your millionaire, Nancy," they would call to her whenever any man who looked the rôle approached her counter. It got to be a habit of men, who were hanging about while their women folk were shopping, to stroll over to the handkerchief counter and dawdle over the cambric squares. Nancy's imitation high-bred air and genuine dainty beauty was what attracted. Many men thus came to display their graces before her. Some of them may have been millionaires; others were certainly no more than their sedulous apes. Nancy learned to discriminate. There was a window at the end of the handkerchief counter; and she could see the rows of vehicles waiting for the shoppers in the street below. She looked and perceived that automobiles differ as well as do their owners.

Once a fascinating gentleman bought four dozen handkerchiefs, and wooed her across the counter with a King Cophetua air. When he had gone one of the girls said:

"What's wrong, Nance, that you didn't warm up to that fellow. He looks the swell article, all right, to me."

"Him?" said Nancy, with her coolest, sweetest, most impersonal, Van Alstyne Fisher smile; "not for mine. I saw him drive up outside. A 12 H. P. machine and an Irish chauffeur! And you saw what kind of handkerchiefs he bought — silk! And he's got dactylis on him. Give me the real thing or nothing, if you please."

Two of the most "refined" women in the store — a forelady and a cashier — had a few "swell gentlemen friends" with whom they now and then dined. Once they included Nancy in an invitation. The dinner took place in a spectacular café whose tables are engaged for New Year's eve a year in advance. There were two "gentlemen friends" — one without any hair on his head — high living ungrew it; and we can prove it — the other a young man whose worth and sophistication he impressed upon you in two convincing ways — he swore that all the wine was corked; and he wore diamond cuff buttons. This young man perceived irresistible excellencies in Nancy. His taste ran to shopgirls; and here was one that added the voice and manners of his high social world to the franker charms of her own caste. So, on the following day, he appeared in the store and made her a serious proposal of marriage over a box of hem-stitched, grass-bleached Irish linens. Nancy declined. A brown pompadour ten feet away had been using her eyes and ears. When the rejected suitor had gone she heaped carboys of upbraidings and horror upon Nancy's head.

"What a terrible little fool you are! That fellow's a millionaire — he's a nephew of old Van Skittles himself. And he was talking on the level, too. Have you gone crazy, Nance?"

"Have I?" said Nancy. "I didn't take him, did I? He isn't a millionaire so hard that you could notice it, anyhow. His family only allows him $20,000 a year to spend. The bald-headed fellow was guying him about it the other night at supper."

The brown pompadour came nearer and narrowed her eyes.

"Say, what do you want?" she inquired, in a voice hoarse for lack of chewing-gum. "Ain't that enough for you? Do you want to be a Mormon, and marry Rockefeller and Gladstone Dowie and the King of Spain and the whole bunch? Ain't $20,000 a year good enough for you?"

Nancy flushed a little under the level gaze of the black, shallow eyes.

"It wasn't altogether the money, Carrie," she explained. "His friend caught him in a rank lie the other night at dinner. It was about some girl he said he hadn't been to the theater with. Well, I can't stand a liar. Put everything together — I don't like him; and that settles it. When I sell out it's not going to be on any bargain day. I've got to have something that sits up in a chair like a man, anyhow. Yes, I'm looking out for a catch; but it's got to be able to do something more than make a noise like a toy bank."

"The physiopathic ward for yours!" said the brown pompadour, walking away.

These high ideas, if not ideals — Nancy continued to cultivate on $8. per week. She bivouacked on the trail of the great unknown "catch," eating her dry bread and tightening her belt day by day. On her face was the faint, soldierly, sweet, grim smile of the preordained man-hunter. The store was her forest; and many times she raised her rifle at game that seemed broad-antlered and big; but always some deep unerring instinct — perhaps of the huntress, perhaps of the woman — made her hold her fire and take up the trail again.

Lou flourished in the laundry. Out of her $18.50 per week she paid $6. for her room and board. The rest went mainly for clothes. Her opportunities for bettering her taste and manners were few compared with Nancy's. In the steaming laundry there was nothing but work, work and her thoughts of the evening pleasures to come. Many costly and showy fabrics passed under her iron; and it may be that her growing fondness for dress was thus transmitted to her through the conducting metal.

When the day's work was over Dan awaited her outside, her faithful shadow in whatever light she stood.

Sometimes he cast an honest and troubled glance at Lou's clothes that increased in conspicuity rather than in style; but this was no disloyalty; he deprecated the attention they called to her in the streets.

And Lou was no less faithful to her chum. There was a law that Nancy should go with them on whatsoever outings they might take. Dan bore the extra burden heartily and in good cheer. It might be said that Lou furnished the color, Nancy the tone, and Dan the weight of the distraction-seeking trio. The escort, in his neat but obviously ready-made suit, his ready-made tie and unfailing, genial, ready-made wit never startled or clashed. He was of that good kind that you are likely to forget while they are present, but remember distinctly after they are gone.

To Nancy's superior taste the flavor of these ready-made pleasures was sometimes a little bitter: but she was young; and youth is a gourmand, when it cannot be a gourmet.

"Dan is always wanting me to marry him right away," Lou told her once. "But why should I? I'm independent. I can do as I please with the money I earn; and he never would agree for me to keep on working afterward. And say, Nance, what do you want to stick to that old store for, and half starve and half dress yourself? I could get you a place in the laundry right now if you'd come. It seems to me that you could afford to be a little less stuck-up if you could make a good deal more money."

"I don't think I'm stuck-up, Lou," said Nancy, "but I'd rather live on half rations and stay where I am. I suppose I've got the habit. It's the chance that I want. I don't expect to be always behind a counter. I'm learning something new every day. I'm right up against refined and rich people all the time — even if I do only wait on them; and I'm not missing any pointers that I see passing around."

"Caught your millionaire yet?" asked Lou with her teasing laugh.

"I haven't selected one yet," answered Nancy. "I've been looking them over."

"Goodness! the idea of picking over 'em! Don't you ever let one get by you Nance — even if he's a few dollars shy. But of course you're joking — millionaires don't think about working girls like us."

"It might be better for them if they did," said Nancy, with cool wisdom. "Some of us could teach them how to take care of their money."

"If one was to speak to me," laughed Lou, "I know I'd have a duck-fit."

"That's because you don't know any. The only difference between swells and other people is you have to watch 'em closer. Don't you think that red silk lining is just a little bit too bright for that coat, Lou?"

Lou looked at the plain, dull olive jacket of her friend.

"Well, no I don't — but it may seem so beside that faded-looking thing you've got on."

"This jacket," said Nancy, complacently, "has exactly the cut and fit of one that Mrs. Van Alstyne Fisher was wearing the other day. The material cost me $3.98. I suppose hers cost about $100. more."

"Oh, well," said Lou lightly, "it don't strike me as millionaire bait. Shouldn't wonder if I catch one before you do, anyway."

Truly it would have taken a philosopher to decide upon the values of the theories held by the two friends. Lou, lacking that certain pride and fastidiousness that keeps stores and desks filled with girls working for the barest living, thumped away gaily with her iron in the noisy and stifling laundry. Her wages supported her even beyond the point of comfort; so that her dress profited until sometimes she cast a sidelong glance of impatience at the neat but inelegant apparel of Dan — Dan the constant, the immutable, the undeviating.

As for Nancy, her case was one of tens of thousands. Silk and jewels and laces and ornaments and the perfume and music of the fine world of good-breeding and taste — these were made for woman; they are her equitable portion. Let her keep near them if they are a part of life to her, and if she will. She is no traitor to herself, as Esau was; for she keeps he birthright and the pottage she earns is often very scant.

In this atmosphere Nancy belonged; and she throve in it and ate her frugal meals and schemed over her cheap dresses with a determined and contented mind. She already knew woman; and she was studying man, the animal, both as to his habits and eligibility. Some day she would bring down the game that she wanted; but she promised herself it would be what seemed to her the biggest and the best, and nothing smaller.

Thus she kept her lamp trimmed and burning to receive the bridegroom when he should come.

But, another lesson she learned, perhaps unconsciously. Her standard of values began to shift and change. Sometimes the dollar-mark grew blurred in her mind's eye, and shaped itself into letters that spelled such words as "truth" and "honor" and now and then just "kindness." Let us make a likeness of one who hunts the moose or elk in some mighty wood. He sees a little dell, mossy and embowered, where a rill trickles, babbling to him of rest and comfort. At these times the spear of Nimrod himself grows blunt.

So, Nancy wondered sometimes if Persian lamb was always quoted at its market value by the hearts that it covered.

One Thursday evening Nancy left the store and turned across Sixth Avenue westward to the laundry. She was expected to go with Lou and Dan to a musical comedy.

Dan was just coming out of the laundry when she arrived. There was a queer, strained look on his face.

"I thought I would drop around to see if they had heard from her," he said.

"Heard from who?" asked Nancy. "Isn't Lou there?"

"I thought you knew," said Dan. "She hasn't been here or at the house where she lived since Monday. She moved all her things from there. She told one of the girls in the laundry she might be going to Europe."

"Hasn't anybody seen her anywhere?" asked Nancy.

Dan looked at her with his jaws set grimly, and a steely gleam in his steady gray eyes.

"They told me in the laundry," he said, harshly, "that they saw her pass yesterday — in an automobile. With one of the millionaires, I suppose, that you and Lou were forever busying your brains about."

For the first time Nancy quailed before a man. She laid her hand that trembled slightly on Dan's sleeve.

"You've no right to say such a thing to me, Dan — as if I had anything to do with it!"

"I didn't mean it that way," said Dan, softening. He fumbled in his vest pocket.

"I've got the tickets for the show tonight," he said, with a gallant show of lightness. "If you —"

Nancy admired pluck whenever she saw it.

"I'll go with you, Dan," she said.

Three months went by before Nancy saw Lou again.

At twilight one evening the shopgirl was hurrying home along the border of a little quiet park. She heard her name called, and wheeled about in time to catch Lou rushing into her arms.

After the first embrace they drew their heads back as serpents do, ready to attack or to charm, with a thousand questions trembling on their swift tongues. And then Nancy noticed that prosperity had descended upon Lou, manifesting itself in costly furs, flashing gems, and creations of the tailors' art.

"You little fool!" cried Lou, loudly and affectionately. "I see you are still working in that store, and as shabby as ever. And how about that big catch you were going to make — nothing doing yet, I suppose?"

And then Lou looked, and saw that something better than prosperity had descended upon Nancy — something that shone brighter than gems in her eyes and redder than a rose in her cheeks, and that danced like electricity anxious to be loosed from the tip of her tongue.

"Yes, I'm still in the store," said Nancy, "but I'm going to leave it next week. I've made my catch — the biggest catch in the world. You won't mind now Lou, will you? — I'm going to be married to Dan — to Dan! — he's my Dan now — why, Lou!"

Around the corner of the park strolled one of those new-crop, smooth-faced young policemen that are making the force more endurable — at least to the eye. He saw a woman with an expensive fur coat, and diamond-ringed hands crouching down against the iron fence of the park sobbing turbulently, while a slender, plainly-dressed working girl leaned close, trying to console her. But the Gibsonian cop, being of the new order, passed on, pretending not to notice, for he was wise enough to know that these matters are beyond help so far as the power he represents is concerned, though he rap the pavement with his nightstick till the sound goes up to the furthermost stars.

The Whirligig Of Life

Justice-of-the-Peace Benaja Widdup sat in the door of his office smoking his elder-stem pipe. Halfway to the zenith the Cumberland range rose blue-gray in the afternoon haze. A speckled hen swaggered down the main street of the "settlement," cackling foolishly.

Up the road came a sound of creaking axles, and then a slow cloud of dust, and then a bull-cart bearing Ransie Bilbro and his wife. The cart stopped at the Justice's door, and the two climbed down. Ransie was a narrow six feet of sallow brown skin and yellow hair. The imperturbability of the mountains hung upon him like a suit of armour. The woman was calicoed, angled, snuff-brushed, and weary with unknown desires. Through it all gleamed a faint protest of cheated youth unconscious of its loss.

The Justice of the Peace slipped his feet into his shoes, for the sake of dignity, and moved to let them enter.

"We-all," said the woman, in a voice like the wind blowing through pine boughs, "wants a divo'ce." She looked at Ransie to see if he noted any flaw or ambiguity or evasion or partiality or self-partisanship in her statement of their business.

"A divo'ce," repeated Ransie, with a solemn nod. "We-all can't git along together nohow. It's lonesome enough fur to live in the mount'ins when a man and a woman keers fur one another. But when she's a-spittin' like a wildcat or a-sullenin' like a hoot-owl in the cabin, a man ain't got no call to live with her."

"When he's a no-'count varmint," said the woman, "without any especial warmth, a-traipsin' along of scalawags and moonshiners and a-layin' on his back pizen 'ith co'n whiskey, and a-pesterin' folks with a pack o' hungry, triflin' houn's to feed!"

"When she keeps a-throwin' skillet lids," came Ransie's antiphony, "and slings b'ilin' water on the best coon-dog in the Cumberlands, and sets herself agin' cookin' a man's victuals, and keeps him awake o' nights accusin' him of a sight of doin's!"

"When he's al'ays a-fightin' the revenues, and gits a hard name in the mount'ins fur a mean man, who's gwine to be able fur to sleep o' nights?"

The Justice of the Peace stirred deliberately to his duties. He placed his one chair and a wooden stool for his petitioners. He opened his book of statutes on the table and scanned the index. Presently he wiped his spectacles and shifted his inkstand.

"The law and the statutes," said he, "air silent on the subjeck of divo'ce as fur as the jurisdiction of this co't air concerned. But, accordin' to equity and the Constitution and the golden rule, it's a bad barg'in that can't run both ways. If a justice of the peace can marry a couple, it's plain that he is bound to be able to divo'ce 'em. This here office will issue a decree of divo'ce and abide by the decision of the Supreme Co't to hold it good."

Ransie Bilbro drew a small tobacco-bag from his trousers pocket. Out of this he shook upon the table a five-dollar note. "Sold a b'arskin and two foxes fur that," he remarked. "It's all the money we got."

"The regular price of a divo'ce in this co't," said the Justice, "air five dollars." He stuffed the bill into the pocket of his homespun vest with a deceptive air of indifference. With much bodily toil and mental travail he wrote the decree upon half a sheet of foolscap, and then copied it upon the other. Ransie Bilbro and his wife listened to his reading of the document that was to give them freedom:

"Know all men by these presents that Ransie Bilbro and his wife, Ariela Bilbro, this day personally appeared before me and promises that hereinafter they will neither love, honour, nor obey each other, neither for better nor worse, being of sound mind and body, and accept summons for divorce according to the peace and dignity of the State. Herein fail not, so help you God. Benaja Widdup, justice of the peace in and for the county of Piedmont, State of Tennessee."

The Justice was about to hand one of the documents to Ransie. The voice of Ariela delayed the transfer. Both men looked at her. Their dull masculinity was confronted by something sudden and unexpected in the woman.

"Judge, don't you give him that air paper yit. 'Tain't all settled, nohow. I got to have my rights first. I got to have my ali-money. 'Tain't no kind of a way to do fur a man to divo'ce his wife 'thout her havin' a cent fur to do with. I'm a-layin' off to be a-goin' up to brother Ed's up on Hogback Mount'in. I'm bound fur to hev a pa'r of shoes and some snuff and things besides. Ef Rance kin affo'd a divo'ce, let him pay me ali-money."

Ransie Bilbro was stricken to dumb perplexity. There had been no previous hint of alimony. Women were always bringing up startling and unlooked-for issues.

Justice Benaja Widdup felt that the point demanded judicial decision. The authorities were also silent on the subject of alimony. But the woman's feet were bare. The trail to Hogback Mountain was steep and flinty.

"Ariela Bilbro," he asked, in official tones, "how much did you 'low would be good and sufficient ali-money in the case befo' the co't?"

"I 'lowed," she answered, "fur the shoes and all, to say five dollars. That ain't much fur ali-money, but I reckon that'll git me to up brother Ed's."

"The amount," said the Justice, "air not onreasonable. Ransie Bilbro, you air ordered by the co't to pay the plaintiff the sum of five dollars befo' the decree of divo'ce air issued."

"I hain't no mo' money," breathed Ransie, heavily. "I done paid you all I had."

"Otherwise," said the Justice, looking severely over his spectacles, "you air in contempt of co't."

"I reckon if you gimme till tomorrow," pleaded the husband, "I mout be able to rake or scrape it up somewhars. I never looked for to be a-payin' no ali-money."

"The case air adjourned," said Benaja Widdup, "till tomorrow, when you-all will present yo'selves and obey the order of the co't. Followin' of which the decrees of divo'ce will be delivered." He sat down in the door and began to loosen a shoestring.

"We mout as well go down to Uncle Ziah's," decided Ransie, "and spend the night." He climbed into the cart on one side, and Ariela climbed in on the other. Obeying the flap of his rope, the little red bull slowly came around on a tack, and the cart crawled away in the nimbus arising from its wheels.

Justice-of-the-peace Benaja Widdup smoked his elder-stem pipe. Late in the afternoon he got his weekly paper, and read it until the twilight dimmed its lines. Then he lit the tallow candle on his table, and read until the moon rose, marking the time for supper. He lived in the double log cabin on the slope near the girdled poplar. Going home to supper he crossed a little branch darkened by a laurel thicket. The dark figure of a man stepped from the laurels and pointed a rifle at his breast. His hat was pulled down low, and something covered most of his face.

"I want yo' money," said the figure, "'thout any talk. I'm gettin' nervous, and my finger's a-wabblin' on this here trigger."

"I've only got f-f-five dollars," said the Justice, producing it from his vest pocket.

"Roll it up," came the order, "and stick it in the end of this here gun-bar'l."

The bill was crisp and new. Even fingers that were clumsy and trembling found little difficulty in making a spill of it and inserting it (this with less ease) into the muzzle of the rifle.

"Now I reckon you kin be goin' along," said the robber.

The Justice lingered not on his way.

The next day came the little red bull, drawing the cart to the office door. Justice Benaja Widdup had his shoes on, for he was expecting the visit. In his presence Ransie Bilbro handed to his wife a five-dollar bill. The official's eye sharply viewed it. It seemed to curl up as though it had been rolled and inserted into the end of a gun-barrel. But the Justice refrained from comment. It is true that other bills might be inclined to curl. He handed each one a decree of divorce. Each stood awkwardly silent, slowly folding the guarantee of freedom. The woman cast a shy glance full of constraint at Ransie.

"I reckon you'll be goin' back up to the cabin," she said, along 'ith the bull-cart. There's bread in the tin box settin' on the shelf. I put the bacon in the b'ilin'-pot to keep the hounds from gittin' it. Don't forget to wind the clock tonight."

"You air a-goin' to your brother Ed's?" asked Ransie, with fine unconcern.

"I was 'lowin' to get along up thar afore night. I ain't sayin' as they'll pester theyselves any to make me welcome, but I hain't nowhar else fur to go. It's a right smart ways, and I reckon I better be goin'. I'll be a-sayin' goodbye, Ranse — that is, if you keer fur to say so."

"I don't know as anybody's a hound dog," said Ransie, in a martyr's voice, "fur to not want to say goodbye — 'less you air so anxious to git away that you don't want me to say it."

Ariela was silent. She folded the five-dollar bill and her decree carefully, and placed them in the bosom of her dress. Benaja Widdup watched the money disappear with mournful eyes behind his spectacles.

And then with his next words he achieved rank (as his thoughts ran) with either the great crowd of the world's sympathizers or the little crowd of its great financiers.

"Be kind o' lonesome in the old cabin tonight, Ranse," he said.

Ransie Bilbro stared out at the Cumberlands, clear blue now in the sunlight. He did not look at Ariela.

"I 'low it might be lonesome," he said; "but when folks gits mad and wants a divo'ce, you can't make folks stay."

"There's others wanted a divo'ce," said Ariela, speaking to the wooden stool. "Besides, nobody don't want nobody to stay."

"Nobody never said they didn't."

"Nobody never said they did. I reckon I better start on now to brother Ed's."

"Nobody can't wind that old clock."

"Want me to go back along 'ith you in the cart and wind it fur you, Ranse?"

The mountaineer's countenance was proof against emotion. But he reached out a big hand and enclosed Ariela's thin brown one. Her soul peeped out once through her impassive face, hallowing it.

"Them hounds shan't pester you no more," said Ransie. "I reckon I been mean and low down. You wind that clock, Ariela."

"My heart hit's in that cabin, Ranse," she whispered, "along 'ith you. I ai'nt a-goin' to git mad no more. Le's be startin', Ranse, so's we kin git home by sundown."

Justice-of-the-peace Benaja Widdup interposed as they started for the door, forgetting his presence.

"In the name of the State of Tennessee," he said, "I forbid you-all to be a-defyin' of its laws and statutes. This co't is mo' than willin' and full of joy to see the clouds of discord and misunderstandin' rollin' away from two lovin' hearts, but it air the duty of the co't to p'eserve the morals and integrity of the State. The co't reminds you that you air no longer man and wife, but air divo'ced by regular decree, and as such air not entitled to the benefits and 'purtenances of the mattermonal estate."

Ariela caught Ransie's arm. Did those words mean that she must lose him now when they had just learned the lesson of life?

"But the co't air prepared," went on the Justice, "fur to remove the disabilities set up by the decree of divo'ce. The co't air on hand to perform the solemn ceremony of marri'ge, thus fixin' things up and enablin' the parties in the case to resume the honour'ble and elevatin' state of mattermony which they desires. The fee fur performin' said ceremony will be, in this case, to wit, five dollars."

Ariela caught the gleam of promise in his words. Swiftly her hand went to her bosom. Freely as an alighting dove the bill fluttered to the Justice's table. Her sallow cheek coloured as she stood hand in hand with Ransie and listened to the reuniting words.

Ransie helped her into the cart, and climbed in beside her. The little red bull turned once more, and they set out, handclasped, for the mountains.

Justice-of-the-peace Benaja Widdup sat in his door and took off his shoes. Once again he fingered the bill tucked down in his vest pocket. Once again he smoked his elder-stem pipe. Once again the speckled hen swaggered down the main street of the "settlement," cackling foolishly.

A Harlem Tragedy

Harlem.

Mrs. Fink had dropped into Mrs. Cassidy's flat one flight below.

"Ain't it a beaut?" said Mrs. Cassidy.

She turned her face proudly for her friend Mrs. Fink to see. One eye was nearly closed, with a great, greenish-purple bruise around it. Her lip was cut and bleeding a little and there were red finger-marks on each side of her neck.

"My husband wouldn't ever think of doing that to me," said Mrs. Fink, concealing her envy.

"I wouldn't have a man," declared Mrs. Cassidy, "that didn't beat me up at least once a week. Shows he thinks something of you. Say! but that last dose Jack gave me wasn't no homeopathic one. I can see stars yet. But he'll be the sweetest man in town for the rest of the week to make up for it. This eye is good for theater tickets and a silk shirt waist at the very least."

"I should hope," said Mrs. Fink, assuming complacency, "that Mr. Fink is too much of a gentleman ever to raise his hand against me."

"Oh, go on, Maggie!" said Mrs. Cassidy, laughing and applying witch hazel, "you're only jealous. Your old man is too frappéd and slow to ever give you a punch. He just sits down and practises physical culture with a newspaper when he comes home — now ain't that the truth?"

"Mr. Fink certainly peruses of the papers when he comes home," acknowledged Mrs. Fink, with a toss of her head; "but he certainly don't ever make no Steve O'Donnell out of me just to amuse himself — that's a sure thing."

Mrs. Cassidy laughed the contented laugh of the guarded and happy matron. With the air of Cornelia exhibiting her jewels, she drew down the collar of her kimono and revealed another treasured bruise, maroon-colored, edged with olive and orange — a bruise now nearly well, but still to memory dear.

Mrs. Fink capitulated. The formal light in her eye softened to envious admiration. She and Mrs. Cassidy had been chums in the downtown paper-box factory before they had married, one year before. Now she and her man occupied the flat above Mame and her man. Therefore she could not put on airs with Mame.

"Don't it hurt when he soaks you?" asked Mrs. Fink, curiously.

"Hurt!" — Mrs. Cassidy gave a soprano scream of delight. "Well, say — did you ever have a brick house fall on you? — well, that's just the way it feels — just like when they're digging you out of the ruins. Jack's got a left that spells two matinees and a new pair of Oxfords — and his right! — well, it takes a trip to Coney and six pairs of openwork, silk lisle threads to make that good."

"But what does he beat you for?" inquired Mrs. Fink, with wide-open eyes.

"Silly!" said Mrs. Cassidy, indulgently. "Why, because he's full. It's generally on Saturday nights."

"But what cause do you give him?" persisted the seeker after knowledge.

"Why, didn't I marry him? Jack comes in tanked up; and I'm here, ain't I? Who else has he got a right to beat? I'd just like to catch him once beating anybody else! Sometimes it's because supper ain't ready; and sometimes it's because it is. Jack ain't particular about causes. He just lushes till he remembers he's married, and then he makes for home and does me up. Saturday nights I just move the furniture with sharp corners out of the way, so I won't cut my head when he gets his work in. He's got a left swing that jars you! Sometimes I take the count in the first round; but when I feel like having a good time during the week or want some new rags I come up again for more punishment. That's what I done last night. Jack knows I've been wanting a black silk waist for a month, and I didn't think just one black eye would bring it. Tell you what, Mag, I'll bet you the ice cream he brings it tonight."

Mrs. Fink was thinking deeply.

"My Mart," she said, "never hit me a lick in his life. It's just like you said, Mame; he comes in grouchy and ain't got a word to say. He never takes me out anywhere. He's a chair-warmer at home for fair. He buys me things, but he looks so glum about it that I never appreciate 'em."

Mrs. Cassidy slipped an arm around her chum. "You poor thing!" she said. "But everybody can't have a husband like Jack. Marriage wouldn't be no failure if they was all like him. These discontented wives you hear about — what they need is a man to come home and kick their slats in once a week, and then make it up in kisses, and chocolate creams. That'd give 'em some interest in life. What I want is a masterful man that slugs you when he's jagged and hugs you when he ain't jagged. Preserve me from the man that ain't got the sand to do neither!"

Mrs. Fink sighed.

The hallways were suddenly filled with sound. The door flew open at the kick of Mr. Cassidy. His arms were occupied with bundles. Mame flew and hung about his neck. Her sound eye sparkled with the love light that shines in the eye of the Maori maid when she recovers consciousness in the hut of the wooer who has stunned and dragged her there.

"Hello, old girl!" shouted Mr. Cassidy. He shed his bundles and lifted her off her feet in a mighty hug. "I got tickets for Barnum & Bailey's, and if you'll bust the string of one of them bundles I guess you'll find that silk waist — why, good evening, Mrs. Fink — I didn't see you at first. How's old Mart coming along?"

"He's very well, Mr. Cassidy — thanks," said Mrs. Fink. "I must be going along up now. Mart'll be home for supper soon. I'll bring you down that pattern you wanted tomorrow, Mame."

Mrs. Fink went up to her flat and had a little cry. It was a meaningless cry, the kind of cry that only a woman knows about, a cry from no particular cause, altogether an absurd cry; the most transient and the most hopeless cry in the repertory of grief. Why had Martin never thrashed her? He was as big and strong as Jack Cassidy. Did he not care for her at all? He never quarrelled; he came home and lounged about, silent, glum, idle. He was a fairly good provider, but he ignored the spices of life.

Mrs. Fink's ship of dreams was becalmed. Her captain ranged between plum duff and his hammock. If only he would shiver his timbers or stamp his foot on the quarter-deck now and then! And she had thought to sail so merrily, touching at ports in the Delectable Isles! But now, to vary the figure, she was ready to throw up the sponge, tired out, without a scratch to show for all those tame rounds with her sparring partner. For one moment she almost hated Mame — Mame, with her cuts and bruises, her salve of presents and kisses; her stormy voyage with her fighting, brutal, loving mate.

Mr. Fink came home at 7. He was permeated with the curse of domesticity. Beyond the portals of his cozy home he cared not to roam, to roam. He was the man who had caught the street car, the anaconda that had swallowed its prey, the tree that lay as it had fallen.

"Like the supper, Mart?" asked Mrs. Fink, who had striven over it.

"M-m-m-yep," grunted Mr. Fink.

After supper he gathered his newspapers to read. He sat in his stocking feet.

Arise, some new Dante, and sing me the befitting corner of perdition for the man who sitteth in the house in his stockinged feet. Sisters of Patience who by reason of ties or duty have endured it in silk, yarn, cotton, lisle thread or woollen — does not the new canto belong?

The next day was Labor Day. The occupations of Mr. Cassidy and Mr. Fink ceased for one passage of the sun. Labor, triumphant, would parade and otherwise disport itself.

Mrs. Fink took Mrs. Cassidy's pattern down early. Mame had on her new silk waist. Even her damaged eye managed to emit a holiday gleam. Jack was fruitfully penitent, and there was a hilarious scheme for the day afoot, with parks and picnics and Pilsener in it.

A rising, indignant jealousy seized Mrs. Fink as she returned to her flat above. Oh, happy Mame, with her bruises and her quick-following balm! But was Mame to have a monopoly of happiness? Surely Martin Fink was as good a man as Jack Cassidy. Was his wife to go always unbelabored and uncaressed? A sudden, brilliant, breathless idea came to Mrs. Fink.

She would show Mame that there were husbands as able to use their fists and perhaps to be as tender afterward as any Jack.

The holiday promised to be a nominal one with the Finks. Mrs. Fink had the stationary washtubs in the kitchen filled with a two weeks' wash that had been soaking overnight. Mr. Fink sat in his stockinged feet reading a newspaper. Thus Labor Day presaged to speed.

Jealousy surged high in Mrs. Fink's heart, and higher still surged an audacious resolve. If her man would not strike her — if he would not so far prove his manhood, his prerogative and his interest in conjugal affairs, he must be prompted to his duty.

Mr. Fink lit his pipe and peacefully rubbed an ankle with a stockinged toe. He reposed in the state of matrimony like a lump of unblended suet in a pudding. This was his level Elysium — to sit at ease vicariously girdling the world in print amid the wifely splashing of suds and the agreeable smells of breakfast dishes departed and dinner ones to come. Many ideas were far from his mind; but the furthest one was the thought of beating his wife.

Mrs. Fink turned on the hot water and set the washboards in the suds. Up from the flat below came the gay laugh of Mrs. Cassidy. It sounded like a taunt, a flaunting of her own happiness in the face of the unslugged bride above. Now was Mrs. Fink's time.

Suddenly she turned like a fury upon the man reading.

"You lazy loafer!" she cried, "must I work my arms off washing and toiling for the ugly likes of you? Are you a man or are you a kitchen hound?"

Mr. Fink dropped his paper, motionless from surprise. She feared that he would not strike — that the provocation had been insufficient. She leaped at him and struck him fiercely in the face with her clenched hand. In that instant she felt a thrill of love for him such as she had not felt for many a day. Rise up, Martin Fink, and come into your kingdom! Oh, she must feel the weight of his hand now — just to show that he cared — just to show that he cared!

Mr. Fink sprang to his feet — Maggie caught him again on the jaw with a wide swing of her other hand. She closed her eyes in that fearful, blissful moment before his blow should come — she whispered his name to herself — she leaned to the expected shock, hungry for it.

In the flat below Mr. Cassidy, with a shamed and contrite face was powdering Mame's eye in preparation for their junket. From the flat above came the sound of a woman's voice, high-raised, a bumping, a stumbling and a shuffling, a chair overturned — unmistakable sounds of domestic conflict.

"Mart and Mag scrapping?" postulated Mr. Cassidy. "Didn't know they ever indulged. Shall I trot up and see if they need a sponge holder?"

One of Mrs. Cassidy's eyes sparkled like a diamond. The other twinkled at least like paste.

"Oh, oh," she said, softly and without apparent meaning, in the feminine ejaculatory manner. "I wonder if — wonder if! Wait, Jack, till I go up and see."

Up the stairs she sped. As her foot struck the hallway above out from the kitchen door of her flat wildly flounced Mrs. Fink.

"Oh, Maggie," cried Mrs. Cassidy, in a delighted whisper; "did he? Oh, did he?"

Mrs. Fink ran and laid her face upon her chum's shoulder and sobbed hopelessly.

Mrs. Cassidy took Maggie's face between her hands and lifted it gently. Tear-stained it was, flushing and paling, but its velvety, pink-and-white, becomingly freckled surface was unscratched, unbruised, unmarred by the recreant fist of Mr. Fink.

"Tell me, Maggie," pleaded Mame, "or I'll go in there and find out. What was it? Did he hurt you — what did he do?"

Mrs. Fink's face went down again despairingly on the bosom of her friend.

"For God's sake don't open that door, Mame," she sobbed. "And don't ever tell nobody — keep it under your hat. He — he never touched me, and — he's — oh, Gawd — he's washin' the clothes — he's washin' the clothes!"

The Making Of A New Yorker

Besides many other things, Raggles was a poet. He was called a tramp; but that was only an elliptical way of saying that he was a philosopher, an artist, a traveller, a naturalist and a discoverer. But most of all he was a poet. In all his life he never wrote a line of verse; he lived his poetry. His Odyssey would have been a Limerick, had it been written. But, to linger with the primary proposition, Raggles was a poet.

Raggles's specialty, had he been driven to ink and paper, would have been sonnets to the cities. He studied cities as women study their reflections in mirrors; as children study the glue and sawdust of a dislocated doll; as the men who write about wild animals study the cages in the zoo. A city to Raggles was not merely a pile of bricks and mortar, peopled by a certain number of inhabitants; it was a thing with a soul characteristic and distinct; an individual conglomeration of life, with its own peculiar essence, flavor and feeling. Two thousand miles to the north and south, east and west, Raggles wandered in poetic fervor, taking the cities to his breast. He footed it on dusty roads, or sped magnificently in freight cars, counting time as of no account. And when he had found the heart of a city and listened to its secret confession, he strayed on, restless, to another. Fickle Raggles! — but perhaps he had not met the civic corporation that could engage and hold his critical fancy.

Through the ancient poets we have learned that the cities are feminine. So they were to poet Raggles; and his mind carried a concrete and clear conception of the figure that symbolized and typified each one that he had wooed.

Chicago seemed to swoop down upon him with a breezy suggestion of Mrs. Partington, plumes and patchouli, and to disturb his rest with a soaring and beautiful song of future promise. But Raggles would awake to a sense of shivering cold and a haunting impression of ideals lost in a depressing aura of potato salad and fish.

Thus Chicago affected him. Perhaps there is a vagueness and inaccuracy in the description; but that is Raggles's fault. He should have recorded his sensations in magazine poems.

Pittsburg impressed him as the play of "Othello" performed in the Russian language in a railroad station by Dockstader's minstrels. A royal and generous lady this Pittsburg, though — homely, hearty, with flushed face, washing the dishes in a silk dress and white kid slippers, and bidding Raggles sit before the roaring fireplace and drink champagne with his pigs' feet and fried potatoes.

New Orleans had simply gazed down upon him from a balcony. He could see her pensive, starry eyes and catch the flutter of her fan, and that was all. Only once he came face to face with her. It was at dawn, when she was flushing the red bricks of the banquette with a pail of water. She laughed and hummed a chansonette and filled Raggles's shoes with ice-cold water. Allons!

Boston construed herself to the poetic Raggles in an erratic and singular way. It seemed to him that he had drunk cold tea and that the city was a white, cold cloth that had been bound tightly around his brow to spur him to some unknown but tremendous mental effort. And, after all, he came to shovel snow for a livelihood; and the cloth, becoming wet, tightened its knots and could not be removed.

Indefinite and unintelligible ideas, you will say; but your disapprobation should be tempered with gratitude, for these are poets' fancies — and suppose you had come upon them in verse!

One day Raggles came and laid siege to the heart of the great city of Manhattan. She was the greatest of all; and he wanted to learn her note in the scale; to taste and appraise and classify and solve and label her and arrange her with the other cities that had given him up the secret of their individuality. And here we cease to be Raggles's translator and become his chronicler.

Raggles landed from a ferryboat one morning and walked into the core of the town with the blasée air of a cosmopolite. He was dressed with care to play the rôle of an "unidentified man." No country, race, class, clique, union, party clan or bowling association could have claimed him. His clothing, which had been donated to him piece-meal by citizens of different height, but same number of inches around the heart, was not yet as uncomfortable to his figure as those speciments of raiment, self-measured, that are railroaded to you by transcontinental tailors with a suit case, suspenders, silk handkerchief and pearl studs as a bonus. Without money — as a poet should be — but with the ardor of an astronomer discovering a new star in the chorus of the milky way, or a man who has seen ink suddenly flow from his fountain pen, Raggles wandered into the great city.

Late in the afternoon he drew out of the roar and commotion with a look of dumb terror on his countenance. He was defeated, puzzled, discomfited, frightened. Other cities had been to him as long primer to read; as country maidens quickly to fathom; as send-price-of-subscription-with-answer rebuses to solve; as oyster cocktails to swallow; but here was one as cold, glittering, serene, impossible as a four-carat diamond in a window to a lover outside fingering damply in his pocket his ribbon-counter salary.

The greetings of the other cities he had known — their homespun kindliness, their human gamut of rough charity, friendly curses, garrulous curiosity and easily estimated credulity or indifference. This city of Manhattan gave him no clue; it was walled against him. Like a river of adamant it flowed past him in the streets. Never an eye was turned upon him; no voice spoke to him. His heart yearned for the clap of Pittsburg's sooty hand on his shoulder; for Chicago's menacing but social yawp in his ear; for the pale and eleemosynary stare through the Bostonian eyeglass — even for the precipitate but unmalicious boot-toe of Louisville or St. Louis.

On Broadway Raggles, successful suitor of many cities, stood, bashful, like any country swain. For the first time he experienced the poignant humiliation of being ignored. And when he tried to reduce this brilliant, swiftly changing, ice-cold city to a formula he failed utterly. Poet though he was, it offered him no color similes, no points of comparison, no flaw in its polished facets, no handle by which he could hold it up and view its shape and structure, as he familiarly and often contemptuously had done with other towns. The houses were interminable ramparts loopholed for defense; the people were bright but bloodless spectres passing in sinister and selfish array.

The thing that weighed heaviest on Raggles's soul and clogged his poet's fancy was the spirit of absolute egotism that seemed to saturate the people as toys are saturated with paint. Each one that he considered appeared a monster of abominable and insolent conceit. Humanity was gone from them; they were toddling idols of stone and varnish, worshipping themselves and greedy for though oblivious of worship from their fellow graven images. Frozen, cruel, implacable, impervious, cut to an identical pattern, they hurried on their ways like statues brought by some miracles to motion, while soul and feeling lay unaroused in the reluctant marble.

Gradually Raggles became conscious of certain types. One was an elderly gentleman with a snow-white, short beard, pink, unwrinkled face and stony, sharp blue eyes, attired in the fashion of a gilded youth, who seemed to personify the city's wealth, ripeness and frigid unconcern. Another type was a woman, tall, beautiful, clear as a steel engraving, goddess-like, calm, clothed like the princesses of old, with eyes as coldly blue as the reflection of sunlight on a glacier. And another was a by-product of this town of marionettes — a broad, swaggering, grim, threateningly sedate fellow, with a jowl as large as a harvested wheat field, the complexion of a baptized infant and the knuckles of a prizefighter. This type leaned against cigar signs and viewed the world with frappéd contumely.

A poet is a sensitive creature, and Raggles soon shrivelled in the bleak embrace of the undecipherable. The chill, sphinx-like, ironical, illegible, unnatural, ruthless expression of the city left him downcast and bewildered. Had it no heart? Better the woodpile, the scolding of vinegar-faced housewives at back doors, the kindly spleen of bartenders behind provincial free-lunch counters, the amiable truculence of rural constables, the kicks, arrests and happy-go-lucky chances of the other vulgar, loud, crude cities than this freezing heartlessness.

Raggles summoned his courage and sought alms from the populace. Unheeding, regardless, they passed on without the wink of an eyelash to testify that they were conscious of his existence. And then he said to himself that this fair but pitiless city of Manhattan was without a soul;

that its inhabitants were manikins moved by wires and springs, and that he was alone in a great wilderness.

Raggles started to cross the street. There was a blast, a roar, a hissing and a crash as something struck him and hurled him over and over six yards from where he had been. As he was coming down like the stick of a rocket the earth and all the cities thereof turned to a fractured dream.

Raggles opened his eyes. First an odor made itself known to him — an odor of the earliest spring flowers of Paradise. And then a hand soft as a falling petal touched his brow. Bending over him was the woman clothed like the princess of old, with blue eyes, now soft and humid with human sympathy. Under his head on the pavement were silks and furs. With Raggles's hat in his hand and with his face pinker than ever from a vehement burst of oratory against reckless driving, stood the elderly gentleman who personified the city's wealth and ripeness. From a nearby café hurried the by-product with the vast jowl and baby complexion, bearing a glass full of a crimson fluid that suggested delightful possibilities.

"Drink dis, sport," said the by-product, holding the glass to Raggles's lips.

Hundreds of people huddled around in a moment, their faces wearing the deepest concern. Two flattering and gorgeous policemen got into the circle and pressed back the overplus of Samaritans. An old lady in a black shawl spoke loudly of camphor; a newsboy slipped one of his papers beneath Raggles's elbow, where it lay on the muddy pavement. A brisk young man with a notebook was asking for names.

A bell clanged importantly, and the ambulance cleaned a lane through the crowd. A cool surgeon slipped into the midst of affairs.

"How do you feel, old man?" asked the surgeon, stooping easily to his task. The princess of silks and satins wiped a red drop or two from Raggles's brow with a fragrant cobweb.

"Me?" said Raggles, with a seraphic smile, "I feel fine."

He had found the heart of his new city.

In three days they let him leave his cot for the convalescent ward in the hospital. He had been in there an hour when the attendants heard sounds of conflict. Upon investigation they found that Raggles had assaulted and damaged a brother convalescent — a glowering transient whom a freight train collision had sent in to be patched up.

"What's all this about?" inquired the head nurse.

"He was runnin' down me town," said Raggles.

"What town?" asked the nurse.

"Noo York," said Raggles.

The Voice Of The City

Twenty-five years ago the school children used to chant their lessons. The manner of their delivery was a singsong recitative between the utterance of an Episcopal minister and the drone of a tired sawmill. I mean no disrespect. We must have lumber and sawdust.

I remember one beautiful and instructive little lyric that emanated from the physiology class. The most striking line of it was this:

"The shin-bone is the longest bone in the hu-man bod-y."

What an inestimable boon it would have been if all the corporeal and spiritual facts pertaining to man had thus been tunefully and logically inculcated in our youthful minds! But what we gained in anatomy, music and philosophy was meagre.

The other day I became confused. I needed a ray of light. I turned back to those school days for aid. But in all the nasal harmonies we whined forth from those hard benches I could not recall one that treated of the voice of agglomerated mankind.

In other words, of the composite vocal message of massed humanity.

In other words, of the Voice of a Big City.

Now, the individual voice is not lacking. We can understand the song of the poet, the ripple of the brook, the meaning of the man who wants $5 until next Monday, the inscriptions on the tombs of the Pharaohs, the language of flowers, the "step lively" of the conductor, and the prelude of the milk cans at 4 a. m. Certain large-eared ones even assert that they are wise to the vibrations of the tympanum produced by concussion of the air emanating from Mr. H. James. But who can comprehend the meaning of the voice of the city?

I went out for to see.

First, I asked Aurelia. She wore white Swiss and a hat with flowers on it, and ribbons and ends of things fluttered here and there.

"Tell me," I said, stammeringly, for I have no voice of my own, "what does this big — er — enormous — er — whopping city say? It must have a voice of some kind. Does it ever speak to you? How do you interpret its meaning? It is a tremendous mass, but it must have a key."

"Like a Saratoga trunk?" asked Aurelia.

"No," said I. "Please do not refer to the lid. I have a fancy that every city has a voice. Each one has something to say to the one who can hear it. What does the big one say to you?"

"All cities," said Aurelia, judicially, "say the same thing. When they get through saying it there is an echo from Philadelphia. So, they are unanimous."

"Here are 4,000,000 people," said I, scholastically, "compressed upon an island, which is mostly lamb surrounded by Wall Street water. The conjunction of so many units into so small a space must result in an identity — or, or rather a homogeneity that finds its oral expression through a common channel. It is, as you might say, a consensus of translation, concentrating in a crystallized, general idea which reveals itself in what may be termed the Voice of the City. Can you tell me what it is?"

Aurelia smiled wonderfully. She sat on the high stoop. A spray of insolent ivy bobbed against her right ear. A ray of impudent moonlight flickered upon her nose. But I was adamant, nickel-plated.

"I must go and find out," I said, "what is the Voice of this City. Other cities have voices. It is an assignment. I must have it. New York," I continued, in a rising tone, "had better not hand me a cigar and say: 'Old man, I can't talk for publication.' No other city acts in that way. Chicago says, unhesitatingly, 'I will;' I Philadelphia says, 'I should;' New Orleans says, 'I used to;' Louisville says, 'Don't care if I do;' St. Louis says, 'Excuse me;' Pittsburg says, 'Smoke up.' Now, New York —"

Aurelia smiled.

"Very well," said I, "I must go elsewhere and find out."

I went into a palace, tile-floored, cherub-ceilinged and square with the cop. I put my foot on the brass rail and said to Billy Magnus, the best bartender in the diocese:

"Billy, you've lived in New York a long time — what kind of a song-and-dance does this old town give you? What I mean is, doesn't the gab of it seem to kind of bunch up and slide over the bar to you in a sort of amalgamated tip that hits off the burg in a kind of an epigram with a dash of bitters and a slice of—"

"Excuse me a minute," said Billy, "somebody's punching the button at the side door."

He went away; came back with an empty tin bucket; again vanished with it full; returned and said to me:

"That was Mame. She rings twice. She likes a glass of beer for supper. Her and the kid. If you ever saw that little skeesicks of mine brace up in his high chair and take his beer and — But, say, what was yours? I get kind of excited when I hear them two rings — was it the baseball score or gin fizz you asked for?"

"Ginger ale," I answered.

I walked up to Broadway. I saw a cop on the corner. The cops take kids up, women across, and men in. I went up to him.

"If I'm not exceeding the spiel limit," I said, "let me ask you. You see New York during its vocative hours. It is the function of you and your brother cops to preserve the acoustics of the city. There must be a civic voice that is intelligible to you. At night during your lonely rounds you must have heard it. What is the epitome of its turmoil and shouting? What does the city say to you?"

"Friend," said the policeman, spinning his club, "it don't say nothing. I get my orders from the man higher up. Say, I guess you're all right. Stand here for a few minutes and keep an eye open for the roundsman."

The cop melted into the darkness of the side street. In ten minutes he had returned.

"Married last Tuesday," he said, half gruffly. "You know how they are. She comes to that corner at nine every night for a — comes to say 'hello!' I generally manage to be there. Say, what was it you asked me a bit ago — what's doing in the city? Oh, there's a roofgarden or two just opened, twelve blocks up."

I crossed a crow's-foot of streetcar tracks, and skirted the edge of an umbrageous park. An artificial Diana, gilded, heroic, poised, wind-ruled, on the tower, shimmered in the clear light of her namesake in the sky. Along came my poet, hurrying, hatted, haired, emitting dactyls, spondees and dactylis. I seized him.

"Bill," said I (in the magazine he is Cleon), "give me a lift. I am on an assignment to find out the Voice of the city. You see, it's a special order. Ordinarily a symposium comprising the views of Henry Clews, John L. Sullivan, Edwin Markham, May Irwin and Charles Schwab would be about all. But this is a different matter. We want a broad, poetic, mystic vocalization of the city's soul and meaning. You are the very chap to give me a hint. Some years ago a man got at the Niagara Falls and gave us its pitch. The note was about two feet below the lowest G on the piano. Now, you can't put New York into a note unless it's better indorsed than that. But give me an idea of what it would say if it should speak. It is bound to be a mighty and far-reaching utterance. To arrive at it we must take the tremendous crash of the chords of the day's traffic, the laughter and music of the night, the solemn tones of Dr. Parkhurst, the ragtime, the weeping, the stealthy hum of cab-wheels, the shout of the press agent, the tinkle of fountains on the roof gardens, the hullabaloo of the strawberry vender and the covers of *Everybody's Magazine*, the whispers of the lovers in the parks — all these sounds must go into your Voice — not combined, but mixed, and of the mixture an essence made; and of the essence an extract — an audible extract, of which one drop shall form the thing we seek."

"Do you remember," asked the poet, with a chuckle, "that California girl we met at Stiver's studio last week? Well, I'm on my way to see her. She repeated that poem of mine, 'The Tribute of Spring,' word for word. She's the smartest proposition in this town just at present. Say, how does this confounded tie look? I spoiled four before I got one to set right."

"And the Voice that I asked you about?" I inquired.

"Oh, she doesn't sing," said Cleon. "But you ought to hear her recite my 'Angel of the Inshore Wind.'"

I passed on. I cornered a newsboy and he flashed at me prophetic pink papers that outstripped the news by two revolutions of the clock's longest hand.

"Son," I said, while I pretended to chase coins in my penny pocket, "doesn't it sometimes seem to you as if the city ought to be able to talk? All these ups and downs and funny business and queer things happening every day — what would it say, do you think, if it could speak?"

"Quit yer kiddin'," said the boy. "Wot paper yer want? I got no time to waste. It's Mag's birthday, and I want thirty cents to git her a present."

Here was no interpreter of the city's mouthpiece. I bought a paper, and consigned its undeclared treaties, its premeditated murders and unfought battles to an ash can.

Again I repaired to the park and sat in the moon shade. I thought and thought, and wondered why none could tell me what I asked for.

And then, as swift as light from a fixed star, the answer came to me. I arose and hurried — hurried as so many reasoners must, back around my circle. I knew the answer and I hugged it in my breast as I flew, fearing lest some one would stop me and demand my secret.

Aurelia was still on the stoop. The moon was higher and the ivy shadows were deeper. I sat at her side and we watched a little cloud tilt at the drifting moon and go asunder quite pale and discomfited.

And then, wonder of wonders and delight of delights! our hands somehow touched, and our fingers closed together and did not part.

After half an hour Aurelia said, with that smile of hers:

"Do you know, you haven't spoken a word since you came back!"

"That," said I, nodding wisely, "is the Voice of the City."

Biography of O. Henry

CHAPTER ONE
The Life And The Story

O. HENRY was once asked why he did not read more fiction. "It is all tame," he replied, "as compared with the romance of my own life." But nothing is more subtly suggestive in the study of this remarkable man than the strange, structural resemblance between the story and the life. Each story is a miniature autobiography, for each story seems to summarize the four successive stages in his own romantic career.

First, the reader notices in an O. Henry story the quiet but arrestive beginning. There is interest, a bit of suspense, and a touch of distinction in the first paragraph; but you cannot tell what lines of action are to be stressed, what complications of character and incident are to follow, or whether the end is to be tragic or comic, a defeat or a victory. So was the first stage of his life. The twenty years spent in Greensboro, North Carolina, were comparatively uneventful. There was little in them of prospect, though they loom large with significance in the retrospect. O. Henry was always unique. When as a freckle-faced boy, freckled even to the feet, he played his childish pranks on young and old and told his marvellous yarns of knightly adventure or Indian ambuscade, every father and mother and boy and girl felt that he was different from others of his kind. As he approached manhood, his "somnolent little Southern town" recognized in him its most skilful cartoonist of local character and its ablest interpreter of local incident. Moliere has been called "the composite smile of mankind." O. Henry was the composite smile of Greensboro.

In the second stage of an O. Henry story the lines begin suddenly to dip toward a plot or plan. Still water becomes running water. It is the stage of the first guess. Background and character, dialogue and incident, sparkle and sly thrust, aspiration and adventure, seem to be spelling out something definite and resultant. You cannot guess the end but you cannot help trying. In terms of his life this was O. Henry's second or Texas period. Had he died at the age of twenty, before leaving Greensboro, he would have left a local memory and a local cult, but they would have remained local. A few would have said that with wider opportunities he would have been heard from in a national way. But when letters began to come from Texas telling of his life on the ranch and later of his adventures in local journalism, and when "W. S. Porter" signed to a joke or skit or squib in Truth or Up to Date or the Detroit Free Press became more and more a certificate of the worth while, those of us who remained in the home town began to prophesy with some assurance that he would soon join the staff of some great metropolitan newspaper or magazine and win national fame as a cartoonist or travelling correspondent.

The third stage of an O. Henry story is reached when you find that your first forecast is wrong. This is the stage of the first surprise. Something has happened that could not or would not have happened if the story was to end as you at first thought. You must give up the role of prophet or at least readjust your prophecy to the demands of an ending wholly different from that at first conjectured. This stage in the life was reached in 1898, when misfortune, swift, pitiless, and seemingly irretrievable, overtook him. His life had hitherto developed uniformly, like the advance of a rolling ball. It had permitted and even invited some sort of conjecture as to his ultimate place in the work of the world. But now his destiny seemed as incalculable as the blind movements of a log in the welter of the sea.

The fourth and last stage in an O. Henry story, the stage of the second surprise, is marked by light out of darkness. Lines of character and characterization, of hap or mishap, converge to a triumphant conclusion.

We are surprised, happily surprised, and then surprised again that we should have been surprised at first. Says Nicholas Vachel Lindsay:

He always worked a triple-hinged surprise
To end the scene and make one rub his eyes.

The end was inherent in the beginning, however, though we did not see it. But the greatest surprise and the happiest surprise is found in the last stage of O. Henry's life. This was his

New York period, the culmination of tendencies and impulses that we now know had stirred mightily within him from the beginning. Eight years had passed, however, years of constant and constantly deepening development, and not a word had drifted back to the home town from him or about him since 1898. His pencil sketches were still affectionately cherished and had grown in historic value as well as in personal significance as the years had passed. They furnished a bond of common memory and happy association wherever Greensboro men foregathered, though the fun and admiration that they occasioned were mellowed by the thought of what might have been. Now came the discovery, through a photograph published in a New York magazine, that O. Henry, variously styled "the American Kipling," "the American de Maupassant," "the American Gogol," "our Fielding a la mode," "the Bret Harte of the city," "the Y. M. C. A. Boccaccio," "the Homer of the Tenderloin," "the 20th century Haroun Al-Raschid," "the discoverer and interpreter of the romance of New Yrork," "the greatest living master of the short story," was Will Porter of Greensboro. No story that he has written quite equals this in reserved surprise or in real and permanent achievement.

The technique of the story, however, is the technique of the life. But the life is more appealing than the story.

CHAPTER TWO
Vogue

WILLIAM SYDNEY PORTER, better known as O. Henry, was born in Greensboro, Guilford County, North Carolina, September 11, 1802. He died in New York City, June 5, 1910. Before the Porter family Bible was found, his birth year varied from 1807 to 1804, from "about the close of the war" to a question mark. There is no doubt that O. Henry used the author's traditional right to mystify his readers in regard to his age and to the unessential facts of his life. An admirer once wrote to him begging to know by return mail whether he was a man or a woman. But the stamped envelope enclosed for reply remains still unused. "If you have any applications from publishers for photos of myself," he wrote to Mr. Witter Bynner, "or 'slush' about the identity of O. Henry, please refuse. Nobody but a concentrated idiot would write over a pen-name and then tack on a lot of twaddle about himself. I say this because I am getting some letters from reviewers and magazines wanting pictures, etc., and I am positively declining in every case."

There has thus grown up a sort of O. Henry myth.

"It threatens to attain," said the New York Sun five years after his death, "the proportions of the Stevenson myth, which was so ill-naturedly punctured by Henley. It appears to be inevitably the fate of 'the writers' writer' — and O. Henry comes under this heading notwithstanding his work's universal appeal — to disintegrate into a sort of grotesque myth after his death. As a matter of fact Sydney Porter was, in a sort of a way, a good deal of a myth before he died. He was so inaccessible that a good many otherwise reasonable people who unsuccessfully sought to penetrate his cordon and to force their way into his cloister drew bountifully upon their imaginations to save their faces and to mask their failure."

But however mythical his personality, O. Henry's work remains the most solid fact to be reckoned with in the history of twentieth-century American literature. "More than any author who ever wrote in the United States," says Mr. Stephen Leacock, "O. Henry is an American writer. And the time is coming, let us hope, when the whole English-speaking world will recognize in him one of the great masters of modern literature." If variety and range of appeal be an indication, O. Henry would seem to be approaching the time thus prophesied. He has won the three classes of readers, those who work with their brains, those who work with their hands, and those who mingle the two in varying but incalculable proportions. The ultra-conservatives and the ultra-radicals, the critical and the uncritical, the bookmen and the business men, the women who serve and those who only stand and wait, all have enlisted under his banner. "The men and women whom I have in mind," writes Mr. W. J. Ghent, author of "Socialism and Success," "are social reformers, socialists, radicals, and progressives of various schools, practical and theoretical workers in the fields of social and political science. Some of these persons read Marx; most of them read H. G. Wells and John Galsworthy; but all of them are much more likely to read bluebooks and the Survey than the current fiction which contains no 'message.' Yet it was just among these persons, so far as my individual acquaintance goes, that O. Henry established himself as a writer almost at the beginning of his career."

"When I was a freshman in Harvard College," writes Mr. John S. Reed in the American Magazine, "I stood one day looking into the window of a bookstore on Harvard Square at a new volume of O. Henry. A quietly dressed, unimpressive man with a sparse, dark beard came up and stood beside me. Said he, suddenly: 'Have you read the new one?' 'No,' I said. 'Neither have I. I've read all the others, though.'

'He's great, don't you think?' 'Bully,' replied the quietly dressed man; 'let's go in and buy this one.'" The quietly dressed man was William James.

A writer is not often called a classic until at least a half century has set its seal upon his best work. But Mr. Edward Garnett, the English author, reviewer, and critic, admits to "the shelf of my prized American classics" seven authors. They are Poe, Thoreau, Whitman, Stephen Crane, Miss Sarah Orne Jewett, Mr. W. D. Ho wells, and O. Henry, though O. Henry published his first book in 1904. Professor Henry Seidel Canby, author of "The Short Story in English," thinks that the technique of the short story has undergone marked changes in recent years, "especially since O. Henry took the place of Kipling as a literary master." Mr. James Lane Allen believes that the golden age of the American short story closed about 1895. "The best of the American short stories," he says, "written during that period [1870-1895], outweigh in value those that have been written later — with the exception of those of one man... the one exception is O. Henry. He alone stands out in the later period as a world within himself, as much apart from any one else as are Hawthorne and Poe."

Mr. Henry James Forman, author of "In the Foot prints of Heine," finds also that, with one exception, there has been a decline in the short story as a distinct genre. "Publishers still look upon it somewhat askance," he writes, "as on one under a cloud, and authors, worldly-wise, still cling to the novel as the unquestioned leader. But here and there a writer now boldly brings forth a book of short tales, and the publisher does his part. The stigma of the genre is wearing off, and for the rehabilitation one man is chiefly responsible. Mr. Sydney Porter, the gentleman who, in the language of some of his characters, is 'denounced' by the euphonious pen-name of O. Henry, has breathed new life into the short story." After a tentative comparison with Frangois Villon, Dickens, and Maupassant, Mr. Forman concludes: "It is idle to compare O. Henry with anybody. No talent could be more original or more delightful. The combination of technical excellence with whimsical sparkling wit, abundant humour, and a fertile invention is so rare that the reader is content without comparisons." The Nation, after indicating the qualities that seem to differentiate him from Kipling and Mark Twain, summarizes in a single sentence: "O. Henry is actually that rare bird of which we so often hear false reports — a born story teller."

Professor William Lyon Phelps in "The Advance of the English Novel" puts O. Henry among the five greatest American short story writers. "No writer of distinction," he continues, "has, I think, been more closely identified with the short story in English than O. Henry. Irving, Poe, Hawthorne, Bret Harte, Stevenson, Kipling attained fame in other fields; but although Porter had his mind fully made up to launch what he hoped would be the great American novel, the veto of death intervened, and the many volumes of his 'complete works' are made up of brevities. The essential truthfulness of his art is what gave his work immediate recognition, and accounts for his rise from journalism to literature. There is poignancy in his pathos; desolation in his tragedy; and his extraordinary humour is full of those sudden surprises that give us delight. Uncritical readers have never been so deeply impressed with O. Henry as have the professional, jaded critics, weary of the old trick a thousand times repeated, who found in his writings a freshness and originality amounting to genius."

There is no doubt that the jaded critics extended a warm welcome to O. Henry, but that they were more hospitable than the uncritical admits of question. For several years I have made it a practice in all sorts of unacademic places, where talk was abundant, to lead the conversation if possible to O. Henry. The result has been a conviction that O. Henry is to-day not less "the writers' writer" but still more the people's writer.

Travelling a few years ago through a Middle Western State, during an intolerable drought, I fell into conversation with a man the burden of whose speech was "I've made my pile and now I'm going away to live." He was plainly an unlettered man but by no means ignorant. He talked interestingly, because genuinely, until he put the usual question: "What line of goods do you carry?" When I had to admit my unappealing profession his manner of speech became at once formal and distant. "Professor," he said, after a painful pause, "Emerson is a very elegant writer, don't you think so?" I agreed and also agreed, after another longer and more painful pause, that Prescott was a very elegant writer. These two names plus "elegant" seemed to exhaust his available supply of literary allusion. "Did you ever read O. Henry?" I asked. At the mention of the name his manner changed instantly and his eyes moistened. Leaning far over he said: "Professor, that's literature, that's literature, that's real literature." He was himself again now. The mask of affectation had fallen away, and the appreciation and knowledge of O. Henry's work that he displayed, the affection for the man that he expressed, the grateful indebtedness that he was proud to acknowledge for a kindlier and more intelligent sympathy with his fellowmen showed plainly that O. Henry was the only writer who had ever revealed the man's better nature to himself.

The incident is typical. The jaded critics and the short story writers read O. Henry and admire him: they find in him what they want. Those who do not criticise and do not write read him and love him: they find in him what they need — a range of fancy, an exuberance of humour, a sympathy, an understanding, a knowledge of the raw material of life, an ability to interpret the passing in terms of the permanent, an insight into individual and institutional character, a resolute and pervasive desire to help those in need of help, in a word a constant and essential democracy that they find in no other short story writer. But the deeper currents in O. Henry's work can be traced only through a wider knowledge of O. Henry the man.

CHAPTER THREE
Ancestry

The O. Henry myth could not forever withstand the curiosity and inquiry begotten by the increasing acclaim that the stories were beginning to receive. O. Henry himself must have recognized the futility of attempting a further mystification, for there is evident in his later years a willingness and even a desire to throw off the mask of the assumed name and thus to link his achievement with the name and fortunes of his family. He had sought freedom and self-expression through his writings rather than fame. In fact, he shunned publicity with the timidity of a child. "What used to strike me most forcibly in O. Henry," writes Mr. John H. Barry, who knew him from the beginning of his career in New York, "was his distinction of character. To those he knew and liked he revealed himself as a man of singular refinement. He had beautiful, simple manners, a low voice, and a most charming air of self-effacement. For the glory of being famous he cared little. He had a dislike of being lionized. Lion-hunting women filled him with alarm. In fact, he was afraid of nearly all women."

But fame had come and with it came a vein of ancestral reminiscence and a return in imagination to the days of childhood. His marriage, in 1907, to the sweetheart and the only sweetheart of the Greensboro years, his visits to Mrs. Porter's home in Asheville, and his affectionate allusions to his father and mother show plainly a tendency to relax the cordon about him and to re-knit the ties and associations of youth. O. Henry was becoming Will Porter again. Even the great American novel, of which Professor Phelps speaks, was to be in the nature of an autobiography. "Let Me Feel Your Pulse," the last complete story that he wrote, was also the most autobiographical. "It was written," says Dr. Pinkney Herbert, of Asheville, "with the aid of my medical books. Sometimes he would take them to his office and again he would sit in my outer office." It was heralded by the magazine announcement, "If you want to get well, read this story." But O. Henry was dead before the story was published. In it he speaks of his ancestors who blended the blood of North and South :

"It's the haemoglobin test," he [the doctor] explained. "The color of your blood is wrong." "Well," said I, "I know it should be blue; but this is a country of mix-ups. Some of my ancestors were cavaliers; but they got thick with some people on Nantucket Island, so"

His forebears were again in his mind when, wrenched with pain but not bowed, he went to the hospital in New York from which he knew he would not return alive. Will Irwin describes the scene as follows :*

Then as he stepped from the elevator to the ward, a kind of miracle came over him. Shy, sensitive, guarding the bare nerve-ends of his soul with an affectation of flippancy, his gait had always been furtive, his manner shrinking. Now he walked nobly, his head up, his chest out, his feet firm — walked as earls walked to the scaffold. Underneath all that democracy of life and love of the raw human heart which made him reject the prosperous and love the chatter of car-conductors and shopgirls — that quality which made Sydney Porter "O. Henry" — lay pride in his good Southern blood. It was as though he summoned all this pride of blood to help him fight the last battle like a man and a Sydney.

Thus
After Last returns the First,
Though a wide compass round be fetched.

William Sydney Porter was named after his mother's father, William Swaim, and his father's father, Sidney Porter.f He was always called Will Porter in the early days except by his grandmother on his father's side who occasionally called him Sydney. He never saw either of his grandfathers, both dying long before he was born. But William Swaim, his mother's father, who died in 1835, left his impress upon the State and was, so far as can be learned, the only journalist or writer among O. Henry's ancestors. The ink in O. Henry's blood came from this Quaker grandparent, *"O. Henry, Man and Writer" (in the Cosmopolitan, September, 1910).

tO.Henry changed thespellingofhis middle name fromSidney to Sydney in 1898. See page 169l whose ancestor, also William Swaim, emigrated from Holland about the year 1700 and is buried in Richmond, Staten Island, his descendants having moved to North Carolina at least ten years before the Revolutionary War. William Swaim, O. Henry's grandfather, did not found the Greensboro Patriot, of which he became editor in 1827, but he had the good sense to change its name from the ponderous Patriot a?id Greensboro Palladium to the simpler title that it has since borne. He does not seem to me to have been as able or as well balanced a man as Lyndon Swaim who, strangely enough, though not ascertainably related, was soon to succeed William Swaim both as editor and as husband and thus to become the only father that O. Henry's mother knew.

William Swaim had convictions and he hewed to the line. When "the nabob gentry" of Greensboro, as he called them, sought to bend the Patriot to their own purposes, he wrote as follows (May 30, 1832):

They soon learned from our tone that we would sooner beg for bread and be free than to compromise our principles for a seat upon a tawdry throne of corruption. Still bent upon the fell purpose of preventing, if possible, an unshackled press from growing into public favor, their last resort was to ransack hell, from the centre to the circumference, for slanderous fabrications; and these have been heaped upon us, without cause and without mercy, even until now. But thanks to a generous public, they have thus far sustained us "through evil as well as through good report," and we would rather bask for one hour in their approving smiles than to spend a whole eternity amidst the damning grins of a concatenation of office-hunters, despots, demagogues, tyrants, fools, and hypocrites.

When subscribers subscribed but took French leave, Editor Swaim threw the lasso after them in this wise:

STOP THE RUNAWAYS!

The following is a list of gentlemen who, after reading our paper for a time, have politely disappeared and left us the "bag to hold." We give the name of each, together with the amount due, and the place of his residence at the time he patronized us. Should this publication meet the eye of any delinquents and should they yet conclude to forward to us the amount due, we will publicly acknowledge the receipt and restore him who sends it to better credit than an act of the legislature could possibly give. Any person who will favor us with information of the residence of any or all of these absentees shall have the right to claim the homage of our sincere thanks:

Joseph Aydelotte, Esq., Guilford County, North Carolina. Twelve dollars.

John Lackey, Tarboro. Nine dollars.

James Hiatt, not recollected. Nine dollars.

"William Atkinson, unknown. Nine dollars.

Jacob Millers, not recollected. Nine dollars.

Joseph Bryan, whipt anyhow and may be hung. Six dollars.

Is there not at least a hint of O. Henry in this "unexpected crack of the whip at the end?"

William Swaim believed that the lines had fallen to him in an evil age. He was an ardent Whig, a bitter opponent of Jackson and all things Jacksonian, a fearless and independent fighter for the right as he saw the right, and an equal foe of fanaticism in the North and of slavery in the South. His style was ponderous rather than weighty, the humour being entirely unconscious. "I am surprised," he writes, "that my old friend Jonathan suffered this limb of the law to put afloat under the sanction of his name such a tissue of falsehood, malignity, and spleen." One must go to Jeff Peters of "The Gentle Grafter" for a sentence the equal of that. "Let me tell you first," said Jeff, "about these barnacles that clog the wheels of society by poisoning the springs of rectitude with their upas-like eye."

The ablest thing that this grandfather of O. Henry ever wrote was a protest against slavery. He was an advocate of the gradual emancipation of the slaves, a society for this purpose having been formed at Center, ten miles from Greensboro, as early as 1816. Center was a Quaker stronghold, its most influential family being the Worth family, to which O. Henry's grandmother on his father's side belonged. Hinton Rowan Helper, the most famous of North

Carolina's abolitionists, refers to the valiant services of Daniel Worth in "The Impending Crisis," a book often compared with "Uncle Tom's Cabin" as a sort of co-herald of the doom of slavery. "William Swaim was greeted," says Cartland,* "with a storm of abuse, but he boldly published his sentiments and often gave the threatening letters *See "Southern Heroes or the Friends in War Time," by Fernando G. Cartland.

which he received a conspicuous place in the Patriot." In 1882 Daniel It. Goodloe writes to Lyndon Swaim from Washington, D. C.:

William Swaim in 1830 published a pamphlet entitled "An Address to the People of North Carolina on the Evils of Slavery" with mottoes in Latin and English. The imprint is "William Swaim, Printer, Greensboro, N. C. 1830." Some twenty-seven or thirty years ago the abolitionists of New York republished, I suppose, a facsimile of the original, and Mr. Spofford, the librarian of Congress, has procured a copy. He asked me who was the author, as it is a rule with him to give, as far as possible, the name of every author. I should have quoted in the title that it purports to be written and published "By the Friends of Liberty and Equality." William Swaim introduces the address with a few words over his signature, stating that it emanates from the "Board of Managers of the Manumission Society of North Carolina." I will thank you to write me all you know of this Manumission Society and of the authorship of this pamphlet. The pamphlet does great honor to all concerned with it, and their names should be known in this day of universal liberty.

O. Henry's grandmother, who married Lyndon Swaim after the death of her husband William Swaim, was Abia Shirley (or Abiah Shirly), daughter of Daniel Shirley, a wealthy planter, of Princess Anne County, Virginia. "The original Abia Shirley," O. Henry once remarked to an intimate friend in New York, "was related to the House of Stuart but she ran off with a Catholic priest." Where O. Henry learned this bit of ancestral history I do not know; but that the Shirley family to which his grandmother traced her lineage was among the most loyal adherents of the Stuarts admits of little doubt. A letter from Charles II to the widow of Sir Robert Shirley, Sir Robert having died in the Tower "after seven times being imprisoned there and suspected to be poisoned by the Usurper Oliver Cromwell," runs as follows:*

Brusselles 20 Oct. 1657.

It hath been my particular care of you that I have this long deferred to lament with you the greate losse that you and I have sustained, least insteede of comforting, I might farther expose you to the will of those who will be glad of any occasion to do you further prejudice; but I am promised that this shall be put safely into your hands, though it may be not so soone as I wish; and I am very willing you should know, which I suppose you cannot doubte, that I bear a greate parte with you of your affliction and whenever it shall be in my power to make it lighter, you shall see I retayne a very kinde memory of your frinde by the care I shall have of you and all his relations: and of this you may depende upon the worde of your very affectionate Frinde Charles R.

This Sir Robert Shirley, who met his death in 1656, was one of the Shirleys of Wiston (or Whiston), in Sussex, though he lived in Leicestershire; and it was after Sir Thomas Shirley of Wiston that Shirley, the beautiful old Virginia place, was named;f Built at an unknown date just above the point where the Appomattox River enters the James, this historic *See "Stemmata Shirleiana" (1841), which makes, however, no references to the American Shirleys.

home, with its three lofty stories and two-storied porches, its widespreading lawn and massive oaks, contests with Monticello the primacy among Virginia's ancestral seats. Here was born Anne Hill Carter, the wife of Light Horse Harry Lee and the mother of Robert E. Lee. As far back as 1(>22, in the history of the Indian massacre of that year, the Plantation of West Shirley in Virginia is mentioned as one of the "five or six well-fortified places" into which the survivors gathered for defense. It was from the Shirleys of Wistoii, who gave the name to the plantation and later to the home, that the Shirley family of Princess Anne County always traced their descent. Though I have been unable to find an Abia Shirley antedating O. Henry's grandmother, William Swaim, in a letter lying before me, dated Greensboro, N. C., May 22,

1830, speaks of Nancy Shirley, his wife's sister, "who had intermarried with Thomas Bray." It is at least a noteworthy coincidence that a sixteenth-century Beatrix Shirley of Wiston married "Sir Edward Bray, the elder, of Vachery, Surrey County, Knight." *

* "Stemmata Shirleiana."

But whether "the original Abia Shirley" was fact or fancy, it is certain that the Abia Shirley, who became O. Henry's grandmother, lived a gracious and exemplary life in Greensboro and bequeathed a memory still cherished by the few friends who survive her.

The following obituary notice, signed "A Friend," appeared in the Patriot of January, 1858:

Died. — In this place on Monday morning, January 18th, Mrs. Abia Swaim, wife of Lyndon Swaim, in the 50th year of her age. For nearly two years Mrs. Swaim had been confined to her room, and most of that time to her bed, by consumption — constantly in pain, which she patiently endured with great Christian fortitude. She leaves an affectionate husband and a devoted daughter to mourn their loss. In her death the "poor and the needy" have been deprived of an invaluable friend; for no one in this community was more ready to contribute to the relief of poverty and hunger than the subject of this notice. She was always ready to watch around the sick bed of her friends, and all who knew her were her friends; I believe she had no enemies.

Mrs. Swaim was a native of Eastern Virginia — her maiden name being Shirly. On arriving to womanhood, she removed to this place with her sister, the late Mrs. Carbry, and was afterward united in marriage with William Swaim. He dying, she remained a widow several years, when she was married to Lyndon Swaim.

She embraced religion in her youth, and for a quarter of a century lived an exemplary and acceptable member of the Methodist Episcopal Church, exhibiting on all occasions a strong and lively faith in the efficacy of the blood of Christ; and while her friends drop many sympathizing tears with her bereaved family, they can in their sorrow' all rejoice in full assurance that her never-dying spirit is now united with that of a sweet infant daughter who preceded her to heaven; and that at the great resurrection morn, her body will be raised to life everlasting. May we all strive to imitate her many virtues, that when the summons of death comes, we may be able to die as she died, at peace with God ana man, and gently close our eyes in sleep.

The "devoted daughter" was Mary Jane Virginia Swaim, O. Henry's mother. She was twenty-five years old at the time of her mother's death and married Dr. Algernon Sidney Porter three months later. Only seven years had passed when the Patriot bore the following announcement:

DIED

In Greensboro, N. C., September 26, 1865, Mrs. Mary V. Porter, wife of Dr. A. S. Porter, and only child of the late William Swaim. Mrs. Porter leaves a devoted husband and three small children, together with numerous friends to mourn her early death. She gave, in her last moments, most satisfactory evidence that she had made her peace with God, and her friends can entertain no doubt of her happiness in the spirit land. She was aged about thirty years; was a graduate of Greensboro Female College; and possessed mental faculties of high order, finely developed by careful training. Her death is a great social loss to our community; but especially to her affectionate husband and three little children. Her disease was consumption.

Whether O. Henry remembered his mother or not it would be impossible to say. Certain it is that he cherished the thought of her with a devotion and pride and sense of temperamental indebtedness that he felt for no one else, nor for all his other relatives put together. Whatever vein of quiet humour marked his allusions to the other members of his family or to his family history, his mother's name was held apart. She was to him "a thing ensky'd and sainted." There was always an aureole about her. The poems that she wrote and the pictures that she painted — or rather the knowledge that she had written poems and painted pictures — exercised a directive and lasting influence upon him. Had she lived she would have given to the Porter home an atmosphere that it never had after 1865. She would have enabled her gifted son to find himself many years earlier than he did and she would have brought him to his goal not "By a route obscure and lonely"but along the broad highway of common tastes and common sympathies.

Lyndon Swaim gave his stepdaughter every educational advantage that Greensboro offered and then as now no town in North Carolina offered as many to women. There were two colleges for women on old West Market Street, both very near and one almost opposite the house in which O. Henry's mother was to spend all of her short married life. Both institutions had already begun to attract students from other Southern States. One was the Greensboro Female College, now the Greensboro College for Women, a Methodist school, the cornerstone of which was laid in 1843 and the later history of which has been the romance of education in North Carolina. The other was the Edgeworth Female Seminary, a Presbyterian school, founded and owned by Governor John Motley Morehead, whose influence on the industrial and cultural development of the State remains as yet unequalled.

Edgeworth opened its doors in 1840 and was burned in 1872. O. Henry's mother attended both schools, graduating from the Greensboro Female College in 1850, the year in which Dr. Charles F. Deems assumed control. Her graduating essay bore the strangely prophetic title, "The Influence of Misfortune on the Gifted."

She entered Edgeworth at the age of twelve and during her one session there she studied Bullion's "English Grammar," Bolmar's "Physics," Lincoln's "Botany," besides receiving "instruction in the higher classes and in the French language." During her four years at the Greensboro Female College she studied rhetoric, algebra, geometry, logic, astronomy, White's "Universal History," Butler's "Analogy of Religion, Natural and Revealed, to the Constitution and Course of Nature," and Alexander's "Evidences of the Authenticity, Inspiration, and Canonical Authority of the Holy Scriptures." She specialized in French and later in painting and drawing. The flyleaves of her copy of Alexander's "Evidences" — and doubtless of Butler's "Analogy" if it could be found — are covered with selections from her favourite poets, while dainty sketches of gates, trees, houses, and flowers, filling the inter-spaces, show that she relieved the tedium of classroom lectures exactly as her son was to do thirty years later.

That O. Henry's mother was an unusually bright scholar is attested by both teachers and classmates. Rev. Solomon Lea, the first President of the Greensboro Female College, writes December 1, 184G, to Lyndon Swaim: "Your daughter Mary ranks No. 1 in her studies, has an excellent mind, and will no doubt make a fine scholar." Says one of her classmates, Mrs. Henry Tate: "Mary Swaim was noted in her school days as a writer of beautiful English and the school girls came to depend upon her for their compositions. She wrote most of the graduating essays for the students." Mrs. Tate adds that O. Henry resembled his mother in personal appearance and in traits of character.

The following letter, written by her at the age of fifteen to her stepfather, almost the only letter of O. Henry's mother that has been preserved, seems here and there to hint if it does not fore-announce something of the humorous playfulness of the son. Note especially the tendency to give an unexpected turn to common sayings and quotations, a device that became in O. Henry's hands an art:

Greensboro, Sept. 21, 1848.

Dear Father: Your letter reached us last Monday, having come by Raleigh as also did Dr. Mebane's. We were very anxious to hear from you before we received your letter, but it came like an "Angel's visit" bringing peace to our anxious minds. We are all well at present and want to see you very much. Your letter was very interesting to us all from its being a description of your travels. From what you wrote I should judge you had not received my letter which I wrote agreeable to your request. Mother says she is very glad to hear that your health is improving and she wants to see you when you come home looking as portly as Dr. Cole* or Governor Morehead. There is no news of interest stirring in town at this time. Last Sunday evening there was a sudden death in the Methodist Church. A negro belonging to Mrs. Bencini was either shouting or talking to the mourners when she fell dead on the spot. Mr. Armfield's daughter died last week. There is little or no sickness in town at present.

Sherwood you know always does keep a "stiff upper lip" for he rarely if ever shaves, only when he is in the neighbourhood of Miss Betsey or Miss Martha or Miss Maria or a dozen of

Misses at whom he casts sheep eyes. You said as you passed through Lexington you saw Miss Salisbury teaching some "young ideas how to shoot." I am sure if they were as large as I they would not have needed her assistance to teach them how to shoot, especially if they shoot with a bow, for generally such ideas learn how to shoot with that sort of a weapon by instinct. All the family send their love to you, and Mother says again: "Take good care of yourself and come home soon." As I am to have this letter finished by twelve o'clock and it is only a few minutes of that time, I must stop here, not before saying, however, to make haste and come home. If you do not start home right off, you must write again.

Yours affectionately Mary V. Swaim.

The resemblances between O. Henry and his mother are still further revealed in these "Memories of the *This was Br. J. L. Cole with whom lived his nephew C. C. Cole. The latter, a young graduate of Trinity College, N. C., was soon to edit the Times of Greensboro, to which William Gilmore Simms, John Esten Cooke, and Mrs. Lydia Huntly Sigourney contributed regularly. C. C. Cole became Colonel of the Twenty-second Regiment and was killed in the Battle of Chancellorsville, May 3, 1863.

Mother of a Gifted Writer," sent me by Mr. William Laurie Hill:

In the days of the old four horse stage coach and the up and down hill stretch of our country roads leading from one town or village to another, there were but fifty miles of road between the old Revolutionary village of Milton, North Carolina, and the more aspiring town of Greensboro. For a high type of social life old Milton, although a village, had no superior in the State, and her people, although "stay at home bodies," claimed many friends even in distant parts. In summer many of her homes were filled with visitors and in those halcyon days of peace and plenty it was a delight to keep open house.

Milton could boast of having a spicy weekly paper known as the Milton Chronicle that carried its weekly message into all the neighboring counties. The editor was Charles Napoleon Bonapart Evans, who originated the character of "Jesse Holmes, the Fool-Killer."*

* Readers of O. Henry will recall that in "The Fool-Killer" he says: "Down South whenever any one perpetrates some particularly monumental piece of foolishness everybody says: 'Send for Jesse Holmes.' Jesse Holmes is the Fool-Killer." It is interesting to note that O. Henry was here quoting, unconsciously I presume, a saying originated by his mother's cousin. Charles Napoleon Bonapart Evans's mother was a Miss Shirley, sister of Abia Shirley. The familiarity of Greensboro boys with "Jesse Holmes" has here led O. Henry to ascribe a wider circuit to the saying than the facts seem to warrant. From queries sent out I am inclined to think that "Jesse Holmes" as a synonym for the Fool-Killer is not widely known in the South and is current in North Carolina only in spots. "I tried it out this morning in chapel," writes President E. K. Graham, of the University of North Carolina, "on perhaps five hundred North Carolinians. Only three had heard of it." One of these was from Greensboro and cited Charles Napoleon Bonapart Evans as the author. This character furnished sarcasm and wit in weekly instalments that kept the young people always on the edge of expectancy. Greensboro also had a paper of no mean pretentions and, perhaps leaving out the Salisbury Watchman and the Hillsboro paper long presided over by that venerable old editor Dennis Heartt, the Greensboro Patriot stood next in age in the State, and the name of William Swaim was almost as widely known as was Edward J. Hale of the Fayetteville Observer. There seemed to be warm and tender social ties that united the Swaim and Evans families and although dwelling fifty miles apart there were frequent interchanges of visits, and Mary Jane Virginia Swaim always enjoyed with a relish her visits to Mrs. Evans and was the recipient of many hospitable attentions whenever she brightened by her presence our little village.

To have a new girl come into our social life was a source of great pleasure to our boys and I well remember the first time I ever saw Mary Swaim, and, had I been just a little older, perhaps there might have been a serious attempt to alter what is now both biography and family history. Calling one evening at the Evans home, which was diagonally across the street from my own,

I was ushered into the presence of one of the most winsome women I ever saw, and from our first introduction we became friends.

Mary Swaim was not a beauty but her eyes could talk and when she became animated in conversation her every feature was instinct with expression and life and with the passing thoughts to which she gave expression. There was a play of color in her cheeks richer than the blush of the peach. She was quick of wit and a match for any would-be iconoclast who undertook to measure repartee with her. She was considerate of even her youngest cavalier and never seemed to shun the attentions of those younger in years than herself. To say that she was a universal favorite in old Milton with young and old, expresses but feebly the impression that she left on the hearts and memories of those who knew her in the happy days of long ago.

The tides of life ebbing and flowing carried this most winsome woman into new and untried paths and she became, as she had given promise to be, a lovely and loving mother. After the pleasant associations of those early days I saw her no more, but I was in the throng that assembled in Raleigh, on December 2, 1914, and witnessed the unveiling of the bronze tablet* in the Library Building, placed there in memory of her illustrious son, William Sydney Porter, more familiarly and affectionately known as O. Henry. Is it any wonder that such a woman as Mary Swaim should have given to the world such a son as William Sydney *Erected by the Literary and Historical Association of North Carolina under the presidency of Dr. Archibald Henderson.

Porter? In him and his wonderful literary work the mother will live on when marble monuments and bronze tablets shall have crumbled into dust.

O. Henry's grandparents on his father's side were Sidney Porter and Ruth Coffyn Worth. They rest side by side in the small and fast diminishing graveyard of the First Presbyterian Church in Greensboro, the headstones bearing the inscriptions:

Sidney Porter was a tall, jolly, heavy-set man but with little of the force or thrift of the family into which he married. He came from Connecticut to North Carolina about the year 1823 as the agent of a clock company. Several of the clocks that he sold are still doing duty in Guilford County and from the firm-name upon them, "Eight day repeating brass clock, made by C. and N. Jerome, Bristol, Conn.," they would seem to indicate that Sidney Porter's home was in Bristol. "C. and N. Jerome," writes Judge Epaph-roditus Peck, of Bristol, "were the principal clock-makers here at that time. They used to send out as travelling sellers of their clocks young men here; and I think that the fact that Sidney Porter was sent out by them probably indicates that he was then living here. Communities were then isolated and self-centred and they were not likely to send men from other towns. I do not find any traces of him, however, on the local records."

Dr. David Worth, father of Ruth, made minute inquiries into the past of his would-be son-in-law and became convinced, writes a descendant, that "Mr. Porter was a man of strictly upright character and worthy of his daughter's hand." The marriage took place at Center, the ancestral home of the Worths, on April 22, 1824, and was really a double celebration. Ruth Worth's brother Jonathan, who was later to become Governor of North Carolina, had married Martitia Daniel of Virginia two days before, and the brother's infare served as wedding reception for the sister. It was a notable occasion for the little Quaker village in more ways than mere festivity. Could I have been present when the infare was at its height, when congratulation and prophecy were bringing their blended tributes to father and mother and to son and daughter, I should not have been an unwelcome visitor, I think, could I have lifted the veil of the future for a moment and said to Doctor Worth and his wife: "Eighty-three years from now a statue will be dedicated in the capital of North Carolina to one of Jonathan's grandsons, the first statue to be erected by popular subscription to a North Carolina soldier, and the name engraved upon it will be that of Worth Bagley; and ninety years from to-day a memorial tablet will be dedicated in the same city to one of Ruth's grandsons, the only monument ever erected in the State to literary genius, and the name engraved upon it will be that of William Sydney Porter." But the roads of destiny along which the two cousins were to travel to their memorial meeting-place were to be strangely diverse.

Sidney Porter, after a few unsuccessful years spent in a neighbouring county, came back to Guilford and opened a carriage-making and general repair shop in Greensboro, where he worked at his trade till his death. His shop stood on West Market Street where his daughter's school was later to be erected, the only school that O. Henry ever attended. Sidney Porter was liked for his genial qualities by his neighbours but his business did not prosper. In 1841 he was compelled to mortgage to James Sloan, "trustee for the benefit of John A. Mebane and others," all that he had even to his working tools except those "allowed to be retained by debtors who are workmen." That the mortgage was not foreclosed was probably due to the standing and aid of his wife's family and especially to his wife's superior thrift and efficiency. It is probable also that slave labour was a handicap not sufficiently taken into account by one whose training had been in a community unaccustomed to the peculiar conditions that confronted the white labourer in the South.

That O. Henry's grandfather was considered a man of at least more than ordinary directive ability, in spite of his habit of frequent tippling which is still remembered, appears from a public record of 1837. The little town, whose corporate limits had just been made one mile square, appointed groups of men to keep the streets in order. Four supervisors, representing the four quarters of the town, were chosen to have control of the new work. The position was one of responsibility and was given only to men of known enterprise, as is shown by the character of the appointees. James Sloan, one of the foremost citizens of the town and later to be Chief Quartermaster of the State during the war, was supervisor of the first division; Sidney Porter, of the second; Henry Humphreys, the richest man in Greensboro, the owner of the Mount Hecla Steam Cotton Mill, and the first to prove that cotton could be profitably manufactured in the State, of the third; and Reuben Dick, pioneer manufacturer of cigars, of the fourth.

Sidney Porter's most characteristic trait, however, the quality that he was to transmit to his grandson, was not business efficiency. It was his sunny good humour.

"He joked and laughed at his work," says an old citizen, "and was especially beloved by children. He would repair their toys for them free of charge and seemed never so happy as when they gathered about him on the street or in his workshop. He even let them tamper with his tools." Fifty years later they were to say of O. Henry in Texas :f " He was a favourite with the children. Those that have grown lip up have pleasant memories of a jolly, big-hearted man who never failed to throw himself unreservedly into their games, to tell them stories that outrivalled in interest those of Uncle Remus, to sing delightfully humorous ongs to the merry jangle of a guitar, or to draw mirth-provoking cartoons."

The memory of Sidney Porter that survives is clear, therefore, in outline, though faint in content. From him O. Henry got also the wanderlust that urged him unceasingly from place to place. Clocks were never as interesting to Grandpa Porter as were the faces and places that he saw on his frequent tours. From Hartford County, Connecticut, to Guilford County, North Carolina, from Guilford to Randolph, from Randolph back to Guilford, Sidney Porter's shifts brought him a widened fellowship but neither prosperity nor geographical contentment. He handed down his name and a goodly share of his disposition to his grandson and, as the original rolling stone, might well typify if he did not suggest the title of the first and only periodical that O. Henry was to edit.

Ruth Worth, wife of Sidney Porter and grandmother of O. Henry, was what is known in North Carolina parlance as "a character," the term implying marked individuality and will power. Her parents were Quakers of honourable ancestry and of distinguished service. David Worth, the father, was a descendant of John Worth who emigrated from England, during Cromwell's reign, and settled in Massachusetts. David Worth became a physician, was active in the Manumission Society of North Carolina, and represented Guilford County in the legislature from 1822 to 1823. Through him O. Henry was eighth in lineal descent from Peter Folger, Benjamin Franklin's grandfather. Eunice Gardner, whom David Worth married in 1798, was born in North Carolina, though her parents came from Nantucket. On the death of her husband she began the practice of medicine, in which she attained notable success. The best-known member of the family was Ruth Worth's brother Jonathan, who was Governor of North Carolina from 1865 to 18G8 and whom the Chronicle, of Charleston, South Carolina, described as "a quiet little old gentleman, sharp as a briar, and with a well of wisdom at the root of every gray hair."

The description fits Ruth Worth though it omits her native kindness of heart. I have found no memorial tribute to this grandmother of O. Henry that does not emphasize her loyalty to her convictions, her practical efficiency, her self-reliance, and her goodness of heart. "So genuine was her kindness of heart and sympathy for suffering," says Church Society, "that the surest passports to her ministry were sickness, poverty, and want, and long will she be remembered." Says another local paper: "She was perhaps the best known and most useful, self-sacrificing woman of her day. A history of her eventful life cannot be given in a few words but it would require a volume to do justice to her honoured career." Six years after her death Mr. J. R. Bulla, in his "Reminiscences of Randolph County," compared her with Pocahontas, Lady Arabella, Flora McDonald, Queen Margaret, and Queen Elizabeth, all of whom were hopelessly and pathetically outclassed. "If Queen Elizabeth," he concludes, "had had as much wisdom as Ruth Porter, her reign would not only be extolled by the English but by all the civilized world. No Queen that Britain has ever had, had the eighth part of the common sense of Ruth Porter."

Left a widow at the age of forty-three with seven children and a mortgaged home she set to work first with her needle and then with a few boarders to earn a support for herself and those dependent on her. To these were later added Shirley Worth Porter, William Sydney Porter [O. Henry], and David Weir Porter, the motherless children of her son, Dr. Algernon Sidney Porter. David Weir died in early childhood but O. Henry lived with his grandmother, his father, his aunt, "Miss Lina," and his brother Shirley till 1882 when he moved to Texas Finding neither her needle nor her table sufficiently remunerative Mrs. Porter studied medicine and drugs under her son and became, as her mother had become before her, a practitioner in many homes.

She also collected or tried to collect the bills due her son. It was not good form in those days for a physician to dun a patient or even to send in a statement of the amount due. The patient was supposed to settle once a year without a reminder. This did not accord with Mrs. Porter's ways of doing business and she used to make out the bills and send them. In return she often received very sharp replies. Doctor Porter had on one occasion visited two maiden ladies and when the bill was sent to their father he replied indignantly that Doctor Porter's visits were only "social calls." "Social calls!" wrote O. Henry's grandmother. "I want you to understand that my son Algernon don't make social calls on maiden ladies at two o'clock in the morning and they a-suffering with cramp colic." The bill was paid.

Her son's practice declined steadily, however, and the household was often in sore straits. Mrs. Porter's rather intermittent calls, Miss Lina's little school, and O. Henry's meagre salary as clerk in his uncle Clark Porter's drug store were practically the only means of family support during the latter years of O. Henry's life in his native State. One cannot but feel a keen regret that neither the grandmother, nor the father, nor the aunt lived to witness or even to fore-glimpse the fame of the youngest member of the Porter household. Indeed the chief trait which Mrs. Sidney Porter saw in her grandson was his constitutional shyness. "I sometimes regret," she remarked, "that we did not send him to Trinity College, for Dr. Braxton Craven makes every student feel that he, Braxton Craven, is the greatest man on earth and the student himself the next greatest." An education away from home, however, could never have been seriously considered. "I would have given my eyes for a college education," O. Henry said, when his daughter Margaret brought home her college diploma.

O. Henry's father, Dr. Algernon Sidney Porter, was the oldest of the seven children. He was born in 1825 and died in 1888. If O. Henry received from his mother his gift of repartee, his artistic temperament, and a certain instinctive shyness, he received from his father his sympathy with all sorts and conditions of men, his overflowing generosity, his utter indifference to caste, in a word a large share of his characteristic and ineradicable democracy. To the same source may also be ascribed, through association at least, some of O. Henry's constructive ingenuity.

Doctor Porter was for several years the best-known and the best-loved physician in Guilford County. An old friend* of his, to whom the memory of Doctor Porter brought tears, said recently: "He was the best-hearted man I ever knew; honest, high-toned, and generous. Rain or shine, sick or well, he would visit the poorest family in the county. He would have been a rich man if he had collected a half of what was due him. His iron-gray hair and the shape of his head reminded you of Zeb Vance." His office, like his father's before him, became a sort of general repair shop, though in a different way. "I shall never forget," said the late Joe Reece, editor of the Daily Record of Greensboro, "something that happened in my boyhood. A giant of a negro had been cut down the back in a street fight. He passed me making straight for Doctor Porter's office, and yelling like a steam piano. Everybody in those days when they got hurt made for Doctor Porter's office as straight as a June shad in fly-time. When I got to the little office, I'll be john-squizzled if Alg. Porter didn't have that darky down on the floor.

He was sitting on him and sewing him up and lecturing to him about the evils of intemperance all at the same time. He lectured sort o' unsteadily on that theme but nobody could beat his sewing."

A few of the older citizens kept Doctor Porter as their physician to the last in spite of his lessening interest in the practice of medicine. "I never knew his equal," said one. "You got better as soon as he entered the room. He was the soul of humour and geniality and resourcefulness and all my children were devoted to him."

My own memory of Doctor Porter is of a small man with a huge head and a long beard; quiet, gentle, soft-voiced, self-effacing, who looked at you as if from another world and who walked with a step so noiseless, so absolutely echo-less, as to attract attention. This characteristic was also inherited by O. Henry who always seemed to me to be treading on down. They used to say of Doctor Porter that he had a far more scientific knowledge of medicine and drugs than any other physician in the community. He had studied under Dr. David P. Weir, in whose drug store he had clerked, and for a time he lectured on chemistry at the Edgeworth Female Seminary, of which Doctor Weir was principal from 1844 to 1845.

Doctor Porter's interests, however, became more and more absorbed in fruitless inventions and remained less and less with the problems or with the actual practice of medicine. A perpetual motion water-wheel, a new-fangled churn, a washing machine, a flying machine, a horseless carriage to be run by steam, and a cotton-picking contrivance that was to take the place of negro labour became obsessions with him. In the winter time his room would be littered with wooden wheels and things piled under the bed, but in the summer time he moved or was moved out to the barn. In one of his last interviews O. Henry said that he often found himself recalling the days when as a boy he used to lie prone and dreaming on the old barn floor while his father worked quietly and assiduously on his perpetual motion water-wheel. "He was so absentminded," O. Henry said, "that he would frequently start out without his hat and we would be sent to carry it to him." A schoolmate of O. Henry writes of those days:

Will [O. Henry] was a great lover of fun and mischief. When we were quite small his father, Dr. A. S. Porter, fell a victim to the delusion that he had solved the problem of perpetual motion, and finally abandoned a splendid practice and spent nearly all his time working on his machines. His mother, who was a most practical and sensible old woman, made him betake himself and his machines to the barn, and these Will and I, always being careful to wait for a time when the doctor was out, would proceed to demolish, destroying often in a few minutes that which it had taken much time and labor to construct. While, of course, I do not know the fact, I strongly suspect that the doctor's mother inspired these outrages.

Scientists distinguish three kinds of inheritance. In the case of "blended" inheritance, the child, like a folk-song, bears the marks of composite authorship; in "prepotent" inheritance, one parent or remoter ancestor is supposed to be most effective in stamping the offspring; and in "exclusive" inheritance, the character of the descendant is definitely that of one ancestor. Though the classification rests on no well-established basis and illustrates the use of three obedient adjectives rather than the operation of ascertained laws, it is at least convenient and may serve pro tern till a wiser survey replaces it. It is easy to see that O. Henry was the beneficiary not of an exclusive but of a blended inheritance. "This is a country," he reminds us, "of mix-ups." But the mother strain, if not prepotent in the sense of science, seems to me to have outweighed that of any other relative of whom we have record.

CHAPTER FOUR
Birthplace And Early Years

O. HENRY once wrote from New York:

I was born and raised in "No'th Ca'llina" and at eighteen went to Texas and ran wild on the prairies. Wild yet, but not so wild. Can't get to loving New Yorkers. Live all alone in a great big two rooms on quiet old Irving Place three doors from Wash. Irving's old home. Kind of lonesome. Was thinking lately (since the April moon commenced to shine) how I'd like to be down South, where I could happen over to Miss Ethel's or Miss Sallie's and sit down on the porch — not on a chair — on the edge of the porch, and lay my straw hat on the steps and lay my head back against the honeysuckle on the post — and just talk. And Miss Ethel would go in directly (they say "presently" up here) and bring out the guitar. She would complain that the E string was broken, but no one would believe her; and pretty soon all of us would be singing the "Swanee River" and "In the Evening by the Moonlight" and — oh, gol darn it, what's the use of wishing?

These words, in which O. Henry almost succeeds in expressing the inexpressible, are cited by Miss Marguerite Campion in Harper's Weekly as an example of "charm." "For charm," she says, "is three parts softness. Did not O. Henry, almost more than any other American writer, possess it, and was he not, until the day of his death, the soft-hearted advocate of humanity, the friend-of-all-the-world, after the only original model of Kim, the vagabond? Charm flowed from him through his peculiarly personal pen into all that he wrote."

PICB 07185, Austin History Center, Austin Public Library

Porter family in early 1890s —Athol, Margaret (daughter), William -

The passage is reproduced here not to illustrate charm — though every word is instinct with it — but as an example of O. Henry's ingrained affection for the place of his birth. A boy's life in a small Southern town immediately after the war, one phase of that life at least, was never better portrayed than these lines portray it, and whatever facts or events may be added in this chapter may best be interpreted against the background of the April moon, the porch, the honeysuckle, and the guitar with the broken E string. A few years later O. Henry said, of the novel that he hoped to write: "The 'hero' of the story will be a man born and 'raised' in a somnolent little Southern town. His education is about a common school one, but he learns afterward from reading and life."

It is of this little town and of the formative influences that passed from it into O. Henry that we purpose in this chapter to write. Had William Sydney Porter not been reared in "a somnolent little Southern town"

he would hardly have developed into the O. Henry that we know to-day. He was all his life a dreamer, and if the "City of Flowers" had already become the "Gate City" during his boyhood, if the wooded slopes had already been covered with the roaring cotton mills, the dreamer whose dreams were to become literature would hardly have found in the place of his birth either the time or the clime in which to develop his dream faculties. The somnolent little Southern town, moreover, which he would have sketched if he had lived to write his literary autobiography, deserves more than a mere mention. Not only was it the place that nurtured him and his forebears, that released his constructive powers, that held a place in his dreams to the end; it had also an individuality of its own and a history not without dignity and distinction.

Greensboro took its name from General Nathanael Greene, of Rhode Island. Five miles northwest of the town, on March 15, 1781, the great Rhode Islander fought his greatest battle, that of Guilford Court House. The fact that the battle was not incontest-ably a victory for either Greene or Cornwallis has, by multiplying discussion, been an advantage in keeping alive the memory of the conflict and of the issues involved. The boys and girls of Greensboro know more about the battle and about the traditions that still hover around the field than they would have known if either Greene or Cornwallis had been decisively and undebatably defeated. Mark Twain says that every American is born with the date 1492 engraved on his brain. The children of Guilford County are born with March 15, 1781, similarly impressed. Since the publication, however, of Schenck's "Memorial Volume of the Guilford Battle Ground Company," in 1893, historians have begun to recognize that in any fair perspective the battle of Guilford Court House must rank as a turning point in the Revolutionary War. Ultimate victory was assured and would have come to the patriot arms without the contribution of this battle, but it would not have come at Yorktown seven months and four days later. A participant in the battle wrote immediately afterward :*

* The letter was published in the New Jersey State Gazette of April 11, 1781.

The enemy were so beaten that we should have disputed the victory could we have saved our artillery, but the General thought that it was a necessary sacrifice. The spirits of the soldiers would have been affected if the cannon had been sent off the field, and in this woody country cannon cannot always be sent off at a critical moment.

The General, by his abilities and good conduct and by his activity and bravery in the field, has gained the confidence and respect of the army and the country to an amazing degree. You would, from the countenances of our men, believe they had been decidedly victorious. They are in the highest spirits, and appear most ardently to wish to engage the enemy again. The enemy are much embarrassed by their wounded. When we consider the nakedness of our troops and of course their want of discipline, their numbers, and the loose, irregular manner in which we came into the field, I think we have done wonders. I rejoice at our success, and were our exertions and sacrifices published to the world as some commanding officers would have published them, we should have received more applause than our modesty claims.

When the battle was fought there was of course no Greensboro. The county seat of Guilford was Martinsville, where the court house was, where the battle took place, and where the court records of November 21, 1787, remind us that "Andrew Jackson produced a license from the judges of the Superior Court of Law and Equity to practise law and was admitted as an attorney of this court." But twenty-eight years after the battle the court records read: "Court adjourned from the town of Martinsville to the town of Greensboro, the centre of the county, to meet at 10 o'clock tomorrow, Friday, 19 May, 1809... . According to adjournment the court met Friday, 19 May, at Greensboro, for the first time." This procedure marked the death of Martinsville and the birth of Greensboro. But the historic old court house at Martinsville was to render a patriotic service that its builders could never have anticipated. Some of the great oak logs of which it was built, long seasoned and carefully hewn, were sold year by year to the builders of new homes in the new county seat. Some of them were sawed up into weatherboarding while others were only shortened or placed just as they were in the new buildings. These scarred memorials of Revolutionary days may not have meant much to the generation that utilized them, but to the younger generation of another age they were as full of historic romance as the Spanish ships that young Longfellow used to gaze at in the wharves of his native Portland. One of these logs formed a part of the Porter home, which was built of logs weatherboarded over, and O. Henry used to exhibit with boyish pride a treasured Indian arrow-head which he had found sticking in it.

Guilford Battle Ground is now covered with stately memorials, more than thirty monuments or shafts testifying to the pride that North Carolina and Virginia and Maryland and Delaware and the national Government itself feel in the service rendered by the men who fell or fought on this field. In addition to the great monument to Nathanael Greene there is a monument to "No North, No South." There is another to the "Hon. Lieut. Colonel Stuart, of the 2nd Battalion of the Queen's Guards"; it was erected on the spot where he fell "by the Guilford Battle Ground Company in honour of a brave foeman." But during O. Henry's boyhood and till he left Greensboro no organized attempt had been made to redeem the field from its century of neglect. It was only an expanse of red soil and woodland, but an expanse that by its very bareness stimulated the constructive imagination.

There was no part of the ground that O. Henry did not know. Bullets, buttons, pieces of swords or shells or flint-locks could be picked up after an hour's search. The visitor to the battlefield does not now lose himself in a reverie; he reads history as recorded and interpreted for him on monument and slab, on boulder and arch. But in the 'seventies the field had to be reconstructed in imagination, the contestants visualized, the lines of battle regrouped, the sound of gun and drum made audible again, the charge and countercharge reenacted. If the field is history now, it was the stuff that dreams are made of then, and to no one was its appeal stronger or more fertile in storied suggestion than to O. Henry. "I have never known any one who read history with such avidity," said Mrs. R. M. Hall, in whose home on the Texas ranch O. Henry lived. "He not only devoured Hume, Macaulay, Green, and Guizot, but made their scenes and characters live again in vivid conversation."

But though General Greene gave Greensboro its name, the real founder of the town was an oldfield school teacher, one of those rare characters who, unknown to history, seem endowed with the power to vitalize every forward-looking agency of their times and to touch constructively every personality that comes within the orbit of their influence. The year 1824, which witnessed the marriage of Sidney Porter and Ruth Worth, O.Henry's grandparents, witnessed the death at the age of one hundred years of David Caldwell, the man who, more than any other, made Guilford County and Greensboro known beyond State lines.

It lias been already said that when the battle of Guilford Court House was fought there was no Greensboro. There was, however, the triangle in which Greensboro was to be placed, a triangle formed by David Caldwell's log schoolhouse and his two Presbyterian churches, Alamance and Buffalo. The schoolhouse, which was also his home, stood on the road between Guilford Court House and what was to be Greensboro. To it came students from every Southern State and from it went five governors, more than fifty ministers, and an uncounted number of teachers and trained citizens. David Caldwell was a Scotch-Irishman from Lancaster County, Pennsylvania, a graduate of Princeton, a teacher, preacher, carpenter, farmer, doctor, and patriot.

David Caldwell had espoused the cause of the Revolution ten years before the storm broke and from his schoolroom and pulpit had prepared his countrymen for the issue which he plainly foresaw. He had reasoned with Tryon and Cornwallis and had given valuable counsel to Greene. Though a price had been set upon his head he was with his two congregations when they faced the British at Alamance and Guilford Court House. The greatest personal loss that had come to him was in the wanton burning of his books, letters, and private papers. Armful after armful of these memorials of an heroic past were dumped by Cornwallis's troopers into the flaming oven in the doctor's backyard. Though his books were his tools, he was often heard to say that he regretted most of all the loss of his private papers which constituted a sort of first-hand history of the times. Had these been preserved Doctor Caldwell's name would probably appear in every record of the original sources of colonial and Revolutionary history, while now it appears in none.

His life was written eighteen years after his death by Dr. Eli \Y. Caruthers, and he appears as one of the characters in at least two historical novels, "Alamance; or, the Great and Final Experiment," written by Dr. Calvin II. Wiley, in 1847, and "The Master of the Red Buck and the Bay Doe," a recent work by Mr. William Laurie Hill. Doctor Wiley's book is mentioned by Mr. William Dean Howells as having "bewitched" him in his boyhood:

At nine years of age he [Mr. Howells] read the history of Greece, and the history of Rome, and he knew that Goldsmith wrote them. One night his father told the boys all about Don Quixote; and a little while after he gave my boy the book. He read it over and over again; but he did not suppose it was a novel. It was his elder brother who read novels, and a novel was like "Handy Andy," or "Harry Lorrequer," or the "Bride of Lammermoor." His brother had another novel which they preferred to either; it was in Harper's old "Library of Select Novels," and was called "Alamance; or, the Great and Final Experiment," and it was about the life of some sort of community in North Carolina. It be witched them, and though my boy could not afterward recall;t single fact or figure in it, he could bring before his mind's eye every trait of its outward aspect.

But David Caldwell lives most securely not in books but in the men that he made and in the widening compass of their influence. The Guilford County of his day was peculiarly cosmopolitan and even international in its make-up. There were the Scotch-Irish in and around Greensboro, then as now the masterful stock; there were the German exiles from the Palatinate in the eastern part of the county; and there were the English Quakers, who came via Nantucket, and a little band of Welshmen to the west and south. Out of the clash or coincidence of these varied racial stocks the history of the county was built. But all elements went to school to David Caldwell or to teachers trained by him.

The Worth and Porter families form no exception. Jonathan Worth, Quaker and future governor, came from Center to Greensboro to be taught and to teach in the Greensboro Academy, a Presbyterian school taught by a pupil and son of David Caldwell. In 1821 "the trustees of the Academy think it necessary to announce to the public that they have employed Mr. Jonathan Worth as an assistant teacher. No young gentleman, we believe, sustains a fairer character than Mr< Worth." When Jonathan Worth began the study of law it was under Archibald D. Murphey, another graduate of David Caldwell's log school. For fifty years after his death the educational currents flowing through the county can be traced back to a common source in David Caldwell.

But the channel through which he was chiefly to exert an influence upon the Porter family was Governor John Motley Morehead, the founder of Edgeworth Female Seminary. Edgeworth, as we have seen, played an important role in the lives of O. Henry's parents, but after the buildings were burned the spacious lawn was to serve in a peculiar way as playground and dreamland for the son. Mr. Morehead attended David Caldwell's school when the old dominie had passed his ninetieth year but when his ability as a teacher and his range of vision as a citizen seemed to have suffered no diminution. Governor Morehead was an admirer and close reader of the novels of Maria Edgeworth and of her earlier "Essays on Practical Education," written in collaboration with her father.

Miss Edgeworth's favourite contrast between the social careers of young women who had been sanely educated at home and those who had not, her constant balancing of the simple affections against false sentiment and sentimentality, her pitting of the "dasher" and "title-hunter" against modesty and native worth appealed strongly to a man who had five daughters to be educated but who could find no girls' school that met the Maria Edgeworth requirements. He founded, therefore, a school between his own residence, Blandwood, and the Porter home, which he called the Edgeworth Female Seminary. It was the only advanced school for women in North Carolina that was founded, owned, and financed not by a board or a church but by an individual. Teachers were brought from France and Germany, the grounds were beautifully kept, new buildings were added, and till the beginning of the war Edgeworth enjoyed a growing and generous patronage from the South and West.

The war converted Edgeworth into a hospital for both Confederate and Federal soldiers. As the buildings were almost opposite the Porter home, O. Henry's father was kept busy in the practice of his profession. The old Presbyterian Church, which O. Henry's grandmother attended, had also to do hospital duty by turns, and thus father and grandmother were not only in constant demand but were laying up a store of interesting reminiscence that was to become a part of O. Henry's heritage in later years. The war took its toll of Greensboro citizens though there was little destruction of property. The town and county and State had been overwhelmingly for union and against secession, but when the order came to North Carolina to send troops with which to fight her seceding neighbours, all parties were united in opposition. The contest then became, as O. Henry puts it, (in "Buried Treasure.) "the rebellion of the abolitionists against the secessionists." No battle was fought in Guilford County, but Greensboro loomed into sudden prominence at the close of the war and again a few years after the close.

Jefferson Davis was in Danville, Virginia, fifty miles from Greensboro, when he heard on April 9, 1865, that General Lee had surrendered. He came immediately to Greensboro where the last conference was held. The members of his cabinet were with him and he was met in Greensboro by General Joseph E. Johnston and General Beauregard. It was perhaps the saddest moment of Mr. Davis's life. Hope was gone, but his instinctive thoughtfulness for others did not desert him. Knowing that the home that should shelter him might be burned the next day by Federal troops he declined all offers of hospitality and remained in the old-fashioned cars that had brought him from Virginia. He was still for fight but consented reluctantly that General Johnston should open correspondence with General Sherman. A little later thirty thousand of Sherman's troops entered the town under General J. D. Cox and soon thirty-seven thousand Confederates under General Johnston were paroled. Greensboro looked like a tiny islet in a sea of mingled blue and gray. The boys of the town gathered up eagerly and wonderingly the old muskets and swords thrown away by the Confederates and built stories about them or fought mimic battles with them long after the hands that had once held them were dust. There was little disorder, for all knew that the end had come and the soldiers were busy fraternizing. Reconciliation, however, was harder to Confederate wives and mothers than to Confederate soldiers. Mrs. Letitia Walker, a daughter of Governor Morehead, describes the scene as follows:

President and Mrs. Davis remained over one night in Greensboro in their car, declining the invitation of my father, for fear the Federal troops should burn the house that sheltered him for one night. TVlemminger and his wife remained over several days with us for a rest, bringing with them Vice-President Alexander H. Stephens, so pale and careworn; but the price was on his head, and we tearfully bade him Godspeed. Never can I forget the farewell scene when the brave and grand Joseph E. Johnston called to say farewell, with tears running down his brown cheeks. Not a word was spoken, but silent prayers went up for his preservation.

But one fine morning, amid the sound of bugles and trumpets and bands of music, the Federals entered Greensboro, fully thirty thousand strong, to occupy the town for some time. General Cox was in command. He, Burnside, Schofield, and Kilpatrick, with their staffs, sent word to the mayor that they would occupy the largest house in town that night, and until their headquarters were established. They came to Blandwood, which already sheltered three families and several sick soldiers. My father received them courteously and received them as guests — an act which General Cox appreciated, and after placing his tent in the rear of Judge Robert P. Dick's house, he rode up every afternoon to consult with the Honourable John A. Gilmer and my father on the conditions of the country. He was a most courteous and elegant man, and in many ways displayed his sympathy with us... . Very soon a note was received announcing the arrival of Mrs Cox and the hope that Mrs. Gilmer and Mrs. Walker would do him the honour to call upon his wife... . She received us in Mrs. Dick's parlor, simple in manner, dignified, bordering on stiffness — in contrast with the genial manners of her husband... . A grand review of all the troops was to be held on the next Saturday, and a pavil on was built in the centre of town — upper seats to be occupied by the Federal ladies. By nine o'clock a four-horse ambulance with outriders was sent with a note from General Cox again "begging the honour of Mrs. Gilmer's and Mrs. Walker's company, with Mrs. Cox to witness the review." Mrs. Gilmer told her husband that she refused to add one more spectator to the pageant, for it was an enemy's bullet that had maimed her only son for life. Violent, decisive words, and very ugly ones, too, were spoken by the other lady; but a peremptory order was given, and with bitter tears, accompanied by one of our soldiers, she went to the pavilion, to be received so graciously by Mrs. Cox.

Three months later there came to Greensboro a man who was to give its Reconstruction history a unique interest and whose departure after a sojourn of thirteen years was to be promptly chronicled by an O. Henry cartoon. Albion Winegar Tourgee, author of "The Fool's Errand, by One of the Fools," was the first carpet-bagger to enter the "somnolent little Southern town" on the heels of the receding armies. But the town was anything but somnolent during his stay. "He was a bold, outspoken, independent kind of man," writes a Confederate soldier of Greensboro who knew him well and opposed his every move. "He did not toady to the better class of citizens but pursued the even tenor of his way, seemingly regardless of public opinion. He had a good mind and exercised it. He was masterful and would be dominating. He was not popular with the other carpet-baggers nor with the prominent native scalawags — which speaks much for his honesty and independence." By the votes of recently enfranchised slaves he was made a judge, an able, fearless, and personally honest one. But he was always an alien, an unwelcome intrusion, a resented imposition, "a frog in your chamber, a fly in your ointment, a mote in your eye, a triumph to your enemy, an apology to your friends, the one thing not needful, the hail in harvest, the ounce of sour in a pound of sweet." O. Henry found a silver lining in his presence but Governor Worth succeeded at last in having a more acceptable judge appointed in his place.

"The Fool's Errand" finds few readers to-day but when it appeared, in 1879, it took the country by storm. "There can be no doubt," said the Boston Traveller of this Greensboro story, "that 'A Fool's Errand' will take a high rank in fiction — a rank like that of 'Uncle Tom's Cabin.'" The Chicago Herald thought that the author must be Mrs. Stowe. "It may be well to inquire," said the Concord Monitor, of New Hampshire, "in view of the power here displayed, whether the long-looked-for native American novelist who is to rival Dickens, and equal Thackeray, and yet imitate neither, has not been found." "The book will rank," said the Portland Advertiser, of Maine, "among the famous novels which represent certain epochs of history so faithfully and accurately that, once written, they must be read by everybody who desires to be well informed."

The story takes place in Greensboro, which is called "Yerdenton"; Judge Tourgee, "the fool," is "Colonel Servosse"; and most of the other characters are Greensboro men easily recognized. It is certainly a noteworthy fact that "John Burleson," a citizen of Greensboro and the hero in "A Fool's Errand," has recently reappeared as "Stephen Hoyle," the villain, in "The Traitor," the novel which Mr. Thomas Dixon has wrought into the vast and stirring historic drama called "The Birth of a Nation." Neither author attempts an accurate appraisal of the character or career of "John Burleson" alias "Stephen Hoyle," both interpreting him only as the rock on which the Ku Klux Ivlan was wrecked.

Judge Tourgee had lain awake many a night in Greensboro expecting a visit from "The Invisible Empire," but it had not come. In place of it there came the conviction, which gives form and substance to his book, that Reconstruction so-called was folly and he a consummate and pluperfect fool to have aided and abetted it. After reading many special treatises and university dissertations on the kind of Reconstruction attempted in the South I find in "The Fool's Errand" the wisest statement of the whole question yet made. Nearly a half century has passed since the events recorded, but in rereading "A Fool's Errand" one feels anew the utter un-Americanism of the whole scheme known as Reconstruction and the Americanism of the author's conclusions. He presents the Greensboro or Southern side as follows:

We were rebels in arms: we surrendered, and by the terms of surrender were promised immunity so long as we obeyed the laws. This meant that we should govern ourselves as of old. Instead of this, they put military officers over us; they imposed disabilities on our best and bravest; they liberated our slaves, and gave them power over us. Men born at the North came among us, and were given place and power by the votes of slaves and renegades. There were incompetent officers. The revenues of the State were squandered. We were taxed to educate the blacks. Enormous debts were contracted. We did not do these acts of violence from political motives, but only because the parties had made themselves obnoxious.

Of the Southern (or shall we call it the American?) resistance to Reconstruction, the author says:

It was a magnificent sentiment that underlay it all — an unfaltering determination, an invincible defiance to all that had the seeming of compulsion or tyranny. One cannot but regard with pride and sympathy the indomitable men, who, being conquered in war, yet resisted every effort of the conqueror to change their laws, their customs, or even the personnel of their ruling class; and this, too, not only with unyielding stubbornness, but with success. One cannot but admire the arrogant boldness with which they charged the nation which had overpowered them — even in the teeth of her legislators — with perfidy, malice, and a spirit of unworthy and contemptible revenge.

Of the Ku Klux Klan more particularly he writes:

It is sometimes said, by those who do not comprehend its purpose, to have been a base, cowardly, and cruel barbarism. "What!" says the Northern man — who has stood aloof from it all, and with Pharisaic assumption, or comfortable ignorance of facts, denounced "Ku-Klux," "carpet-baggers," "scalawags," and "niggers" alike, — "was it a brave thing, worthy of a brave and chivalric people, to assail poor, weak, defenceless men and women with overwhelming forces, to terrify, maltreat, and murder? Is this brave and commendable?"

Ah, my friend! you quite mistake. If that were all that was intended and done, no, it was not brave and commendable. But it was not alone the poor colored man whom the daring band of night-riders struck, as the falcon strikes the sparrow; that indeed would have been cowardly: but it was the Nation which had given the victim citizenship and power, on whom their blow fell. It was no brave thing in itself for Old John Brown to seize the arsenal at Harper's Ferry; considered as an assault on the almost solitary watchman, it was cowardly in the extreme: but, when we consider what power stood behind that powerless squad, we are amazed at the daring of the Hero of Ossawattomie. So it was with this magnificent organization. It was not the individual negro, scalawag, or carpet-bagger, against whom the blow was directed, but the power — the Government — the idea which they represented. Not unfrequently, the individual victim was one toward whom the individual members of the Klan who executed its decree upon him had no little of kindly feeling and respect, but whose influence, energy, boldness, or official position, was such as to demand that he should be "visited." In most of its assaults, the Klan was not instigated by cruelty, nor a desire for revenge; but these were simply the most direct, perhaps the only, means to secure the end it had in view. The brain, the wealth, the chivalric spirit of the South, was, restive under what it deemed degradation and oppression. This association offered a ready and effective method of overturning the hated organization, and throwing off the rule which had been imposed upon them. From the first, therefore, it spread like wildfire. It is said that the first organization was instituted in May, or perhaps as late as the 1st of June, 1868; yet by August of that year it was firmly established in every State of the South.

O. Henry was seventeen years old when Judge Tourgee left Greensboro, never to return. Reconstruction was a thing of the past and the Ku Klux, of whom there were about eight hundred in Guilford County, had become but a memory. There was romance and mystery in it all to the younger generation, and O. Henry shows the traces of it in his later work. "I'm half Southerner by nature," says Barnard O'Keefe in "Two Renegades." "I'm willing to try the Ku Klux in place of the khaki." That was what Guilford County did in O. Henry's boyhood. In "The Rose of Dixie" Beauregard Fitzhugh Banks was engaged as advertising manager of the new Southern magazine because his grandfather had been "the Exalted High Pillow-slip of the Ku Klux Klan." When the Spanish War came, says O. Henry in "The Moment of Victory," "The old party lines drawn by Sherman's march and the Ku Ivlux and nine-cent cotton and the Jim Crow streetcar ordinances faded away."

Of course Judge Tourgee's residence was to the boys of the town a sort of demon's haunt. We never passed it without shuddering. Dr. Rufus W. Weaver, of Nashville, Tennessee, gives his impressions as follows : (See "A Story of Dreams and Deeds: The Awakening of O. Henry's Town.")

The first money which I, a country boy, ever made was acquired by the picking and the selling of cherries, and since I retailed them, going from house to house, I grew familiar with all the streets of this little town. There was one house, standing far back from the street, its yard thickly shaded by elms and oaks, which was to me a place of mystery, for here there lived that one-eyed scoundrel, that old carpet-bagger, Judge Tourgee, the Republican boss of the State, who had sought, so we are told, to introduce social equality among negroes and whites; who had wrecked the good name and the financial integrity of our fair State by his unexampled extravagance when he was in control of the State legislature, and who had brought about almost a reign of terror, so that he was justly considered by all good people to be a veritable monster.

But to O. Henry, Ku Klux and Judge Tourgee were only so many more challenges to the innate romanticism of his nature. His most intimate boyhood friend, Mr. Thomas H. Tate, writes of those days:

Of course Will [O. Henry] and I played Ku Klux. My mother was a past master at making masks out of newspapers which she folded and cut out with her scissors. I remember how the negroes used to pretend to be terribly frightened and how pleased we were with our efforts. The old Presbyterian High School [a child of David Caldwell] used to be the meeting place of the genuine article and was always held in awe by us boys for a long time on that account. You will remember that it stood vacant and gloomy in the grove just opposite our home place for many years. As to Judge Tourgee, we looked upon him as some sort of a pirate, mysterious and blackened by a thousand crimes, and we glanced at him covertly when he happened around. He was a sort of an ogre, but even then we admired him for his courage and wondered at it, coming as he did from the North. Very dark stories were whispered of his doings out in far-off Warnersville, the negro settlement out by the Methodist graveyard. He held meetings out there that we were almost prepared to say were a species of voodooism.

You will remember that he had a beautiful country place out on the Guilford College Road. There was a greenhouse, flowers, shrubbery, and an immense rustic arbor there and it was used for dances and had an upper and lower floor. Miss Sallie Coleman was visiting in Greensboro and either expressed a desire for magnolias or Will conceived that she would like to have some, so we started about midnight on the six miles' "hike" to West Green to spoil and loot. Strange to say, the memory of the moonlit night is with me now even after all these years. It was a perfect night. The moon was full and showering down her mellow radiance in great floods. I can see the long white line of road stretching out, hear the whippoorwills and smell the good night air laden with its species and fragrance and I can see the long row of magnolia trees out in the wheat field and orchard with their great white flowers gleaming out from the dark foliage. I can also feel the creepy sensation that I felt when we mounted the fence and started across the open field for the trees and the relief that came when we crossed that fence with the loot. We carried them back and laid them on Miss Sallie's doorstep.

The incident is peculiarly characteristic There were plenty of magnolias nearer O. Henry's home than West Green and they could have been had in broad daylight for the asking. What his nature craved was an opportunity to play the knight, to steep himself in romance, to dare the forbidden, to imagine himself for six glorious miles one of the venturers of whom he was afterward to write:("The Venturers.")

The Venturer is one who keeps his eye on the hedgerows and wayside groves and meadows while he travels the road to Fortune. That is the difference between him and the Adventurer. Eating the forbidden fruit was the best record ever made by a Venturer. Trying to prove that it happened is the highest work of the Adventuresome. To be either is disturbing to the cosmogony of creation.

The man who was in later years to be hailed as "the discoverer of the romance in the streets of New York," who, as the Atlantic Monthly put it, "seems to possess the happy gift of picking up gold pieces from the asphalt pavement," was a pursuivant of romance all his life.

Sometimes the sources from which he drew his romantic inspiration could hardly in themselves be called romantic. A playmate writes:

When Will [O. Henry] was about eight years old, he and I were riding around my mother's garden on stick horses, when we found a conical mound where potatoes or turnips had been "holed up .

for winter use. His fertile imagination at once converted this into a great castle inhabited by a cruel giant who kept imprisoned within its grim walls a beautiful maiden whom he and I, after doing valiant battle as her loyal knights, were to triumphantly rescue At this remote period I cannot of course recall all the details of this wonderful story as he told it, but I feel sure that if it could be faithfully reproduced, it would make thrillingly interesting reading of its kind.

But in these early days playing Indian was O. Henry's favourite pastime. Indian arrow-heads were plentiful around Greensboro and O. Henry, it will be remembered, treasured above all others one that he had found sticking in the Revolutionary log that formed a part of his home. The Indian game took many forms but all gave scope and career to his imagination as well as zest and vividness to his early reading. Mr. Thomas H. Tate describes two forms of the Indian play as follows:

My father kept a large flock of turkeys and the tail feathers of these furnished us material for our "war bonnets" when we played Indian, much to the detriment of the turkeys' appearance and to my father's displeasure. We played this game more than any other. Our bows were of our own make as were the arrows, and were quite effective as the Poland Chinas, Berkshires, and Chester Whites could testify if they had not long since gone the way of all good hogs — which is not Jerusalem. These hogs acted in turns the part of grizzlies, deer, horses, etc., and often in the excitement of the chase an arrow would be shot just a little harder than we intended and we would thereupon chase the poor unfortunate to exhaustion to get the arrow out of its mark before my father returned We were always successful is my recollection and I am most sure that it does not fail me for any omission would certainly have been visited by such a forcible reminder that it would have remained fresh and green in my memory to this day and beyond. Another feature of the Indian play, or rather another setting to our action, was on a muddy bank down at the creek. We would take our toy gun, owned in common, go down to the soft, slippery bank — strip and paint up properly and wage warfare on each other. Dying a thousand deaths was a small item to us; we did it thoroughly that many times each day.

During these years O. Henry cared little for indoor games and sports. In chess he could hold his own with the veterans of the town before he had reached his teens and in roller-skating he won the championship prize. He was also a good boxer and a trained fencer. But his favourite recreation was to roam around the fields and woods with a congenial companion. A book was usually taken along and was read in some shady spot or, in winter time, beneath the shelter of pines and broomsedge on a favourite hillside overlooking old Caldwell's Pond. Even when he went fishing or swimming or hunting for chinquapins or hickory nuts, he found his chief exhilaration in the breadth and freedom of out of doors rather than in the nominal object of the jaunt. An outing with a set purpose was never to his liking. His pleasure was in merely being in the woods or on the bank of a stream, in surrendering himself to the mood rather than to the purpose of the occasion, and in interpreting in waggish ways everything said or done or seen. He was always shy, his exuberant humour and rare gift of story telling seeming to take flight within the walls of a house. He preferred the front gate or, as a halfway station, the porch. Even in a small group out of doors, if there was a stranger or one uncongenial companion, O. Henry would not be heard from. But the next day he would tell you what happened and with such a wealth of original comment and keenness of insight and alchemy of exaggeration, all framed in a droll or dramatic story, that you would think you had missed the time of your life in not being present.

"His education is about a common school one," said O. Henry of himself in the words already cited, "but he learns afterward from reading and life." His teacher and his only teacher was his aunt, Miss Evelina Maria Porter, known to every one in Greensboro as Miss Lina. Hers was undoubtedly the strongest personal influence brought to bear on O. Henry during his twenty years in North Carolina. The death of his mother when he was only three years old and the increasing absorption of his father in futile inventions resulted in Miss Lina's taking the place of both parents, and this she did not only with whole-souled devotion but with rare and efficient intelligence. She was a handsome woman with none of her father's happy-go-lucky disposition but with much of her mother's directive ability and with a profound sense of responsibility for the welfare of every boy and girl that entered her school. She had been educated at Edgeworth Female Seminary and in the late 'sixties opened a small school in one of the rooms of her mother's home. Her mother assisted her and in a few years, the school having outgrown its accommodations, a small building was erected on the Porter premises. Here Miss Lina taught until the growth of the public graded school system, which Greensboro was the first town in the State to adopt, began to encroach upon her domain and to render her work less remunerative and less needful.

When she closed her school she carried with her the love and the increasing admiration of all whom she had taught. No teacher of a private preparatory school in Greensboro ever taught as many pupils as Miss Lina or was followed by a heartier plaudit of "Well done." She did not, of course, spare the rod. It was not the fashion in those days to spare it. At a Friday afternoon speech-making one of her pupils started gayly off with

One hungry day a summer ape.

The emendation must have appealed to the youthful O. Henry. Of that, however, we are not informed, but we are informed that the perpetrator had hardly reached "ape" before he had a lesson impressed upon him as to the enormity of adjectival transposition that he will carry with him into the next world.

But there was no cruelty in Miss Lina's disposition. She tempered justice if not with mercy at least with rigid impartiality and with hearty laughter. I have never known a pupil of her school, whether doctor, teacher, preacher, merchant, lawyer, or judge, who did not say that every application of the rod, so far as he was concerned, was amply and urgently deserved. To have been soundly whipped by Miss Lina is still regarded in Greensboro as a sort of spiritual bond of union, linking together the older citizens of the town in a community of cutaneous experience for which they would not exchange a college diploma. The little schoolroom was removed many years ago but it still lives in the grateful memory of all who attended it and has attained a new immortality in the fame of its most illustrious pupil.

O. Henry attended no other school, and he attended this only to the age of fifteen. He was always a favourite with Miss Lina and with the other pupils. The gentleness of his disposition and his genius for original kinds of play won his schoolmates while his aunt held up his interest in his books, his good deportment, and his skill in drawing as worthy of all emulation. Miss Lina taught drawing, but O. Henry's sketches were almost from the start so far superior to hers that they were generally selected as the models. Some of his best freehand sketches Miss Lina never saw, though she deserves the credit of having inspired them. She had a way of sending the arithmetic class to the blackboard while she paced the floor with the bundle of switches. O. Henry would work his "sum" with his right hand and sketch Miss Lina with his left at the same time. The likeness was perfect, not a feature or switch being omitted. The whole thing had to be done as she walked from one side of the little room to the other with her back to the blackboard. To insure safety through instantaneous erasure the fingers of the left hand held not only the rapidly moving crayon but also the erasing rag. O. Henry's ear, long practised told him accurately how near Miss Lina was to the end of her promenade, and just before her last step was taken and the return trip begun the rag would descend and she would behold only a sum so neatly worked that it would become the subject of another address on good work and model workers.

But we are more concerned here with Miss Lina's method of teaching literature. She had a method, and O. Henry's lifelong love of good books was in part the fruitage of her method. She did not teach the history of literature, but she laboured in season and out of season to have her pupils assimilate the spirit of literature. Her reading in the best English literature was, if not wide, at least intimate and appreciative. She loved books as she loved flowers, because her nature demanded them. Fiction and poetry were her means of widening and enriching her own inner life, not of learning facts about the world without. Scott and Dickens were her favourite novelists and Father Ryan her favourite poet. She did not measure literature by life but life by literature. So did O. Henry at that time, but he was later to transpose his standards, putting life first. I have often thought that Miss Lina must have been in O. Henry's mind when he wrote those suggestive words about Azalea Adair in "A Municipal Report":

She was a product of the old South, gently nurtured in the sheltered life. Her learning was not broad, but was deep and of splendid originality in its somewhat narrow scope. She had been educated at home, and her knowledge of the world was derived from inference and by inspiration. Of such is the precious, small group of essayists made. While she talked to me I kept brushing my fingers, trying, unconsciously, to rid them guiltily of the absent dust from the half-calf backs of Lamb, Chaucer, Hazlitt, Marcus Aurelius, Montaigne, and Hood. She was exquisite; she was a valuable discovery. Nearly everybody nowadays knows too much — oh, so much too much — of real life.

Miss Lina used regularly to gather her boys about her at recess and read to them from some standard author. When she saw that she had caught their interest she would announce a Friday night meeting in the schoolroom at which they would pop corn and roast chestnuts and she would continue the readings.

"I did more reading," says O. Henry, "between my thirteenth and nineteenth years than I have done in all the years since, and my taste at that time was much better than it is now, for I used to read nothing but the classics. Burton's 'Anatomy of Melancholy' and Lane's translation of 'The Arabian Nights' were my favourites." During his busy years in New York he often remarked to Mrs. Porter: "I never have time to read now. I did all my reading before I was twenty." This did not, of course, refer to newspapers, which he devoured three or four times a day.

But Miss Lina believed that the best way to learn or to appreciate the art of narration was to try your hand at it yourself. You might never become a great writer, but you would at least have a first-hand ac-=quaintance with the discipline that well-knit narrative involves. In the intervals, therefore, between chestnut roastings and classic readings an original story would be started, every one present having to make an impromptu contribution when called on. Each contribution, being expected to grow naturally out of the incidents that preceded it, demanded, of course, the closest attention to all that had hitherto been said. The most difficult role in this narrative program fell, of course, to the pupil who tried to halt the windings of the story by an interesting and adequate conclusion. To do this required not only a memory that retained vividly the incidents and characters already projected into the story, but a constructive imagination that could interpret and fuse them. Need I say that the creator of "The Four Million" found his keenest delight in this exercise or that his contributions were those most eagerly awaited by teacher and pupil?

In the long summer evenings after school Miss Lina's boys would gather on the old Edgeworth grounds for a kind of recreation which the contracted Porter premises did not permit. In an English magazine O. Henry had read two serial stories called "Jack Hark-away" and "Dick Lightheart." These gave him the suggestion for two clubs or societies into which the more congenial of Miss Lina's pupils were forthwith divided. One was the Brickbats, the other the Union Jacks. The Union Jacks, to which O. Henry belonged, had selected for their armory one of the few minor buildings on the Edgeworth campus which had been spared by the fire. Here they had stored a rich collection of wooden battleaxes, shields, spears, helmets, cavalry sabres, and all other things Jane Porterish, and here they held nightly conclave. The planning of raids which never took place, the discussion of the relative values of medieval weapons of which they had read, the facile citation of well-known non-existent authorities on attack and counter-attack, the bestowal of knightly titles on themselves and of less knightly on their imagined foes, and the generous use of "Hist!" "Zounds!" "Hark ye!" and "By my halidome!" make the Union Jacks and the Edgeworth grounds not the least of the formative influences that wrought upon O. Henry during his more malleable years.

"On Friday nights,"* says one of the Union Jacks, "it was their custom to sally forth armed and equipped from their castle in search of adventure, like knights of old, carefully avoiding the dark nooks where there were gloomy shadows. Porter was the leading spirit in the daring enterprises and many were the hair-raising adventures these ten-year-old heroes encountered. The shields and battleaxes were often thrown hastily aside when safety lay in flight. Ghosts were not uncommon in those days, or rather nights, and only good, sturdy legs could cope with the supernatural."

Two other incidents of O. Henry's brief school days will illustrate the artistic use that he so often makes in his stories of scraps of verse stored in the memory as well as the longing that he had to play the venturer beyond the confines of his native town and State. By way of introduction the reader will recall the dramatic manner in which O. Henry uses in "The Caballero's Way" these lines:

Don't you monkey with my Lulu girl
Or I'll tell you what I'll do

Only these two lines are given in the story, once by way of prophecy and at the end by way of fulfilment; but the character of the singer and the way in which the lines are sung enable the reader who is unfamiliar with the remaining two lines to guess their import. Mr. J. D. Smith, of Mount Airy, North Carolina, writes:

The first recollection that I can recall of William Porter was when I was going to school to Miss Lina Porter. I went to jump out of the window and in doing so dislocated my ankle. Not being able to walk Will and his brother Shirley carried me into the house, and sent for old Doctor Porter. He had about quit practising, but the ankle had to be set at once, so Shirley held me on the floor while Will seized my leg and the old doctor started to twist my ankle off, it seemed to me. I began to cry out, and then Will began to sing, and you know he could not sing, but this was his song:

If you don't stop fooling with my Lula
  I tell you what I'll do;
  I'll feel around your heart with a razor
  And I'll cut your liver out too.

The next adventure that I can recall was: There was a boy who lived opposite the school by the name of Robertson, whose father was a dentist. He ran away and went on a whaling vessel, but finally came back, and we would meet around and hear him tell about the sea, and how much money he made catching whales. Will and Tom Tate and I would meet and caucus whether we would go and catch whales or fight the Indians. Tom was for fighting the Indians, and Will and I decided that we would make our fortunes catching whales, so we started for the sea. Our money gave out at Raleigh and, after spending all we had for something to eat, we decided to go home if we could get there. We went to the depot and, as luck would have it, we saw a freight conductor that we knew in Greensboro, and asked him if he would let us "brake" for our fare home. He told us to crawl up on the box cars, and that two blows meant put on brakes, and one to take them off, and for us to mind or he would put us off. That is the first and last time I have ever been on top of a box car running. After we had gotten up good speed I saw the engine disappear around a curve, and it seemed to me that the box car that Will and I were on was going direct to the woods. Then we both gave up as lost, and lay right down on the running board, and Will began to repeat what Miss Lina Porter had taught him, "Now I lay me down to sleep," *etc.* I had my eyes closed, expecting the car to hit the woods every minute. Finally, when nothing happened, it seemed that we both raised up about the same time, and just looked at each other. Then Will began his song, If you don't stop fooling with my Lula, but in rather a sheepish manner.

But when O. Henry's boyhood friends recall him it is not usually as a pupil in Miss Lina's school; nor is it as the writer in the great city. It is as the clerk in his uncle Clark Porter's drug store on Elm Street, opposite the old Benbow Hotel. Here he was known and loved by old and young, black and white, rich and poor. He was the wag of the town, but so quiet, so unobtrusive, so apparently preoccupied that it was his pencil rather than his tongue that spread his local fame. His youthful devotion to drawing was stimulated in large part by the pictures painted by his mother. Many of these hung in the Porter home. Some were portraits and some landscapes. They were part of the atmosphere in which O. Henry was reared. One of his own earliest sketches was made when Edgeworth was burned. O. Henry was then only ten years old but the picture that he drew of a playmate rescuing an empty churn from the basement of the burning building, with the milk spilled all over him, is remembered for its ludicrous conception and for its striking fidelity to the boy and to the surroundings.

His five years in his uncle's drug store meant much to him as a cartoonist. His feeling for the ludicrous, for the odd, for the distinctive, in speech, tone, appearance, conduct, or character responded instantly to the appeal made by the drug store constituency. Not that he was not witty; he was. But his best things were said with the pencil. There was not a man or woman in the town whom he could not reproduce recognizably with a few strokes of a lead pencil. Thus it was a common occurrence, when Clark Porter returned to the store from lunch, for a conversation like this to take place: O. Henry would say: "Uncle Clark, a man called to see you a little while ago to pay a bill.'" It should be premised that it was not good form in those days to ask a man to stand and deliver either his name or the amount due. "Who was it?" his uncle would ask. "I never saw him before, but he looks like this," and the pencil would zigzag up and down a piece of wrapping paper. " Oh, that's Bill Jenkins out here at Reedy Fork. He owes me $7.25."

Several years before he left Greensboro the fame of his cartoons had spread to other towns, and he was urged by Colonel Robert Bingham, a relative by marriage and Superintendent of the famous Bingham School, then at Mebane, North Carolina, to come at once to Bingham's where an education free of charge would be given him. "My only direct connection with William Sydney as a boy," writes Colonel Bingham, "was to offer him his tuition and board in order to get the use of his talent as a cartoonist for the amusement of our boys. He was an artist with chalk on a blackboard. But he could not accept my offer for lack of means to provide for his uniform and books." This must have been a bitter disappointment though O. Henry was never heard to allude to it.

His pencil sketches sometimes gave offence, especially when some admirer would hang them in the store window, but rarely. He was absolutely without malice. There was about him also a gentleness of manner, a delicacy of feeling, a refinement in speech and demeanour that was as much a part of him as his humour. I have received no reminiscences of him that do not make mention of his purity of speech and thought. Yet he was never sissy. He could be genuinely funny so easily himself without striking beneath the belt that a resort to underhand tactics seemed crude and awkward to him. It betrayed poverty of resources. In the presence of such methods he seemed to me uneasy and bored rather than indignant or shocked. No one at least who knew him in the old days will wonder at the surprise with which in later years he resented the constant comparison of his work with that of De Maupassant, though toward the last he kept a copy of De Maupassant always at hand. No two writers ever lived more diametrically opposed than O. Henry and De Maupassant except in technique. "I have been called," he said, "the American De Maupassant. Well, I never wrote a filthy word in my life, and I don't like to be compared to a filthy writer." Like Edgar Allan Poe, with whom he had little else in common, O. Henry was honoured during his whole life with the understanding friendship of a few noble-spirited women who in the early days, as in the later, helped, I think, to keep his compass true.

After Miss Lina's school the drug store was to O. Henry a sort of advanced course in human nature and in the cartoonist's art. George Eliot tells in "Romola" of the part played in medieval Florence by the barber shop. A somewhat analogous part was played in Greensboro forty years ago by Clark Porter's drug store. It was the rendezvous of all classes, though the rear room was reserved for the more elect. The two rooms constituted in fact the social, political, and anecdotal clearing house of the town. The patronage of the grocery stores and drygoods stores was controlled in part by denominational lines, but everybody patronized the drug store. It was also a sort of physical confessional. The man who would expend only a few words in purchasing a ham or a hat would talk half an hour of his aches and ills or those of his family before buying twenty-five cents' worth of pills or a tencent bottle of liniment. When the ham or the hat was paid for and taken away there was usually an end of it. Not so with the pills or the liniment. The patient usually came back to continue his personal or family history and to add a sketch of the character and conduct of the pills or liniment. All this was grist to O. Henry's mill.

No one, I think, without a training similar to O. Henry's, would be likely to write such a story as "Makes the Whole World Kin." It is not so much the knowledge of drugs displayed as the conversational atmosphere of the drug store in a small Southern town that gives the local flavour. A burglar, you remember, has entered a house at night. "Hold up both your hands," he said. "Can't raise the other one," was the reply. "What's the matter with it?" "Rheumatism in the shoulder." "Inflammatory?" asked the burglar. "Was. The inflammation has gone down." " 'Scuse me," said the burglar, "but it just socked me one, too." "How long have you had it?" inquired the citizen. "Four years." "Ever try rattlesnake oil?" asked the citizen. "Gallons. If all the snakes I've used the oil of was strung out in a row they'd reach eight times as far as Saturn, and the rattles could be heard at Valparaiso, Indiana, and back." In the end the burglar helps the citizen to dress and they go out together, the burglar standing treat.

The drawings that O. Henry used to make of the characters that frequented the drug store were not caricatures. There was usually, it is true, an overemphasis put upon some one trait, but this trait was the central trait, the overemphasis serving only to interpret and reveal the character as a whole. Examining these sketches anew, when the characters themselves are thirty odd years older than they were then, one is struck with the resemblance still existing. In fact, O. Henry's sketches reproduce the characters as they are to-day more faithfully than do the photographs taken at the same time. The photographs have been outgrown, but not the sketches; for the sketches caught the central and permanent, while the photographs made no distinction. In O. Henry's story called "A Madison Square Arabian Night," an artist, picked at random from the "freebed line," is made to say:

Whenever I finished a picture people would come to see it, and whisper and look queerly at one another. I soon found out what the trouble was. I had a knack of bringing out in the face of a portrait the hidden character of the original. I don't know how I did it — I painted what I saw.

But O. Henry's distinctive skill, the skill of the story teller that was to be, is seen to better advantage in his pictures of groups than in his pictures of individuals. Into the group pictures, which he soon came to prefer to any others, he put more of himself and more of the life of the community. They gave room for a sort of collective interpretation which seems to me very closely related to the plots of his short stories. There is the same selection of a central theme, the same saturation with a controlling idea, the same careful choice of contributory details, the same rejection of non-essentials, and the same ability to fuse both theme and details into a single totality of effect. "He could pack more of the social history of this city into a small picture," said a citizen of Austin, Texas, "than I thought possible. Those of us who were on the inside could read the story as if printed. Let me show you," and he entered into an affectionate rhapsody over a little pen and ink sketch which he still carried in his inside coat pocket.

An illustration is found in a sketch of the interior of Clark Porter's drug store. The date is 1879. Every character is drawn to the life, but what gives unity to the whole is the grouping and the implied comment, rather than criticism, that the grouping suggests.

The picture might well be called, to borrow one of O. Henry's story names, "The Hypothesis of Failure." Indeed Clark Porter's expression, as he gazes over the counter, signifies as much. But the failure is due to good-natured foibles rather than to faults. The central figure is the speaker. He was a sign painter in Greensboro, a dark, Italianate-looking man, whose shop was immediately behind the drug store. He was one of the first to recognize O. Henry's genius and treasured with mingled affection and admiration every drawing of the master's that he could find. He did not rightfully belong, however, to the inner circle of the drug store habitues. If he had, he would never have said "I'll pay you for it." He is here shown on his way to the rear room. His ostensible quest is ice, but the protrusions from the pitcher indicate that another ingredient of "The Lost Blend" is a more urgent necessity. His plaintive query about cigars finds its answer in the abundant remains, mute emblems of hospitality abused, that already bestrew the floor. On the right is the Superintendent of the Presbyterian Sunday School. He was also a deacon and kept a curiosity shop of a store. His specialties were rabbit skins and Mason and Hamlin organs. But he made his most lasting impression on O. Henry as a dispenser of kerosene oil.

It happened in this way: the Pastor of the Presbyterian Church had always carried his empty oil can, supposed to hold a gallon, to be replenished at the Superintendent's font. But one day the Superintendent's emporium was closed and the pastoral can journeyed on to the hardware store of another deacon. "Why," said the latter, after careful measurement, "this can doesn't hold but three quarts." "That's strange," said the minister pensively; "Brother M. has been squeezing four quarts into it for twenty years." The reply went the rounds of the town at once and O. Henry, who no more doubted Brother M's good intentions than he did his uncle's or the sign painter's, put him promptly into the picture as entitled to all the rights and privileges of the quartette. The venerable figure on the left is Dr. James K. Hall, the Nestor of the drug store coterie and the leading physician of Greensboro. He was a sort of second father to O. Henry, whom he loved as a son, though O. Henry drew about as many cartoons of him as he filled prescriptions made by him. Three years later Doctor Hall was to take O. Henry with him to Texas where the second chapter in his life was to begin. Doctor Hall was the tallest man in Greensboro and the stoop, the pose of the head, the very bend of the knee in the picture are perfect. He is sketched at the moment when, having contributed his full quota of cigar stumps, he is writing a prescription for Clark or O. Henry to fill.

O. Henry's reading at this time as well as his drawing had begun to widen and deepen. At first he had been gripped by the dime novel. He was four years old when George Munro began to issue his "Ten Cent Novels." These became to O. Henry what Skelt's melodramas were to Robert Louis Stevenson. "In this roll-call of stirring names," says Stevenson,* "you read the evidences of a happy childhood." The roll-call included "The Red Rover," "The Wood Demon," "The Miller and His Men," "Three-fingered Jack," and "The Terror of Jamaica." "We had the biggest collection of dime novels," says Mr. Thomas H. Tate, O. Henry's schoolmate and co-reader, "I have ever seen outside of a cigar stand, and I don't think we could have been over seven or eight years old. Will soon imbibed the style and could tell as good a thriller as the author of 'RedEyed Rube.' I can see the circle of wide-eyed little fellows lying around in the shade on the grass as he opened up with: 'If you had been a close observer you might have descried a solitary horseman slowly wending his way' or 'The sun was sinking behind the western hills,' and so on."

Stevenson's early favourites were plays while O. Henry's were stories, but by acting on the banks of Caldwell's Pond the more romantic episodes in the Munro tales O. Henry turned the dime novel into a sort of homemade melodrama. If we may make the distinction between the acquisitive reader and the assimilative reader we should say that O. Henry was first and last assimilative. For facts as facts in books he cared but little, but for the way they were put together, for the way they were fused and used, for the after-tones and afterglow that the writer's personality imparted, he cared everything. We have often wondered what effect a college education would have had upon him. The effect, we think, that it would have had upon Bret Harte or Joel Chandler Harris or Mark Twain, that of making each more acquisitive and less assimilative.

After the dime novel came the supernatural story, when "the clutch of a clammy hand" replaced the solitary horseman and the dutiful sun. Before leaving Greensboro, however, O. Henry had passed to the stage represented in his own statement: "I used to read nothing but the classics." But to "The Arabian Nights," a lifelong inspiration, and Burton's "Anatomy of Melancholy," must be added the novels of Scott, Dickens, Thackeray, Charles Reade, Bulwer Lytton, Wilkie Collins, Auerbach, Victor Hugo, and Alexander Dumas. His love of Scott came via an interest which he soon outgrew in "Thaddeus of Warsaw" and "The Scottish Chiefs." He considered "Bleak House" the best of Dickens's works and "Vanity Fair" of Thackeray's. Dickens's unfinished story, "The Mystery of Edwin Drood," occupied much of his thought at this time and he attempted more than once to complete the plot but gave it up. Of Charles Reade's masterpiece he said later: "If you want philosophy well put up in fiction, read 'The Cloister and the Hearth.' I never saw such a novel. There is material for dozens of short stories in that one book alone."

Three other novels made a deep impression upon him at this time: Spielhagen's "Hammer and Anvil," Warren's "Ten Thousand a Year," and John Esten Cooke's "Surry of Eagle's Nest." He thought Warren's character of "Oily Gammon" the best portrait of a villain ever drawn and always called one of Greensboro's lawyers by that name. Stonewall Jackson and Jeb Stuart, among the characters introduced by Cooke, were the Confederate heroes of whom he talked with most enthusiasm.

In fact, his reading and his close confinement in the drug store had begun to threaten his health. His mother and grandmother had both died of consumption and O. Henry, never robust, was under the obsession that he had already entered upon his fateful inheritance. He took no regular exercise. An occasional fishing or seining jaunt out to Caldwell's or OrreH's or Donnell's Pond, a serenade two or three times a week, and a few camping-out trips to Pilot Mountain and beyond made almost the only breaks in the monotony of the drug store regime. But however many or few fish might be caught on these jaunts O. Henry was always more of a spectator and commentator than participant; on the serenades he played what he called "a silent tenor" violin or twanged indifferently a guitar, the E string of which was usually broken;

and on the camping-out expeditions his zest and elation were due more to freedom from pills and prescriptions than to the love of mountain scenery.

But he did not slight his work in the drug store and never intimated that it was distasteful. It was only in later years that he said: "The grind in the drug store was agony to me." It doubtless was, not so much in itself as in the utter absence of outlook. No profession attracted him, and there was no one in Greensboro doing anything that O. Henry would have liked to do permanently. The quest of ' What's around the corner," a theme that he has wrought into many stories and that grew upon him to the last, was his nearest approach to a vocation and he had about exhausted the possibilities of his birthplace. Sixteen years later, at the darkest moment of his life, his skill as a pharmacist was to help him as no other profession could have helped him. But even if the future had been known, there was nothing more to be learned about drugs in his uncle's drug store, nor would added knowledge have proved an added help.

The release came unexpectedly. Three sons of Dr. James K. Hall, Lee, Dick, and Frank, had gone to Texas to make their fortunes. They were tall, lithe, blond, iron-sinewed men, and all had done well. Lee, the oldest, had become a noted Texas Ranger. As "Red Hall" his name was a terror to evil-doers from the Red River to the Rio Grande. Though Red Hall himself was a modest and silent man, his brief letters to his parents, his intermittent visits to Greensboro, and the more detailed accounts of his prowess that an occasional Texas newspaper brought, kept us aglow with excitement. Whenever it was known that Red Hall and his wife were visiting in Greensboro there was sure to be a gratifying attendance of boys at the morning service of the Presbyterian Church. To see him walk in and out, to wonder what he was thinking about, to speculate on the number of sixshooters that he had with him, were opportunities not lightly disregarded. The drug store was, of course, headquarters for the latest from Texas and O. Henry used to hold us breathless as he retailed the daring arrests and hair-breadth 'scapes of this quiet Greensboro man whom the citizens of the biggest State in the Union had already learned to lean upon in time of peril.

In March, 1882, Doctor and Mrs. Hall were planning to visit their sons in Texas. O. Henry at this time had a hacking cough and Doctor Hall used to wince as if struck whenever he heard it. "Will," he said, a few days before starting on the long trip, "I want you to go with us. You need the change, and ranch life will build you up." Never in his life had O. Henry received an invitation that so harmonized with every impulse of his nature. It meant health and romance. It was the challenge of all that he had read and dreamed. It was the call of "What's around the corner" with Red Hall as guide and co-seeker.

CHAPTER FIVE
Ranch And City Life In Texas

If O. HENRY could have chosen the ranch and the ranch manager that he was to visit in Texas he could not have done better than to choose the ranch in La Salle County that had Lee Hall at its head. He was to see much more of Dick Hall than of Lee, but it was Lee's personality and Lee's achievement that opened the doors of romance to him in Texas and contributed atmosphere and flavour to the nineteen stories that make up his "Heart of the West."

Red Hall, as we prefer to call him, was now at the height of his fame. The monument erected to him in the National Cemetery, in San Antonio, contains only the brief inscription:

Jesse Lee Hall
   1849-1911
   Captain Co. M., 1st U. S. Vol. Inf.
   War with Spain

But had there been no war with Spain Red Hall's claim on the gratitude of the citizens of the Lone Star State would have been almost equally well founded. "He was the bravest man I ever knew," said the old Comanche chief against whose warriors Red Hall had led the Texans in the last battle with the tribe in northeast Texas. "He did more to rid Texas of desperadoes/' wrote Mr. John E. Elgin, "to establish law and order, than any officer that Texas ever had. He has made more bad men lay down their guns and delivered more desperadoes and outlaws into the custody of the courts, and used his own gun less, than any other officer in Texas." "I have known him intimately for twenty-five years," wrote Major-General Jesse M. Leef, United States Army Retired, "in peace and in war. No braver spirit, no more devoted friend ever passed from earth. He was 'the bravest of the brave,' and his heart was as tender as that of the most lovable woman. His heroic deeds would fill a volume."

Ten years before O. Henry went to Texas Red Hall's name had become one to conjure with. When Edward King, at the instance of Scribner's Month!?/, visited the fifteen ex-slave States in 1873-1874, he met Red Hall and paid prompt tribute to his daring and to his unique success in awing and arresting men without using his pistol. The desperado problem was especially acute along the Red River because the thieves could cross into Indian Territory where arrest was almost impossible. Mr. King describes the situation as follows: ("The Great South" (1874))

So frequent had this method of escape become at the time of the founding of Denison, that the law-abiding citizens were enraged; and the famous deputy-sheriff, "Red Hall," a young man of great courage and unflinching "nerve," determined to attempt the capture of some of the desperadoes. Arming himself with a Winchester rifle, and with his belt garnished with navy revolvers, he kept watch on certain professional criminals. One day, soon after a horse-thief had been heard from in a brilliant dash of grand larceny, he repaired to the banks of the Red River, confident that the thief would attempt to flee.

In due time, the fugitive and two of his friends appeared at the river, all armed to the teeth, and while awaiting the ferryboat, were visited by Ilall, who drew a bead upon them, and ordered them to throw down their arms. They refused, and a deadly encounter was imminent; but he finally awed them into submission, threatening to have the thief's comrades arrested for carrying concealed weapons. They delivered up their revolvers and even their rifles, and lied, and the horse-thief, rather than risk a passage-at-arms with the redoubtable Hall, returned with him to Denison, after giving the valiant young constable some ugly wounds on the head with his fist. The passage of the river having thus been successfully disputed by the law, the rogues became somewhat more wary.

"Red Hall" seemed to bear a charmed life. He moved about tranquilly every day in a community where there were doubtless an hundred men who would have delighted to shed his blood; was often called to interfere in broils at all hours of the night; yet his life went on. He had been ambushed and shot at and threatened times innumerable, yet had always exhibited a scorn for his enemies, which finally ended in forcing them to admire him.

Red Hall was made Lieutenant of the Texas Rangers in April, 1877, and received his commission as Captain in the same year. Of his life in 1882 and of O. Henry's association with him, Mrs. Lee Hall has k'ndly written a short sketch from which I am permitted to quote:

At the time Willie Porter was with us in Texas, Captain Hall had charge of the ranch in La Salle County belonging to the Dull Brothers, of Harrisburg, Pennsylvania. He had a contract with these gentlemen to buy the land, fence and stock it, and then operate the ranch as Superintendent. And it is this ranch and his life thereon that O. Henry has immortalized in many of his Texas stories. Captain Hall had to rid La Salle County of a notorious band of fence-cutting cattle thieves, and his famous result is chronicled in the Bexar County Courts of 1882. He finally succeeded in electing "Charlie" McKinney, a former member of his company of Rangers, as sheriff of La Salle County, and this officer proved himself most efficient and capable, securing peace to that community until his untimely death.

When we first went to the ranch, we occupied a small frame house of one room, about 12 x 8 feet in size. This room was sitting-room, bedroom, dining-room, etc., in fact the whole house. They then built a log house, about 12 x 35 feet, for Captain Hall and myself, and Mr. and Mrs. Dick Hall took possession of the log house, and it was here that Willie Porter first stayed with them.

We lived a most unsettled exciting existence. Captain Hail was in constant danger. His life was threatened in many ways, and the mail was heavy with warnings, generally in the shape of crude sketches, portraying effigies with ropes around the necks, and bearing the unfailing inscription "Your Necktie." We usually travelled at night, nearly always with cocked guns. It was at this period of our life, during the struggle between the legitimate owners and the cattle thieves, that O. Henry saw something of the real desperado.

Willie Porter himself had a most charming but shy personality at this time. I remember him very distinctly and pleasantly. At the time he was 011 the ranch with us he was really living with Mr. and Mrs. Dick Hall, though he was a frequent visitor at our house. The intercourse between O. Henry and Captain Hall was more of a social than a business nature, though he acted as cowboy for a period under Captain Hall about the year 1882.

One does not have to read O. Henry's Texas stories very closely to detect the presence of Red Hall. Whenever a Ranger officer is mentioned there is a striking absence of the strident, swash-buckling, blood-and- thunder characteristics that are popularly supposed to go with the members of the famous force, but there stands before us a calm and determined man who uses his pistol with instant precision but only as a last resort. This is the real type of the Ranger officer, dime novels to the contrary notwithstanding, and this is the type that O. Henry has portrayed. In "The Caballero's Way," Lieutenant Sandridge of the Rangers is described as "six feet two, blond as a Viking, quiet as a deacon, dangerous as a machine gun."

In "An Afternoon Miracle," the conversation falls on Bob Buckley, another Ranger Lieutenant:

"I've heard of fellows," grumbled Broncho Leathers, "what was wedded to danger, but if Bob Buckley ain't committed bigamy with trouble, I'm a son of a gun."

"Peculiarness of Bob is," inserted the Nueces Kid, "he ain't had proper trainin'. He never learned how to git skeered. Now a man ought to be skeered enough when he tackles a fuss to hanker after readin' his name on the list of survivors, anyway."

"Buckley," commented Ranger No. 3, who was a misguided Eastern man, burdened with an education, "scraps in such a solemn manner that I have been led to doubt its spontaneity. I'm not quite onto his system, but he fights, like Tybalt, by the book of arithmetic."

"I never heard," mentioned Broncho, "about any of Dibble's ways of mixin' scrappin' and cipherin'."

"Triggernometry?" suggested the Nueces infant.

"That's rather better than I hoped from you," nodded the Easterner, approvingly. "The other meaning is that Buckley never goes into a fight without giving away weight. He seems to dread taking the slightest advantage. That's quite close to foolhardiness when you are dealing with horse-thieves and fence-cutters who would ambush you any night, and shoot you in the back if they could."

O. Henry was to remain on the La Salle County ranch for two years. Both Mrs. Dick Hall and Mrs. Lee Hall were fond of books and, though their libraries were constantly augmented by visits to Austin and San Antonio, O. Henry more than kept pace with the increase. "His thirst for knowledge of all kinds," says Mrs. Dick Hall, "was unquenchable. History, fiction, biography, science, and magazines of every description were devoured and were talked about with eager interest." Tennyson became now his favourite poet and, as O. Henry's readers would infer, remained so to the end. Webster's "Unabridged Dictionary" was also a constant companion. He used it not merely as a reference book but as a source of ideas. It became to him in the isolation of ranch life what Herkimer's "Handbook of Indispensable Information" had been to Sanderson Pratt and "The Rubaiyat" of Omar Khayyam to Idaho Green in "The Handbook of Hymen." Mrs. Hall championed Worcester while O. Henry believed Worcester a back number and Webster the only up-to-date guide. The Webster-Worcester differences in spelling and pronunciation were at his tongue's end and when he went to Austin he used to challenge the boys in the Harrell home to "stump" him on any point on which Webster had registered an opinion. "I carried Webster's 'Unabridged Dictionary' around with me for two years," he said, "while herding sheep for Dick Hall."

There is more than humour in his review of Webster published in the Houston Daily Post:

We find on our table quite an exhaustive treatise on various subjects written in Mr. Webster's well known, lucid, and piquant style. There is not a dull line between the covers of the book. The range of subjects is wide, and the treatment light and easy without being flippant. A valuable feature of the work is the arranging of the articles in alphabetical order, thus facilitating the finding of any particular word desired. Mr. Webster's vocabulary is large, and he always uses the right word in the right place. Mr. Webster's work is thorough, and we predict that he will be heard from again.

Dick Hall had been educated at Guilford College, a well-known Quaker school near Greensboro, and had learned French and Spanish from a Monsieur Maurice of the old Edgeworth Female Seminary. O. Henry began now the study of French and German but more persistently of Spanish. French and German were taken up as diversions but, as Mexican-Spanish was spoken all around him, he absorbed it as a part of his environment and in three months was the best speaker of it on the ranch. Not content with the "Greaser" dialect he bought a Spanish grammar and learned to read and speak Castilian Spanish. There is no evidence that he studied Latin after leaving Greensboro. The knowledge of it that he took with him was only that of a well-trained drug clerk and enough of Caesar to enable him to misquote accurately.

He had not been long on the ranch before he received his cowboy initiation, "the puncher's accolade." The ritual varies but the treatment of Curly in "The Higher Abdication" typifies the general aim and method:

Three nights after that Curly rolled himself in his blanket and went to sleep. Then the other punchers rose up softly and began to make preparations. Ranse saw Long Collins tie a rope to the horn of a saddle. Others were getting out their sixshooters.

"Boys," said Ranse, "I'm much obliged. I was hoping you would. But I didn't like to ask."

Half a dozen sixshooters began to pop — awful yells rent the air — Long Collins galloped wildly across Curly's bed, dragging the saddle after him. That was merely their way of gently awaking their victim. Then they hazed him for an hour, carefully and ridiculously, after the code of cow camps. Whenever he uttered protest they held him stretched over a roll of blankets and thrashed him woefully with a pair of leather leggings.

And all this meant that Curly had won his spurs, that he was receiving the puncher's accolade. Nevermore would they be polite to him. But he would be their "pardner" and stirrup-brother, foot to foot.

But O. Henry was still the dreamer and onlooker rather than the active or regular participant in the cowboy disciplines. He learned or rather absorbed with little effort the art of lassoing cattle, of dipping and shearing sheep, of shooting accurately from the saddle, of tending and managing a horse. Even the cowboys conceded his premiership as a broncho-buster. He became also a skilled amateur cook, than which no other accomplishment was more serviceable on the La Salle County ranch. But he had no set or regular tasks. He lived with the Halls not as an employee but as one of the family. He rode regularly once a week to Fort Ewell fifteen miles away and occasionally to Cotulla which was forty miles from the ranch house. But his interest was mainly in the novelty of ranch life, in the contrast between it and the Greensboro life, in the strange types of character that he learned to know, and in the self-appointed task of putting what he saw into paragraphs or pictures which lie promptly destroyed.

This blend of close observation, avid reading, varied experience, and self-discipline in expression was an incomparable preparation for his future work. No occasional visitor on a ranch, no man who had not learned to hold the reins and the pen with equal mastery, could have described Raidler's ride in "Hygeia at the Solito":

If anything could, this drive should have stirred the acrimonious McGuire to a sense of his ransom. They sped upon velvety wheels across an exhilarant savanna. The pair of Spanish ponies struck a nimble, tireless trot, which gait they occasionally relieved by a wild, untrammelled gallop. The air was wine and seltzer, perfumed, as they absorbed it, with the delicate redolence of prairie flowers. The road perished, and the buckboard swam the uncharted billows of the grass itself, steered by the practised hand of Raidler, to whom each tiny distant mott of trees was a signboard, each convolution of the low hills a voucher of course and distance.

None but a sensitive nature, gifted but disciplined, could achieve a paragraph like this from "The Missing Chord":

The ranch rested upon the summit of a lenient slope. The ambient prairie, diversified by arroyos and murky patches of brush and pear, lay around us like a darkened bowl at the bottom of which we reposed as dregs. Like a turquoise cover the sky pinned us there. The miraculous air, heady with ozone and made memorably sweet by leagues of wild flowerets, gave tang and savour to the breath. In the sky was a great, round, mellow searchlight which we knew to be no moon, but the dark lantern of summer, who came to hunt northward the cowering spring. In the nearest corral a flock of sheep lay silent until a groundless panic would send a squad of them huddling together with a drumming rush. For other sounds a shrill family of coyotes yapped beyond the shearing-pen, and whippoorwills twittered in the long grass. But even these dissonances hardly rippled the clear torrent of the mocking-birds' notes that fell from a dozen neighbouring shrubs and trees. It would not have been preposterous for one to tiptoe and essay to touch the stars, they hung so bright and imminent.

An interesting impression of O. Henry at this time is given by Mr. Joe Dixon* who had written "Carbonate Days," which he was later to destroy, and was looking around for some one to draw the pictures:

One day John Maddox came in and said: "See here, Joe — there is a young fellow here who came from North Carolina with Dick Hall, named Will Porter, who can draw like blazes. I believe he would be the very one to make the illustrations for your book. Dick Hall owns a sheep ranch out not very far from here, and Porter is working for him. Now, you might go out there and take the book along and tell him just about what you want, and let him have a crack at it."

It looked like a pretty good idea to me, for it seemed to me that a man who had seen something of the same life might better be able to draw the pictures.

I found Porter to be a young, silent fellow, with deep, brooding, blue eyes, cynical for his years, and with a facile pen, later to be turned to word-painting instead of picture-drawing.

I would discuss the story with Will in the daytime, and at night he would draw the pictures. There were forty of them in all. And while crude, they were all good and true to the life they depicted.

The ranch was a vast chaparral plain, and for three weeks Porter worked on the illustrations, and he and I roamed about the place and talked together. We slept together in a rude little shack. I became much interested in the boy's personality. He was a taciturn fellow, with a peculiar little hiss when amused, instead of the boyish laugh one might have expected, and he could give the queerest caustic turn to speech, getting off epigrams like little sharp bullets, every once in a while, and always unexpectedly.

One night Mrs. Hall said to me: "Do you know that that quiet boy is a wonderful writer? He slips in here every now and then and reads to me stories as fine as any Rider Haggard ever wrote."

Mrs. Hall was a highly cultivated woman and her words deeply impressed me. After I had gained Will's confidence he let me read a few of his stories, and I found them very fine.

"Will," I said to him one day, "why don't you try your hand at writing for the magazines?" But he had no confidence in himself, and destroyed his stories as fast as he wrote them.

"Well, at any rate," I said, "try your hand at newspaper work." But he couldn't see it, and went on writing and destroying.

Only a few of O. Henry's letters from the ranch to friends in Greensboro have been preserved. Most of these were written to Mrs. J. K. Hall, mother of Dick and Lee, and to Dr. W. P. Beall. Dr. Beall had recently moved to Greensboro from Lenoir, North Carolina, to practise medicine with Doctor Hall. He became a staunch friend of O. Henry and suggested to the Vesper Reading Club, of Lenoir, that they elect the young ranchman to honourary membership. Following are extracts from O. Henry's letter of acknowledgment :

Ladies and Gentlemen of the Vesper Reading Club :

Some time ago I had the pleasure of receiving a letter from the secretary of your association which, on observing the strange postmark of Lenoir, I opened with fear and trembling, although I knew I didn't owe anybody anything in that city. I began to peruse the document and found, first, that I had been elected an honourary member of that old and world-renowned body amidst thunders of applause that resounded far among the hills of Caldwell County, while the deafening cheers of the members were plainly heard above the din of the loafers in the grocery store. When I had somewhat recovered from the shock which such an unexpected honor must necessarily produce on a person of delicate sensibilities and modest ambition, I ventured to proceed and soon gathered that I was requested to employ my gigantic intellect in writing a letter to the club. I again picked myself up, brushed the dust off, and was disappointed not to find a notice of my nomination for governor of North Carolina.

The origin of the idea that I could write a letter of any interest to any one is entirely unknown to me. The associations with which I have previously corresponded have been generally in the dry goods line and my letters for the most part of a conciliatory, pay-you-next-week tendency, which could hardly have procured me the high honors that your club has conferred upon me. But I will try and give you a truthful and correct account in a brief and condensed manner of some of the wonderful things to be seen and heard in this country. The information usually desired in such a case is in regard to people, climate, manners, customs, and general peculiarities.

The people of the State of Texas consist principally of men, women, and children, with a sprinkling of cowboys. The weather is very good, thermometer rarely rising above 2,500 degrees in the shade and hardly ever below 212. There is a very pleasant little phase in the weather which is called a "norther" by the natives, which endears the country very much to the stranger who experiences it. You are riding along on a boiling day in September, dressed as airily as etiquette will allow, watching the fish trying to climb out of the pools of boiling water along the way and wondering how long it would take to walk home with a pocket compass and 75 cents in Mexican money, when a wind as cold as the icy hand of death swoops down on you from the north and the "norther" is upon you.

Where do you go? If you are far from home it depends entirely upon what kind of life you have led previous to this time as to where you go. Some people go straight to heaven while others experience a change of temperature by the transition. "Northers" are very useful in killing off the surplus population in some degree, while the remainder die naturally and peacefully in their boots.

After a long imaginary interview with a citizen of Texas whose picture was enclosed but has been lost, the letter ends:

But I must bring this hurried letter to a close. I have already written far into the night. The moon is low and the wind is still. The lovely stars, the "forget-me-nots of the angels," which have blossomed all night in the infinite meadows of heaven, unheeded and unseen by us poor sleepy mortals for whom they spread their shining petals and silvery beams in vain, are twinkling above in all their beauty and mystery. The lonely cry of the coyote is heard mingling with the noise of a piece of strong Texas bacon trying to get out of the pantry. It is at a time like this when all is quiet, when even nature seems to sleep, that old memories come back from their graves and haunt us with the scenes they bring before us. Faces dead long ago stare at us from the night and voices that once could make the heart leap with joy and the eye light up with pleasure seem to sound in our ears. With such feelings we sit wrapped in thought, living over again our youth until the awakening comes and we are again in the present with its cares and bitterness. It is now I sit wondering and striving to recall the past. Longingly I turn my mind back, groping about in a time that is gone, never more to return, endeavoring to think and convene my doubting spirit whether or not I fed the pup at supper. But listen! I hear the members of the V. R. C. rushing to the door. They have torn away the man stationed there to keep them inside during the transactions of the evening, and I will soon close with the request that the secretary in notifying me not to send any more letters may break the terrifying news as gently as possible, applying the balm of fair and delusive sentences which may prepare me at first by leading up gradually to the fearful and hope-destroying announcement.

In a letter* to Mrs. J. Iv. Hall he confines himself to the two ranches of her sons.

La Salle Co., Texas, January 20, 1883.

Dear Mrs. Hall: Your welcome letter which I received a good while ago was much appreciated, and I thought I would answer it in the hopes of getting another from you. I am very short of news, so if you find anything in this letter rather incredible, get Doctor Beall to discount it for you to the proper size. He always questions my veracity since I came out here. Why didn't he do it when I was at home? Dick has got his new house done, and it looks very comfortable and magnificent. It has a tobacco-barn-like grandeur about it that always strikes a stranger
*The Bookman, New York, August, 1913.
with awe, and during a strong north wind the safest place about it is outside at the northern end.

A coloured lady is now slinging hash in the kitchen and has such an air of command and condescension about her that the pots and kettles all get out of her way with a rush. I think she is a countess or a dukess in disguise. Cotulla has grown wonderfully since you left; thirty or forty new houses have gone up and thirty or forty barrels of whiskey gone down. The barkeeper is going to Europe on a tour next summer, and is thinking of buying Mexico for his little boy to play with. They are getting along finely with the pasture; there are sixty or seventy men at work on the fence and they have been having good weather for working. Ed. Brockman is there in charge of the commissary tent, and issues provisions to the contractors. I saw him last week, and he seemed very well.

Lee came up and asked me to go down to the camps and take Brockman's place for a week or so while he went to San Antonio. Well, I went down some six or seven miles from the ranch. On arriving I counted at the commissary tent nine niggers, sixteen Mexicans, seven hounds, twenty-one sixshooters, four desperadoes, three shotguns, and a barrel of molasses. Inside there were a good many sacks of corn, flour, meal, sugar, beans, coffee and potatoes, a big box of bacon, some boots, shoes, clothes, saddles, rifles, tobacco and some more hounds. The work was to issue the stores to the contractors as they sent for them, and was light and easy to do. Out at the rear of the tent they had started a graveyard of men who had either kicked one of the hounds or prophesied a norther. When night came, the gentleman whose good fortune it was to be dispensing the stores gathered up his saddle-blankets, four old corn sacks, an oil coat and a sheepskin, made all the room he could in the tent by shifting and arranging the bacon, meal, etc., gave a sad look at the dogs that immediately filled the vacuum, and went and slept outdoors. The few days I was there I was treated more as a guest than one doomed to labour. Had an offer to gamble from the nigger cook, and was allowed as an especial favour to drive up the nice, pretty horses and give them some corn. And the kind of accommodating old tramps and cowboys that constitute the outfit would drop in and board, and sleep and smoke, and cuss and gamble, and lie and brag, and do everything in their power to make the time pass pleasantly and profitably — to themselves. I enjoyed the thing very much, and one evening when I saw Brockman roll up to the camp, I was very sorry, and went off very early next morning in order to escape the heartbreaking sorrow of parting and leave-taking with the layout.

Now, if you think this fine letter worth a reply, write me a long letter and tell me what I would like to know, and I will rise up and call you a friend in need, and send you a fine cameria obscuria view of this ranch and itemised accounts of its operations and manifold charms. Tell Doctor Beall not to send me any cake; it would make some postmaster on the road ill if he should eat too much, and I am a friend to all humanity. I am writing by a very poor light, which must excuse bad spelling and uninteresting remarks.

I remain, Very respectfully yours, W. S. Porter.
Everybody well.

The following letter to Mrs. Hall indicates that O. Henry had determined to leave the ranch and to strike out for the city. It is his last ranch letter:La Salle Co., Texas.
March 13th '84.
My Dear Mrs. Hall:
As you must be somewhat surprised that I haven't been answering your letters for a long time, I thought I would write and let you know that I never got any of them and for that reason have not replied. With the Bugle, Patriot, and your letters stopped, I am way behind in Greensboro news, and am consumed with a burning desire to know if Julius A. Gray has returned from Fayetteville, if Caldcleugh has received a fresh assortment of canary bird cages, or if Fishblate's clothing is still two hundred percent below first cost of manufacturing, and I know that you will take pity on the benighted of the far southwest and relieve the anxiety. Do you remember the little hymn you introduced into this country?

Far out upon the prairie,
  How many children dwell,
  Who never read the Bible
  Nor hear the sabbath bell!

Instead of praying Sundays,
  You hear their firearms bang,
  They chase cows same as Mondays
  And whoop the wild mustang.

And seldom do they get, for
  To take to church a gal,
  It's mighty hard you bet, for
  Them in the chaparral.

But I will not quote any more as of course you know all the balance, and will proceed to tell you what the news is in this section. Spring has opened and the earth is clothed in verdure new. The cowboy has doffed his winter apparel and now appeareth in his summer costume of a blue flannel shirt and spurs. An occasional norther still swoops down upon him, but he buckles on an extra six shirts and defies the cold. The prairies are covered with the most lovely and gorgeous flowers of every description — columbine, jaspers, junipers, hollyhocks, asteroids, sweet-marjoram, night-blooming cereus, anthony-overs, percolators, hyoscyamuses, bergamots, crystallized anthers, fuchsias, and horoscopes. The lovely and deliciously scented meningitis twines its clustering tendrils around the tall mesquites, and the sweet little purple thanatopsis is found in profusion on every side. Tall and perfumed volutas wave in the breeze while the modest but highly-flavored megatherium nestles in the high grass. You remember how often you used to have the train stopped to gather verbenas when you were coming out here? Well, if you should come now, the engineer would have to travel the whole distance in Texas with engine reversed and all brakes down tight, you would see so many rare and beautiful specimens.

I believe everybody that you take any interest in or know is well and all right. Everything is quiet except the wind, and that will stop as soon as hot weather begins. I am with Spanish like Doctor Hall's patients, still "progressing," and can now tell a Mexican in the highest and most grammatical Castilian to tie a horse without his thinking I mean for him to turn him loose. I would like to put my knowledge of the language into profitable use, but am undecided whether consulship to Mexico or herd sheep. Doctor Beall suggests in his letter to me the other day that I come back to North Carolina and buy a shovel and go to work on the Cape Fear and Yadkin Valley Railroad, but if you will examine a map of your State you will see a small but plainly discernible line surrounding the State and constituting its border. Over that border I will cross when I have some United States bonds, a knife with six blades, an oroide watch and chain, a taste for strong tobacco, and a wild western manner intensely suggestive of cash.

I figure up that I made two thousand five hundred dollars last spring by not having any money to buy sheep with; for I would have lost every sheep in the cold and sleet of last March and a lamb for each one besides. So you see a fellow is sometimes up and sometimes down, however large a capital he handles, owing to the fluctuations of fortune and the weather.

This is how I console myself by philosophy, which is without a flaw when analyzed; but you know philosophy, although it may furnish consolation, starts back appalled when requested to come to the front with such little necessaries as shoes and circus tickets and clothes and receipted board bills, etc.; and so some other science must be invoked to do the job. That other science has but four letters and is pronounced Work. Expect my next letter from the busy marts of commerce and trade.

I hope you will write to me soon, when you have time. Give ' Doctor Hall my highest regards, and the rest of the family.

I remain Very truly yours W. S. Porter.

This letter had hardly reached Mrs. Hall before O. Henry found himself in Austin, the county seat of Travis and the capital of Texas. Dick Hall had moved to a new ranch in Williamson County, which forms the northern boundary of Travis County, and O. Henry had decided to give up ranch life and to live in Austin. Here he remained until October, 1895, when he went to Houston as reporter for the Houston Daily Post. Dick Hall had many friends in Austin, among them Mr. Joe Harrell, a retired merchant. Mr. Harrell was born near Greensboro, in 1811, and every fellow Carolinian found a hospitable welcome under his roof. When it was decided, therefore, that O. Henry was to remain in Austin, Mr. Harrell invited the young Tar-Heel and fellow countryman to come to his home, and here he lived for three years. Mr. Harrell and his three sons became devoted friends of the newcomer, whom they found to be timid and retiring but an unequalled entertainer in a coterie of intimates and a genius with his pencil. Mr. Harrell would accept nothing for board or lodging but regarded O. Henry as an adopted son.

O. Henry's stay in Austin was marked by the same sort of quick and wide-reaching reaction to his environment that had already become characteristic and that was to culminate during his eight years in New York. As the confinement in the Greensboro drug store had whetted his appetite for the freedom of the ranch, so the isolation of ranch life had made him all the more eager for the social contacts of city life. "A man may see so much," says O. Henry, in "The Hiding of Black Bill," "that he'd be bored to turn his head to look at a $3,000,000 fire or Joe Weber or the Adriatic Sea. But let him herd sheep for a spell, and you'll see him splitting his ribs laughing at 'Curfew Shall Not Ring Tonight,' or really enjoying himself playing cards with ladies." Austin had only about ten thousand inhabitants in 1884 but as the capital of the great State, and the seat of the rapidly growing State University, it was peculiarly representative of the old and the new, of the East and the West and the Southwest. To the knight-errant of "What's around the corner" it offered if not a wide at least a varied field of opportunity, and he proceeded forthwith to occupy.

His friends in Austin say that no one ever touched the city at so many points or knew its social strata as familiarly as O. Henry. Occasional clerk in a tobacco store and later in a drug store, bookkeeper for a real estate firm, draftsman in a land office, paying and receiving teller in a bank, member of a military company, singer in the choirs of the Presbyterian, Baptist, and Episcopal churches, actor in private theatricals, editor of a humorous paper, serenader and cartoonist, O. Henry would seem to have viewed the little city from all possible angles. The only segment of the life that he seems not to have touched was the University.

And yet he can hardly be said to have identified himself with Austin or with Austin interests. Everybody who knew him liked him and felt his charm, but few got beneath the surface. "Our times lapped by only one year," says Harry Peyton Steger, "and the freshman knew not that the wizard was around the corner, but my acquaintance there helped me in my search when I went there in January of this year. The first ten days on the ground showed me that Will Porter (it was only in his post-Texan days that people called him 'Sydney,' I believe) was known to hundreds and that few knew him. In his twenties and later in New York, he was the same lone wolf. But to his charm and brilliance all bear witness." In "The Man about Town," O. Henry questions four classes of people about his multiform subject only to find at last that the real man about town is the one who puts the questions.

But O. Henry differed from his typical man about town as widely as Jaques differed from Hamlet, or as a yachtsman differs from a seasoned tar. He worked hard when he did work and went "bumming," as he called it, by way of recreative reaction To go bumming was his phrase for a sort of democratic romancing. One of his Austin intimates, Dr. D. Daniels, says:

Porter was one of the most versatile men I had ever met. He was a fine singer, could write remarkably clever stuff under all circumstances, and was a good hand at sketching. And he was the best mimic I ever saw in my life. He was one of the genuine democrats that you hear about more often than you meet. Night after night, after we would shut up shop, he would call to me to come along and "go bumming." That was his favorite expression for the night-time prowling in which we indulged. We would wander through streets and alleys, meeting with some of the worst specimens of down-and-outers it has ever been my privilege to see at close range. I've seen the most ragged specimen of a bum hold up Porter, who would always do anything he could for the man. His one great failing was his inability to say "No" to a man.

He never cared for the so-called "higher classes," but watched the people on the streets and in the shops and cafes, getting his ideas from them night after night. I think that it was in this way he was able to picture the average man with such marvellous fidelity.

Another chum of those days writes :(The Bookman, New York, July)
  As a business man, his face was calm, almost expressionless; his demeanour was steady, even calculated. He always worked for a high class of employers, was never wanting for a position, and was prompt, accurate, talented, and very efficient; but the minute he was out of business — that was all gone. He always approached a friend with a merry twinkle in his eye and an expression which said: "Come on, boys, we are going to have a lot of fun," and we usually did... . He lived in an atmosphere of adventure that was the product of his own imagination. He was an inveterate story-teller, seemingly purely from the pleasure of it, but he never told a vulgar joke, and as much as he loved humour he would not sacrifice decency for its sake and his stories about women were always refined.

The first paying position that O. Henry held in Austin was that of bookkeeper for the real estate firm of Maddox Brothers and Anderson. He worked here for two years at a salary of a hundred dollars a month. "He learned bookkeeping from me," said Mr. Charles E. Anderson, "and I have never known any one to pick it up with such ease or rapidity. He was number one, and we were loath to part with him." Mr. Anderson persuaded O. Henry to live with him after his resignation as bookkeeper, and Mr. John Maddox offered him the money to go to New York and study drawing but O. Henry declined.

In the meantime, Dick Hall had been elected Land Commissioner of Texas and O. Henry applied for a position under him. "The letter of application," said Mrs. Hall, "was a masterpiece. Nothing that I have since seen from his pen seemed so clever. We kept it and re-read it for many years but it has mysteriously disappeared." Dick replied that if O. Henry could prepare himself in three months for the office of assistant compiling draftsman, the position would be given him. "It was wonderful how he did it," said Dick, "but he was the most skilful draftsman in the force."

O. Henry remained in the General Land Office for four years, from January, 1887, to January, 1891. The building stands just across from the Capitol on a high hill, and both its architecture and its storied service moved O. Henry's pen as did no other building in Texas. Many years after he had left the State he was to reproduce in "Georgia's Ruling," "Witches' Loaves," and "Buried Treasure" either the General Land Office itself or some tradition or experience associated with it. "People living in other States," he writes, "can form no conception of the vastness and importance of the work performed here and the significance of the millions of records and papers composing the archives of this office. The title deeds, patents, transfers, and legal documents connected with every foot of land owned in the State of Texas are filed here." The building he describes as follows:

Whenever you visit Austin you should by all means go to see the General Land Office. As you pass up the avenue you turn sharp round the corner of the court house, and on a steep hill before you you see a mediaeval castle. You think of the Rhine; the "castled crag of Drachenfels"; the Lorelei; and the vine-clad slopes of Germany. And German it is in every line of its architecture and design. The plan was drawn by an old draftsman from the " Vaterland," whose heart still loved the scenes of his native land, and it is said he reproduced the design of a certain castle near his birthplace with remarkable fidelity.

Under the present administration a new coat of paint has vulgarized its ancient and venerable walls. Modern tiles have replaced the limestone slabs of its floors, worn in hollows by the tread of thousands of feet, and smart and gaudy fixtures have usurped the place of the time-worn furniture that has been consecrated by the touch of hands that Texas will never cease to honor. But even now, when you enter the building, you lower your voice, and time turns backward for you, for the atmosphere which you breathe is cold with the exudations of buried generations. The building is stone with a coating of concrete; the walls are immensely thick; it is cool in the summer and warm in the winter; it is isolated and sombre; standing apart from the other state buildings, sullen and decaying, brooding on the past.

But the happiest event of O. Henry's life in Texas was his marriage on July 5, 1887, to Miss Athol Estes, the seventeen-year-old daughter of Mrs. G. P. Roach. It was a case of love at first sight on O. Henry's part but he deferred actual courtship until Miss Athol had finished school. Mr. and Mrs. Roach, however,

entered a demurrer on the score of health. Miss Athol's father had died of consumption as had O. Henry's mother and grandmother. But the young lovers were not to be denied. An elopement was instantly planned and romantically carried out. Borrowing a carriage from Mr. Charles E. Anderson they drove out at midnight to the residence of Dr. R. K. Smoot, the Presbyterian minister in whose choir they both sang. Mr. Anderson was dispatched to the

Roach home to sue for peace. Forgiveness was at last secured, and O. Henry never had two stauncher friends than Mr. and Mrs. Roach. In the darkest hours of his life their love for him knew no waning and their faith in him neither variableness nor the shadow of turning.

To the manner of his marriage O. Henry occasionally referred in later years and always with the deepest feeling and the tenderest memory. The moonlight drive under the trees, the borrowed carriage, the witticisms on the way, the parental opposition, the feeling of romantic achievement, the courage and serenity and joy of the little woman at his side, his own sense of assured and unclouded happiness for the future — these came back to him touched with pathos but radiant and hallowed in the retrospect. Surely a whiff of that July night transfigures these words, written eighteen years later:

On the highest rear seat was James Williams, of Cloverdale, Missouri, and his Bride. Capitalize it, friend typo — that last word — word of words in the epiphany of life and love. The scent of the flowers, the booty of the bee, the primal drip of spring waters, the overture of the lark, the twist of lemon peel on the cocktail of creation — such is the bride. Holy is the wife; revered the mother; galliptious is the summer girl — but the bride is the certified check among the wedding presents that the gods send in when man is married to mortality... . James Williams was on his wedding trip. Dear kind fairy, please cut out those orders for money and 40 H. P. touring cars and fame and a new growth of hair and the presidency of the boat club. Instead of any of them turn backward — oh, turn backward and give us just a teeny-weeny bit of our wedding trip over again. Just an hour, dear fairy, so we can remember how the grass and poplar trees looked, and the bow of those bonnet strings tied beneath her chin — even if it was the hatpins that did the work. Can't do it? Very well; hurry up with that touring car and the oil stock, then.

O. Henry found in his married life not only happiness but the incentive to effort that he had sorely lacked. It was an incentive that sprang from perfect congeniality and from the ambition to make and to have a home. Mrs. Porter was witty and musical. She was also stimulatively responsive to the drolleries of her husband. She cooperated with him in his sole journalistic venture and helped him with the society items of the Houston Daily Post. If the thought of her did not shape the character of Delia in "The Gift of the Magi," it might have done so. She did not live to see him become famous but, if she had, she would have been the first to say "I told you so." It is certainly no accident that the year of his marriage is also the year in which he begins to rely on his pen as a supplementary source of income. The editor of the Detroit Free Press writes, September 4, 1887:

My Dear Sir:
Please send your string for month of August. And it would please me to receive further contributions at once. Send a budgetevery week.

    A. Sincerely, Mosley.

    B.

And again three months later:

My Dear Mr. Porter:
Your string for November just in. Am sorry it is not longer.
Check will be sent in a few days.
Can you not send more matter — a good big installment every week? I returned everything that I felt I could not use, in order that we might resume operations on a clear board. Hereafter all unavailable matter shall be sent back within two or three days. After you get a better idea of the things we do not want, the quantity to be returned will be very small.

About the same time presumably, though the note is undated, the editors of Truth write from New York:

We have selected "The Final Triumph" and "A Slight Inaccuracy," for which you will receive a check for $6.

In the printed form used by the editors of Truth, contributions were classified as Jokes, Ideas, Verses, Squibs, Poems, Sketches, Stories, and Pictures. The two contributions accepted from O. Henry were entered 011 the line reserved for Sketches. The earliest record of an accepted short story that I have found, the earliest evidence that O. Henry had turned from paragraph writing to really constructive work, is in the following note written ten years later:

New York, Dec. 2, 1897.

W. S. Porter, Esq., 211 E. 0th St., Austin, Texas.

Dear Sir: Your story, "The Miracle of Lava Canon,"* is excellent. It has the combination of humane interest with dramatic incident, which in our opinion is the best kind of a story. If you have more like this, we should be glad to read them. We have placed it in our syndicate of newspapers. The other stories we return herewith. They are not quite available.

Very truly yours The S. S. McClure Co.

* This story, which deserves all that is here said of it, was entered for copyright by the McClure Syndicate, September 11, 1898, marked " for publication September 18, 1898." It was undoubtedly to this story that O. Henry referred in later years when he said: "My first story was paid for but I never saw it in print."

The four years in the General Land Office were the happiest years of O. Henry's life in Texas. The work itself was congenial, he found time for drawing, his coworkers in the office were his warm personal friends, and his occasional contributions of jokes, squibs, sketches, etc., could be counted upon whenever needed to help out the family larder. There was born to him also at this time a daughter, Margaret Worth Porter, whom the proud parents journeyed twice to Greensboro to exhibit and whose devotion to her father was to equal, though it could not surpass, that of the father to his only child.

But a change was imminent. Dick Hall ran for governor of Texas in 1891 but by a close margin was defeated by James Hogg. His term as Land Commissioner had expired, and, on January 21, O. Henry resigned his position as assistant compiling draftsman and entered the First National Bank of Austin as paying and receiving teller. The change, as will be seen, was to prove a disastrous one, the only rift in the cloud being that the new position was to widen his range of story themes and to force him to rely wholly upon his pen for a living. He had hitherto coquetted with his real calling, using it in Scott's words "as a staff, not as a crutch," as a buffet lunch rather than as a solid meal. Early in December, 1894, he resigned his position in the bank but not until he had begun to edit a humorous weekly which he called the Rolling Stone.

The first issue of the Rolling Stone appeared in Austin on April 28, 1894, and the last on April 27, 1895. It can hardly be said to have flourished between these dates: it only flickered. "It rolled for about a year," said O. Henry, "and then showed unmistakable signs of getting mossy. Moss and I never were friends, and so I said goodbye to it." "It was one of the means we employed," writes Mr. James P. Crane, of Chicago, one of the editors, "to get the pleasure out of life and never appealed to us as a money-making venture. We did it for the fun of the thing." This may have been O. Henry's motive in the beginning, but after resigning his position in the bank the financial side of the Rolling Stone assumed a new importance. In fact, the following letter to Mr. Crane shows that O. Henry was looking to his little paper for income:

San Antonio, Dec. 20, 1894.

Dear Jeems :

I am writing this in the City of Tomales. Came over last night to work up the Rolling Stone a little over here. Went over the city by gaslight. It is fearfully and wonderfully made. I quit the bank a day or two ago. I found out that the change was going to be made, so I concluded to stop and go to work on the paper.

Are you still in Chicago and what are the prospects? I tell you what I want to do. I want to get up in that country somewhere on some kind of newspaper. Can't you work up something for us to go at there? If you can I will come up there any time at one day's notice. I can worry along here and about live but it is not the place for one to get ahead in. You know that, don't you? See if you can't get me a job up there, or if you think our paper would take, and we could get some support, what about starting it up there?

I'm writing you on the jump, will send you a long letter in a few days which will be more at length than a shorter one would.

Yours as ever Bill.

The visit to San Antonio was the beginning of the end of the Rolling Stone. In the issue of January 2G, 1895, the announcement is made that the paper is "published simultaneously in Austin and San Antonio, Texas, every Saturday." Encouraging letters had been received from Bill Nye and John Kendrick Bangs but when O. Henry was overpersuaded to launch the Rolling Stone into the Callaghan mayoralty fight in San Antonio its doom was sealed. The Austin end of the little weekly had already lost heavily through a picture with a humorous underline which O. Henry had innocently inserted. The picture was of a German musician brandishing his baton. Underneath were the lines:

With his baton the professor beats the bars,
'Tis also said he beats them when he treats;

But it made that German gentleman see stars When the bouncer got the cue to bar the beats.

"For some reason or other," says Doctor Daniels,* "that issue alienated every German in Austin from the Rolling Stone and cost us more than we were able to figure out in subscriptions and advertisements."

But the by-products of the visits to San Antonio were later to reimburse O. Henry far over and beyond the immediate loss incurred. Cities were always in a peculiar sense his teachers, and from his editorial trips to the most interesting city of the Southwest he was later to find material for " Hygeiaat]the Solito," "The Enchanted Kiss," "The Missing Chord," "The Higher Abdication," "Seats of the Haughty," and "A Fog in Santone."

After the demise of the Rolling Stone, the opportunity "to get on some kind of newspaper," about which he had written to Mr. Crane, did not present itself until nearly six months had passed. In the meantime he was supporting himself by writing for any paper that paid promptly for humorous contributions. The Rolling Stone had given him the opportunity of a tryout and he seems never afterward to have doubted that writing of some sort was the profession for which he was best fitted. His experience in the bank had also convinced him that business was not his calling. "Frequently when I entered the bank," said a citizen of Austin, "O. Henry would put hastily aside some sketch or bit of writing on which he was engaged, before waiting on me." He had lived in his writings long before he attempted to live by them.

In July, 1895, O. Henry decided to accept a call to Washington, D. C. His household furniture was sold by way of preparation and he was on the eve of starting when Mrs. Porter became ill. The doctors found that the long-dreaded blow had fallen. She had consumption. O. Henry was unwilling to leave her or to attempt so long a journey with her. He continued, therefore, his contribution of odds and ends to newspapers and in October was writing chiefly for the Plain Dealer of Cleveland, Ohio, but hoping in the meanwhile to secure a more permanent position nearer home.

The opportunity came when Colonel R. M. Johnston offered him a position on the Houston Daily Post. Mrs. Porter was not well enough at first to accompany her husband to Houston but in a little while she was pronounced much better and joined him. Prospects were brighter now than they had been since his resignation from the General Land Office. The Post was one of the recognized moulders of public opinion in the Southwest and O. Henry's work gained for it new distinction. "The man, woman, or child," wrote an exchange, "who pens 'Postscripts' for the Houston Post, is a weird, wild-eyed genius and ought to be captured and put on exhibition."

"He became," said an editorial in the Post at the time of O. Henry's death, "the most popular member of the staff." "As a cartoonist," continues the Post, "Porter would have made a mark equal to that he attained as a writer had he developed his genius; but he disliked the drudgery connected with the drawing and found that his sketches were generally spoiled by any one else who took them to finish. In the early days he illustrated many of his stories. Those were days before the present development of the art of illustration, whether for magazine or newspaper, and he did most of the work on chalk, in which the drawing was made, a cast of lead being afterward made with more or less general results of reproducing the drawing in the shape of printing. The generality of the result was at times disheartening to the artist and Porter never followed his natural knack for embodying his brilliant ideas in drawings." His salary was quickly raised from fifteen to twenty-five dollars a week and he was advised by Colonel Johnston to go to New York where his talents would be more adequately rewarded.

O. Henry's first column appeared in the Post on October 18, 1895, his last on June 22, 1896. He began with "Tales of the Town" but changed quickly to "Some Postscripts and Pencillings," ending with "Some Postscripts." But the names made no difference. O. Henry wrote as he pleased. The cullings that follow will give a better idea of his matter and manner at this time than mere comment, however extended, could do. The tribute to Bill Nye lias the added interest of containing O. Henry's only known reference to American humour as a whole:

(October 18, 1895) Of an editor: He was a man apparently of medium height, with light hair and dark chestnut ideas.

(October 21, 1895) "Speaking of the $140,000,000 paid out yearly by the government in pensions," said a prominent member of Hood's Brigade to the Post's representative, "I am told that a man in Indiana applied for a pension last month on account of a surgical operation lie had performed on him during the war. And what do you suppose that surgical operation was?" "Haven't the least idea."

"He had his retreat cut off at the battle of Gettysburg!"

(November 3, 1895)
LOOKING FORWARD

> Soft shadows grow deeper in dingle and dell,
> Night hawks are beginning to roam; The breezes are cooler; the owl is awake, The whippoorwill calls from his nest in the brake;
> When
> the
> cows
> come
> home.
> The cup of the lily is heavy with dew;
>
> In heaven's aerial dome
> Stars twinkle; and down in the darkening swamp
> The fireflies glow, and the elves are a-romp;
> When
> the
> cows
> come
> home.
> And the populist smiles when he thinks of the time

That unto his party will come;
When at the pie counter they capture a seat,
And they'll eat and eat and eat and eat Till
the
cows
come
home.

(November 6, 1895)
   EUGENE FIELD

      No gift bis genius might have had,
      Of titles high in church or State,
      Could charm him as the one he bore
      Of children's poet laureate.
      He smiling pressed aside the bays

      And laurel garlands that he won,
      And bowed his head for baby hands
      To place a daisy wreath upon.
      He found his kingdom in the ways

      Of little ones he loved so well;
      For them he tuned his lyre and sang
      Sweet simple songs of magic spell.
      Oh, greater feat to storm the gates

      Of children's pure and cleanly hearts,
      Than to subdue a warring world
      By stratagems and doubtful arts!
      So, when he laid him down to sleep

      And earthly honors seemed so poor;
      Methinks he clung to little hands
      The latest, for the love they bore.
      A tribute paid by chanting choirs

      And pealing organs rises high;
      But soft and clear, somewhere he hears
      Through all, a child's low lullaby.

(November 27, 1895)

      An old woman who lived in Fla.
      Had some neighbors who all the time ba.
      Tea, sugar, and soap,
      Till she said: "I do hope I'll never see folks that are ha."

(December 1, 1895)

"You're at the wrong place," said Cerberus. "This is the gate that leads to the infernal regions, while this is a passport to heaven that you've handed me."

"I know it," said the departed Shade wearily, "but it allows a stop-over here. You see, I'm from Galveston, and I've got to make the change gradually."

(December 12, 1895)

A young lady in Houston became engaged last summer to one of the famous shortstops of the Texas baseball league. Last week he broke the engagement, and this is the reason why:

He had a birthday last Tuesday, and she sent him a beautiful bound and illustrated edition of Coleridge's famous poem, "The Ancient Mariner." The hero of the diamond opened the book with a puzzled look.

"What's dis bloomin' stuff about anyways?" he said. He read the first two lines:

" It is the Ancient Mariner, And he stoppeth one of three" — The famous shortstop threw the book out the window, stuck out his chin, and said: "No Texas sis can't gimme de umpire face like dat. I swipes nine daisy cutters outer ten dat comes in my garden, dat's what."

(February 26, 1896)

Bill Nye, who recently laid down his pen for all time, was a unique figure in the field of humor. His best work probably more nearly represented American humor than that of any other writer. Mr. Nye had a sense of the ludicrous that was keen and judicious. His humor was peculiarly American in that it depended upon sharp and unexpected contrasts and the bringing of opposites into unlooked for comparison for its effect. Again he had the true essence of kindliness, without which humor is stripped of its greatest component part. His was the child's heart, the scholar's knowledge, and the philosopher's view of life. The world has been better for him, and when that can be said of a man, the tears that drop upon his grave are more potent than the loud huzzas that follow the requiem of the greatest conqueror or the most successful statesman. The kindliest thoughts and the sincerest prayers follow the great humanitarian — for such he was — into the great beyond, and such solace as the hearty condole-ment of a million people can bring to the bereaved loved ones of Bill Nye, is theirs.

When O. Henry ceased to write for the Houston Daily Post he had closed a significant chapter in his life. Had he died at this time those who had followed his career closely would have seen in him a mixture of Bill Nye and Artemus WTard with an undeveloped vein of Eugene Field. There was a hint of many things which he was later to use as embellishments of his art, but there was no indication of the essential nature of the art that was to be embellished. A character in Fletcher's "Love's Pilgrimage" is made to say:

Portly meat, Bearing substantial stuff, and fit for hunger, I do beseech you, hostess, first; then some light garnish, Two pheasants in a dish.

But O. Henry served the "light garnish" first. His "two pheasants" were the Rolling Stone and his column in the Houston Daily Post. His more "substantial stuff" came after these, but was not the natural outgrowth from them.

Nothing that he had written for these two publications was selected by him for reproduction in the volumes of his short stories. The so-called stories that he read to Mrs. Hall on the ranch and those that appeared now and then in the Rolling Stone were sketches or extravaganzas rather than real stories at grips with real life. "I was amazed," said Mrs. Hall, "when I learned that O. Henry was our Will Porter. I had thought that he might be a great cartoonist but had never thought of his being a master of the modern short story."

O. Henry was now to begin a period of severe trial and of prolonged and unmerited humiliation. But he was to come out of it all with purpose unified and character deepened. Experience with the seamy side of life was to do for him what aimless experimentation with literary forms would never have done.

CHAPTER SIX
The Shadowed Years

When O. Henry left Houston, never to return, he left because he was summoned to come immediately to Austin and stand trial for alleged embezzlement of funds while acting as paying and receiving teller of the First National Bank of Austin. The indictments charged that on October 10, 1894, he misappropriated $554.48; on November 12, 1894, $299.60; and on November 12, 1895, $299.60.

Had he gone he would certainly have been acquitted. He protested his innocence to the end. "A victim of circumstances" is the verdict of the people in Austin who followed the trial most closely. Not one of them, so far as I could learn after many interviews, believed or believe him guilty of wrong doing. It was notorious that the bank, long since defunct, was wretchedly managed. Its patrons, following an old custom, used to enter, go behind the counter, take out one hundred or two hundred dollars, and say a week later: "Porter, I took out two hundred dollars last week. See if I left a memorandum of it. I meant to." It must have recalled to O. Henry the Greensboro drug store. Long before the crash came, he had protested to his friends that it was impossible to make the books balance. " The affairs of the bank," says Mr.' Hyder E. Rollins, of Austin, "were managed so loosely that Porter's predecessor was driven to retirement, his successor to attempted suicide."

There can be no doubt that O. Henry boarded the train at Houston with the intention of going to Austin. I imagine that he even felt a certain sense of relief that the charge, which had hung as a dead albatross about his neck, was at last to be unwound, and his innocence publicly proclaimed. His friends were confident of his acquittal and are still confident of his innocence. If even one of them had been with O. Henry, all would have been different. But when the train reached Hempstead, about a third of the way to Austin, O. Henry had had time to pass in review the scenes of the trial, to picture himself a prisoner, to look into the future and see himself marked with the stigma of suspicion. His imagination outran his reason, and when the night train passed Hempstead on the way to New Orleans, O. Henry was on it.

His mind seems to have been fully made up. He was not merely saving himself and his family from a public humiliation, he was going to start life over again in a new place. His knowledge of Spanish and his ignorance of Honduras made the little Central American republic seem just the haven in which to cast anchor. How great the strain was can be measured in part by the only reference of the sort, so far as I know, that O. Henry ever made to his life in the little Latin American country: "The freedom, the silence, the sense of infinite peace, that I found here, I cannot begin to put into words." His letters to Mrs. Porter from Honduras show that he had determined to make Central America his home, and that a school had already been selected for the education of his daughter.

How long O. Henry remained in New Orleans, on his way to or from Honduras, is not known; long enough, however, to draw the very soul and body of the Crescent City into the stories that he was to write years afterward. With his usual flair for originality, he passes by Mardi Gras, All Saints' Day, Quatorze Juillet, and crevasses; but in "Whistling Dick's Christmas Stocking," "The Renaissance of Charleroi," "Cherchez La Femine," and "Blind Man's Holiday," he has pictured and interpreted New Orleans and its suburbs as only one who loved and lived the life could do.

It is probable that he merely passed through New Orleans on his way to Honduras and took the first available fruit steamer for the Honduran coast, arriving at Puerto Cortez or Criba or Trujillo. At any rate, he was in Trujillo and was standing on the wharf when he saw a man in a tattered dress suit step from a newly arrived fruit steamer. "Why did you leave so hurriedly?" asked O. Henry. "Perhaps for the same reason as yourself," replied the stranger. "What is your destination?" inquired O. Henry. "I left America to keep away from my destination," was the reply; "I'm just drifting. How about yourself?" "I can't drift," said O. Henry; "I'm anchored."

The stranger was Al Jennings, the leader of one of the most notorious gangs of train robbers that ever infested the Southwest. In "Beating Back," which Mr. Jennings was to publish eighteen years later, one may read the frank confession and life story of an outlaw and ex-convict who at last found himself and "came back" to live down a desperate past. That he has made good may be inferred from the spirit of his book, from the high esteem in which he is held by friends and neighbours, and from the record of civic usefulness that has marked his career since his return.

But when he and O. Henry met at Trujillo Mr. Jennings was still frankly a fugitive outlaw. He and his brother Frank had chartered a tramp steamer in Galveston, and the departure had been so sudden that they had not had time to exchange their dress suits and high hats for a less conspicuous outfit. Mr.

Jennings and his brother had no thought of continuing their career of brigandage in Latin America. They were merely putting distance between them and the detectives already on their trail. O. Henry joined them and together they circled the entire coast of South America. This was O. Henry's longest voyage and certainly the strangest. When the money was exhausted, "Frank and I," says Mr. Jennings, "decided to pull off a job to replenish the exchequer. We decided to rob a German trading store and bank in northern Texas, and I asked Porter if he would join us. 'No,' he said, 'I don't think I could.' 'Well, Bill,' I said, 'you could hold the horses, couldn't you?' 'No,' said Porter, 'I don't think I could even hold the horses.'"

In these wanderings together Mr. Jennings probably saw deeper into one side of O. Henry's life than any one else has ever seen. In a letter to Harry Peyton Steger, he writes: "Porter was to most men a difficult proposition, but when men have gone hungry together, feasted together, and looked grim death in the face and laughed, it may be said they have a knowledge of each other. Again, there is no period in a man's life that so brings out the idiosyncrasies as gaunt and ghastly famine. I have known that with our friend and could find no fault. If the world could only know him as I knew him, the searchlight of investigation could be turned on his beautiful soul and find it as spotless as a bar of sunlight after the storm-cloud had passed." In a letter just received Mr. Jennings says: "Porter joined with Frank in urging me to leave the 'Trail,' establish ourselves in Latin America, and forget the past. Quite often, indeed, he spoke of his wife and his child and there was always a mist in his eye and a sob in his throat."

O. Henry's letters to Mrs. Porter came regularly after the first three weeks. The letters were inclosed in envelopes directed to Mr. Louis Ivreisle, in Austin, who handed them to Mrs. Porter. "Mrs. Porter used to read me selections from her husband's letters," said Mrs. Kreisle. "They told of his plans to bring Athol [Mrs. Porter] and Margaret to him as soon as he was settled. He had chosen a school for Margaret in Honduras and was doing everything he could to have a little home ready for them. At one time he said he was digging ditches. He also mentioned a chum whom he had met. Sometimes they had very little to eat, only a banana each. He had a hard time but his letters were cheerful and hopeful and full of affection. Mr. and Mrs. Roach were, of course, willing to provide for Athol and Margaret but Athol did not want to be dependent. She said she did not know how long they would be separated, so she planned to do something to earn some money. She commenced taking a course in a business college but ill health interfered. When Christmas came she made a point lace handkerchief, sold it for twenty-five dollars, and sent her husband a box containing his overcoat, fine perfumery, and many other delicacies. I never saw such will power. The only day she remained in bed was the day she died."

O. Henry did not know till a month later that this box was packed by Mrs. Porter when her temperature was 105. As soon as he learned it, he gave up all hope of a Latin American home and started for Austin, determined to give himself up and to take whatever medicine fate or the courts had in store for him. He passed again through New Orleans, and, according to the trial reports, arrived in Austin on February 5, 1897. His bondsmen were not assessed, but the amount of the bond was doubled and O. Henry went free till the next meeting of the Federal Court.

All of his time and thought was now given to Mrs. Porter. When she was too weak to walk O. Henry would carry her to and from the carriage in which they spent much of their time. His wanderlust seemed stilled at last and these days of home-keeping and home-tending were happy days to both, though they knew that the end was near. Mrs. Porter had been almost reared in the Sunday-school and the neighbours say that it was a familiar sight on Sunday mornings, in the last spring and summer, to see O. Henry and his wife driving slowly beneath the open windows of the Presbyterian Church. Here they would remain unseen by the congregation till the service was nearly over. Then they would drive slowly back. Each service, it was feared, might be the last. The end came on July 25th.

After many postponements O. Henry's case came to trial in February, 1898. He pleaded not guilty but seemed indifferent. "I never had so non-communicative a client," said one of his lawyers. "He would tell me nothing." O. Henry begged his friends not to attend the trial and most of them respected his wishes. In fact, he seemed, as usual, to be only a spectator of the proceedings. He was never self-defensive or even self-assertive, and at this crisis of his life he showed an aloofness which, however hard to understand by those who did not know him, was as natural to him as breathing. He simply retreated into himself and let the lawyers fight it out.

One error in the indictment was so patent that it is hard to understand how it could have gone unchallenged. He was charged, as has been stated, with having embezzled $299.60 on November 12, 1895, "the said W. S. Porter being then and there the teller and agent of a certain National Banking Association, then and there known and designated as the First National Bank of Austin." Nothing in O. Henry's life is better substantiated than that on November 12, 1895, he was living in Houston and had resigned his position in the Austin bank early in December, 1894. And yet the reader will hardly believe that this flagrant inconsistency in the charge against him has remained to this moment unnoticed. The foreman of the grand jury and the foreman of the trial jury are reported to have regretted afterward that they had voted to convict. "O. Henry was an innocent man," said the former, "and if I had known then what I know now, I should never have voted against him." As the contradiction in time and place was not one of the things that either foreman learned later, one cannot help asking what it was that led to conviction.

The answer is easy. O. Henry lost his case at Hempstead, not at Austin. "Your Grand Jurors," so runs the charge, "further say that between the days the sixth (6th) of July a. d. 1896 and the fifth (5th) of February a. d. 1897 the aforesaid W. S. Porter was a fugitive and fleeing from justice and seeking to avoid a prosecution in this court for the offense hereinbefore set out." This was true, and the humiliation of it and the folly of it were so acutely felt by O. Henry that he remained silent. I think it unlikely that he noticed the impossible date, November 12, 1895, for a more dateless and timeless man never lived. To a trusted friend in New York, O. Henry declared that Conrad's "Lord Jim" made an appeal to him made by no other book. "I am like Lord Jim," he added, "because we both made one fateful mistake at the supreme crisis of our lives, a mistake from which we could not recover."

"Lord Jim" has been called the greatest psychological study of cowardice that modern literature has to its credit. But Lord Jim was no coward. When he knew that the ship was about to sink, a certain irresolution took possession of him and he did not and could not wake the passengers. He did not think of saving himself, but his mind conjured up the horrors of panic, the tumult, the rush, the cries, the losing fight for place, and it seemed infinitely better to him that they should all go down in peace and quiet. "Which of us," says Conrad, "has not observed this, or maybe experienced something of that feeling in his own person — this extreme weariness of emotions, the vanity of effort, the yearning for rest? Those striving with unreasonable forces know it well — the shipwrecked castaways in boats, wanderers lost in a desert, men battling against the unthinking might of nature or the stupid brutality of crowds."

Like Lord Jim, O. Henry was governed more by impulse than by reason, more by temperament than by commonsense. The sails ruled the rudder in his disposition, not the rudder the sails. When he changed trains at Hempstead it was not cowardice that motivated his action. It was the lure of peace and quiet under Honduran skies, the call of a new start in life, the challenge of a novel and romantic career. The same faculties that were to plot his stories were now plotting this futile jaunt to Central America. The vision swept him along till, like Lord Jim, he had time to reflect and still longer time to regret.

The jury rendered its verdict of guilty on February 17, 1898, and on March 25, O. Henry was sentenced to imprisonment in the Ohio Penitentiary at Columbus for the period of five years. Immediately after being sentenced he wrote from the jail in Austin the following letter to his motherin-law, Mrs. G. P. Roach:'

Dear Mrs. Roach:

I feel very deeply the forbearance and long suffering kindness shown by your note, and thank you much for sending the things. Right here I want to state solemnly to you that in spite of the jury's verdict I am absolutely innocent of wrong doing in that bank matter, except so far as foolishly keeping a position that I could not successfully fill. Any intelligent person who heard the evidence presented knows that I should have been acquitted. After I saw the jury I had very little hopes of their understanding enough of the technical matters presented to be fair. I naturally am crushed by the result, but it is not on my own account. I care not so much for the opinion of the general public, but I would have a few of my friends still believe that there is some good in me.

O. Henry entered the penitentiary on April 25, 1898, and came out on July 24, 1901. On account of good behaviour his term of confinement was reduced from five years to three years and three months. There was not a demerit against him.

When O. Henry passed within the walls of the Ohio prison he was asked: "What is your occupation?" "I am a newspaper reporter," he replied. There was little opportunity for that profession in that place, but the next question may be said to have saved his life: "What else can you do?" "I am a registered pharmacist," was the reply, almost as an afterthought. The profession which he loathed in Greensboro because it meant confinement was now, strangely enough, to prove the stepping-stone to comparative freedom. His career as a drug clerk in the prison, his fidelity to duty, the new friendships formed, the opportunity afforded him to write, and his quick assimilation of short story material from the life about him are best set forth in the testimony of those who knew him during these years of seeming eclipse.

Dr. John M. Thomas was then chief physician at the prison. His letter is especially interesting for the light that it throws on the origin of the stories contained in "The Gentle Grafter":

Druggists were scarce and I felt I was fortunate in securing the services of Sydney Porter, for he was a registered pharmacist and unusually competent. In fact, he could do anything in the drug line. Previous to his banking career in Texas he had worked in a drug store in North Carolina, so he told me. While Porter was drug clerk Jimmie Consedine, one time proprietor of the old hotel Metropole in New York, was a muse. Consedine spent all his time painting. Out of this came a falling out with O. Henry. Consedine painted a cow with its tail touching the ground. Porter gave a Texas cowman's explanation of the absurdity of such a thing and won Consedine's undying hatred.

After serving some time as drug clerk O. Henry came to me and said: "I have never asked a favor of you before but there is one I should like to ask now. I can be private secretary to the steward outside [meaning that he would be outside the walls and trusted]. It depends on your recommendation." I asked him if he wanted to go. When he said he did, I called up the steward, Mr. C. N. Wilcox, and in twenty minutes O. Henry was outside.

He did not associate very much with any of the other inmates of the prison except the western outlaws. A ery few of the officers or attendants at the prison ever saw him. Most convicts would tell me frankly how they got into jail. They did not seem to suffer much from mortification. O. Henry, on the other hand, was very much weighed down by his imprisonment. In my experience of handling over ten thousand prisoners in the eight years I was physician at the prison, I have never known a man who was so deeply humiliated by his prison experience as O. Henry. He was a model prisoner, willing, obedient, faithful. His record is clear in every respect.

It was very seldom that he mentioned his imprisonment or in any way discussed the subject. One time we had a little misunderstanding about some alcohol which was disappearing too rapidly for the ordinary uses to which it was put. I requested that he wait for me one morning so that I could find out how much alcohol he was using in his night rounds, and after asking him a few questions he became excited when he thought I might be suspicion-ing him. "I am not a thief," he said, "and I never stole a thing in my life. I was sent here for embezzling bank funds, not one cent of which I ever got. Some one else got it all, and I am doing time for it."

You can tell when a prisoner is lying as well as you can in the case of anybody else. I believed O. Henry implicitly. I soon discovered that he was not the offender in the matter of the alcohol. But the question disturbed him and he asked me once or twice afterward if I really thought that he ever stole anything.

Once in a long while he would talk about his supposed crime and the great mistake he made in going to Central America as soon as there was any suspicion cast on him. When he disappeared suspicion became conviction. After his return from Central America, when he was tried, he never told anything that would clear himself. While he was in Central America he met Al Jennings who was likewise a fugitive from justice. After they returned to the States they renewed their friendship at the prison, where both eventually landed. Jennings was also one of the trusted prisoners and in the afternoon they would often come into my office and tell stories.

O. Henry liked the western prisoners, those from Arizona, Texas, and Indian Territory, and he got stories from them all and retold them in the office. Since reading his books I recognize many of the stories I heard there. As I mentioned before, he was an unusually good pharmacist and for this reason was permitted to look after the minor ills of the prisoners at night. He would spend two or three hours on the range or tiers of cells every night and knew most of the prisoners and their life stories.

"The Gentle Grafter" portrays the stories told him on his night rounds. I remember having heard him recount many of them. He wrote quite a number of short stories while in prison and it was a frequent thing for me to find a story written on scrap paper on my desk in the morning, with a note telling me to read it before he sent it out. We would often joke about the price the story would bring, anything from twenty-five to fifty dollars. He wrote them at night in from one to three hours, he told me.

The night doctor at the penitentiary was Dr. George W. Williard. He also became a friend and admirer of O. Henry and was the first to recognize the original of Jimmy Valentine, the leading character in "A Retrieved Reformation." Dr. Williard contributes the following reminiscences:

He was the last man in the world you would ever pick for a crook. Toward every one he was quiet, reserved, almost taciturn. He seldom spoke unless in answer. He never told me of his hopes, his aims, his family, his crime, his views of life, his writing, in fact, he spoke of little save the details of his pharmaceutical work in which he was exceptionally careful and efficient. The chief means by which I judged his character was by the way he acted and by one or two little incidents which brought out the man's courage and faithfulness.

I respected him for his strict attention to business, his blameless conduct, and his refusal to mix in the affairs of other prisoners. He seemed to like me personally because I did not ask him personal questions and because I showed that I felt as one intelligent man must feel toward another under such circumstances. So we grew to be friends.

He was as careful and conscientious as if the drug store at the prison had been his own property. His hours were from six in the evening to six in the morning. Often I left at midnight with Porter in charge and I knew things would run as regularly and effectively until morning as if I had remained. Porter was almost as free from prison life as any one on the outside. He received all the magazines and did lots of reading. He did not sleep in a cell but on a cot in the hospital during the day time. His ability and conduct were such that, once he had demonstrated them, there was never any danger that he would have to eat and sleep and work in the shops with other prisoners.

Convicts who were ill or who claimed to be ill would be brought into the hospital in charge of a guard and, ranging themselves along the front of the drug counter, would be given medicines by the drug clerk according to my instructions. It was part of Porter's duties to know a couple of hundred drugs by number as well as by name and to be able to hand them out without mistake quickly. Constant desire of prisoners to escape work by feigning illness necessitated the physician and his clerk being always on their guard against shams. Often some violent convict, when refused medicine, would rebel.

One night a huge negro to whom I refused a drug became abusive. The guard who had brought him in had stepped away for a moment and the prisoner directed at me a fearful torrent of profanity. I was looking around for the guard when Sydney Porter, my drug clerk, went over his counter like a panther. All of his hundred and seventy or eighty pounds were behind the blow he sent into the negro's jaw. The negro came down on the floor like a ton of brick. Instantly Porter was behind his counter again. He did not utter a word.

Another time a certain piece of equipment was stolen from the penitentiary hospital. There had been a good deal of stealing going on and I was responsible when it happened during my "trick." I mentioned this to Porter and he gave me the name of a certain official of the prison who, he said, had stolen the property. I told the warden who had taken the property and said it would have to come back at once. In twelve hours it was back. Porter said in his quiet way: "Well, I see you got in your work." It was the only time he ever told on any one and he did it merely out of loyalty to me. Although nearly every drug clerk at the prison was at some time or other guilty of petty trafficking in drugs or whisky, Porter was always above reproach. He always had the keys to the whisky cabinet, yet I never heard of his taking a drink.

The moment I read O. Henry's description and character delineation of Jimmy Valentine in "A Retrieved Reformation," I said, "That's Jimmy Connors through and through." Connors was in for blowing a postoffice safe. He was day drug clerk in the prison hospital at the same time Porter was night clerk. The men were friendly and often, early in the evening, before Connors went to bed, he would come and talk to Porter and tell him of his experiences.

Although Connors admitted himself guilty of many other jobs he claimed not to be guilty of the one for which he was serving time. Another man who resembled Connors had blown a safe and Connors was arrested and sent to prison for it. Because of fear of implicating himself in other jobs of which he was guilty, he said, he never told on the other man but went to prison innocent. This statement was borne out early in his term in the penitentiary by the arrival of the sheriff who had sent him up and who, in the meantime, had arrested the real culprit and secured from him a confession. To right his wrong the sheriff went to Washington, but the inspectors knew Jimmy Connors and said he doubtless was guilty of some other jobs and had best stay in prison for safekeeping. He did stay, giving O. Henry the chance to meet him and find inspiration for "A Retrieved Reformation."

Porter never said a word to me about his own crime, but another man once told me that Porter had told him that he had been "railroaded" to prison, so I think that he secretly held himself unjustly dealt with. The fact that he and Jimmy Connors agreed on this point in their respective cases doubtless drew them together.

Poor Jimmy! He never lived to try any sort of reformation on the outside. He died of kidney trouble in the penitentiary hospital, May 19, 1902, which was after Porter left and before Jimmy Valentine became famous in story, play, and song. He was a wonderful chemist and I still, in my daily practice, use one formula he gave me. It is not saying too much, I am sure, to state that the recent craze for "crook" plays in the theatrical world may be traced directly to this dead prisoner, for from him O. Henry drew the character which made the story famous, and from the story came the first "crook" play which won wide success, leading the way to the production of many similar plays. You would recognize instantly, if you knew customs and conditions, that the prison atmosphere at the beginning of the story was gathered bodily from Ohio penitentiary life as Porter knew it.

Mr. J. B. Rumer, a night guard at the penitentiary, was thrown with O. Henry during the latter's working hours, from midnight till dawn. There was little conversation between them, O. Henry being absorbed in his stories. Mr. Rumer says:

After most of his work was finished and we had eaten our midnight supper, he would begin to write. He always wrote with pen and ink and would often work for two hours continuously without rising. He seemed oblivious to the world of sleeping convicts about him, hearing not even the occasional sigh or groan from the beds which were stretched before him in the hospital ward or the tramp of the passing guards. After he had written for perhaps two hours he would rise, make a round of the hospital, and then come back to his work again. He got checks at different times and once told me that he had only two stories rejected while he was in prison.

Another side of O. Henry impressed Alexander Hobbs, a coloured prisoner who acted as valet to one of the physicians. Hobbs was afterward the political boss of the coloured voters of Columbus:

Mr. Porter was from the South and he always called colored men niggers. I never got fresh with him. I treated him with respect but let him alone. One day he asked me about it and I said: "Mr. Porter, I know you all don't want nothing to do with no black folks." He laughed and after that we always got along fine.

Mr. Porter was a nurse over in the hospital and he hadn't been in long when by mistake one day WTarden E. G. Coffin was given an overdose of Fowler's solution of arsenic. The right antidote couldn't be found and the day physician, the nurses, and all the prison officers were crowded around the bed on which the warden was lying, in great fright. Everybody was panic-stricken and it looked like the warden, who was unconscious, was going to die with doctors and a drug store right there beside him.

Then Mr. Porter, who had been upstairs nursing a sick prisoner, came walking down. He had learned what was the matter. I can just see him yet, as he came down them stairs, as quiet and composed as a free citizen out for a walk. "Be quiet, gentlemen," he says, and walks over to the drug store and takes charge, just as easy as if he owned the prison. Then he mixes a little drink, just like mixing a soda water. In an hour the warden was out of danger and the next day Mr. Porter was made night drug clerk.

O. Henry's letters from prison tell their own story. The life was intolerable at first but he lived in constant expectation of a pardon. When this hope failed he turned all the more wholeheartedly to story writing. His appointment by Doctor Thomas, in October, 1900, to a position in the steward's office (see page 148) was evidently a turning-point in his life and was so recognized by him. It is needless to say, as the letters show, that Margaret did not know where her father was. From the moment of his sentence O. Henry's chief concern was that she should never know. And she did not know till he told her face to face.

May 18, 1898.

Dear Mr. Roach:

I wrote you about ten days ago a letter which I sent through the office of this place. I could not say in it what I wanted to as the letters are all read here and they are very strict about what is in them. I now have the opportunity to send an occasional letter by a private way, and to receive them by the same means. I want to give you some idea of the condition of things here.

I accidentally fell into a place on the day I arrived that is a light one in comparison with others. I am the night druggist in the hospital, and as far as work is concerned it is light enough, and all the men stationed in the hospital live a hundred per cent, better than the rest of the 2,500 men here. There are four doctors and about twenty-five other men in the hospital force. The hospital is a separate building and is one of the finest equipped institutions in the country. It is large and finely finished and has every appliance of medicine and surgery.

We men who are on the hospital detail fare very well comparatively. We have good food well cooked and in unlimited abundance, and large clean sleeping apartments. We go about where we please over the place, and are not bound down by strict rules as the others are. I go on duty at five o'clock p. m. and off at five a. m. The work is about the same as in any drug store, filling prescriptions, *etc.* and is pretty lively up to about ten o'clock. At seven p. m. I take a medicine case and go the rounds with the night physician to see the ones over in the main building who have become sick during the day.

The doctor goes to bed about ten o'clock and from then on during the night I prescribe for the patients myself and go out and attend calls that come in. If I find any one seriously ill I have them brought to the hospital and attended to by the doctor. I never imagined human life was held as cheap as it is here. The men are regarded as animals without soul or feeling. They carry on all kinds of work here; there are foundries and all kinds of manufacturing done, and everybody works and works twice as hard as men in the same employment outside do. They work thirteen hours a day and each man must do a certain amount or be punished. Some few strong ones stand the work, but it is simply slow death to the majority. If a man gets sick and can't work they take him into a cellar and turn a powerful stream of water on him from a hose that knocks the breath out of him. Then a doctor revives him and they hang him up by his hands with his feet off the floor for an hour or two. This generally makes him go to work again, and when he gives out and can't stand up they bring him on a stretcher to the hospital to get well or die as the case may be.

The hospital wards have from one hundred to two hundred patients in them all the time. They have all kinds of diseases — at present typhus fever and measles are the fashion. Consumption here is more common than bad colds are at home. There are about thirty hopeless cases of it in the hospital just now and nearly all the nurses and attendants are contracting it. There are hundreds of other cases of it among the men who are working in the shops and foundries. Twice a day they have a sick call at the hospital, and from two hundred to three hundred men are marched in each day suffering from various disorders. They march in single file past the doctor and he prescribes for each one "on the fly." The procession passes the drug counter and the medicines are handed out to each one as they march without stopping the line.

I have tried to reconcile myself to remaining here for a time, but am about at the end of my endurance. There is absolutely not one thing in life at present or in prospect that makes it of value. I have decided to wait until the New Orleans court decides the appeal, provided it is heard within a reasonable time, and see what chance there conies out of it.

I can stand any kind of hardships or privations on the outside, but I am utterly unable to continue the life I lead here. I know all the arguments that could be advanced as to why I should endure it, but I have reached the limit of endurance. It will be better for every one else and a thousand times better for me to end the trouble instead of dragging it out longer.

July 8, 1898.

Dear Mrs. R.

I have little to say about myself, except that as far as physical comfort goes I am as well situated as any one here. I -attend to my business (that of night druggist) and no one interferes with me, as the doctor leaves everything in my hands at night. I attend to sick calls and administer whatever I think proper unless it happens to be a severe case and then I wake up the doctor. I am treated with plentiful consideration by all the officials, have a large, airy, clean sleeping room and the range of the whole place, and big, well kept yard full of trees, flowers, and grass. The hospital here is a fine new building, fully as large as the City Hall in Austin, and the office and drug store is as fine and up-to-date as a first class hotel. I have my desk and office chair inside the drug store railing, gas lights, all kinds of books, the latest novels, *etc.* brought in every day or two, three or four daily papers, and good meals, sent down the dumb waiter from the kitchen at ten o'clock and three p. m. There are five wards in the hospital and they generally have from fifty to two hundred patients in them all the time.

The guards bring in men who are sick at all hours of the night to the hospital which is detached some one hundred yards from the main buildings. I have gotten quite expert at practicing medicine. It's a melancholy place, however — misery and death and all kinds of suffering around one all the time. We sometimes have a death every night for a week or so. Yery little time is wasted on such an occasion. One of the nurses will come from a ward and say — "Weil, So and So has croaked." Ten minutes later they tramp out with So and So on a stretcher and take him to the dead house. If he has no friends to claim him — which is generally the case — the next day the doctors have a dissecting bee and that ends it. Suicides are as common as picnics here. Every few nights the doctor and I have to strike out at a trot to see some unfortunate who has tried to get rid of his troubles. They cut their throats and hang themselves and stop up their cells and turn the gas on and try all kinds of ways. Most of them plan it well enough to succeed. Night before last a professional pugilist went crazy in his cell and the doctor and I, of course, were sent for. The man was in good training and it took eight of us to tie him. Seven held him down while the doctor climbed on top and got his hypodermic syringe into him. These little things are our only amusements. I often get as blue as any one can get and I feel as thoroughly miserable as it is possible to feel, but I consider that my future efforts belong to others and I have no right to give way to my own troubles and feelings.

Hello, Margaret:

Don't you remember me? I'm a Brownie, and my name is Aldibirontiphostiphornikophokos. If you see a star shoot and say my name seventeen times before it goes out, you will find a diamond ring in the track of the first blue cow's foot you see go down the road in a snowstorm while the red roses are blooming on the tomato vines. Try it some time. I know all about Anna and Arthur Dudley, but they don't see me. I was riding by on a squirrel the other day and saw you and Arthur Dudley give some fruit to some trainmen. Anna wouldn't come out. Well goodbye, I've got to take a ride on a grasshopper. I'll just sign my first letter — "A".

July 8, 1898.

My Dear Margaret :

You don't know how glad I was to get your nice little letter to-day. I am so sorry I couldn't come to tell you goodbye when I left Austin. You know I would have done so if I could have.

Well, I think it's a shame some men folks have to go away from home to work and stay away so long — don't you? But I tell you what's a fact. When I come home next time I'm going to stay there. You bet your boots I'm getting tired of staying away so long.

I'm so glad you and Munny are going to Nashville. I know you'll have a fine ride on the cars and a good time when you get to Uncle Bud's. Now you must have just the finest time you can with Anna and the boys and tumble around in the woods and go fishing and have lots of fun. Now, Margaret, don't you worry any about me, for I'm well and fat as a pig and I'll have to be away from home a while yet and while I'm away you can just run up to Nashville and see the folks there.

And not long after you come back home I'll be ready to come and I won't ever have to leave again.

So you be just as happy as you can, and it won't be long till we'll be reading Unclc Remus again of nights.

I'll see if I can find another one of Uncle Remus's books when I come back. You didn't tell me in your letter about your going to Nashville. When you get there you must write me a long letter and tell me what you saw on the cars and how you like Uncle Bud's stock farm.

When you get there I'll write you a letter every week, for you will be much nearer to the town I am in than Austin is.

I do hope you will have a nice visit and a good time. Look out pretty soon for another letter from me.

I think about you every day and wonder what you are doing. Well, I will see you again before very long.

Your loving Papa.

August 16, 1898.

My Dear Margaret :

I got your letter yesterday, and was mighty glad to hear from you. I think you must have forgotten where you were when you wrote it, for you wrote "Austin, Texas" at the top of it. Did you forget you had gone to Tennessee?

The reason why I have not written you a letter in so long is that I didn't know the name of the postoffice where you and Munny were going until I got her letter and yours yesterday. Now that I know how to write I will write you a letter every Sunday and you will know just when you are going to get one every week. Are you having a nice time at Aunt Lilly's?

Munny tells me you are fat and sassy and I am glad to hear it. You always said you wanted to be on a farm. You must write and tell me next time what kind of times you have and what you do to have fun.

I'd have liked to see the two fish you caught. Guess they were most as long as your little finger, weren't they? You must make Munny keep you up there till the hot weather is over before you go back to Austin. I want you to have as good times as you can, and get well and strong and big but don't get as big as Munny because I'm afraid you'd lick me when I come home.

Did you find Dudley and Arthur much bigger than they were when they were in Austin? I guess Anna is almost grown now — or thinks she is — which amounts to about the same thing.

April 5, 1899.

Dear Mrs. R.:

One thing I am sorry for is that we are about to lose Dr. Reinert, our night physician. He has been my best friend and is a thoroughly good man in every way. He will resign his place in about a month to accept a better position as Police Surgeon. You can still address in his care until May 1st, and in the meantime I will make other arrangements. I believe, though, that I will be able to hold my own after he leaves, as I have the confidence and good will of all the officers. Still we never can tell here, as everything is run on political and financial lines. Of course, all the easy positions are greatly in demand, and every variety of wirepulling and scheming is used to secure them. As much as a thousand dollars have been offered by men here for such places as the one I hold, and as I hold mine simply on my own merits I have to be on the lookout all the time against undermining.

I have abundant leisure time at night and I have been putting-it to best advantage studying and accumulating manuscript to use later.

February 14, 1900.

Dear Margaret :

It has been quite a long time since I heard from you. I got a letter from you in the last century, and a letter once every hundred years is not very often. I have been waiting from day to day, putting off writing to you, as I have been expecting to have something to send you, but it hasn't come yet, and I thought I would write anyhow.

I am pretty certain I will have it in three or four days, and then I will write to you again and send it to you.

I hope your watch runs all right. When you write again be sure and look at it and tell me what time it is, so I won't have to get up and look at the clock.

With much love, Papa.

May 17, 1900.

Dear Margaret :

It has been so long since I heard from you that I'm getting real anxious to know what is the matter. Whenever you don't answer my letters I am afraid you are sick, so please write right away when you get this. Tell me something about Pittsburg and what you have seen of it. Have they any nice parks where you can go or is it all made of houses and bricks? I send you twenty nickels to spend for anything you want.

Now, if you will write me a nice letter real soon I will promise to answer it the same day and put another dollar in it. I am very well and so anxious to be with you again, which I hope won't be very long now.

With much love, as ever Papa.

October 1, 1900.

Dear Margaret:

I got your very nice, long letter a good many days ago. It didn't come straight to me, but went to a wrong address first. I was very glad indeed to hear from you, and very, very sorry to learn of your getting your finger so badly hurt. I don't think you were to blame at all, as you couldn't know just how that villainous old "lioss" was going to bite. I do hope that it will heal up nicely and leave your finger strong. I am learning to play the mandolin, and we must get you a guitar, and we will learn a lot of duets together when I come home, which will certainly not be later than next summer, and maybe earlier. I suppose you have started to school again some time ago. I hope you like to go, and don't have to study too hard. When oue grows up, a thing they never regret is that they went to school long enough to learn all they could. It makes everything easier for them, and if they like books and study they can always content and amuse themselves that way even if other people are cross and tiresome, and the world doesn't go to suit them.

You mustn't think that I've forgotten somebody's birthday. I couldn't find just the thing I wanted to send, but I know where it can be had, and it will reach you in a few days. So, when it comes you'll know it is for a birthday remembrance.

I think you write the prettiest hand of any little girl (or big one, either) I ever knew. The letters you make are as even and regular as printed ones. The next time you write, tell me how far you have to go to school and whether you go alone or not.

I am busy all the time writing for the papers and magazines all over the country, so I don't have a chance to come home, but I'm going to try to come this winter. If I don't I will by summer sure, and then you'll have somebody to boss and make trot around with you.

Write me a letter whenever you have some time to spare, for I am always glad and anxious to hear from you. Be careful when you are on the streets not to feed shucks to strange dogs, or pat snakes on the head or shake hands with cats you haven't been introduced to, or stroke the noses of electric car horses.

Hoping you are well and your finger is getting all right, I am, with much love, as ever, Papa.
November 5, 1900.
Dear Mrs. R.:

I send you an Outlook by this mail with a little story of mine in it. I am much better situated now for work and am going to put in lots of time in writing this winter.

About two weeks ago I was given what I consider the best position connected with this place. I am now m the steward s office keeping books, and am very comfortably situated. The office is entirely outside and separate from the rest of the institution. It is on the same street, but quite a distance away I am bout as near free as possible. I don't have to go near the other buildings except sometimes when I have business with some of the departments inside. I sleep outside at the office -d am absolutely without supervision of any kind. I go in and out as I please. At night I take walks on the streets or go down to the t and walk along the paths there. The steward's office is a two-story building containing general stores and provisions There arc two handsomely furnished office rooms with up-to-date fixtures — natural gas, electric lights, 'phones, etc have a big fine desk with worlds of stationery and everything I need We have a fine cook out here and set a table as good as a good hotel steward and the storekeeper very agreeable gentlemen both of them — leave about four p.m. and I am my own boss till next morning. In fact, I have my duties and attend to, hem, and am much more independent than an employer would be. I take my hat and go out on the street whenever I please. I have a good wire cot which I rig up in the office at night, and altogether no one could ask for anything better under the circumstances.

DEAR MARGARET, Here are three more pictures, hut they are not very good Munny says you are learning very fast at school I'm sure you re te a very smart girl, and I guess I'd better study a lot more myself or you will know more than I will I was reading to day about a cat a lady had that was about the smartest cat I ever heard of. One day the cat was asleep and woke up. He didn't see his mistress, so he ran to a bandbox where she kept the hat she wore when she went out, and knocked the top oft to ee ift was there. When he found it was there he contented and lay down and went to sleep again. Wasn't that pretty bright for a eat? Do you think Nig would do anything that smart?

You must plant some seeds and have them growing so you can water them as soon as it gets warm enough. Well, I'll write you another letter in a day or two. So goodbye till then.
Your loving Papa.
My Dear Margaret :

I ought to have answered your last letter sooner, but I haven't had a chance. It's getting mighty cool now. It won't be long before persimmons are ripe in Tennessee. I don't think you ever ate any persimmons, did you? I think persimmon pudden (not pudding) is better than cantaloupe or watermelon either. If you stay until they get ripe you must get somebody to make you one.

If it snows while you are there you must try some fried snowballs, too. They are mighty good with Jack Frost gravy.

You must see how big and fat you can get before you go back to Austin.

When I come home I want to find you big and strong enough to pull me all about town on a sled when we have a snow storm. Won't that be nice? I just thought I'd write this little letter in a hurry so the postman would get it and when I'm in a hurry I never can think of anything to write about. You and Munny must have a good time, and keep a good lookout and don't let tramps or yellowjackets catch you. I'll try to write something better next time. Write soon.

Your loving Papa.

November 12.

My Dear Margaret :

Did you ever have a pain right in the middle of your back between your shoulders? Well, I did just then when I wrote your name, and I had to stop a while and grunt and twist around in my chair before I could write any more. Guess I must have caught cold. I haven't had a letter from you In a long time. You must stir Munny up every week or two and make her send me your letter. I guess you'd rather ride the pony than write about him, wouldn't you? But you know I'm always so glad to get a letter from you even if it's only a teentsy weentsy one, so I'll know you are well and what you are doing.

You don't want to go to work and forget your old Pop just because you don't see much of him just now, for he'll come in mighty handy some day to read Uncle Remus to you again and make kites that a cyclone wouldn't raise off the ground. So write soon.

With love as ever, Papa.

My Dear Margaret :

I ought to have answered your letter some time ago, but you know how lazy I am. I'm very glad to hear you are having a good time, and I wish I was with you to help you have fun. I read in the paper that it is colder in Austin than it has been in many years, and they've had lots of snow there too. Do you remember the big snow we had there once? I guess everybody can get snow this winter to fry. Why don't you send me some fried snow in a letter? Do you like Tennessee as well as you did Texas? Tell me next time you write. Well, old Christmas is about to come round again. I wish I could come and light up the candles on the Christmas tree like we used to. I wouldn't be surprised if you haven't gotten bigger than I am by now, and when I come back and don't want to read Uncle Remus of nights, you can get a stick and make me do it. I saw some new Uncle Remus books a few days ago and when I come back I'll bring a new one, and you'll say "thankydoo, thankydoo." I'm getting mighty anxious to see you again, and for us to have some more fun like we used to. I guess it won't be much longer now till I do, and I want to hear you tell all about what times you've had. I'll bet you haven't learned to button your own dress in the back yet, have you?

I hope you'll have a jolly Christmas and lots of fun — Geeminy! don't I wish I could eat Christmas dinner with you! Well, I hope it won't be long till we all get home again. Write soon and don't forget your loving, Papa.

My Dear Margaret :

Here it is summertime, and the bees are blooming and the flowers are singing and the birds making honey, and we haven't been fishing yet. Well, there's only one more month till July, and then we'll go, and no mistake. I thought you would write and tell me about the high water around Pittsburg some time ago, and whether it came up to where you live, or not. And I haven't heard a thing about Easter, and about the rabbits' eggs — but I suppose you have learned by this time that eggs grow on egg plants and are not laid by rabbits.

I would like very much to hear from you oftener; it has been more than a month since you wrote. Write soon and tell me how you are, and when school will be out, for we want plenty of holidays in July so we can have a good time. I am going to send you something nice the last of this week. What do you guess it will be?

Lovingly, Papa.

When O. Henry passed out of the prison walls of Columbus, he was a changed man. Something of the old buoyancy and waggishness had gone, never to return. He was never again to content himself with random squibs or jests contributed to newspapers or magazines. Creation had taken the place of mere scintillation. Observation was to be more and more fused with reflection. He was to work from the centre out rather than from the circumference in. The quest of "What's around the corner" was to be as determined as before but it was to be tempered with a consciousness of the under-side of things. The hand that held the pen had known a solemnizing ministry and the eye that guided it had looked upon scenes that could not be expunged from memory.

The old life was to be shut out. He had written to none of his earlier friends while in prison and he hoped they would never know. The work that he had elected to do could be done in silence and separation and, so far as in him lay, he would start life over again once more. Explanations would be useless. He had his secret and he determined to keep it. He had been caught in the web of things but he had another to live for and hope was strong and confidence still stronger within him. If a sense of pervading romance had buoyed him before his days of testing, it had not deserted him when he passed within the shadows. It had been not only his pillar of cloud by day but his pillar of fire by night.

There are men, says O. Henry, in one of his vivid characterizations, to whom life is "a reversible coat, seamy on both sides." His had been seamy on only one side; the inner side was still intact. The dream and the vision had remained with him. He had suffered much, but the texture of life still seemed sound to him.

There was no sense of disillusionment. No friend had failed him; no friend ever failed him. So far from losing interest in life, he was rather re-dedicated to it.

Nothing so testifies to the innate nobleness of O. Henry's nature as the utter absence of bitterness in his disposition after the three years in Columbus. These years had done their work, but it was constructive, not destructive. His charity was now as boundless as the air and his sympathy with suffering, especially when the sufferer was seemingly down and out, as prompt and instinctive as the glance of the eye. He was talking to a friend once on the streets of New York when a beggar approached and asked for help. O. Henry took a coin from his pocket, shielded it from the view of his friend, and slipped it into the beggar's hand, saying, "Here's a dollar. Don't bother us any more." The man walked a few steps away, examined the coin, and seemed uncertain what to do. Then he came slowly back. "Mister," he said, "you were good to me and I don't want to take advantage of you. You said this was a dollar. It's a twenty-dollar gold piece." O. Henry turned upon him indignantly: "Don't you think I know what a dollar is? I told you not to come back. Get along!" He then continued his conversation, but was plainly mortified lest his friend should have detected his ruse. A woman whom he had helped over many rough places in New York said: " His compassion for suffering was infinite. He used to say' I know how it is.' That was his gift. He had a genius for friendship." The first step in putting the past irrevocably behind him was to write under an assumed name. The pen-name of O. Henry may have been thought of while he was in New Orleans; it may have been suggested by the names found in a New Orleans daily, the Times-Democrat or the Picayune. O. Henry, I believe, is reported to have said as much. But the evidence is that he did not adopt and use the name until he found himself in prison. When the S. S. McClure Company wrote to him about "The Miracle of Lava Canon" (see page 124), he had been out of New Orleans nearly a year and was never to see the city again, but he was addressed as W. S. Porter and the story was published as W. S. Porter's. On April 25, 1898, the day on which he arrived in Columbus, the S. S. McClure Company wrote to him in Austin, addressing him as Sydney Porter. It was his first change of signature and was adopted in the month between his conviction and his commitment. It was also the name to be engraved upon his visiting cards in New York. But after reaching Columbus, not before, he took the pen-name O. Henry and kept it to the end.*

* So far as I can discover, only three stories were signed Sydney Porter and these are not reproduced in O. Henry's collected works. They were "The Cactus" and "Round the Circle," both published in Everybody's for October, 1902, and "Hearts and Hands," published in Everybody's for December of the same year. Other names occasionally signed were Olivier Henry, S. H. Peters, James L. Bliss (once), T. B. Dowd, and Howard Clark.

One of the most interesting odds and ends found among O. Henry's belongings is a small notebook used by him in prison. In it he jotted down the names of his stories and the magazines to which he sent them. It is not complete, the first date being October 1, 1900. It contains, therefore, no mention of " Whistling Dick's Christmas Stocking," which appeared in McClures Magazine for December, 1899, or of "Georgia's Ruling," to which he alludes in the letter to Mrs. Roach (see page 162). Of the stories now grouped into books, these two were the first written. The stories listed in the prison notebook and now republished in book form are, in chronological order, "An Afternoon Miracle,"* "Money Maze," "No Story," "A Fog in Santone," "A Blackjack Bargainer," "The Enchanted Kiss," "Hygeia at the Solito," "Rouge et Noir," "The Duplicity of Hargraves," and "The Marionettes."

*This is a reshaping of his first story, "The Miracle of Lava Canon."

These twelve stories, three of which were picked as among O. Henry's best in the plebiscite held by the Bookman, June, 1914, show a range of imagination, a directness of style, and a deftness of craftsmanship to which little was to be added. In the silent watches of the night, when the only sound heard was "the occasional sigh or groan from the beds which were stretched before him in the hospital ward or the tramp of the passing guard," O. Henry had come into his own. He had passed from journalism to literature. He had turned a stumbling-block into a stepping-stone. And his mother's graduating essay, "The Influence of Misfortune on the Gifted," written a half century before, had received its strangest and most striking fulfilment.

CHAPTER SEVEN
Finding Himself In New York

On July 24, 1901, the day of his liberation, O. Henry went to Pittsburg where his daughter and her grandparents were then living. Mr. and Mrs. Roach had moved from Austin immediately after the trial. Mr. Roach was now the manager of the Iron Front Hotel in Pittsburg, and here O. Henry improvised an office in which he secluded himself and wrote almost continuously. The stories that had issued from the prison in Columbus had gone first to New Orleans and had been re-mailed there. Now the stories were sent direct from Pittsburg.

The call or rather invitation to New York came in the spring of 1902. Mr. Gilinan Hall, associate editor of Everybody's Magazine but at that time associate editor of Ainslee's, had written an appreciative letter to O. Henry before the prison doors had opened. The letter was directed, of course, to New Orleans where the stories were thought to originate. "The stories that he submitted to Duffy and myself," said Mr. Hall, "both from New Orleans and Pittsburg were so excellent that at least the first seven out of eight were immediately accepted. For these first stories we gave him probably seventy-five dollars each." O. Henry did not go to New York under contract. He went because Mr. Hall, quick to discover merit and unhappy till he has extended a helping hand, urged him to come.

New York needed him and he needed New York. How great the need was on both sides it is not likely that Mr. Hall or Mr. Duffy or O. Henry himself knew. During the eight years of his stay, however, O. Henry was to get closer to the inner life of the great city and to succeed better in giving it a voice than any one else had done. To O. Henry this last quest of "What's around the corner," confined now to a city that was a world within itself, was to be his supreme inspiration. Very soon he found that he could not work outside of New York. "I could look at these mountains a hundred years," he said to Mrs. Porter in Asheville, "and never get an idea, but just one block downtown and I catch a sentence, see something in a face — and I've got my story." If ever in American literature the place and the man met, they met when O. Henry strolled for the first time along the streets of New York.

"Of the writing men and women of the newer generation," says Mr. Arthur Bartlett Maurice,* "the men and women whose trails are the subject of these papers, there are many who have staked claims to certain New *See "The New York of the Novelists" (the Bookman, New York, October, 1915).

York streets or quarters. There has been but one conqueror of Alexander-like ambitions, that is, of course, the late O. Henry, and Sydney Porter's name will naturally appear again and again in these and in ensuing papers. To north, east, south, and west, stretch his trails; to north, east, south, and west, he wandered like a modern Haroun al Rascliid. And like a conqueror he rechristened the city to suit his whimsical humour. At one moment it is his 'Little Old Bagdad-on-the-Subway'; at another, 'The City of Too Many Caliphs'; at another, 'Noisyville-on-the-Hudson'; or, ' Wolfville-on-the-Subway'; or, 'The City of Chameleon Changes.'"

The acceptance of the invitation to come to New York without a definite engagement is evidence that O. Henry had at last gained confidence in himself as a writer. This confidence was a fruit of the years spent in Columbus. Without faith in himself no power of persuasion could, I think, have induced him to launch himself in a city where he had not only no assured position but no friends or acquaintances. Like Childe Roland's acceptance of the challenge on the occasion of his memorable first visit to the Dark Tower, O. Henry's acceptance of the invitation to come to New York was in itself the pledge of ultimate victory. It is certain that he took with him to New York short story material not yet worked up, but that he had any definite plan of publication, any particular plots that could be more easily completed in the more favourable atmosphere of a great city, is not likely. It is more probable that the desire to get into the game and the consciousness that he could play it now or never, if given a chance, were the ruling forces in the decision. The passion for self-expression which began in his earliest youth had grown with every later experience, and there was now added the determination, come what might, to give his daughter the best education possible. The road lay through the short story with New York as his workshop.

Nobody except the family trio in Pittsburg and the editors and publishers of Ainslees Magazine knew that O. Henry was going to New York. He had spent a day or two in the city before he called at Duane and William streets to make himself known. "As happens in these matters," writes Mr. Richard Duffy,* "whatever mind picture Gilman Hall or I had formed of him from his letters, his handwriting, his stories, vanished before the impression of the actual man. To meet him for the first time you felt his most notable quality to be reticence, not a reticence of social timidity, but a reticence of deliberateness. If you also were observing, you would soon understand that his reticence proceeded from the fact that civilly yet masterfully he was taking in every item of the 'y°u' being presented to him to the accom * See the Bookman, New York, October, 1913.

paniment of convention's phrases and ideas, together with the 'y°u' behind this presentation. It was because he was able thus to assemble and sift all the multifarious elements of a personality with sleight-of-hand swiftness that you find him characterising a person or a neighbourhood in a sentence or two; and once I heard him characterise a list of editors he knew each in a phrase."

No one in New Y^ork came to know him better or felt a warmer affection for him than Mr. Gilman Hall. "I was sure," said Mr. Hall, "that he had a past, though he did not tell me of it and I did not inquire into it. It was not till after his death that I learned of the years spent in Columbus. I used to notice, however, that whenever we entered a restaurant or other public place together he would glance quickly around him as if expecting an attack. This did not last long, however. I thought that he had perhaps killed some one in a ranch fight, for he told me that he had lived on a ranch in Texas. This inference was strengthened by finding that he was a crack shot with a pistol, being very fond of shooting-galleries as well as of bowling alleys. But when I found that he did not carry a pistol, I began to doubt the correctness of my theory."

Mr. Duffy relates that he found O. Henry a man with whom you could sit for a long time and feel no necessity for talking, though a passerby would often evoke from him a remark that later reappeared as the basis of a story. "Any one who endeavoured to question him about himself," continues Mr. Duffy, "would learn very little, especially if he felt he was being examined as a4literary' exhibit; although when he was in the humour he would give you glimpses of his life in Greensboro and on the ranch to which he had gone as a young man, because he had friends there and because he was said to be delicate in the chest. He would never, however, tell you 'the story of his life' as the saying is, but merely let you see some one or some happening in those days gone by that might fit in well with the present moment, for always he lived emphatically in the present, not looking back to yesterday, not very far ahead toward tomorrow. For instance, I first heard of a doctor in Greensboro, who was his uncle, I believe, and something of a character to O. Henry at least, when I inquired about a story he was writing, — how it was coming along. Then he told me of the doctor who, when asked about any of his patients, how they, Mr. Soandso or Mrs. Soandso, were getting along, would invariably reply with omniscience: 'Oh, Mrs. Soandso is progressing!' But as O. Henry said: 'He never explained which way the patient was progressing, toward better or worse.' It was here in Greensboro naturally that he began to have an interest in books, and I recall among those he used to mention as having read at the time, that one night he spoke to me of a copybook of poems written by his mother. He spoke with shy reverence about the poems, which he no doubt remembered, but he did not speak of them particularly. They were merely poems, written by her in her own hand, and as a young man they had come to him."

O. Henry could not be prevailed upon to meet a man simply because the man was a celebrity nor, when he himself became a celebrity, would he permit himself to be visited as such if he could help it. There was never a moment of his stay in New York when the four million were not more interesting to him than the four hundred. One self-protective device that stood him in good stead was a sort of pan-American dialect which he adopted on such occasions and which served as a deterrent to future offenders. Thus a woman who had written to him about his stories and who insisted on bringing a friend to meet the great man said to him afterward: "You mortified me nearly to death, you talked so ungrammatical." Another method of evasion was to drop into a perfectly serious vein of Artemus Ward rusticity. There was fun in it to those who understood, but it was meant for those who did not and could not understand and it had the desired effect.

But with a congenial companion, O. Henry was more interesting than his stories. Almost all, however, who have written about him mention his barrier of initial reserve. Till this was penetrated — and he had to penetrate it himself by sensing a potential friend in the casual acquaintance — there was no flow. "My first impression of O. Henry," writes Mrs. Wilson Woodrow, "andan impression which lasted during half the evening at least, was one of disappointment. This wonderful story teller struck me as stolid and imperturbable in appearance and so unresponsive and reserved in manner that I had a miserable feeling that I was a failure as a guest, and nothing hurts a writer's vanity, a woman writer's anyway, so much as to have her work considered more interesting and attractive than herself. But presently Mr. Porter began to sparkle. He was unquestionably a great raconteur. I am sure that if his table-talk had ever been taken down in shorthand, it would have sounded very much like his written dialogue, only it was not circumscribed and curbed by the limits of the story and the necessity of keeping the narrative uppermost.

"His wit was urban, sophisticated, individual; entirely free from tricks and the desire to secure effects. It was never mordant nor corrosive; it did not eat nor fester; it struck clean and swift and sure as a stroke of lightning. It was packed with world-knowledge, designed to delight the woman of thirty, not of twenty, and yet I never heard him tell a story even faintly risque. He was the most delightful of companions, thoughtful to a degree of one's comfort and enjoyment, and his wit never flagged; quite effortless, it bubbled up from an inexhaustible spring. Most brilliant talkers are quite conscious of their gift; they put it through all its paces, and you are expected to award the blue ribbon of appreciation. Not so O. Henry. He treated it as carelessly and casually as an extravagant and forgetful woman does her jewels. He was absolutely free from any pose, and he would tolerate none. He gave and he exacted always the most punctilious courtesy. But more, I think that his was one of the proudest spirits, so sensitive, too, that he protected himself from the crude and rude touch of the world in a triple-plated armour of mirth and formality."

O. Henry's friends soon found that money went through his hands like water through a sieve. He simply could not keep it. His tips were often twice the amount of the bill. The view has been expressed more than once in print that O. Henry was the victim while in New York of some sort of blackmail, that on no other theory could his constant pennilessness be accounted for. Those who knew him best, however, not only discredit the theory but find no reason to invoke it. Money was not squeezed from him — he gave it away, willingly, bounteously, gladly. "He would share his last dollar," writes Mrs. Porter, "with a fellow who came to him with a hard-luck story. He would give away the clothes he needed himself to a man poorer than himself." He not only gave freely to any beggar or street waif or hobo that called upon him, says Mr. Hall, but as he showed them to the door he would ask them to call again.

As penniless as he usually was, however, and as eager as he always was to know the feel of money in his pocket, you could not move him a hair's-breadth by dangling money before him. When publishers and periodicals that had turned a deaf ear to him in his struggling days sought to capitalize his fame by patronizing him he assumed their former rule. He did the declining. Mr. Clarence L. Cullen narrates the following incident: (The New York Sun, January 10, 1915)

I was with him at the Twenty-sixth Street place one afternoon when a batch of mail was brought to him. One of the envelopes caught his eye. On the envelope was printed the name of one of the leading fiction publications in all the world, if not indeed the most important of them all. Many times during the years when he had been struggling for a foothold as a writer of short stories he had submitted his tales, including the best of them, to the editor of this publication. Always had they come back with the conventional printed slip. When he reached the topmost rung of the ladder he meticulously refrained from submitting anything to that particular publication, the writers for which comprised the leading "names" in the world of fiction.

He ripped open this envelope which attracted his eye. There was a note and a check for $1,000. The note asked him briefly for something from his pen — anything — with that word underscored — check for which was therewith enclosed. If the thousand dollars were not deemed sufficient, the note went on, he had only to name what sum he considered fair and the additional amount would be remitted to him.

Porter, who probably was the least vainglorious writer of equal fame that ever lived, smiled a sort of cherubic smile as he passed the note over to me. When I had finished reading it, without comment, he, saying never a word, addressed an envelope to the editor of the publication, slipped the check into the envelope, stamped the envelope and went out into the hall and deposited it in the drop. Not a word passed between us about the offer.

If O. Henry's chief quest in New York was for "What's around the corner," his underlying purpose was to get first-hand material for short stories. Those who knew him most intimately believe that he never borrowed a plot. "Two things," says Mr. Hall, "stirred his indignation: a salacious story and the proffer of a plot. 'Don't you know better,' he would say, 'than to offer me a plot?'" It was a necessity of his nature to manufacture his products from the raw material.

Hints he took and from all conceivable sources. "Once at a dinner," says Mrs. Porter, "my brother told him of a man who hated the particular locality in which he lived so bitterly that he had gone far away, but at death his body had been brought back to the very spot he disliked for burial." O. Henry was seen to jot down the idea on his cuff, but it does not reappear in any of his stories. Nor does an earlier incident of which he made at least a mental note at the time. A prisoner convicted of murder had been electrocuted in Columbus and his last words were, "a curse upon the warden and all of his." Two weeks afterward the warden dropped dead. There was much talk and still more excitement about it among the prisoners. "As we were repeating this to Dr. Thomas," writes Mr. J. Clarence Sullivan, a reporter in Columbus, "O. Henry remarked: 'So you see a story to-day, do you?' and then, as usual, went from the room." It was the only time that the reporters in Columbus had heard him utter a word, for he avoided them sedulously. But no story that he wrote, so far as I recall, turns upon the fulfilment of a malediction. O. Henry found his usable material in things seen rather than in things heard, or, if heard, they were heard at first-hand.

The two incidents mentioned, moreover, illustrate human destiny rather than human character, and O. Henry's quest was for character manifestations. These he sought in the mass rather than in rare or abnormal displays. "When I first came to New York," he once said, "I spent a great deal of time knocking around the streets. I did things then that I wouldn't think of doing now. I used to walk at all hours of the day and night along the river fronts, through Hell's Kitchen, down the Bowery, dropping into all manner of places, and talking with any one who would hold converse with me. I never met any one but what I could learn something from him; he's had some experience that I have not had; he sees the world from his own viewpoint. If you go at it in the right way, the chances are that you can extract something of value from him. But whatever else you do, don't flash a pencil and notebook; either he will shut up or he will become a Hall Caine."

There is evidently a rich vein of autobiography in the words with which he introduces "He Also Serves":

If I could have a thousand years — just one little thousand years — more of life, I might, in that time, draw near enough to true Romance to touch the hem of her robe.

Up from ships men come, and from waste places and forest and road and garret and cellar to maunder to me in strangely distributed words of the things they have seen and considered. The recording of their tales is no more than a matter of ears and fingers. There are only two fates I dread — deafness and writer's cramp.

From what O. Henry himself said of his way of getting story material and from what those closest to him in New York have reported, it would seem that two kinds of the city's population, two strata of its society, interested him most: those who were under a strain of some sort and those who were under a delusion. The first stirred his sympathy; the second furnished him unending entertainment. Both are abundantly represented in his stories, and both marked out trails that he followed eagerly to the end.

Of his efforts to know the life of the working girls of New Yrork before writing about them, no one ean speak more authoritatively than Miss Anne Partlan. "He told me," she writes, "that the hand-to-mouth life that girls led in New York interested him and when he came to New York he looked me up. I used to have parties of my friends up to meet him and they never dreamed that this Mr. Porter, who fitted so well into our queer makeshift life, was a genius. He had absolutely no pose. 'The Unfinished Story' and 'The Third Ingredient' were taken straight from life. That is why there is never anything sordid in the little stories. We were poor enough in our dingy rooms but he saw the little pleasures and surprises that made life bearable to us."

O. Henry's general manner at such times is thus described by Miss Partlan :

There was nothing of the brilliant wit about the great story writer when in the atmosphere of the shopgirl, clerk, or salesman. Instead, there was a quiet, sympathetic attitude and, at times, a preoccupied manner as if their remarks and chatter reminded him of his old days of bondage in the country drug store, and the perpetual pillmaking which he was wont to describe with an amusing gesture, indicating the process of forming the cure-all.

One evening a group of department store employees were having dinner with me. Among them were salesgirls, an associate buyer, and one of the office force. I asked O. Henry to join us so that he might catch the spirit of their daily life. He leavened their shop-talk with genial, simple expressions of mirth as they told their tales of petty intrigue and strife for place amid the antagonism and pressure which pervades the atmosphere of every big organization. On leaving, he remarked to me: "If Henry James had gone to work in one of those places, he would have turned out the great American novel."

On another occasion, the conversation turned to feather curling, and he astonished me with his detailed knowledge of the craft. I asked him where he had learned so much about the work and he told me that in one of his first months in New York he was living in very humble lodgings and one evening found him without funds. He became so hungry that he could not finish the story on which he was working, and he walked up and down the landing between the rooms. The odor of cooking in one of the rooms increased his pangs, and he was beside himself when the door opened and a young girl said to him, "Have you had your supper? I've made hazlett stew and it's too much for me. It won't keep, so come and help me eat it."

He was grateful for the invitation and partook of the stew which, she told him, was made from the liver, kidneys, and heart of a calf. The girl was a feather curler and, during the meal, she explained her work and showed him the peculiar kind of dull blade which was used in it. A few days later he rapped at her door to ask her to a more substantial dinner, but he found that she had gone and left no address.

Miss Partlan's father, an expert mechanic and an inventor of blacksmith's tools, asked O. Henry to accompany him to a meeting of master workmen. Miss Partlan continues:

Speeches were made by masters of their craft, filled with references to "side hill plows," "bolt cutters," and "dressing chisels for rock use." The speeches referred to the most humane make of horse shoes, bar iron, toe calks, and hoof expanders. All of this fell on no more attentive ears than O. Henry's. A Scotchman presently arose and spoke on coach building. He told of a wood filling which he once made of the dust gathered from forges, mixed with a peculiar sort of clay. His enunciation was not clear and more than once O. Henry turned to me to ask me if I had caught the indistinct word.

After the speeches came dancing of the Lancers and the Virginia Reel. O. Henry threw himself into the spirit like a boy. He danced and whistled and called out numbers, laughing heartily when in the maze of a wrong turn. No one there dreamed he was other than a fellow-working man.

"Where do you keep shop, Mr. Porter?" asked the wife of a Missouri mechanic.

"Mr. Porter is an author," I replied impulsively.

"Well, I can do other things," he retorted with a note of defense as he continued, "I can rope cows, and I tried sheep raising once."

But O. Henry's favourite coign of vantage was the restaurant. From his seat here, as from his broad window in the Caledonia on West Twenty-sixth Street, he gazed at his peep-show with a zest and interpretative insight that never flagged. Henry James says somewhere: "It is an incident for a woman to stand up with her hand resting on a table and look at you in a certain way." O. Henry would have preferred that she sit down and order something. Restaurant tables mirrored better for him than centre tables. The more individual hotels, restaurants, and cabarets of New York were ticketed and classified in his mind as men classify bugs or books. Their patrons he divided into two classes: those who knew and those who thought they knew, the real thing and those who would be considered the real thing. If the "has-been's" had free access to O. Henry's pockets, the " would-be's" occupy almost an equal space in his pages; and among the "would-be's" the would-be Bohemians come first.

"Thrice in a lifetime," says O. Henry, "may woman walk upon the clouds — once when she trippeth to the altar, once when she first enters Bohemian halls, the last when she marches back across her first garden with the dead hen of her neighbour." Miss Medora Martin had the Bohemian craze. She had come to New York from the village of Harmony, at the foot of the Green Mountains, Vermont. One rainy day Mr. Binkley, a fellow boarder, who was forty-nine and owned a fishstall in a downtown market, had gone with her to "one of the most popular and widely patronized, jealously exclusive Bohemian resorts in the city." This is what took place:*

Binkley had abandoned art and was prating of the unusual spring catch of shad. Miss Elise arranged the palette-and-maul-stick tie pin of Mr. Vandyke. A Philistine at some distant table was maundering volubly either about Jerome or Gerome. A famous actress was discoursing excitably about monogrammed hosiery. A hose clerk from a department store was loudly proclaiming his opinions of the drama. A writer was abusing Dickens.

A magazine editor and a photographer were drinking a dry brand at a reserved table. A 36-25-42 young lady was saying to an eminent sculptor: "Fudge for your Prax Italys! Bring one of your Venus Anno Dominis down to Cohen's and see how quick she'd be turned down for a cloak model. Back to the quarries with your Greeks and Dagos!"

Thus went Bohemia.

Scenes of this sort were dear to O. Henry's heart. Not as a satirist but as a genial and immensely amused spectator he would sit night after night amid these children of illusion and find a satisfaction and stimulation in their behaviour that real Bohemia was powerless to furnish. "He watched them," writes an associate, "at their would-be Bohemian antics with his broad face creased with merriment, and I would that it had been possible to get phonographic records of his comments made in his extraordinarily lowpitched voice."

Though O. Henry's studies of New York life began as soon as he arrived in the city, it is not till 1904 that his stories are found to reflect in a marked degree his new environment. The intervening stories dealt with the West or Southwest and with Central or South America. One of these early Texas stories, "Madame Bo-Peep, of the Ranches," deserves more than a passing notice. It is a satisfying love story, redolent of happiness, of genuineness, of green prairies, temperate winds, and blue heavens, with just enough "centipedes and privations" to bring together at last two lives that New York had put apart. It is mentioned here because it was to bring together two other lives that are of more concern to us just now than either Octavia Beaupree or Teddy Westlake.

The story was published in the Smart Set for June, 1902. How many readers treasured it for the beauty of its simple plot and the balm of its wide and flowered spaces, I do not know. Among the letters written to O. Henry by admirers of his stories and preserved among his effects, there is none that mentions "Madame Bo-Peep." But one letter at least was written, and through it this story was to link the past and the present of O. Henry's life. It was to do more than any other one story to bridge the chasm between Will Porter of Greensboro and O. Henry of New York. It was ultimately to reveal to the friends of boyhood days that the youthful cartoonist of the "somnolent little Southern town" was now the short story interpreter of Bagdad-on-the-Subway.

Mrs. Thaddeus Coleman, of Asheville, North Carolina, the mother of Miss Sallie Coleman, for whom O. Henry at the age of six had looted the magnolias (see page 67), had been visiting in New York in the spring of 1905. There she learned that O. Henry was Will Porter. The news brought to Miss Coleman not only surprise but eager delight and a train of long-slumbering memories. "In my desk," writes Mrs. Porter, "lay 'Madame Bo-Peep' and I loved her. I wrote O. Henry a note. 'If you are not Will Porter, don't bother to answer,' I said. He answered but does not seem to have bothered. 'Some day,' he wrote, 'when you are not real busy, won't you sit down at your desk where you keep those antiquated stories and write to me? I'd be so pleased to hear something about what the years have done for you, and what you think about when the tree frogs begin to holler in the evening.'

A little later, when Miss Coleman had mentioned her ambition to write, came a more urgent letter:

Now I'll tell you what to do. Kick the mountains over and pack a kimono and a lead-pencil in a suit-case and hurry to New York. Get a little studio three stories up with mission furniture and portieres, a guitar and a chafing-dish and laugh at fate and the gods. There are lots of lovely women here leading beautiful and happy lives in the midst of the greatest things in this hemisphere of art and music and literature on tiny little incomes. You meet the big people in every branch of art, you drink deep of the Pierian spring, you get the benefit of earth's best. —

They were married in Asheville on November 27, 1907.

Another one of these early Western stories, "A Retrieved Reformation," has probably had a wider vogue and caused its author to be pointed out more frequently in the restaurants and theatres of New York than anything else that he wrote, though it can hardly be classed among his best. The suggestion of the leading character came, doubtless, as Dr. Williard says (see page 151), from Jimmy Connors of the Columbus prison, and O. Henry may have sketched the story before leaving Columbus. It first appeared, however, in the Cosmopolitan of April, 1903, and was republished as "Mr. Valentine's New Profession" in the London Magazine of the following September. The phraseology is changed here and there in the English version and always for the worse, the plot and incidents remaining the same. On May 5, 1909, Curtis Brown and Massie, of London, wrote to O. Henry thanking him for "the [enclosed] authorization which we shall have pleasure in forwarding to the French translator." The money received for the rights of French translation was donated by O. Henry to the Children's Country Holiday Fund of England.

The French translator was Mr. A. Foulcher, a civil engineer now in the French army. This translation, says Mr. Foulcher, was, "without my knowledge or consent," promptly adapted and put upon the Paris stage. "Some five or six years ago," he writes,* "entering by chance the Vaudeville one fine evening, I had the pleasure of witnessing the performance of Mr. Valentine's feats, in which of course I found neither glory nor profits. Mr. Valentine had once more changed his name, but he was the same man and played the same trick on the safe." A French stage version, by the way, which, like Mr. Paul Armstrong's American stage version, was called "Alias Jimmy Valentine," was made by Mr. Maurice Tourneur, who later filmed the play for the United States. As both of these versions preserve the original name Valentine, it must have been still another French adaptation that Mr. Foulclier saw. In fact, the London stage version is known as "Jimmy Samson" and it was probably a re-adaptation of this version that Mr. Foulcher saw played in Paris.

A Spanish translation of the English "Jimmy Samson" was made by Senor Alberti and acted at the Teatro Espanol in Madrid. O. Henry would hardly recognize his work in either its English or its Spanish form till the curtain goes up for the last time. "The author," writes a Spanish critic, "has saved for this point his most effective stroke. A little girl has got shut up in the safe and is in peril of being asphyxiated. Samson, actuated by his good heart, hastens to open the safe and thus shows to the police who are following him that he really is the famous thief who is clever enough to open safes with a 'twist of the wrist.' The sacrifice might have cost him his happiness, since the daughter of the minister was in love with him, and also his liberty, since the police have at last discovered him; but the latter show themselves generous and the girl continues loving him in spite of all, and so all of us are satisfied."

But Latin America had laid its spell on O. Henry, and when "A Retrieved Reformation" was published the author was better known as a writer of Central and South American tales than of those dealing with the West or with New York. "He is threatening the supremacy of Mr. Richard Harding Davis in a field in which for several years the more widely known writer has been absolutely alone," wrote Mr. Stanhope Searles. O. Henry was urged to put his Latin American stories together, to add others, and to publish the whole as a novel. This was the origin of "Cabbages and Kings," published late in 1904 and O. Henry's first book. It shows on every page a first-hand acquaintance with coastal Latin America. Mr. John Ewing, Minister to Honduras, writes from Tegucigalpa, December 16, 1915:

From conversations with people who have lived there and who have read "Cabbages and Kings," which I have in my library and which, by the way, is in constant demand, I understand that it is recognized and admitted to be true to life as conditions then existed in that section.

Dr. B. E. Washburn, of the International Health Commission, writes from Port of Spain, Trinidad, August 26, 1915:

During a recent journey through the West Indies and the Guianas I visited the booksellers and made inquiries as to which American authors were popular in each country. At St. Thomas, a Danish possession (where English is the language used, however), I found the works of Longfellow and Poe for sale. At Dominica only Poe was represented in the small stock of books. The visit to the bookseller in Barbados was much more encouraging for here I found not only Poe and Longfellow, but also Bret Harte, Hawthorne, Mary Johnston, and O. Henry. At Georgetown, in British Guiana, I also found O. Henry, as well as many of the modern American novelists, especially Mark Twain, Booth Tark-ington, Opie Read, James Lane Allen, and Anna Katharine Green. At New Amsterdam, a city of 10,000 people in the far off province of Berbice, in Guiana, I found only Poe. When I asked the bookseller and "critique," as he termed himself, about the works of O. Henry, he drew a long breath and said, "They are finished," meaning he had sold out.

This particular "critique" had reviewed "Cabbages of ze King," but "with ze failure to recognize an interest." It was too literal, too much a bare recital of things as they are. "Senor O. Henry is no storie escritor," he continued. "Anybody can see things happen an' write 'em down. You exclaim to me zat he is popular in ze America. Excuse me, an' a t'ousan' pardons ef I offend, but ze Americanos can be no judge of ze traits of ze imagination. No matter ef ze Americanos, ze Ingles, or ze whole world entire like ze Senor Henry, he is no storie escritor. But ze books of him do sell!"

The London Spectator noted in " Cabbages and Kings"

"not only an individual point of view but a remarkable gift of literary expression." In fact, almost every characteristic that O. Henry was later to develop may here be found in embryo. There is the apparent turning aside from the main narrative to indulge in a little philosophy, a sort of hide-and-seek played by the short story and its ancestor, the essay: see the passage on pages 53-54 about the "quaint old theory that man may have two souls — a peripheral one which serves ordinarily, and a central one which is stirred only at certain times, but then with activity and vigour."

There is the portrayal of character by a few significant details:

The fact that he did not know ten words of Spanish was no obstacle; a pulse could be felt and a fee collected without one being a linguist. Add to the description the facts that the doctor had a story to tell concerning the operation of trepanning which no listener had ever allowed him to conclude, and that he believed in brandy as a prophylactic; and the special points of interest possessed by Dr. Gregg will have become exhausted.

There is a beauty of style here and there, a tropic exuberance of colour, a wealth of leisurely description, that he never again equalled. Could a Honduran sunset be better photographed than in these words? —

The mountains reached up their bulky shoulders to receive the level gallop of Apollo's homing steeds, the day died in the lagoons and in the shadowed banana groves and in the mangrove swamps, where the great blue crabs were beginning to crawl to land for their nightly ramble. And it died, at last, upon the highest peaks. Then the brief twilight, ephemeral as the flight of a moth, came and went; the Southern Cross peeped with its topmost eye above a row of palms, and the fireflies heralded with their torches the approach of soft-footed night.

There is the trick of the diverted and diverting quotation:

"Then," says I, "we'll export canned music to the Latins; but I'm mindful of Mr. Julius Ctesar's account of 'em where he says: 'Onmis Gallia in tres partes divisa est'; which is the same as to say, 'We will need all of our gall in devising means to tree them parties.'"

There is the pitting of city against city:

"Yes, I judge that town was considerably on the quiet. I judge that after Gabriel quits blowing his horn, and the car starts, with Philadelphia swinging to the last strap, and Pine Gully, Arkansas, hanging onto the rear step, this town of Solitas will wake up and ask if anybody spoke.

There is the art of hitting the target by seeming to aim above it, a sort of calculated exaggeration:

"Twice before," says the consul, "I have cabled our government for a couple of gunboats to protect American citizens. The first time the Department sent me a pair of gum boots. The other time was when a man named Pease was going to be executed here. They referred that appeal to the Secretary of Agriculture."

And there is the love of street scenes in New York which was to grow with him to his last moment:

I get homesick sometimes, and I'd swap the entire perquisites of office for just one hour to have a stein and a caviare sandwich somewhere on Thirty-fourth Street, and stand and watch the street cars go by, and smell the peanut roaster at old Giuseppe's fruit stand.

But with all these divertissements and many more, "Cabbages and Kings" was, comparatively, a failure. It is not equal to the sum total of its seventeen constituent parts. It has unity, but it is the unity of a sustained cleverness carried to an extreme. Suspense is preserved but interest is sacrificed. Chapters XII and XIII, called respectively "Shoes" and "Ships," will illustrate. These two stories had not been previously published. They were fashioned and put in after the author had decided to amplify his title by giving prominence to the stanza —

"The time has come," the Walrus said,
"To talk of many things;
Of shoes and ships and sealing-wax,
And cabbages and kings."

Sealing-wax had been already incidentally mentioned in "The Lotus and the Bottle" which was published in January, 1902, and which forms the second chapter of "Cabbages and Kings." But "shoes and ships" must be accounted for, though the natives of Coralio went barefooted. So five hundred pounds of stiff, dry cockleburrs are shipped from Alabama and sprinkled by night along the narrow sidewalks of Coralio. Shoes become a necessity and ships bring them, along with more cockleburrs. But, in the meanwhile, the two central characters of the novel, Goodwin and his wife, are dropped from the story. They must wait till the exactions of line three of our prefatory stanza are met and resolved. But, more disconcerting still, Mr. and Mrs. Goodwin are presented as charlatans and thieves. It is not till the seventeenth chapter is reached that we find we have been deceived. Mr. and Mrs. Goodwin are neither charlatans nor thieves. They are honest, clever, and likable. We must reread the whole story to reinstate them. Clever? Too clever.

By the time "Cabbages and Kings" was published, New York life had gripped O. Henry and he had entered upon his most prolific period. During 1904, if we omit the stories published in

"Cabbages and Kings" and count only those that have since appeared in book form, the total is sixty-five; the total for 1905 is fifty. No other years of his life approximated such an output. Of these hundred and fifteen stories all but twenty-one appeared in the columns of the New York World and all but sixteen deal directly or indirectly with New York City. O. Henry's contract with the World called for a story a week, the payment for each being one hundred dollars. They would bring now at the lowest estimate, writes a New York editor, between a thousand and fifteen hundred dollars each. IVlien we consider not only the number of these stories but their differences of mood and manner, their equal mastery of humour and pathos, their sheer originality of conception and execution, and their steadily increasing appeal in book form to every grade of reader, it becomes evident that a new chapter has been added to the annals of narrative genius in this country. The short story in 1904 and 1905 developed a new flexibility, established new means of communication between literature and life, and, as a mirror of certain aspects of American society, attained a fidelity and an adequacy never before achieved.

In 1906, O. Henry's second book appeared, "The Four Million." It stamped the author as the foremost American short story writer of his time and furnished also in its famous prefatory note a clue to his activities and interests during 19041905:

Not very long ago some one invented the assertion that there were only "Four Hundred" people in New York City who were really worth noticing. But a wiser man has arisen — the census taker — and his larger estimate of human interest has been preferred in marking out the field of these little stories of the "Four Million."

Each succeeding year until 1911 was to be marked by the publication of two collections of his stories: "The Trimmed Lamp" and "Heart of the West" in 1907, "The Voice of the City" and "The Gentle Grafter" in 1908, "Roads of Destiny" and "Options" in 1909, "Strictly Business" and "Whirligigs" in 1910. A year after his death "Sixes and Sevens" appeared, and in 1913 "Rolling Stones," the latter being chiefly a collection of early material with an Introduction by the lamented Harry Peyton Steger.

"The Trimmed Lamp," "The Voice of the City," and "Strictly Business" are "more stories of the four million" and were written for the most part in 19041905. "Heart of the West" is the fruit of the years spent in Texas, most of the stories having appeared before 1905. "The Gentle Grafter" found its inspiration in the stories told to O. Henry from 1898 to 1901. The first eleven stories in this book had not before been published. They probably belong, as do some of the stories in "Cabbages and Kings," to the accumulation of manuscript mentioned by O. Henry in his letter to Mrs. Roach (see page 160), though they could hardly have been made ready for publication before 1908.

"The Gentle Grafter" is not a novel. It is a kind of "mulct'em in parvo," a string of "Autolycan adventures" told by one whose vocabulary consisted chiefly of "contraband sophistries" and whose life conformed to "the gilded rule." "I never skin a sucker," says Jeff, in an autobiographic confession, "without admiring the prismatic beauty of his scales. I never sell a little auriferous trifle to the man with the hoe without noticing the beautiful harmony there is between gold and green." The stories take place in the South, in the West, and in New York. In each of the succeeding collections, "Roads of Destiny," "Options," "Strictly Business," "Whirligigs," and "Sixes and Sevens," O. Henry mingles Latin America, the South, the West, and New York. The titles, however, are arbitrary and are not intended as keynotes to the contents.

But the real life of O. Henry in New York is to be sought in the ideas out of which the stories grew rather than in the succession of incidents that happened to him or in the names of the books that he published. A rereading of the stories in the order in which they were written seems to show that from first to last he moved from theme to theme. Character, plot, and setting were ancillary to the central conception — were but the concrete expressions of the changing ideas that he had in mind. Only a few of these will be traced, enough to indicate, however, that his real biography, the biography of his mind, is to be found in his work.

CHAPTER EIGHT
Favourite Themes

Every one who has heard O. Henry's stories talked about or has talked about them himself will recall or admit the frequent recurrence of some such expression as, "I can't remember the name of the story but the point is this." Then will follow the special bit of philosophy, the striking trait of human nature, the new aspect of an old truth, the novel revelation of character, the wider meaning given to a current saying, or whatever else it may be that constitutes the point or underlying theme of the story. Of no other stories is it said or could it be said so frequently, "The point is this," because no other writer of stories has, I think, touched upon such an array of interesting themes.

Most of those who have commented upon O. Henry's work have singled out his technique, especially his unexpected endings, as his distinctive contribution to the American short story. "I cannot drop this topic," says Professor Walter B. Pitkin, author of "The Art and the Business of

Story Writing," "without urging the student to study carefully the maturer stories of O. Henry, who surpasses all writers, past and present, in his mastery of the direct denouement."

The unexpected ending, however, is not, even technically, the main point in the structural excellence of a short story. Skill here marks only the convergence and culmination of structural excellencies that have stamped the story from the beginning. The crack of the whip at the end is a mechanical feat as compared with the skilful manipulation that made it possible. Walter Pater speaks somewhere — and O. Henry's best stories are perfect illustrations — of "that architectural conception of the work which perceives the end in the beginning and never loses sight of it, and in every part is conscious of all the rest, till the last sentence does but, with undiminished vigor, unfold and justify the first." In fact, it is not the surprise at the end that reveals the technical .mastery of O. Henry or of Poe or of De Maupassant. It is rather the instantly succeeding second surprise that there should have been a first surprise: it is the clash of the unexpected but inevitable.

It is not technique, however, that has given O. Henry his wide and widening vogue. Technique starts no after-tones. It flashes and is gone. It makes no pathways for reflection. If a story leaves a residuum, it is a residuum of theme, bared and vivified by technique but not created by it. It is O. Henry's distinction that he has enlarged the area of the American short story by enriching and diversifying its social themes. In his hands the short story has become the organ of a social consciousness more varied and multiform than it had ever expressed before. Old Sir John Davies once said of the soul that it was:

Much like a subtle spider which doth sit
In middle of her web, which spreadeth wide;
If aught do touch the utmost thread of it,
She feels it instantly on every side.

So was O. Henry. Whether in North Carolina or Texas or Latin America or New York an instant responsiveness to the humour or the pathos or the mere human interest of men and women playing their part in the drama of life was always his-distinguishing characteristic. It was not merely that he observed closely. Beneath the power to observe and the skill to reproduce lay a passionate interest in social phenomena which with him no other interest ever equalled or ever threatened to replace.

Man in solitude made little appeal to O. Henry, though he had seen much of solitude himself. But man in society, his "humours" in the old sense, his whims and vagaries, his tragedies and comedies and tragi-comedies, his conflicts with individual and institutional forces, his complex motives, the good underlying the evil, the ideal lurking potent but unsuspected within — whatever entered as an essential factor into the social life of men and women wrought a sort of spell upon O. Henry and found increasing expression in his art. It was not startling plots that he sought: it was human nature themes, themes beckoning to him from the life about him but not yet wrought into short story form.

Take the theme that O. Henry calls "turning the tables on Haroun al Raschid." It emerges first in "While the Auto Waits," published in May, 1903, a month after "A Retrieved Reformation." As if afraid that his pen-name was becoming unduly prominent, O. Henry signs the story James L. Bliss. "We do not know who James Bliss is," wrote the critic of the New York Times. "The name is a new one to us. But we defy any one to produce a French short story writer of the present day who is capable of producing anything finer than 'While the Auto Waits.'" O. Henry had discovered a little unexploited corner of human nature which he was further to develop and diversify in "The Caliph and the Cad," "The Caliph, Cupid, and the Clock," "Lost on Dress Parade," and "Transients in Arcadia."

The psychology is sound. Shakespeare would have sanctioned it.
Look, what thy soul holds dear, imagine it
To lie the way thou go'st, not whence thou comest.
Browning's Pippa would have approved.
For am I not, this day,

Whate'er I please? What shall I please to-day?
My morn, noon, eve and night — how spend my day?
Tomorrow I must be Pippa who winds silk,
The whole year round, to earn just bread and milk:
But, this one day, I have leave to go,
And play out my fancy's fullest games.

If Haroun al Rasehid found it diverting to wander incognito among his poor subjects, why should not "the humble and poverty-stricken" of this more modern and self-expressive age play the ultra-rich once in a while? They do, but they had lacked a spokesman till O. Henry appeared for them. He, by the way, goes with them in spirit and they all return to their tasks happy and refreshed. They have given their imagination a surf bath.

Habit is another favourite theme. A man believes that he has conquered a certain deeply rooted habit, or hopes he has. By a decisive act or experience he puts a certain stage of his life, as he thinks, behind him. O. Henry is not greatly interested in how he does this: he may change from a drifting tramp to a daring desperado; he may marry; he may undergo an emotional reformation which seems to run a line of cleavage between the old life and the new; a woman may bid farewell to her position as cashier in a downtown restaurant and enter the ranks of the most exclusive society.

But, however the break with the past comes about, O. Henry is profoundly interested in the possibilities of relapse. Such stories, to mention them in the order of their writing, as "The Passing of Black Eagle," "A Comedy in Rubber," "From the Cabby's Seat," "The Pendulum," "The Romance of a Busy Broker," "The Ferry of Unfulfilment," "The Girl and the Habit," and "The Harbinger" would form an interesting pendant to William James's epochal essay on habit. Indeed I have often wondered whether the great psychologist's fondness for O. Henry was not due, in part at least, to the freshness and variety of the story teller's illustrations of mental traits and mental whimsies. No one, at any rate, can read the stories mentioned without concluding that O. Henry had at least one conviction about habit. It is that when the old environment comes back the old habit is pretty sure to come with it.

Of these particular stories, "The Pendulum" makes unquestionably the deepest impression. O. Henry at first called it "Katy of Frogmore Flats" but reconsidered and gave it its present name, thus indicating that the story is a dramatization of the measured to-and-fro, the monotonous tick-tock of a life dominated by routine. "The Pendulum" should be read along with the story by De Maupassant called "An Artist." Each has habit as its central theme, and the two reveal the most characteristic differences of their authors. In the setting, the tone, the story proper, the conversations, the characters, the attitude of the author to his work, there is hardly an element of the modern short story that is not sharply contrasted in these two little masterpieces, neither of which numbers two thousand words.

"Man lives by habits indeed, but what he lives for is thrills and excitements." These words are Professor James's, not O. Henry's, but O. Henry would have heartily applauded them. "What's around the corner" seems at first glance too vague or too inclusive to be labelled a distinctive theme. But it was distinctive with O. Henry, distinctive in his conduct, distinctive in his art. What was at first felt to be an innate impulse, potent but indefinable, came later to be resolutely probed for short story material. "At every corner," he writes,f "handkerchiefs drop, fingers beckon, eyes besiege, and the lost, the lonely, the rapturous, the mysterious, the perilous, changing clues of adventure are slipped into our fingers. But few of us are willing to hold and follow them. We are grown stiff with the ramrod of convention down our backs. We pass on; and some day we come, at the end of a very dull life, to reflect that our romance has been a pallid thing of a marriage or two, a satin rosette kept in a safe-deposit drawer, and a lifelong feud with a steam radiator."

From "The Enchanted Kiss," written in prison, to "The Venturers," written a year before his death, one may trace the footprints of characters who, in dream or vision, in sportive fancy or earnest resolve, traverse the far boundaries of life, couching their lances for routine in all of its shapes, seeking "a subject without a predicate, a road without an end, a question without an answer, a cause without an effect, a gulf stream in life's ocean." Fate, destiny, romance, adventure, the lure of divergent roads, the gleam of mysterious signals, the beckonings of the Big City — these are the signs to be followed. They may lead you astray but you will at least have had the zest of pursuit without the satiety of conquest.

"Nearly all of us," says O. Henry, of the unheroic hero of "The Enchanted Kiss," "have, at some point in our lives — either to excuse our own stupidity or placate our consciences — promulgated some theory of fatalism. We have set up an intelligent Fate that works by codes and signals. Tansey had done likewise; and now he read, through the night's incidents, the finger-prints of destiny. Each excursion that he had made had led to the one paramount finale — to Katie and that kiss, which survived and grew strong and intoxicating in his memory. Clearly, Fate was holding up to him the mirror that night, calling him to observe what awaited him at the end of whichever road he might take. He immediately turned, and hurried homeward."

Fate did her part but Tansey, a "recreant follower of destiny," did not do his. In his absinthe-born dreams he had tried two roads and found knightly exploits and Katie's lips waiting for him at the end of each. Now, though unaided by absinthe, it is no wonder that he takes confidently the homeward road, the road leading to the Peek boardinghouse. Katie was waiting, but —

The fault, dear Brutus, is not in our stars,

But in ourselves that we are underlings.

"The Roads of Destiny," the most carefully wrought out of O. Henry's longer stories, is an answer to the question with which it begins:

I go to seek on many roads

What is to be.

True heart and strong, with love to light-

Will they not bear me in the fight

To order, shun or wield or mould

My Destiny?

The answer is: No. Take what road you please, the right or the left or the home-faring, the same destiny awaits you. You cannot "order, shun or wield or mould" it. The story has an Alexander Dumas exterior, a Poe structure, and an Omar Khayyam interior.

In "The Roads We Take," Shark Dodson says:

I was born on a farm in Ulster County, New York. I ran away from home when I was seventeen. It was an accident my comin' West. I was walkin' along the road with my clothes in a bundle, makin' for New York City. I had an idea of goin' there and makin' lots of money. I always felt like I could do it. I came to a place one even in' where the road forked and I didn't know which fork to take. I studied about it for half an hour, and then I took the left-hand. That night I run into the camp of a Wild West show that was travelin' among the little towns, and I went West with it. I've often wondered if I wouldn't have turned out different if I'd took the other road.

The reply sums up O. Henry's last word on fate, destiny, and roads:

"Oh, I reckon you'd have ended up about the same," said Bob Tidball, cheerfully philosophical. "It ain't the roads we take; it's what's inside of us that makes us turn out the way we do."

It was certainly so with Shark Dodson. He "wouldn't have turned out different." He only dreamed that he took the left-hand road and became the murderer of his friend. He took, in fact, the right-hand road, came to New York, and became a Wall Street broker. But on awaking from his dream he sacrificed a friend to inexorable cupidity, thus doing as a broker what he dreamed that he had done as a bandit.

In "The Complete Life of John Hopkins," fate and destiny give place to pure romance. "There is a saying," begins the author, "that no man has tasted the full flavor of life until he has known poverty, love, and war." But the three dwell in the city rather than in the country:

In the Big City large and sudden things happen. You round a corner and thrust the rib of your umbrella into the eye of your old friend from Kootenai Falls. You stroll out to pluck a

Sweet William in the park — and lo! bandits attack you — you are ambulanced to the hospital — you marry your nurse; are divorced — get squeezed while short on U. P. S. and D. O. W. N. S. — stand in the bread line — marry an heiress, take out your laundry and pay your club dues — seemingly all in the wink of an eye. You travel the streets, and a finger beckons to you, a handkerchief is dropped for you, a brick is dropped upon you, the elevator cable or your bank breaks, a table d'hote or your wife disagrees with you, and Fate tosses you about like cork crumbs in wine opened by an un-feed waiter. The City is a sprightly youngster, and you are red paint upon its toy, and you get licked off.

John Hopkins experienced poverty, love, and war between the lighting and relighting of a five-cent cigar. But they were thrust upon him. He was no true adventurer. The first true adventurer is Rudolf Steiner of "The Green Door." Here is the test:

Suppose you should be walking down Broadway after dinner with ten minutes allotted to the consummation of your cigar while you are choosing between a diverting tragedy and something serious in the way of vaudeville. Suddenly a hand is laid upon your arm. You turn to look into the thrilling eyes of a beautiful woman, wonderful in diamonds and Russian sables. She thrusts hurriedly into your hand an extremely hot buttered roll, flashes out a tiny pair of scissors, snips off the second button of your overcoat, meaningly ejaculates the one word, "parallelogram!" and swiftly flies down a cross street, looking back fearfully over her shoulder.

That would be pure adventure. Would you accept it? Not you. You would flush with embarrassment; you would sheepishly drop the roll and continue down Broadway, fumbling feebly for the missing button. This you would do unless you are one of the blessed few in whom the pure spirit of adventure is not dead.

But the venturer is a finer fellow than the adventurer, and in "The Venturers" O. Henry tilts for the last time at a theme which, if health had not failed, says Mr. Gil-man Hall, would have drawn from him many more stories. In a little backless notebook which O. Henry used in New York I find the jotting from which "The Venturers" grew. The notebook kept in Columbus gives only the titles of completed stories and the names of the magazines to which they were forwarded. The New York notebook mentions no magazines but contains in most cases only the bare theme or motif that was later to be elaborated into a story. Many of these jottings proved unmanageable and left no story issue. But "The Venturers" harks back to this entry, the last in the book: "Followers of chance — Two knights-errant — One leaves girl and other marries her for what may be 'around the corner.'"

Of the two characters in the story, Forster and Ives, the latter is the better talker. The essayist in O. Henry never appeared to better advantage than in the resourceful way in which Ives is made to expound the nature of a venturer:

I am a man who has made a lifetime search after the to-be- continued-in-our-next. I am not like the ordinary adventurer who strikes for a coveted prize. Nor yet am I like a gambler who knows he is either to win or lose a certain set stake. What I want is to encounter an adventure to which I can predict no conclusion. It is the breath of existence to me to dare Fate in its blindest manifestations. The world has come to run so much by rote and gravitation that you can enter upon hardly any footpath of chance to which you do not find signboards informing you of what you may expect at its end... . Only a few times have I met a true venturer — one who does not ask a schedule and map from Fate when he begins a journey. But, as the world becomes more civilized and wiser, the more difficult it is to come upon an adventure the end of which you cannot foresee. In the Elizabethan days you could assault the watch, wring knockers from doors and have a jolly set-to with the blades in any convenient angle of a wall and "get away with it." Nowadays, if you speak disrespectfully to a policeman, all that is left to the most romantic fancy is to conjecture in what particular police station he will land you... . Things are not much better abroad than they are at home. The whole world seems to be overrun by conclusions. The only thing that interests me greatly is a premise. I've tried shooting big game in Africa. I know what an express rifle will do at so many yards; and when an elephant or a rhinoceros falls to the bullet, I enjoy it about as much as I did when I was kept in after school to do a sum in long division on the blackboard... . The sun has risen on the Arabian nights. There are no more caliphs. The fisherman's vase is turned to a vacuum bottle, warranted to keep any genie boiling or frozen for forty-eight hours. Life moves by rote. Science has killed adventure. There are no more opportunities such as Columbus and the man who ate the first oyster had. The only certain thing is that there is nothing uncertain.

In fact, the central idea of "The Venturers," the revolt against the calculable, seems at times to run away with the story itself. Ives marries Miss Marsden at last because he became convinced that marriage is the greatest "venture" of all. But what convinced him? The expository part of the narrative has put the emphasis elsewhere. The centre of the story seems not quite in the middle.

Another theme, one that O. Henry has almost preempted, is the shopgirl.

Five years — the pencil and the yellow pad
Are laid away. Our changes run so swift
That many newer pinnacles now lift
Above the old four million he made glad.
But still the heart of his well-loved Bagdad
Upon-the-Subway is to him renewed.
He knew, beneath her harmless platitude,
The gentler secrets that the shopgirl had.*

*Mr. Christopher Morley in the New York Evening Post, June 5, 1915.

Mr. Nicholas Vachel Lindsay calls him " the little shopgirl's knight":

And be it said, 'mid these his pranks so odd, With something nigh to chivalry he trod, And oft the drear and driven would defend — The little shopgirl's knight, unto the end.*

*"The Knight in Disguise" (the American Magazine, June, 1912). t The Bookman, New York, January, 1916.

Certainly no other American writer has so identified himself with the life problems of the shopgirl in New York as has O. Henry. In his thinking she was an inseparable part of the larger life of the city. She belonged to the class that he thought of as under a strain and his interest in her welfare grew with his knowledge of the conditions surrounding her. "Across every counter of the New York department store," writes Mr. Arthur Bartlett Maurice,f "is the shadow of O. Henry." It has been said that O. Henry laughs with the shopgirl rather than at her, but the truth is that he does not laugh at all when she is his theme; he smiles here and there but the smile is at the humours of life itself rather than at the shopgirl in particular.

His first shopgirl story, "A Lickpenny Lover," was written in the summer of 1904. There are thousands of working girls in New York whose world is bounded bv Coney Island. From some such commonplace of daily speech O. Henry took his cue. Masie, a shopgirl, is courted by Irving Carter, artist, millionaire, traveller, poet, gentleman. He had fallen in love at first sight. When he asks if he may call at her home she laughs and proposes a meeting at the corner of Eighth Avenue and Forty-eighth Street. He is troubled but accepts.

Carter did not know the shopgirl. He did not know that her home is often either a scarcely habitable tiny room or a domicile filled to overflowing with kith and kin. The street-corner is her parlor, the park is her drawing-room, the avenue is her garden walk; yet for the most part she is as inviolate mistress of herself in them as is my lady inside her tapestried chamber.

Two weeks later he courts her with all the ardour of his nature and all the resources of his vocabulary. "Marry me, Masie," he whispered, "and we will go away from this ugly city to beautiful ones. I know where I should take you," and he launched into an impassioned picturing of palaces, towers, gondolas, India and her ancient cities, Hindoos, Japanese gardens — but Masie had risen to her feet. The next morning she scornfully remarked to her chum Lu: "What do you think that fellow wanted me to do? He wanted me to marry him and go down to Coney Island for a wedding tour!"

So the Hostess in "Henry V" thought that the dying Falstaff only "babbled of green fields," but he was repeating or trying to repeat the Twenty-third Psalm.

Words meant to Masie and to the poor Hostess only what their experience would let them mean. And words mean no more than that to any of us. The pathos as well as the humour of speech as a social instrument is that the appeal of every word is measured not by its formal definition but by our orbit of experience and association. The tragedy of the circumscribed life is not that it occasionally mistakes the imitation world for the real world but that the imitation world is its all. There is humour in the story but it is close to pathos. It is furnished by life rather than by Masie.

"The Lickpenny Lover" was followed by four stories which established O. Henry's right to be called the knight of the shopgirl. These stories are constructive in aim and are energized by a mingled sympathy and indignation that recall Dickens on every page. In the first, "Elsie in New York," O. Henry, recognizing that he is in Dickensland, ends the story not with a sudden surprise but with a quotation from "him of Gad's Hill, before whom, if you doff not your hat, you shall stand with a covered pumpkin":

Lost, Your Excellency. Lost, Associations and Societies. Lost, Right Reverends and Wrong Reverends of every order. Lost, Reformers and Lawmakers, born with heavenly compassion in your hearts, but with the reverence of money in your souls. And lost thus around us every day.

But where Dickens wrote "Dead," O. Henry writes "Lost." It is the key word to all of these stories. Elsie was lost before she became a shopgirl. She was only seeking a position, and she found three. But at the very threshold of each she was met and shooed away by the agent of some self-styled charitable organization. "But what am I to do?" asks Elsie. The agents had nothing to suggest. They knew nothing more than that the places had been ticketed as potentially bad. They could only say "Go," not "Come." If one had forgotten the name of this story he would doubtless say and say rightly: "The point of it is that many charitable organizations of New York are very successful in preventing girls from securing positions but do nothing to secure other positions for them."

In "The Guilty Party, an East Side Tragedy," Liz drifts to the street and ruin because her father would do nothing to make home attractive for her. She is not a shopgirl but she belongs here: she is one of the lost whom the world judged wrongly. The action of the story begins:

A little girl of twelve came up timidly to the man reading and resting by the window, and said:
" Papa, won't you play a game of checkers with me if you aren't too tired?"

The red-haired, unshaven, untidy man, sitting shoeless by the window, answered with a frown:

"Checkers! No, I won't. Can't a man who works hard all day have a little rest when he comes home? Why don't you go out and play with the other kids on the sidewalk?"

The woman who was cooking came to the door.

"John," she said, "I don't like for Lizzie to play in the street. They learn too much there that ain't good for 'em. She's been in the house all day long. It seems that you might give up a little of your time to amuse her when you come home."

"Let her go out and play like the rest of 'em if she wants to be amused," said the red-haired, unshaven, untidy man, "and don't bother me."

Like its more famous successor, "The Guilty Party" ends in a dream. The case is tried in the next world. The celestial court-officer discharges Liz, though she had killed her betrayer and committed suicide. He then pronounces the verdict:

The guilty party you've got to look for in this case is a red-haired, unshaven, untidy man, sitting by the window reading in his stocking feet, while his children play in the streets. Get a move on you.

Now, wasn't that a silly dream?

"An Unfinished Story," framed on the model of "The Guilty Party," is O. Henry's indictment of employers who cause the ruin of working girls by underpaying them. It is probably the most admired of O. Henry's stories. In the ten lists of the ten preferred stories sent to the Bookman, this story of less than two thousand five hundred words was mentioned seven times, "A Municipal Report" coming next with six mentions. Some one has said that Dickens'

"Christmas Carol" has done more good than any other story ever written. As the years go by will not the "Christmas Carol" be overtaken by "An Unfinished Story?" It was not hunger, it was not the need of the so-called necessities that wrecked Dulcie's life. The cause lay deeper than that; it belonged not to the eternal-human but to the eternal-womanly. It was neither food nor clothing; it was the natural love of adornment. Dulcie received $G a week. The necessities amounted to $4.70. "I hold my pen poised in vain," says O. Henry, "when I would add to Dulcie's life some of those joys that belong to woman by virtue of all the unwritten, sacred, natural, inactive ordinances of the equity of heaven." There is no crack of the whip at the end: there is the ring of steel:

As I said before, I dreamed that I was standing near a crowd of prosperous-looking angels, and a policeman took me by the wing and asked if I belonged with them.

"Who are they?" I asked.

"Why," said he, "they are the men who hired working girls, and paid 'em five or six dollars a week to live on. Are you one of the bunch?"

"Not on your immortality," said I. "I'm only the fellow that set fire to an orphan asylum, and murdered a blind man for his pennies."

In "Brickdust Row" indictment is brought not against guardians of the young who are found to be prohibitive rather than cooperative; it is not against the careless father, nor the miserly employer. The shaft is aimed at the owners of houses tenanted by working-girls. These houses, having no parlours or reception rooms, compel the occupants to meet their friends " sometimes on the boat, sometimes in the park, sometimes on the street." Blinker, another Irving Carter, falls in love with Florence, another Masie. But Florence lives in Brickdust Row. "They call it that," says Florence, "because there's red dust from the bricks crumbling over everything. I've lived there for more than four years. There's no place to receive company. You can't have anybody come to your room. What else is there to do? A girl has got to meet the men, hasn't she?... The first time one spoke to me on the street, I ran home and cried all night. But you get used to it. I meet a good many nice fellows at church. I go on rainy days and stand in the vestibule until one comes up with an umbrella. I wish there was a parlour, so I could ask you to call, Mr. Blinker." Blinker owns Brickdust Row. "Do what you please with it," he says to his lawyer the next morning. "Remodel it, burn it, raze it to the ground. But, man, it's too late I tell you. It's too late. It's too late. It's too late."

But the greatest of the shopgirl stories as a story is, to my thinking, "The Trimmed Lamp." It is the only one written for the shopgirl rather than about her. But it is not for her alone; it is for all, of whatever age or sex, who work at tasks not commonly rated as cultural. Much has been said and written in recent years about "self-culture through the vocation," but nothing so apt and adequate, I think, as this little story about Nan and Lou and Dan. Froude touched the rim of it when he wrote, fifty years ago:

Every occupation, even the meanest — I don't say the scavenger's or the chimney-sweep's — but every productive occupation which adds anything to the capital of mankind, if followed assiduously with a desire to understand everything connected with it, is an ascending stair whose summit is nowhere, and from the successive steps of which the horizon of knowledge perpetually enlarges.

But Froude limited his occupations too narrowly. He did not quite glimpse the vision of "The Trimmed Lamp." He was afraid to break away from the old and minutely graduated scale of vocations with their traditional degrees of respectability. But this is just what "The Trimmed Lamp" does. It dramatizes the truth that, in spite of inherited divisions and subdivisions, there are only two occupations worth thinking about, and these are one too many. Everybody who has an occupation uses it as a means of subsisting or as a means of growing, as a treadmill or as a stairway, as a shut door or as an open window, as a grindstone or as a stepping-stone.

Every worker may learn from his occupation, "even the meanest," the difference between good work and bad work in his particular calling. But the difference between good work and bad work here is the difference between good work and bad work everywhere. Once erect the standard — and it may be erected by the chimney-sweep as well as by the artist — growth is assured. The lever of Archimedes finds its analogue to-day in such a conception of one's work as moves him to say, "I will examine the universe as it is related to this." Culture is not in the job; it is in the attitude to the job.

Nan illustrates every stage in the upward transition. "'The Trimmed Lamp,'" said O. Henry, "is the other side of 'An Unfinished Story.'" It is the other side of all the stories in which the light is focussed on the downward slope. Nan is the ascending shopgirl. Lou, a piecework ironer in a hand laundry, is her antithesis. Dan is what Coventry Patmore somewhere calls the punctum indifferens, "the point of rest." He is what Kent is in "King Lear," Friar Laurence in "Romeo and Juliet," Horatio in "Hamlet." "He was of that good kind," says O. Henry, "that you are likely to forget while they are present, but to remember distinctly after they are gone." "Faithful? Well, he was on hand when Mary would have had to hire a dozen subpoena servers to find her lamb." Lou has him on her string at first but casts him off.

Three months pass. Nancy and Lou meet accidentally on the border of a little quiet park and Nancy notices that "prosperity had descended upon Lou, manifesting itself in costly furs, flashing gems, and creations of the tailors' art."

"Yes, I'm still in the store," said Naney, "but I'm going to leave it next week. I've made my catch — the biggest catch in the world. You won't mind now, Lou, will you? I'm going to be married to Dan — to Dan! — he's my Dan now — why, Lou!"

Around the corner of the park strolled one of those new-crop, smooth-faced young policemen that are making the force more endurable — at least to the eye. He saw a woman with an expensive fur coat and diamond-ringed hands crouching down against the iron fence of the park sobbing turbulently, while a slender, plainly-dressed working girl leaned close, trying to console her. But the Gibsonian cop, being of the new order, passed on, pretending not to notice, for he was wise enough to know that these matters are beyond help, so far as the power he represents is concerned, though he rap the pavement with his nightstick till the sound goes up to the furthermost stars.

But the shopgirl is a part of a larger theme and that theme is the city.

What a world he left behind him, what
a web of wonder tales,
Fact and fiction subtly woven on the
spinning wheel of Truth!
How he caught the key of living in
the noises of the town,
Major music, minor dirges, rhapsodies
of Age and Youth!
In the twilight of the city,
as I dreamed, as I dreamed,
Watching that eternal drama in the
ever-pulsing street,
All about me seemed to murmur of the
master passed away,
And his requiem was sounded in the
city's fever beat.*

*"O. Henry: In Memoriam," by Mr. Elias Lieberman.

A city was to O. Henry not merely a collective entity, not merely an individuality; certainly not a municipality: it was a personality. In "The Making of a New Yorker," it is said of Raggles:

He studied cities as women study their reflections in mirrors; as children study the glue and sawdust of a dislocated doll; as the men who write about wild animals study the cages in the zoo. A city to Raggles was not merely a pile of bricks and mortar, peopled by a certain number of inhabitants; it was a thing with a soul, characteristic and distinct; an individual conglomeration of life, with its own peculiar essence, flavor, and feeling.

The words are as true of O. Henry himself as any that he ever wrote. And he was always so. When he was eighteen years old, six of us went on a camping trip from Greensboro to old Pilot Mountain and on to the Pinnacles of the Dan. Brief stops were made at Kernersville, Mount Airy, Danbury, and intervening villages. O. Henry, it is needless to say, was the life of the party and, though much has been forgotten, none of us will forget his peculiar interest in these little towns or his quaint, luminous, incisive comments on them as we drove to the next camping place. It was not so much the intensity of his interest that impressed us or that lingers in the memory still. It was that he was interested at all in places so much smaller and, as we thought, less worth while than our own native Greensboro. But interested he was, keenly and steadfastly, and in every book that he has written towns and cities loom large in his survey of human life.

His Latin American stories may serve as illustrations. They deal sparingly with native characters. O. Henry evidently felt some hesitation here, for in his rapid journey from Honduras around both coasts of South America the unit of progress was the coastal town. There was little time to study native character as he studied it on his own soil. The city, therefore, rather than the citizen, is made prominent. An American doctor, for example, who has travelled widely in Latin America, considers O. Henry's description of Espiritu unequalled in accuracy and vividness as a sketch of the typical Latin American coastal town. Certainly no one of his Latin American character portraits is as detailed or as intimate. Sully Magoon is talking:

Take a lot of Filipino huts and a couple of hundred brick-kilns and arrange 'em in squares in a cemetery. Cart down all the conservatory plants in the Astor and Vanderbilt greenhouses, and stick em about wherever there's room. Turn all the Bellevue patients and the barbers' convention and the Tuskegee school loose in the streets, and run the thermometer up to 120 in the shade Set a fringe of the Rocky Mountains around the rear, et it rain, and set the whole business on Rockaway Beach m the middle of January-and you'd have a good imitation of Espintu.*

*From "On Behalf of the Management."

But it is in his references to American cities that O. Henry's feeling for the city as a unit is best revealed. It has been said of George Eliot that her passion for individualizing was so great that a character is rarely introduced in her stories, even if he only says "Breakfast is served," without being separated in some way from the other characters. The same may be said of O Henry's mention of American towns and cities. Sometimes the differentiation is diffused through the story from beginning to end. Sometimes it is summarized in a phrase or paragraph. Of our same Raggles it is said:

Chicago seemed to swoop down upon him with a breezy suggestion of Mrs. Partington, plumes, and patchouli, and to disturb his rest with a soaring and beautiful song of future promise. But Raggles would awake to a sense of shivering cold and a haunting impression of ideals lost in a depressing aura of potato salad and fish.

Pittsburg impressed him as the play of "Othello" performed in the Russian language in a railroad station by Dockstader's minstrels. A royal and generous lady this Pittsburg, though — homely, hearty, with flushed face, washing the dishes in a silk dress and white kid slippers, and bidding Raggles sit before the roaring fireplace and drink champagne with his pigs' feet and fried potatoes.

New Orleans had simply gazed down upon him from a balcony. He could see her pensive, starry eyes and catch the flutter of her fan, and that was all. Only once he came face to face with her. It was at dawn, when she was flushing the red bricks of the banquette with a pail of water. She laughed and hummed a chansonette and filled Raggles's shoes with ice-cold water. Allons!

Boston construed herself to the poetic Raggles in an erratic and singular way. It seemed to him that he had drunk cold tea and that the city was a white, cold cloth that had been bound tightly around his brow to spur him to some unknown but tremendous mental effort. And, after all, he came to shovel snow for a livelihood; and the cloth, becoming wet, tightened its knots and could not be removed.

In "A Municipal Report," O. Henry answers the challenge of Frank Norris who had said:

Fancy a novel about Chicago or Buffalo, let us say, or Nashville, Tennessee! There are just three big cities in the United States that are "story cities" — New York, of course, New Orleans, and. best of the lot, San Francisco.

O. Henry replies:

But, dear cousins all (from Adam and Eve descended), it is a rash one who will lay his finger on the map and say: "In this town there can be no romance — what could happen here? Yes, it is a bold and a rash deed to challenge in one sentence history, romance, and Rand and McNally.

Then follows a story of Nashville, Tennessee, which O. Henry had visited when his daughter was attending Belmont College. "For me," writes Mr. Albert Frederick Wilson, of New York University, "it is the finest example of the short story ever produced in America." "If the reader is not satisfied," says Mr. Stephen Leacock, after attempting to summarize "Jeff Peters as a Personal Magnet" and "The Furnished Room," "let him procure for himself the story called 'A Municipal Report' in the volume 'Strictly Business.' After he has read it he will either pronounce O. Henry one of the greatest masters of modern fiction or else, well, or else he is a jackass. Let us put it that way."

The story ends on the note with which it began: "I wonder what's doing in Buffalo?" It is O. Henry's most powerful presentation of his conviction that to the seeing eye all cities are story cities. It is the appeal of an interpretative genius from statistics to life, from the husks of a municipality as gathered by Rand and McNally to the heart of a city as seen by an artist.

But it happened to O. Henry as it had happened to Raggles:

One day he came and laid siege to the heart of the great city of Manhattan. She was the greatest of all; and he wanted to learn lier note in the scale; to taste and appraise and classify and solve and label her and arrange her with the other cities that had given him up the secret of their individuality.

In "The Voice of the City," O. Henry approaches New York as did Raggles via other cities: "I must go and find out," I said, "what is the Voice of this city. Other cities have voices. It is an assignment. I must have it. New York," I continued, in a rising tone, "had better not hand me a cigar and say: 'Old man, I can't talk for publication.' No other city acts in that way. Chicago says, unhesitatingly, 'I will'; Philadelphia says, 'I should'; New Orleans says, 'I used to'; Louisville says, 'Don't care if I do'; St. Louis says, 'Excuse me'; Pittsburg says, 'Smoke up.' Now, New York"

O. Henry's synonyms for New York and his photographic descriptions of special streets and squares have often been commented upon. Mr. Arthur Bartlett Maurice says again:

In the course of this rambling pilgrimage, the name of Sydney Porter has appeared, and will very likely continue to appear, two or three times to one mention of any other one writer. This is due not only to the high esteem in which the pilgrim holds the work of that singular and gifted man, but also to the fact that the dozen volumes containing the work of O. Henry constitute a kind of convenient bank upon which the pilgrim is able to draw in the many moments of emergency. Perfect frankness is a weapon with which to forestall criticism, and so, to express the matter very bluntly, whenever the writer finds himself in a street or a neighbourhood about which there is little apparent to say, he turns to "The Four Million," or "The Trimmed Lamp," or "The Voice of the City," or "Whirligigs," or "Strictly Business," and in one of these books is able to find the rescuing allusion or descriptive line.

But O. Henry's study went far deeper than "the rescuing allusion or descriptive line." "I would like to live a lifetime," he once said to Mr. Gilman Hall, "on each street in New York. Every house has a drama in it." Indeed the most distinctive and certainly the most thought-provoking aspect of O. Henry's portrayal of New York is not to be found in his descriptions. It lies rather in his attempt to isolate and vivify the character, the service, the function of the city. Streets, parks, squares, buildings, even the multitudinous life itself that flowed ceaselessly before him were to him but the outward and visible signs of a life, a spirit, that informed all and energized all.

But what was it? O. Henry would seem to say, "It is not a single element, like oxygen or hydrogen or gold. It is a combination, a formula, compounded of several elements." In "Squaring the Circle" we learn that a Kentucky feud of forty years' standing had left but a single member of each family, Cal Harkness and Sam Folwell. Cal has moved to New York. Sam, armed to the teeth, follows him. It was Sam's first day in New York. Loneliness smote him; a fat man wouldn't answer him; a policeman told him to move along; an immense engine, "running without mules," grazed his knee; a cab-driver bumped him and "explained to him that kind words were invented to be used on other occasions"; a motorman went the cab-driver one better; a large lady dug an elbow into his back. But at last the bloody and implacable foe of his kith and kin is seen.

He stopped short and wavered for a moment, being unarmed and sharply surprised. But the keen mountaineer's eye of Sam Folwell had picked him out.

There was a sudden spring, a ripple in the stream of passers-by, and the sound of Sam's voice crying:

"Howdy, Cal! I'm durned glad to see ye."

And in the angles of Broadway, Fifth Avenue and Twenty-third Street the Cumberland feudists shook hands.

The city had achieved in one day what a whole State had been powerless to do in forty years. It had done the impossible: it had squared the circle. No mere description could set New York forth as does this story. We have here to do not with the form of a great city but with its function.

Let us return to Raggles once more. The story is " The Making of a New Yorker." Raggles was a tramp.

His specialty was cities. But New York was impenetrable.

Other cities had been to him as long primer to read; as country maidens quickly to fathom; as send-price-of-subscription-with answer rebuses to solve; as oyster cocktails to swallow; but here was one as cold, glittering, serene, impossible as a four-carat diamond in a window to a lover outside fingering damply in his pocket his ribbon-counter salary.

The greetings of the other cities he had known — their homespun kindliness, their human gamut of rough charity, friend y curses, garrulous curiosity, and easily estimated credulity or indifference. This city of Manhattan gave him no clue; it was walled against him. Like a river of adamant it flowed past him in the streets. Never an eye was turned upon him; no voice spoke to him. His heart yearned for the clap of Pittsburg's sooty hand on his shoulder; for Chicago's menacing but social yawp in his ear; for the pale and eleemosynary stare through the Bostonian eyeglass — even for the precipitate but unmalicious boot-toe of Louisville or St. Louis.

Three types of character seem to Raggles about all that New York has: the elderly rich gentleman; the beautiful, steel-engraving woman; the swaggering, grim, threateningly sedate fellow; but all are heartless, frigid, unconcerned. He hates them and the city that produces them. A roar, a hiss, a crash — and Raggles has been struck by an automobile. The three impersonal types are at his side in a moment. They bend over him, put silks and furs under his head, and the threateningly sedate fellow brings a glass full of a crimson fluid that suggested infinite things to the fractured Raggles. A reporter, a surgeon, and an ambulance take him in tow.

In three days they let him leave his cot for the convalescent ward in the hospital. He had been in there an hour when the attendants hear sounds of conflict. Upon investigation they found that Raggles had assaulted and damaged a brother convalescent — a glowering transient whom a freight train collision had sent in to be patched up.

"What's all this about?" inquired the head nurse.

"He was runnin' down me town," said Raggles.

"What town?" asked the nurse.

"Noo York," said Raggles.

Is not that a gaze into the very heart of the city? On the surface, cold, hard, oblivious, greedy; but beneath the surface, kindly, cooperative, organized for every need, efficient for instant help, human to the core.

Read again "The Duel" in which O. Henry declares his theme to be the one particular in which "New York stands unique among the cities of the world." Turn once more to the volume called "The Voice of the City," and weigh it as an answer to the query propounded in the story from which it takes its name. Beneath the humour of stories like these, beneath the cleverness of phrase and the fitness of epithet, there is a solid substratum of thought, a determined attempt to body forth the thing as it really is, a saturation with a central idea, unequalled, we believe, by any other writer who has tried to find adequate predicates for city subjects.

But before O. Henry had seen New York, he was busy with another theme that was to occupy much of his thought in later years. Some one said to him shortly before the end: "Your heart is in your Western stories." "My heart is in heaven," he replied. Had he committed himself I think he would have said: "My heart just now is neither in my Western nor my Northern nor my Southern stories. It is in the stories that are not exclusively any one of the three. I mean the stories that try to contrast the South with the North or the North with the West and to indicate what is separate and characteristic in each." Here again both notebooks bear testimony to the tenacity with which this subject laid hold upon O. Henry's thinking. The Columbus notebook contains the entry:

Duplicity of Hargraves

Munsey 8/16

The New York notebook reads:

Old darkey — difference between Yankee and Southerner — N. Y.

That there is a difference every lover of his country ought to be glad to admit. Time was when we called these differences sectional. A better term is regional.

156

Sectional implies not only difference but antagonism; it recalls oratory, war, and politics. Regional differences suggest neither actual nor potential conflict. Such differences are allies of literature. They make for variety in unity and unity in variety. Sectional differences mean "We dislike one another." Regional differences mean "We are unlike one another." Nowhere does O. Henry's insight into human nature, his breadth and depth, his pervasive humour, or his essential Americanism show more clearly than in such stories as "The Duplicity of Hargraves," "The Champion of the Weather," "New York by Campfire Light," "The Pride of the Cities," "From Each According to His Ability," "The Rose of Dixie," "The Discounters of Money," "Thimble, Thimble," and "Best-Seller." In each of these he stages a contrast between the North and the South or the North and the West.

The task was not an original one but he did it in an original way. Since 1870 American literature has abounded in short stories, novels, and plays that are geographical not only in locale but in spirit and content. "If the reader," writes Mr. Howells, "will try to think what the state of polite literature (as they used to call it in the eighteenth century) would now be among us, if each of our authors had studied to ignore, as they have each studied to recognize, the value of the character and tradition nearest about them, I believe he will agree with me that we owe everything that we now are in literature to their instinct of vicinage." But the "instinct of vicinage" usually confines the author to a single place or a single section. His work attempts to portray Western life or Southern life or New England life, but one at a time. The actual contrasting is done by the reader, who compares author with author or story with story and passes judgment accordingly.

A notable exception is " The Great Divide." William Vaughn Moody has here in a single brief play not only represented the West in Stephen Ghent and New England in Ruth Jordan but himself outlined the contrast in their blended careers. "If Massachusetts and Arizona ever get in a mix-up in there," says Mrs. Jordan, pointing toward Ruth's heart, "woe be!" They do get in a mix-up in there and every American is the gainer. Our very Americanism and sense of national solidarity are quickened and clarified as we watch the struggle between these two characters. Their union at last seems to assure the worth of our constituent parts and to prophesy a nationalism that will endure.

A somewhat similar contest is fought out in Owen Wister's novel, "The Virginian." Molly Wood, of Bennington, Vermont, and the Virginian, of Wyoming, have more than a purely individual interest. They stand for two kinds of regional fidelity that have gone into the very fibre of American life. Mr. Wister even makes the Virginian himself essay a distinction between the East and the West:

Now back East you cau be middling and get along. But if you go to try a thing on in this Western country, you've got to do it well. You've got to deal cyards well; you've got to steal well; and if you claim to be quick with your gun you must be quick, for you're a public temptation, and some man will not resist trying to prove he is the quicker. You must break all the Commandments well in this Western country, and Shorty should have stayed in Brooklyn, for he will be a novice his livelong days.

And over Shorty's dead body the Virginian remarks: "There was no natural harm in him, but you must do a thing well in this country," meaning in Wryoming.

Before the advent of O. Henry, however, short story writers had fought shy of essaying such a contrast within the narrow limits of a single story, a contrast for which the drama and the novel seemed better fitted. Bret Harte and Hamlin Garland, Sarah Orne Jewett and Mrs. Wilkins-Freeman, Thomas Nelson Page and Joel Chandler Harris, and a score of others had proved that the short story could be made to represent as large a territory as the novel. But as an instructed delegate each short story preferred to speak for only one constituency. When it tried to represent two at the same time, there was apt to be a glorification of the one and a caricature of the other.

It is one of O. Henry's distinctions that he is fair to both. The Nation called attention a few months be fore his death to his "genial and equal-handed satire of the confronted Northern and Southern foibles." Western foibles might also have been included. O. Henry is "genial and equal-handed" not only in the characteristics selected but in the way he pits characteristic against characteristic, foible against foible, an excess against a defect, then again a defect against an excess. Art and heart are so blended in these contrasts, wide and liberal observation is so allied to shrewd but kindly insight, that the reader hardly realizes the breadth of the theme or the sureness of the author's footing.

O. Henry was not a propagandist, but one cannot reread these stories without feeling that here as elsewhere the story teller is much more than a mere entertainer. He has suggested a nationalism in which North, West, and South are to play their necessary parts. It is not a question of surrender or abdication; it is a question rather of give and take. We may laugh as we please at Major Pendleton Talbot of "the old, old South" in "The Duplicity of Hargraves." He erred no more on one side than did Hargraves on the other. That Hargraves should not have known that he was wounding the Major's feelings shows a want of tact as onesided on his part as was the Major's excess of pride on his.

"I am truly sorry you took offence," said Hargraves regretfully. "Up here we don't look at things just as you people do. I know men who would buy out half the house to have their personality put on the stage so the public would recognize it."

"They are not from Alabama, sir," said the Major haughtily.

And every reader applauds. But the applause at the end, where Hargraves shows a tact and nobleness beyond what we had thought possible, is still more prompt and generous. The keynote of the story is not sectionalism but reciprocity.

There is the same absence of mere caricature in "The Rose of Dixie." In his New York notebook O. Henry made the entry: "Southern Magazine. All contributors relatives of Southern distinguished men." But the story as it shaped itself in his mind became not merely a burlesque of the hopelessly provincial magazine but a contrast between authorship by ancestry and publication by push. Is not the laugh genially distributed between Colonel Aquila Telfair, of Toombs City, Georgia, and T. T. Thacker, of New York?

Perhaps in "The Pride of the Cities" the reader will be inclined to think that the man from Topaz City, Arizona, overplays the Westernism of his part. Perhaps he does. But his provocation was great. The conversation, you remember, had opened as follows:

"Been in the city long?" inquired the New Yorker, getting ready the exact tip against the waiter's coming with large change from the bill.

"Me?" said the man from Topaz City. "Four days. Never in Topaz City was you?"

"I'" said the New Yorker. "I was never farther west than Eighth Avenue. I had a brother who died on Ninth, but I met the cortege at Eighth. There was a bunch of violets on the hearse, and the undertaker mentioned the incident to avoid mistake. I cannot say that I am familiar with the West."

But each theme that has been mentioned is but an illustration of that larger quest in which all of O. Henry's stories find their common meeting-place — the search for those common traits and common impulses which together form a sort of common denominator of our common humanity. Many of his two hundred and fifty stories are impossible; none, rightly considered, are improbable. They are so rooted in the common soil of our common nature that even when dogs or monuments do the talking we do the thinking. The theme divisions that we have attempted to make are, after all, only subdivisions. The ultimate theme is your nature and mine.

It is too soon to attempt to assign O. Henry a comparative rank among his predecessors. We may attempt, however, to place him if not to weigh him. It was Washington Irving who first gave the American short story a standing at home and abroad. There is a calm upon Irving's pages, an easy quiet grace in his sentences, an absence of restlessness and hurry, that give him an unquestioned primacy among our masters of an elder day. He was more meditative and less intellectual than Scott but, like Scott, he was essentially retrospective. He used the short story to rescue and re-launch the small craft of legend and tradition which had already upon their sails the rime of eld. He leg-endized the short story.

Poe's genius was first and last constructive. It was the build of the short story rather than its historical or intellectual content that gripped his interest. Poe's art, unlike that of Irving, is identified with no particular time or place. He was always stronger on moods than on tenses, and his geography curtsied more to sound than to Mercator or Maury. But in the mathematics of the short story, in the art of making it converge definitely and triumphantly to a preordained end, in the mastery of all that is connoted by the word technique, Poe's is the greatest name. The short story came from his hands a new art form, not charged with a new content but effectively equipped for a new service. In his equal exercise of executive, legislative, and judicial authority, Poe standardized the short story.

Hawthorne made the short story a vehicle of symbolism. Time and place were only starting-points with him. He saw double, and the short story was made to see double, too. Puritan New England, New England of the past, was his locale; but his theme was spiritual truth, a theme that has always had an affinity for symbols and symbolism. Hawthorne allegorized the short story.

With Bret Harte the short story entered a new era. He was the first of our short story writers to preempt a definite and narrowly circumscribed time and place and to lift both into literature. Dialect became for the first time an effective ally of the American short story, and local colour was raised to an art. Though Bret Harte's appeal is not and has never been confined to any one section or to any one country, it is none the less true that he first successfully localized the American short story.

A glance through O. Henry's pages shows that his familiarity with the different sections of the United States was greater than that of any predecessor named. He had lived in every part of the country that may be called distinctive except New England, but he has not preempted any locality. His stories take place in Latin America, in the South, in the West, and in the North. He always protested against having his stories interpreted as mere studies in localism. There was not one of his New York stories, he said, in which the place was essential to the underlying truth or to the human interest back of it. Nor was his technique distinctive. It is essentially the technique of Poe which became later the technique of De Maupassant but was modified by O. Henry to meet new needs and to subserve diverse purposes. O. Henry has humanized the short story.

CHAPTER NINE
Last Days

"I CANNOT help remarking," wrote Alexander Pope to a Mr. Blount, "that sickness, which often destroys both wit and wisdom, yet seldom has power to remove that talent which we call humour." In O. Henry's case sickness affected neither his wit nor his humour but it made creative work hard and irksome. There is as much wit and humour in his last complete story, "Let Me Feel YTour Pulse," or "Adventures in Neurasthenia," as in any story that he wrote, but the ending of no other story was so difficult to him. Plans for a novel and a play were also much in his mind at this time but no progress was made in actual construction.

In fact, O. Henry had been a very sick man for more than a year before his death. "He had not been well for a long time," writes Mrs. Porter, referring to the time of their marriage, "and had got behind with his work." He did not complain but sought creative invigoration in frequent changes of environment. Early in 1909, however, his letters begin to show that writer's cramp was with him only another name for failing health. From his workshop in the Caledonia, he writes to Mr. Henry W. Lanier, who was then secretary to Doubleday, Page & Company:

February 13, 1909.

My Dear Mr. Lanier:

I've been ailing for a month or so — can't sleep, etc.; and haven't turned out a piece of work in that time. Consequently there is a hiatus in the small change pocket. I hope to be in shape Monday so that I can go to Atlantic City, immure myself in a quiet hotel, and begin to get the "great novel" in shape.

March 16, 1909.

It seems that the goddess Hygiene and I have been strangers for years; and now Science must step in and repair the damage. My doctor is a miracle worker and promises that in a few weeks he will doable my working capacity, which sounds very good both for me and for him, when the payment of the bill is considered.

April 6, 1909.

I hope to get the novel in good enough shape to make an "exhibit" of it to you soon. I've been feeling so rocky for so long that I haven't been able to produce much. In fact, I've noticed now and then some suspicious tracks outside the door that closely resembled those made by Lupus Americanus. Has anything accrued around the office in the royalty line that you could put your finger on to-day?

In the fall of 1909, broken in health and suffering greatly from depression, he went to Asheville to be with his wife and daughter. Here on the fifth story of a building on Patton Avenue he set up his workshop. Ideas were plentiful but the power to mould them as he knew he once could have moulded them lagged behind.

Many themes appealed alternately to him for his proposed novel and play but only bare outlines remain. "I want to get at something bigger," he would say. "What I have done is child's play to what I can do, to what I know it is in me to do. If I would debase it, as some of the fellows do, I could get out something. I could turn out some sort of trash but I can't do that."

To Harry Peyton Steger he writes from Asheville, November 5, 1909:

My Dear Colonel Steger: I'd have answered your letter but I've been under the weather with a slight relapse. But on the whole I'm improving vastly. I've a doctor here who says I have absolutely no physical trouble except neurasthenia and that outdoor exercise and air will fix me as good as new. I am twenty pounds lighter and can climb mountains like a goat.

But his Little Old Bagdad-on-the-Subway was calling to him and had called during every waking hour of his absence. He had made his last attempt to write beyond the sound of her voice. In March he was back in his old haunts. To Mr. James P. Crane, of Chicago, he writes. April 15, 1910:

I'm back in New York after a six months' stay in the mountains near Asheville, North Carolina. I was all played out — nerves, *etc.* I thought I was much better and came back to New York about a month ago and have been in bed most of the time — didn't pick up down there as well as I should have done. There was too much scenery and fresh air. What I need is a steam-heated flat with no ventilation or exercise.

The end was near but not much nearer, I think, than he knew. To Mr. Moyle he remarked with a shrug of the shoulders and a whimsical smile: "It'll probably be 'In the Good Old Summer Time.'" A few years before, the question of the after-life had come up casually in conversation and O. Henry had been asked what he thought of it. His reply was:

I had a little dog
  And his name was Rover,
  And when he died
  He died all over.

During the last months the question emerged again. An intimate friend's father had died and O. Henry was eager to know how he had felt about the hereafter. "For myself," he said, "I think we are like little chickens tapping on their shells."

On the afternoon of June 3, Mr. Gilman Hall received a telephone message: "Can you come down right away, Colonel?" His friends were all Colonel or Bill to him. He had collapsed after sending the message and was lying on the floor when Mr. Hall arrived. Dr. Charles Russell Hancock was sent for and O. Henry was taken at once to the Polyclinic Hospital on East Thirty-fourth Street. "You're a poor barber, Doc," he whispered, as Dr. Hancock was brushing his hair; "let me show you." He insisted on stopping to shake hands with the manager of the Caledonia and to exchange a cheery goodbye. He asked that his family be sent for and then quietly gave directions about the disposition of his papers.

Just before entering the hospital the friend who was with him, anticipating his aversion to the newspaper publicity inseparable from his pen-name, asked what name should be announced. "Call me Dennis," he said; "my name will be Dennis in the morning." Then becoming serious he added: "No, say that Will S. — Parker is here." The taking again of the old initials and the name "Will," said O. Henry's friend, was a whim of the moment and a whim of the most whimsical of men, but it was "prompted by the desire to die with the name and initials given him at birth and endeared by every memory of childhood and home."

"He was perfectly conscious until within two minutes of his death Sunday morning," said Doctor Hancock, "and knew that the end was approaching. I never saw a man pluckier in facing it or in bearing pain. Nothing appeared to worry him at the last." There was no pain now and just before sunrise he said with a smile to those about him: "Turn up the lights; I don't want to go home in the dark." He died as he had lived. His last words touched with new beauty and with new hope the refrain of a concert-hall song, the catch-word of the street, the jest of the department store. He did not go home in the dark. The sunlight was upon his face when he passed and illumins still his name and fame.

After the funeral in the Little Church Around the Corner, a woman was seen to remain alone kneeling in prayer. She was one whom O. Henry had rescued from the undertow of the city and restored. "I have always believed," says a gifted writer, "that it was not by accident that a wreath of laurel lay at the head of his coffin and a wreath of lilies at his feet."

THE END

www.ingramcontent.com/pod-product-compliance
Lightning Source LLC
LaVergne TN
LVHW011943070526
838202LV00054B/4778